MOONLIT PASSION

Brad's breath lodged in his throat as he stood just outside the partially opened French doors of the balcony. Silhouetted by the moon, Kathlyn presented a provocative picture. The glow of the lamp inside the suite bathed her form in golden beams. The pale yellow fabric of her nightclothes hugged her delicate curves. "Kat." He spoke her name softly so as not to startle her.

Kathlyn wheeled in surprise. "Good evening, Mr. Hampton. I didn't expect you back tonight."

Obviously not, Brad thought, or else she wouldn't be standing on the balcony half naked. "I've been in for hours."

"Oh? I thought you had plans."

"No, I had no plans. Other than to share a few drinks with the captain. Which I did. Right before I came upstairs — alone."

"What you do is none of my affair, Brad. I'm sure I couldn't care less." The desire in her eyes belied her weak denial.

"Well, at least we're back on a first name basis. And I don't believe you, Kat. I think you care a great deal." Slowly lowering his lips to hers, Brad initiated a passionate kiss. Kathlyn tilted her head back, giving his lips greater access to travel down her bare, slender throat. When she opened her eyes, the stars overhead seemed to burst into a blaze of sensation . . .

CAPTURE THE GLOW OF
ZEBRA'S *HEARTFIRES!*

Teresa Howard
Desire's Bride

ZEBRA BOOKS
KENSINGTON PUBLISHING CORP.

ZEBRA BOOKS

are published by

Kensington Publishing Corp.
475 Park Avenue South
New York, NY 10016

First Printing: November, 1992

Printed in the United States of America

There is nothing holier, in this life of ours, than the first consciousness of love — the first fluttering of its silken wings.

— Henry Wadsworth Longfellow

Prologue

River's Edge Plantation
Athens, Georgia
July 4, 1855

The soft summer night was made for love, which was as it should be, for Christopher Bradley Hampton and Elora Kathlyn McKinney were snared in the web of first love. Hopelessly.
And it was wonderful . . .

The Independence Day picnic had been a rousing success; the celebratory ball was in full swing. Discreetly, Brad and Kathlyn slipped through the garden doors, stealing away for a moment of privacy.

A full moon overhead bathed them in rays of silver as they ran hand-in-hand toward the mammoth greenhouse. Their carefree laughter floated on cool night breezes, lost over the lazy Oconee River. They were deliriously happy. Just being together.

Yet tonight their moonlight tryst had an air of desperation about it; they had come to say goodbye. Their laughter died as the enormity of the occasion settled upon them.

"I wish you didn't have to go, Kat," Brad confessed as they entered the fragrant glass-house.

Kathlyn tilted her head back, until she could look him full in the face. The love warming her heart was evident in her eyes. "I don't want to leave." She raised a gentle hand and touched Brad's full, sensual lips.

He kissed her fingertips then pulled her into his arms. He lowered his head, claiming her mouth, sipping, tasting, savoring, devouring, capturing her breath and returning it to

7

her, mingled with his own.

Many frantic moments later he buried his face in her fiery hair. "I didn't know it would be this hard to say goodbye." For a long moment he just stood there, holding her. Finally, he stepped back.

He wanted to commit every inch of her to memory. Standing in a pool of light, she was so lovely: a halo of sun-kissed ebony hair, liquid iris eyes, pale porcelain skin delicately translucent, and rosy lips swollen and moist from his kisses. When her eyes filled with tears he cradled her head against his heart.

She grasped the back of his evening coat and pressed him ever closer. He was so big, so warm, so solid; he was her lifeline. What would she do without him? She was convinced that her innocent, young heart would shatter into a million pieces before the night was through. She squeezed her eyes shut against the pain. Tears sliding down her cheeks soaked into his pearl gray waistcoat.

"Ah, honey, don't cry," Brad crooned. At a loss with any crying woman, but more so with this fragile beauty, he ran his hand down Kathlyn's spine, gentling her as if she were a skittish filly. She snuggled trustingly closer; waves of affection surged over him. He felt as if a giant fist were squeezing his insides. Past the lump forming in his throat, he tried to soothe her. "Shh, baby."

"I'm sorry to carry on so." Kathlyn sniffled, raising her head and losing herself in tender brown eyes.

Her breath stilled. He was too perfect to be mortal: six foot, two inches of rock-hard muscle, raven's wing black hair, brown eyes that looked clear through to her soul, and animal white teeth flashing against his swarthy complexion when he smiled at her in that heart-stopping way of his. Could such a man really love her? It seemed too good to be true.

"The last three months have been the happiest days of my life," she confessed with the honesty of a child. "I'm going to miss you so."

Brad palmed her trembling chin with one hand and rested his other possessively on the small of her back. "I'm going to miss you too, sweetheart. You've become very precious to me."

The heavy summer heat, trapped in the glasshouse after a day of brilliant sunshine, was cool compared to the scorching kiss he bestowed upon her then. She grew dizzy, wondering if her vertigo was caused by the heat in the room or by the cloying smell of hundreds of gardenias that weighted the air around them.

When Brad slipped his tongue past her lips, deepening the kiss, she knew full well that her vertigo was caused by the passionate ministrations of this man she loved. And she couldn't get enough of him. Instinctively, she strained toward him, giving and taking what would soon be denied her.

The night sounds along the Oconee provided a symphony of nature for the young lovers. Their low moans and inhalations of breath deepened and accelerated in concert with God's creatures.

Suddenly, Kathlyn pulled back to catch her breath, her hands resting lightly on his broad shoulders. "You will visit at Christmas, won't you?"

"If your Uncle Roth doesn't get wind of my plans and shoot me first," he said, only half teasing.

She smiled weakly. "I think he would find it difficult to out-shoot Clarke County's prize-winning marksman." Not meeting his eyes, she fingered the blue ribbon he had just been awarded for the Fourth of July marksmanship contest.

Brad heard the tension in Kathlyn's voice and regretted mentioning Roth. It bothered him more than a little that her uncle opposed their relationship.

He cursed silently. Why he brought up the only sore spot in their otherwise perfect relationship, he couldn't fathom. He had wanted this night to be perfect, a night to remember in the lonely months ahead.

Dipping his head, he tried to kiss away the unpleasantness. It worked partially at best.

"Uncle Roth only wants what's best for me."

"I know, honey. And he might be right. Perhaps I am too old for you." There was a seductive smile in his voice. "But you sure feel like a woman fully grown to me," he growled, nuzzling her bare neck. He kissed his way up the column of her throat, paying homage to her cheeks, eyelids, and forehead. Until finally he took her lips beneath his own again.

Without removing his mouth from hers, he slid one arm beneath her hips, and captured her wasp-like waist with the other. Effortlessly, he lifted her to his chest.

The dark silence was broken only by the soft, moist

sounds of their caressing mouths, the swish of her lavender silk gown against the white blooms, and his sure footfalls upon the stone floor, as with a singleness of purpose, Brad carried his love to a secluded corner . . . where their lives would be changed forever.

"We can lie on my coat," he whispered, setting Kathlyn to her feet and shrugging out of his coat.

The obvious implication caused Kathlyn's cheeks to burn. Before she had fallen in love with Brad, she had never even been kissed romantically. But as the summer had advanced, and her time left visiting with her cousin's family had grown short, they had become quite daring in their expressions of love.

Still, thus far they had restricted their nightly rendezvous to kissing and caressing while fully clothed. When her shawl slithered to the floor with a seductive whisper, they both knew that tonight would be different.

Brad caressed her delicate features as if she were fashioned from the finest china. She moaned and closed her eyes. "Sweetheart, open your eyes." She complied. Very, very softly, he confessed, "I love you, Kat."

Kathlyn's breath lodged in her throat. Finally, she breathed, "I love you too."

He swept her against him. Joyously, they shared physically what was in their hearts. Panting, Brad held her with arms of steel. "I want you so much it hurts," he moaned.

Kathlyn smiled against his shoulder. Her heart was pounding so hard she was sure he could hear it. "I want you too."

Brad jerked his head back, staring intently into her upturned face. "Are you sure?" She was so young, so innocent. He didn't want to pressure her to do anything against her will. At least his mind wanted to do the honorable thing. Various muscles throughout his body had different ideas; he was a mass of aching need.

Kathlyn felt Brad's need as if it were a tangible thing. He was so close she could feel the heat from his body seeping through her thin gown. She felt as if she were a part of him, as if she didn't know where his desire ended and hers began.

She was a lady, but with every frantic beat of her heart she wanted to become a woman. Brad's woman. After all, she had given him her heart, she reasoned. Was her body more sacred than that?

So in answer to his query, she raised up on the tips of her toes and lightly pressed her lips to his. That chaste kiss was more erotic to him than any he had ever experienced. It prophesied the rapture ahead.

In one swift movement, steel-like bands bound her to his throbbing body; a low groan evinced the depth of his desire. Together, they sank to the floor, their world consisting only of the passion engulfing them and the love flowing between their naive hearts.

In their haste, Brad and Kathlyn didn't take the time to undress. They merely shed or pushed aside those articles of clothing as necessary to complete their frantic coupling.

He skimmed her body with his strong hands, pleasuring her until she writhed and pleaded, for what she knew not. She grasped the front of his waistcoat and pulled him closer. He trembled with desire as he settled himself between her thighs.

He didn't want to hurt her, but he knew that it was inevitable. "It'll hurt at first, baby." His mouth was against her ear when he spoke, though she didn't hear him. She was too enraptured.

Slowly, he entered her, groaning from the exquisite sensation and the need to maintain control. He wanted to love her slowly, to initiate her gently, but in her excitement she arched against him, splitting the sheath that proclaimed her pure.

She gasped, stilling instantly. One lone tear told of her discomfort. When the pain subsided she moved gingerly.

Brad set the pace. Thrusting rhythmically, fanning the flames of desire. All too soon sensation exploded into a fiery inferno. Clinging and gasping, they sailed over the abyss . . . together.

They lay partially clothed, their cooling bodies still joined. Shaken, Brad acknowledged that Kathlyn had given him her most precious gift. "Thank you, sweetheart," was his husky whisper.

He had been intimate with many women before. This, however, was the first time he'd truly made love. Unwittingly, Kat had taught him that lovemaking was not the same as having sex. Sex was exhilarating, but the physical expression of love brought with it a sense of responsibility.

A responsibility Brad warmed to. He was stunned by the

intensity of these feelings. He brushed the damp hair off her brow and looked into her face. "Are you all right?"

"Oh yes." Her face glowed with discovery.

Brad understood. Their eyes met and held. He experienced a wave of guilt. A lady as delicate and refined as Kat did not deserve to lose her virginity on the floor like an animal, with her maiden's blood soiling the petticoats she still wore.

In that instant, he decided what he must do. He would declare his intentions to her uncle at the train station in the morning and ask her parents for her hand as soon as he could make the trip to Union Point. Then, he would ask her to be his bride.

Considering the degree of intimacy they had achieved, it was what any Southern gentleman would do; it was what Brad wanted to do; it was the least a lady like Kathlyn would expect.

A Christmas wedding would be beautiful. With the thought of having her as his wife forever warming his heart, he slid from her body. "I'd best get you back inside before they turn the dogs loose on me."

At Kathlyn's disappointed pout, Brad flashed her a very masculine smile. He was quite pleased with himself. And he wanted her again . . . already. Nevertheless, he would wait; Christmas wasn't so far off . . . was it? Groaning, he set about rearranging his clothes before he lost his resolve, before he gave in and loved her as his eager body demanded.

Once they were dressed, he took her in his arms. "Let's not say goodbye, just good night. Tomorrow . . . at the train station . . ."

He held her as if he would never let her go. She responded in kind.

Desperately, they shared one last kiss. Then without another word they walked from the place they would long remember. Never would either of them smell the sweet scent of gardenias without remembering the night they had lost a part of their hearts . . . forever.

The smell of gardenias would also evoke powerful memories in the mind of the enraged woman who remained behind. Trembling, Rachel Jackson, Kathlyn's cousin, stood behind a shelf laden with overflowing pots.

12

She had witnessed the touching scene with murderous eyes. She wasn't sure how, but somehow, she had managed to watch in silence.

"Slut!" — she hissed at her absent cousin — "I'll teach you to steal what's mine."

Rachel's father had cautioned her for a year now that Brad was just being polite in his reaction to her advances. But she hadn't believed him, until now.

She stood with clenched fists at her sides, a look of grim determination sculpting her face. "Damn you, Kathlyn. I'll make you sorry you ever met Brad Hampton and lay under him like a common trollop."

July 5, 1855
Brad:
   Last night was a terrible mistake. You took unfair advantage of my youth and inexperience. I can never forgive you for that. If you possess a shred of honor, do not attempt to contact me in any way. Kathlyn

July 5, 1855
Kathlyn:
   Last night was a terrible mistake. I take full responsibility for my actions. Nonetheless, I don't wish to see you again. Please allow us a shred of dignity and do not contact me in any way. Brad

"There, that oughta do it," Rachel said smugly.

Folding the notes, she went in search of a messenger to deliver them to the unsuspecting couple.

Part One
The South

The mind has a thousand eyes, and the heart but one; yet the light of a whole life dies when love is done.

— Frances William Bourdillon

Chapter One

Athens, Georgia
July 3, 1866
Eleven years later . . .

Elegant. *That was the word to describe the Bank of Georgia.*

And quiet. *The cavernous structure was as quiet as a tomb. So quiet the silence seemed to press down from the chandelier-decked ceilings to the parquet-tiled floors.*

Both words — elegant and quiet — registered simultaneously in Kathlyn McKinney's mind as the bank clerk stretched forth his blue-veined hand. She settled into the chair he indicated, her gaze traveling throughout the bank.

The elegance of the bank surprised her. Surprised her, and quite frankly, repulsed her. In *Reconstruction* Georgia one would hardly expect a financial institution to reek of money. Old money, new money, Yankee money, whatever. But the Bank of Georgia did; it definitely reeked. And this irritated Kathlyn.

Actually, she never had liked banks, to say nothing of bankers. Even before the war she had believed these wealthy men and the institutions they headed were crooked.

Now since the South had gone to hell in a hand-basket and decent people were all but starving in the streets, she had developed a considerable distrust for anyone who had more than two coins to rub together.

Obviously the owner of this bank had a sight more than two coins and had no qualms about flaunting it. *The crook.*

Tilting her head, her glance continued about the room. A tall man with muttonchop whiskers leaned close to a teller's cage and spoke in soft tones. She was amused, finding it funny how people speak quietly in a bank, almost as if it were a church.

Turning to Mr. Simon Percy, banker *extraordinaire,* she peeked at him through a thick fringe of lashes. That one would be totally out of place in a church. Saintly, he was not.

It was something about his eyes; she had always believed you could measure a person by the look in his eyes.

"I'm sure Mr. Dunn will be along shortly." The slightly balding banker referred to the man purchasing Kathlyn's property. "In the meantime, we can become better acquainted."

Kathlyn's eyes widened. There was no mistaking Percy's subtle innuendo. His voice reminded her of a snake-oil salesman who had passed through Union Point when she was a child. She grew nauseated, raking him with her gaze.

Misinterpreting her intense scrutiny as a sign of interest, Simon flashed her a suggestive grin. The early morning sunlight, filtering through the floor-to-ceiling windows, reflected off an enormous golden tooth in the front of his mouth, momentarily blinding her.

There was movement behind his back. Squinting, Kathlyn watched a large, oaken door slowly open. Due to the glare, she couldn't see who opened it, but apparently Simon noticed and knew. She caught the anxious — or was it irritated — look in his eyes.

Suddenly, he became unfailingly polite, washing the suggestive tone from his voice. Even the hungry look flashing in his ferret-like eyes dimmed.

Still, Kathlyn felt uneasy. Her black-gloved hands trembled — much to her chagrin. She despised weakness, especially in herself. Even if she did have a good reason to be distressed, she couldn't afford the luxury of weakness.

If only she could . . .

She sighed. "I trust all the papers are in order for the liquidation of my family's property," she queried, striving to keep her voice steady.

She managed to maintain a grip on her self-control, but not without a struggle. After all, it wasn't everyday that a person disposed of the sum total of her ancestors' holdings. A familiar sense of guilt assailed her. She pressed her reticule against her midriff, applied pressure to her steel stays, halting the flight of butterflies — butterflies the size of river-boats.

Just sign the papers, take the money, and go, she chanted in her mind for the umpteenth time. *Don't think, don't feel, just do it! You have no other choice. It's miraculous you've held on this long. Papa would understand.*

The thought of her late father brought a sheen to Kathlyn's eyes. *Stop this nonsense!* she ordered herself silently, clenching her teeth until her jaw ached. Tears, she simply wouldn't allow.

She had cried only four times since she was sixteen years old; at the deaths of both her parents and each of her two younger brothers. Through the years she had taught herself to withdraw, to insulate her emotions from the cruel realities of the world. She had survived the war by doing it. And she would maintain control of her emotions and survive this.

"I assure you they're in order," the banker answered finally, barely keeping the defensive edge from his voice. "Why else would I have asked you to come here?"

Why else indeed? Simon could think of another reason, but it wouldn't bear close scrutiny. Just looking at the ethereal beauty across from him was painfully arousing. Her rigid posture and bland expression were a blatant challenge to his seductive powers.

But he would have to wait until later. He knew his boss, whose office was located at his back, could hear every word he said. So for now he would play the chivalrous gent.

Not only could Brad Hampton hear every word Simon uttered, but by opening his office door and placing himself in a position to get a clear view of his clerk, he could see every movement the weasel made. He couldn't see the unsuspecting customer.

Brad ran an agitated hand through his dark hair and stiffened with resolve. Just because the war had destroyed nearly everything else in the South was no reason for its inhabitants to abandon the genteel manners and devotion to honor generations of Southern parents had instilled in them. And as long as he owned the Bank of Georgia, he would see to it that this bit of the Old South was not forgotten.

Idly smoothing the folds of his elaborately tied cravat, he leaned a muscled hip against the windowsill, peering around the drapes that covered the windows fronting his office. Then he shifted, stared blankly at the tanned hand that held the burgundy velvet aside, and winced at the thought of eavesdropping on an employee. Various complaints had been leveled against Simon, so Brad felt compelled to keep an eye on him. Still, he didn't like engaging in such a questionable practice as spying.

But the honor of his bank was at stake.

Muffling an oath, he pinched the bridge of his nose and closed his eyes. He had had this argument with himself all week. It always ended the same; the honor of his bank must be upheld. Keeping an eye on Percy was the lesser of two evils in his estimation.

That resolved once again, he tuned in the conversation taking place beyond the curtains.

Simon's customer was a woman. Her soft voice was husky and decidedly southern. There was an edge to it, as if she were holding herself in check. It sounded vaguely familiar, but Brad couldn't place it.

She was probably just some poor widow whose husband had died during the war, he decided. A ray of sunlight kissed the plain gold band Brad wore on his left hand, drawing his attention.

She could be Celia. If he had died and his wife had lived, that woman could be Celia, at the mercy of a man like Simon Percy. His grip tightened on the drapes.

It was an unsettling thought. Not because he was unduly disturbed by the remembrance of his wife's death; he had come to grips with his loss.

A smile softened his masculine features. The memory of his life with Celia was more like a beautiful dream now than a tangible part of his everyday existence. It no longer hurt to think of her. Rather it provided a pleasant, sweet sensation, like so many memories of life before the war.

After returning from the war, Brad had taken the money he had invested in California and Europe and worked sixteen hours a day to reestablish his bank. No doubt, it was this hard work and the love of his daughter, Annadru, that had healed the scars left by Celia's passing.

What sickened him most was, now that the war was over, women like Simon's customer had no one to protect them. Instinctively, his chivalrous nature came to the fore. Dragging his eyes from his wedding band, he listened more intently.

It was then that Simon and the woman stood to greet the buyer and Brad saw the object of his concern. His jaw dropped open. Straightening away from the window, he scanned her from head to toe—a relatively short span—with his smoldering brown eyes.

Nostalgia tugged sharply and the eleven years since their separation melted away. Brad was affected more than he cared to acknowledge.

She had been a girl then; now she was a woman. He'd thought her lovely before; now she was beautiful.

She wasn't a classic beauty, however; she was more. Her heart-shaped face was so delicately sculpted that at first glance it seemed unable to contain those starry-lashed eyes and full, pouting lips.

How well he remembered the perfectly arched brows that cut across her lily-white skin—skin which Brad knew she guarded with bonnet and parasol as Southern women were wont to do.

Her face was framed by a soft profusion of mahogany wisps. Beyond that he couldn't see her hair, for it was netted into a chignon. Instead of disguising her beauty, her primly concealed hair only added an element of mystery to her allure. But it was no mystery to him. Many was the time he'd freed that hair from its demure prison, spilling the silken mass over his hands. His skin tingled with the remembrance.

He stood mesmerized. Her deep ebony hair and violet-blue eyes brought to his mind a brilliant kaleidoscope of colors shot through with golden streaks of illumination. Surely it was an illusion created by the light slanting through the windows, but she looked so compelling, so vibrantly alive, that, involuntarily, he took a step toward her.

Introductions of buyer and seller were made, pleasantries halfheartedly observed, and once again she was seated, out of his sight. Brad was stunned by the bereft feeling he experienced when he could no longer see her. Kathlyn McKinney had been a summer fling to him, nothing more, he scolded.

There he was, congratulating himself for being over his wife's death, and then longing for a woman he hadn't seen in eleven years. A woman who had acted as if she loved him, a woman who had cast him aside like yesterday's newspaper. He deemed such feelings unacceptable. Actually, they scared the hell out of him.

In self defense, the slight cynicism he'd developed during the war reared its head. He had been without the pleasures of a woman too long. He would visit Lois after he and Jared finished at the tavern tonight and not give Kathlyn McKinney another thought. Lois was the kind of woman who satisfied a man's needs for a coin, without emotions getting in the way. Yes, that's all he needed, a torrid session with Lois.

"Would you care to read the contracts before you sign them?" Simon asked Kathlyn weakly, his voice penetrating Brad's thoughts.

Something about his employee's tone of voice alerted the businessman in Brad. He wondered if Kathlyn detected it. *Dammit! why doesn't she have a man conducting her affairs?*

Despite the belligerent tilt of her jaw, she had looked so helpless standing between Simon and the flashily dressed carpetbagger. Didn't she know how treacherous business in the South had become? Uncharacteristically, Brad cursed again.

All three men waited expectantly for Kathlyn's answer. She wasn't as naive as they supposed. She knew that women, far more worldly than she, were easy prey to men with far less intelligence and financial stability than the two confronting her.

No, her problem wasn't naivete. The sad fact was that women of her generation had not been taught to exist in a post-war world, if such a skill was possible.

Yet while she was a victim of her background, she readily detected the reluctance with which Simon made the offer to view the contracts. Obviously, he had something to hide.

She perceived the same wariness in the buyer, Mr. Dunn. She cut her eyes in his direction, purposefully delaying her answer.

She didn't like the man to whom she was selling her home any more than she liked the banker orchestrating the transaction. The fact that Dunn was a Yankee had nothing to do with it. Her father and younger brothers had fought valiantly for the Union themselves, so Kathlyn had no aversion to Yankees. Quite the contrary.

She disliked him, among other reasons, because he was the head of the local Freedman's Bureau. This Federal agency, established in 1865 by the U.S. Department of War, was admirable in its aim. Ostensibly, it was to provide assistance to the newly emancipated Negroes and needy whites as well.

In reality, the local agency was nothing more than an instrument of power for unscrupulous carpetbaggers and scalawags; they used it for their own economic and political gain. It was rumored that the funds earmarked for food and medical supplies lined the pockets of men like Percy and Dunn—and probably the owner of this ostentatious bank—while the unfortunates being denied these resources were packed into squalid cabins where smallpox, tuberculosis, and typhoid ran rampant.

Rage at these men and disgust at herself for dealing with them licked at the edges of her self-control like tongues of fire devouring dry leaves. She trembled as if she were chilled, yet was cognizant of the perspiration pooling beneath her arms.

For a split second she entertained the idea of bolting to her feet, hitching her skirts above her knees, and running out the door; transaction be damned.

Don't be a goose. Sign the papers, take what little money they offer, and go. Don't think, don't feel, just do it! You've got debts to pay and the only way to pay them is to deal with the devil . . . or devils as the case may be. You have no choice; honest people don't have any money these days. You deal with crooks or not at all.

These sentiments mortally wounded Kathlyn's pride. But more was at stake than her own self-esteem; her family's reputation was in jeopardy. She was the only McKinney left now. She was responsible for the McKinney's debts and only she could clear the McKinney name.

Then she would be free to move on. She could make a new life for herself, away from the unhappy memories of the South.

Remember, it's the beginning of your life. It feels like the end, but it isn't. True—your family's dead, your home's being sold to strangers—but it's the beginning. . . . Right! Somehow she wasn't convinced. She only hoped she wasn't selling a part of herself along with her home.

Kathlyn hated feeling uncertain. If only there was someone she could trust, someone to turn to, someone to advise her. But there wasn't. Her uncle was too ill, and her cousin, Rachel, was no wiser in the business world than she.

In the back of her mind she remembered trusting someone in Athens a long time ago, and getting a broken heart for her efforts. Kathlyn felt a familiar pit forming in her stomach.

Why did she have to think of him now? As if things weren't bad enough, she had to remember the time in her life when she had been most gullible, the time she had been betrayed in the most heinous fashion. It was probably her overwhelming sense of impotence that brought it to mind now, she decided.

Well, she was no longer an innocent, ignorant girl, anxious to trust the first man with a kind word and a handsome face. She was a woman now. And she didn't trust men like the two confronting her—or the one who had betrayed her—any further than she could throw them. And she never would.

Still, there was no point in delaying the inevitable; the die was cast. "No," she refused Simon's offer of reading the contracts in a clipped tone.

"I would like to see them," came a deep voice from the office of the president, drawing three sets of widened eyes in that direction.

Kathlyn's hand flew to her throat.

"You!" she accused.

Chapter Two

Years later, when Kathlyn recalled this moment in time, she was quite certain the earth ceased its rotation. Everything froze: the customers milling throughout the bank, Simon and Dunn, the breath in her lungs, her mind, her heart.

Everything, but Brad Hampton. As if from a great distance, he moved toward her, growing larger and more threatening with each step. Until finally, he stood before her.

So close she could smell his familiar scent of soap, spicy cologne, and fine tobacco. How could she remember a fragrance she hadn't smelled in eleven years? And how could it still affect her so?

Damning her eyes, she drank in the sight of him: he was larger than she remembered, taller, more imposing. The years had been kind to him. His wide shoulders stretched the fine navy fabric of his frockcoat, his impossibly flat stomach looked as if it were made of steel, his muscular thighs were encased in rich, fawn trousers, and his hips . . .

Her heart raced with the speed of a runaway freight train; he resembled a Greek god even more now than he had then. She had hoped a young girl's impressionable heart and the intervening years had distorted her memory. But such was not the case.

Brad Hampton was everything she remembered and more: a man born to wealth and position, a man whose every word went unchallenged, a man who possessed more than his share of panache.

Like a kettle of boiling water, emotions churned through her. Feelings she'd thought long since buried rose and threatened the carefully constructed wall she existed behind. Instinctively, she placed her hand on her lower abdomen.

The gesture, full of meaning to her alone, jolted her to her senses. She stiffened ramrod straight, a full six inches separating her back from the chair she perched on. With a force of will, she schooled her expression and raised her gaze to his eyes.

Her earlier thoughts came back to taunt her: *You can always measure a person by the look in his eyes.* Brad Hampton was a flesh and blood exception to that rule.

In their black depths she saw everything and nothing: charm, cynicism, concern, indifference, strength, vulnerability, intelligence, arrogance, and ruthless determination softened by exquisite tenderness. Almost any emotion one could imagine could be found in those hypnotic eyes, blended together to be totally undecipherable. *Damn him.*

Brad watched the emotions slide across Kathlyn's face and wondered at the thoughts that gave rise to them. If possible, the haughty expression she was struggling with now intrigued him most. Fool that he was.

He didn't want to be intrigued by this woman. He wanted only to see that she was treated fairly and thereby preserve the honor of his bank.

Turning away from Kathlyn abruptly, he spoke to Simon. "Please bring those papers into my office."

How dare he dismiss her so casually! Kathlyn surged to her feet. Steadying herself, she braced her calves against the chair at her back and clasped trembling hands in the folds of her wear-softened gown. "You really shouldn't trouble yourself on my account, sir." Kathlyn's voice was loud in the stillness.

"Mr. Hampton, I assure you everything is in order," Simon sputtered as he jumped to his feet.

"I'm quite certain it is," Brad drawled with exaggerated politeness, ignoring Kathlyn's interruption. "But then one can't be too careful, can one?" The taunting elevation of an ebony brow dared Simon to balk.

Brad looked completely in command, but standing alongside Kathlyn—so close he could feel the heat of her indignation—he was forced to take a deep, cleansing breath. A sense of exhilaration at her nearness rose in his breast. Determinedly, he suppressed it.

"Just who the hell do you think you are, meddling in my business?" Dunn hissed.

Brad turned slowly. "I'm Brad Hampton." It was a declaration. Arrogantly offered. As if the very name should strike fear in the hearts of the unjust.

Kathlyn found herself listening for the sound of trumpets.

Then his voice softened. "You're standing in *my* bank." His gentlemanly demeanor and Southern drawl didn't disguise the menace clearly reflected in his chocolate brown eyes.

The deceptively bored expression on his face, coupled with his confident stance, labeled him as a formidable foe. And all parties recognized this, particularly Kathlyn.

Loathe to admit it, she was impressed. *That* was what she was lacking. The self-assured arrogance that came from being competent in business and possessing the wealth and power to manipulate matters to one's own advantage. Brad exuded it from every pore. Obviously she didn't exhibit a shred. No wonder the three Neanderthals acted as if she were invisible.

"Percy's taking care of my affairs, so you just run on back to your plantation and plot another doomed rebellion or whatever you *Southern gentlemen* find to do these days," Dunn sneered.

The carpetbagger hated Southern aristocracy, but Brad's ominous expression made him reluctant to bait him further. So angrily, Dunn turned on Simon.

Before he could speak, however, Simon intervened. "I was just about to inform Miss McKinney and Mr. Dunn that I've been unable to complete the necessary paperwork for their transaction when you offered your assistance."

Brad and Kathlyn both responded. "You said they were in order."

"That's not what you said."

Brad detected strength in Kathlyn's voice. He almost wished he had not intervened, but Simon's reluctance to show him the contracts could not go unchallenged. "Nevertheless, bring them into my office."

Exhibiting inborn Southern charm, Brad placed his hand quite properly beneath Kathlyn's elbow, to escort

27

her into his office.

His touch seared her flesh. Jerking her arm out of his grasp, she turned her spinning head toward him. That was a mistake. He was so close she felt his warm breath on her cheek.

All she wanted now was to flee—flee this damnable deal, these unscrupulous men, and most of all this man who had betrayed her so long ago. When she whirled away from him, her caged crinoline caught on the edge of her chair and threw her off balance. The floor rushed up to meet her.

Brad caught her around the waist as she grasped handfuls of empty air. Circling her arms with strong yet gentle hands, he pulled her against his chest.

"Let me go," it was as much a plea as an order. Her indifferent facade was in serious danger of cracking.

Abruptly, Brad released her. She tottered, and, stifling a curse, he grabbed her again. As he held her flush against him, he became painfully aware that everyone in the bank was watching them. How had he gotten into such a mess? All he had wanted to do was make sure a helpless woman wasn't being cheated, he lied to himself again.

She had appeared so vulnerable earlier, giving rise to his well-developed chivalrous instincts. But this? *This* development caused instincts to rise that had little to do with chivalry. Quite the contrary.

Galvanized into action by the response of his body to her nearness, he untangled her hoop, spun on his heel, and disappeared into his office, dragging her behind him. She was too appalled to resist.

He seated her in a chair a safe distance from his own, then stepped to the door and spoke to Simon in a tone that brooked no argument. "The young lady will require a few moments to catch her breath. After that, bring the contracts into my office."

Brad stepped into his office and closed the door behind him. Kathlyn was standing across the room now, silhouetted by a partially opened window.

He was pulled to her by invisible hands. Sympathy welled in him when he dropped his gaze and noticed the band of black crepe that edged her gown, trapped beneath his shoe.

She was in half-mourning. He wondered if she had lost her husband. Somehow the thought of Kathlyn mourning a lost love bothered him.

Shaking his head, he realized the absurdity of such feelings. She had spurned him years ago. Why shouldn't she find someone else? He had.

The past was behind them. But if he were to help her now, he had to clear the air. And for reasons he didn't care to examine too closely, he wanted very much to help her.

Gently, he touched her shoulder, turning her toward him. He flashed her his most platonic smile. "I'm sorry if I embarrassed you."

Kathlyn looked into his eyes, softened with compassion. She nodded slightly. His widening smile showed a dimple, so at odds with his masculine appearance. Funny, but she didn't remember his dimple. Her fingers tingled with the urge to caress the fetching indentation.

She suppressed the urge and looked away. She wished he would step back; he was standing much too close for her peace of mind.

"How have you been, Kathlyn?"

What did he care how she'd been? He acted as if they were merely casual acquaintances, renewing an old friendship. She had given him her innocence, for heaven's sake. Had it been so meaningless to him?

Oh God, she had a painful thought, *he doesn't even remember. He doesn't remember making love to me.* No doubt, she was just one in a long line of maidens the dashing young Brad Hampton had deflowered.

Her sense of hurt was quickly replaced by anger. If she were given to such *missish* outbursts, she would have stamped her foot. Instead, she just glared at him.

Her flare of emotion pleased him. She didn't look vulnerable now. In fact, she looked downright sexy. In spite of his best intentions, the look in his eyes changed. He remembered making love to her; the erotic memory darkened his piercing gaze.

That was a look Kathlyn had seen before. Feeling threatened, she side-stepped him and crossed over to a vacant chair.

"Look, Mr. Hampton," she emphasized the formal address, leaning against the high back and fixing Brad with her gaze. "I don't want your apology for embarrassing me . . . or anything else from you.

"I appreciate your offer to read my contracts and to see that I'm being treated fairly . . . just as you would do for any other customer in your bank. But that's all. This is a business deal, so let's leave it at that. Shall we?" Kathlyn's voice sounded raspy even to her own ears.

Brad wasn't angered by her response. She was right. Considering their past, the sooner their business was completed, the better it would be for both of them.

Sighing, he stepped back. By the time he had seated himself in his massive chair, he was the picture of a professional banker. He shifted papers about on his desk. The silence in the room was oppressive, broken only by the soft rustle of Kathlyn's petticoat as she settled into the seat fronting his desk.

Finally, their eyes met again. This time, they looked away immediately.

Then Simon knocked on the door and Kathlyn jumped. When Brad heard her muffle an unladylike curse, he smiled. He crossed the room to the door and touched her shoulder in a reassuring gesture as he passed. She flinched, but he didn't notice.

"You wanted to see Miss McKinney's contracts," Simon accused mildly when Brad opened the door.

Bristling at Simon's impertinence, Brad invited both his employee and the buyer into the room in a less than hospitable tone. Once they were all seated, he carefully studied Kathlyn's contracts.

It was just as he suspected. They had planned to cheat Kathlyn. The sum—that Simon had obviously just altered—was still far too low a price for the Union Point property. He could only imagine the paltry amount they had planned to offer her originally.

The tension in the room was fairly tangible. With unseeing eyes aimed at the contracts, Brad was aware of every breath Kathlyn drew. A protective impulse such as he had not known in a long while surprised him with its intensity. In spite of his need to keep her at arm's length, he warmed to the feeling.

He raised his gaze and looked her full in the face. Her expression was closed, but her eyes looked like nothing so much as those of a frightened fawn. Then the iris pools darkened, resembling the surface of the Oconee River on a January morning, still and cold. Icy. He couldn't look away.

Unnerved by Brad's scrutiny, Kathlyn began removing her gloves. Her hands trembled as she lay them on his desk.

He noticed her outward sign of distress. She wasn't the ice maiden she portrayed. She was a scared little girl, playing in a man's world. And she was about to be eaten alive. Unless he intervened.

Pushing the contracts away from him forcefully, he ground out each word, "Miss McKinney cannot possibly accept this offer!" Determination hardened his eyes to shards of black ice.

In tandem, Simon and Dunn gaped in disbelief at the enraged president of the Bank of Georgia.

"What the hell?" Dunn was the first to find his voice. Sweat popped out on his forehead. "I wasn't aware that this was any concern of yours," he spat. "This business affair is between me and Miss McKinney and your bank is merely providing us a service. We are customers here, no more and no less."

Dunn turned and pinned Simon with his glare. "Simon, we had a deal." It was clearly a threat.

But Simon didn't spare him a glance. His eyes alternated from Brad to Kathlyn. At long last, that which he had feared most had occurred. He had been caught with his hand in the till, so to speak. From the look on Brad's face, he was certain he would be looking for employment elsewhere before the day was out.

No matter. He had fleeced a host of customers since the war; he would live comfortably whether he found gainful employment elsewhere or not.

But he didn't intend to leave quietly. Remembering the intimate way Brad had held Kathlyn earlier, Simon taunted his boss. "Perhaps you have a special interest in this particular customer?" He leered at Kathlyn. "Are the words *affair* and *service* particularly apt when it comes to describing your relationship with Miss McKinney?"

Kathlyn's cheeks flamed, and she locked her gaze on the flowered Aubusson rug beneath her feet. It was fortuitous that Simon could not guess how close to the truth he had come.

Brad's rage grew to enormous proportions. "You bastard," he growled, lunging to his feet. He rounded the desk in a blur. Before Simon could react, Brad grabbed him by the collar. Jerking him to his feet, Brad hissed, "You miserable piece of scum, apologize to Miss McKinney now!"

Simon paled visibly. He had never seen any side of Brad Hampton, save that of a soft-spoken, Southern gentleman. Iron-willed, but a gentleman, nonetheless. He had expected his boss to be angry, but not violent. Perhaps he would do well to apologize and leave quietly after all.

Still, Simon hated Brad so, detested him for his excellent pedigree, for his inordinate success. Good sense fled his mind.

The grip Brad had on his collar made it difficult for Simon to turn his head toward Kathlyn. So he merely slanted his eyes in her direction. "I'm sorry," he whispered, "that you're his slut and not mine."

Growling like an enraged grizzly, Brad backhanded Simon, knocking him through a large window, showering glass throughout the spacious office.

As his unconscious partner hung half-in, half-out of the window, Dunn shrank back against his chair. His eyes darted about, searching for an avenue of escape.

Brad stepped forward. Gently, he pulled Kathlyn to her feet. He examined her clothing for fragments of glass, running shaky hands over her gown, skimming her slight curves. His heart lurched when he noticed how much thinner she was now than when she was sixteen. Obviously, the war had taken its toll on her.

Kathlyn brushed Brad's hands aside. "Mr. Hampton, remember yourself." She wasn't sure, but she could have sworn he blushed. Surely not.

Brad cleared his throat, muffling a chuckle at his outrageous behavior. So much for genteel manners . . .

Regaining his composure, he turned on Dunn. "Do you

want the same as Percy, or shall I rewrite the contracts for Miss McKinney's property?" He didn't wait for an answer. "I think after all she has endured, she should get fair market value, plus ten percent. Don't you?" Brad's soft tone was clearly threatening. The only softness in his demeanor was the slight wink he gave Kathlyn when he noticed the flush on her cheeks and the look of appreciation in her eyes.

"Whatever you say, Mr. Hampton," the buyer said, shaking his head up and down like a puppet.

"Well then, it seems that everything is in order," Brad spoke calmly, as if nothing untoward had happened. One would think he sent employees sailing through his office window on a regular basis. "You may leave now, Mr. Dunn. I'll send a runner around when the contracts are ready for your signature."

Dunn was frozen to the spot, not wanting to pass Brad even to get to the door.

Kathlyn recognized this and smiled. She was enthralled; having a man like Brad fight for her was heady stuff. And her body was still tingling from his touch. Perhaps all the romantic heroes weren't to be found in dime novels and love sonnets, she dared to dream.

But they're not to be found in your life either, a nagging voice intruded, reminding her of the many reasons she couldn't believe in knights in shining armor, heroes rescuing damsels in distress, or even honorable bank executives protecting their customers from greedy employees and avaricious carpetbaggers. Especially this particular banker. And this particular customer.

Pragmatically accepting the obvious, she shelved her romantic musings. She cast Simon's body a satisfied glance, then lifted her skirts slightly, and crossed the room to Dunn.

"This is for all the McKinney's you tried to cheat today," she said softly. Then she drew back her bare hand and slapped the shocked carpetbagger's face with all the force her slender arm could wield.

Brad's eyes widened with surprise. Obviously, she was not the same naive, angelic, sixteen-year-old he had known all those years ago. When she returned to his side, he smiled down into her upturned face. He wouldn't mind seeing more of this Kathlyn McKinney.

"It would seem that my office will have to be set to rights before I'm able to work on your contracts. Could I interest you in a glass of lemonade at Hannah's Sweetery?"

The self-confident look on Brad's face shook Kathlyn to her toes. Was he crazy, actually thinking she would see him socially? Was she crazy, actually wanting to?

Yes, on both accounts.

She wanted to say yes with a fierceness that took her breath. But she had given in to him before and had almost died as a result of her foolishness. Crazy or not, she wouldn't make that mistake again.

She chafed her arms, shivering, suddenly enraged—enraged by this terrible longing she felt for Brad, enraged at him for making her feel it. No, enraged at him for *expecting* her to feel it. Almost as if it were his due.

Arrogant jackass. He didn't deserve an answer to his insane invitation. Jerking her chin, she backed toward the door, shards of the broken window crunching beneath her feet.

"You don't care to go with me," Brad verbalized the obvious. "Do you?"

She rolled her eyes heavenward. What did it take with some people? Did a house need to fall on him? Well, if he wanted an answer, she would give him one. "I'd rather chew glass." With that, she spun on her heel and exited the office, head held high.

"Oh would you?" he whispered to her retreating figure. Brad wondered if the lady was saying one thing, and feeling another. In fact, he was quite certain she was.

Smiling, he settled his gaze on Simon's inert form, then shifted it to Dunn. He noticed, with some satisfaction, the small red handprint that had already formed on the carpetbagger's cheek.

Feeling Brad's eyes on him, Dunn hunched his shoulders and scampered from the room.

Brad dropped his head back on his shoulders and laughed for the sheer pleasure of it. All in all it had been one hell of a day.

34

Chapter Three

Paradise Manor stood proud and tall in the midst of a summer thunderstorm when Brad returned home late that afternoon. Purposefully pushing thoughts of his encounter with Kathlyn from his mind, he dashed through the double entry doors, soaked to the skin.

Heavy sheets of rain enclosed the lovely mansion, creating a sense of total isolation. Brad did not find it an unpleasant feeling, however. Since Reconstruction had blown into Georgia on the heels of the American Civil War, families like his valued their solitude.

"Mistah Brad, you're wastin' water all over my clean floor!" Mammy Mae feigned sternness.

He deposited his Adelaide-blue hat, gloves, and silver-topped cane on the entrance table. Smiling, he strode toward his scowling nanny.

"Now is that any way for a lady to talk to her best beau?"

The young charmer bent at the waist and kissed the old woman's dusky cheek. He mounted the stairs two at a time and entered his bedchamber with Mammy's laughter floating in his wake.

Before shucking his wet, clinging clothes, Brad removed his pocket watch from his waistcoat pocket. Pressing a button, he flipped the lid open and checked the time. Then he lay the timepiece on the bureau, considering the evening ahead.

It was almost dark and his brother, Jared, was waiting for him downstairs. They were going to their favorite tavern to discuss a joint business venture which Brad had decided to postpone. Jared wasn't going to like that bit of news and Brad didn't want to make matters worse by leaving him cooling his heels in the parlor. So he dressed quickly.

It was an overcast night and twilight blanketed the pine-ringed clearing as the Hampton brothers approached Eagle Tavern. The rain had stopped, but the gloaming cast its shadows about the handsome twosome.

Despite the ominous clouds overhead, the tavern was doing a booming business. Jared and Brad made their way up the steps. Passing through a sea of ale-soaked revellers, they found an empty table. Neither brother spoke until they were seated.

"When do you leave?" Jared asked, removing his hat and gloves.

"I'm not exactly sure," Brad said evasively. Avoiding Jared's eyes, he drew circles with his gloved finger on the damp tabletop.

Knowing his brother well, Jared was suspicious. "What do you mean you're not exactly sure? In his last letter, Chase said he needed you in Fort Smith right away. He's counting on you to make the arrangements to buy the cattle. He's hired on extra hands for the drive, and all they need now is the beef."

Brad raised his clear brown eyes and fixed them on his physician brother. "I just can't get away right now." He made somewhat of a production of removing his gloves.

"Is it that confounded bank of yours? Smith knows as much about the bank as you do. He *can* get along without you, Brad."

Brad knew full well his Vice President, Morgan Smith, could handle the bank. Morgan had been a friend of his for years. Before the war, Morgan, Brad, and their good friend, Bill Sherman, had engaged in business on numerous occasions. In their past dealings Morgan had more than proven himself to be a man of both honor and competence.

Morgan had been an officer of Bill's bank in San Francisco, Lucas Turner & Co., and he had also been

36

an associate in his law firm, Sherman and Ewing, in Kansas. Unfortunately, he had been with Bill during the war as well, when the famous Union general had marched through Georgia, burning everything in his path.

The devastation they left behind was more than a man of Morgan's sensibilities could accept. After the war he had approached Brad, saying he wanted to stay in the South, to help rebuild it.

Understanding his feelings and appreciating his desire to help, Brad hired him as his Vice President. Brad feared the residents of Athens would have him tarred and feathered, but he stood behind Morgan just the same. He was glad he had. Together, they had built the Bank of Georgia into the growing concern it was today.

"Dammit Brad," cursed Jared, breaking in to Brad's musings. "I thought everything was settled. What could be more important than this deal?"

"What'll y'all have?" a slovenly attired barmaid asked.

Brad blessed the distraction. He felt guilty, disappointing Jared and his brother-in-law, Chase, but he just didn't want to leave Georgia at present.

And he refused to consider that Kathlyn's reappearance in his life could account for his change of heart.

Mentally shaking himself, he observed the serving girl and pasted a pleasant expression on his face. Her vacant stare, greasy, matted hair, and emaciated form were all too familiar to him. The poverty and absolute hopelessness that plagued most Southerners these days tore at his gut.

"What'll it be," she asked again, scratching her scalp with dirty fingers.

"Just a smile from a lovely lady." Brad winked.

All of a sudden, the girl's expression wasn't quite so blank. Her head lifted now, a faint smile touched her face.

"I fear that a smile will do nothing to quench your thirst, sir." Noticing Brad's immaculate appearance, she wiped her hands on a stained apron.

He cocked his head. "Ah, but there are thirsts, and there are thirsts." Meaningless flirtation was something

37

Brad felt comfortable with. Kathlyn, however, was another story. He shifted uneasily at the thought.

The waitress giggled at Brad's words; her hollow cheeks grew pink.

Jared shook his head in amazement. What his roguish brother could do with a lazy stare and a few well-chosen words would put Romeo to shame. Jared wasn't so easily charmed by the handsome rake.

"I thirst for a pint of ale," Jared said flatly, anxious to get back to the subject at hand.

Brad rolled his eyes heavenward and explained to the girl in a stage whisper, "He's married. What does he know of romance?" As an afterthought he added, "I'll take a drink too."

She tittered as she bustled around the table, providing both men with their requests. For Jared, she brought a pint of ale. Then on Brad she bestowed a brilliant smile, along with his drink.

With a wistful glance at Brad, the girl moved on to her other customers. Jared resumed his interrogation. "What's gotten into you? The last time we talked you were all for this trip. You were saying you couldn't wait to see the ranch, to visit with Lacy and her family, not to mention making a fortune.

"And what are you going to tell Annadru? All she's talked about for weeks is finally meeting her Aunt Lacy and Uncle Chase—a real-live Indian. She'll be crushed."

"I know." Brad held his hands up in a placating gesture. Jared was bringing out the big guns, using Annadru as an argument.

"Well, what's so important that you can't make the trip?"

"I'll be danged. If it ain't the darkie-lovin' Hamptons," a taunting voice intruded. "Brad, I'm surprised that a high falutin' banker like you would rub shoulders with poor nabs like us. What's wrong? All your Yankee friends busy?"

The brothers locked gazes and raised their mugs in salute, appearing to ignore the ape towering above them. Jared might be put out with his younger brother, but when it came to outsiders, Hamptons pulled together.

For a long moment, the air crackled with anticipation, not unlike the atmosphere preceding a violent thunderstorm. Jared's muffled curse was drowned out as Brad came uncoiled.

The ape intended to spit another invective, but before he could speak, Brad wielded his silver-topped cane, cracking him across the mouth. Spewing blood and teeth on Brad's blinding white shirt, the ape bellowed in pain and called for assistance.

Instantly, Brad and Jared found themselves confronted by four, foul-smelling, scowling ruffians. They recognized the leader as the thief Brad had fired from Paradise Manor a week earlier.

"Damn Brad, I'm too old for this foolishness," Jared mumbled out of the corner of his mouth.

"Nah, there are only four of 'em. Besides, think of the story we'll have to tell Melinda and the kids."

"Now, gentlemen." Jared extended his hand. "I'm sure we can solve this peacefully, without any more violence."

The ape spat on Jared's boots.

Grinning, Brad raised an ebony brow at his brother and shrugged. Never one to favor inactivity, the promise of a good fight had raised his spirits immensely.

Taking the measure of their opponents, Jared breathed a short prayer requesting that he and his irrepressible brother lived to tell his wife and kids *anything*.

"Ain't they purty all duded up in them fine clothes? Don't know whether to hit 'em or to kiss 'em!" a redheaded ogre goaded.

Red's companions hooted and whistled as if Brad and Jared were sensuous Southern belles, not six-foot-plus specimens of barely contained anger.

In a deceptively calm voice, Brad retorted, "I'd rather kiss a sow."

"So much for a peaceful resolution," Jared yelled, as all hell broke loose.

With macabre excitement, the other patrons of the tavern stepped aside, forming a loose circle around the six combatants.

39

Three of the smelly, cursing louts jumped Brad, while the ape leveled a punch at Jared's chiseled jaw. Failing to connect, the forward movement of the ape's meaty arm propelled him right smack into Jared's clenched fist. Before Jared could think of what he'd done, the ape's second swing connected and pain exploded in his head. Toe to toe, the refined physician and his uncivilized opponent battled, trading blow for blow.

Meanwhile, with arms pumping, Brad fended off the efforts of his trio of attackers. Throwing a powerful right, he caught one man under the chin, then twisted and smashed his fist deep into another's protruding belly. Finally, he planted a well-aimed kick between the remaining goon's legs.

By the time the third man bent double, the first one had recovered. The power of his rush drove all four men to the floor, with Brad trapped at the bottom of a sea of riffraff.

With strength borne of desperation, Brad lunged to his feet, scattering the men all around him. The ape who started the ruckus hurried to their aid.

"Watch out!" the barmaid shrieked from behind.

Brad whirled about just as she expertly wielded a pewter pitcher, cracking the ape over the head. The man's knees buckled and he fell backwards, knocking the woman off balance.

When Brad pulled her to her feet and smiled his thanks, a silver streak flashed in the corner of his eye. Sensing that he was about to be stabbed, he pushed the woman safely to the floor and at the same time raised his forearm to shield his face. The moment the razor-sharp knife sank into his flesh, a gun shot exploded in his ear.

The knife-wielding brigand pitched forward, landing at Brad's feet. After a quick glance to reassure himself that his assailant was still alive, Brad jerked his head in the direction of the blast. Across the room, Jared held a smoking gun.

By the time Jared reached him, Brad's arm was pumping blood. Pressing the wound firmly to staunch the flow, Jared uttered, "Little brother, next time you invite me out for a drink, remind me to decline."

"Now do you see why I can't leave town?" Brad asked, his face paling from loss of blood.

"This fight is no reason to stay."

"Do you actually think this is an isolated incident? Ever since I got back from the war I've been under suspicion. Hell, we all have. They're actually saying we came by our wealth dishonestly, by robbing the Confederacy or some such nonsense.

"You'd think I'd joined the Republican Party the way people are talking. What are you going to do when our self-righteous neighbors stop gossiping and start shooting? What will happen to Melinda and the kids when they have only a peace-loving physician between them and an enraged mob?"

Jared sighed and bowed his head over Brad's wound. His shoulders slumped forward. At thirty-five he suddenly felt like a very old man.

Automatically, he tore a strip of cloth from his shirt and bound the ragged gash on Brad's arm. "The people around here are not, I repeat, are *not* going to do violence to the doctor who cared for their sons during the war. The same doctor, I might add, who treats them and their families even now. In short, they need me. They will not hurt my wife and children because I care for theirs."

Brad couldn't argue with that. For forty years, the Hampton's liberal leanings had been tolerated, albeit grudgingly, because the people of Clarke County needed the medical care and attention three generations of Hampton doctors had provided.

Unfortunately, since the war, their neighbors' long-suffering tolerance didn't encompass Brad and his youngest brother, Jay. Especially not Jay!

"That's blasted hypocritical if you ask me." The thread of tension running the length of Brad was fairly tangible. Both men were so intent on their debate that it didn't occur to them that perhaps they should leave the tavern and continue the discussion once Brad's injury had been closed.

"Hypocritical or not, it's the truth. This fiasco tonight wouldn't have happened if I had been alone, and you know it. Those men were out to get you."

Jared hated being so blunt. It was obvious to anyone who knew Brad, that he was hurting inside. Although he tended to deny it, even to himself. But he was a proud man who had suffered during the war just like everybody else. His way of life had disappeared and his wife had died; a man couldn't lose much more than that.

"I've already checked the schedule. There's a train leaving for Memphis on the fifteenth. You should be able to make it."

Brad leveled Jared a withering glare. "You never give up, do you?" Then, he winced in pain. "If you don't mind, brother, I'd appreciate you patching me up before I bleed to death," he said.

Jared nodded. "If the authorities have any questions, they know where to find us," he called over his shoulder to the barkeep as he helped Brad exit the tavern. In his mind he acknowledged that Brad was right about one thing; he wasn't going to give up. Somehow, he'd manage to get Brad on that train.

After Brad and Jared disappeared through the door, a huge, rough-bearded man, filling the corner of the tavern, stood. Slowly, he crossed over to the unconscious ruffians who littered the floor.

"Damn fools," he spat, kicking them as they began moving about. "Four of you against two, and they walked away." He addressed the man who had been shot, "Wish he'd killed you."

A chilling hatred sparked in the man's pale blue eyes as he left the tavern. "It's not over," he vowed to the night air. "Next time, Brad Hampton won't walk away."

Chapter Four

Mindful of her somewhat stained reputation, Rachel
Jackson came by cover of darkness to the Franklin
Hotel. In her reticule, she carried the note she received
from Stuart Shephard that afternoon.

It read simply: *Rachel: It's time to put the plan into
action. The train leaves for Memphis on the fifteenth.
Have Kathlyn on it. Stuart*

Not until I get some answers, she huffed silently, entering the lobby. Quietly, she passed the dining room
to her left, hoping to go unnoticed. The clink of ster-
ling silver and the tinkle of fine crystal floated to her
ears, reassuring her that no one was paying her any
mind. The diners were too occupied with the hotel's
gourmet fare.

Mounting the marble steps to the second floor, her
heart accelerated. Her footsteps faltered as Stuart's ominous appearance came to mind.

Undoubtedly, she would be in his bed before the
night was through, but she would delay it. This time,
she would insist that he reveal his entire nefarious
scheme and make her a full partner.

Only then would she allow herself the carnal release
to be gained thrashing around in his bed, only then
would she allow herself to enjoy coupling with this
savage lover.

Eventually she would get what she wanted. Physically and otherwise. She always did. Unbidden, Brad
Hampton's face appeared in her mind's eye, taunting

her, reminding her of the time she had not gotten her way. Well, she wasn't through with him yet.

Tamping down her quicksilver rage, she dropped her lace mantle away from her bare shoulders.

She knocked on the hollow pine door and Stuart swung it open a crack.

"My dear," he greeted in cultured tones, stepping aside to allow her entry. His courtly manners and sophisticated drawl were in sharp contrast to his wild appearance.

The sap of desire rushed to Rachel's loins. She stepped inside the room and, for a moment, surveyed her surroundings. The room was nice enough, with the usual furnishings: feather bed, ladder-backed chairs, floral settee, and cherry-wood commode, complete with a zinc basin and one tap.

In the center of the room was a round table with a flask of brandy and two snifters, placed upon a lace runner. A sputtering gas light was suspended from the ceiling, surrounded by a Tiffany lead-crystal shade. Stuart's damp greatcoat was draped over a massive armoire. Obviously, he had just returned to the room. "Where have you been tonight?"

"Out," he answered crisply, drawing her eyes to him.

His hair, prematurely gray, hung over his massive shoulders. An angry scar, trailed from the corner of his right eye, down to his full beard. He was dressed in unrelieved black.

She could hardly believe this was Stuart Shephard, aristocratic gentleman. The rich plantation owner, who, before the war, had wielded such power in the Georgia General Assembly.

She wondered, not for the first time, what the Hamptons had done to Stuart that wrought such a change. How they had brought him so low.

He interrupted her musings when he reached out and boldly fondled her breast. "Not now." She pushed his hand away. "Not until you answer a few questions."

He threw back his head and laughed. "I wondered how you'd play it"—he withdrew his hand—"at least,

44

you're not going to be coy. I give you what you want, and you give me what I want. Rather like a business deal." He pinned her with a suggestive gaze. "But perhaps we want the same thing."

Rachel elevated her carefully tweezed brows, yet said nothing.

He led her to the table, seated her, poured their drinks and took the chair opposite her. His movements were catlike, sleek, graceful, surprisingly agile for a man of his size. "What if I just answer your questions, then send you on your way?" he taunted.

Rachel didn't like the turn of things. She needed a man desperately; she just didn't want Stuart to know. She shrugged, feigning nonchalance.

"Now, my dear. What is it you want to know?"

She leaned forward, placing her palms facedown on the table. "I want to know your . . . our"—she corrected herself—"whole plan, with all the gory details."

"I see. I had hoped to spare you the particulars in order to protect you from the authorities. You see, you can't be prosecuted for something you don't know."

Rachel straightened. "How very noble of you," she drawled sarcastically. "And I thought you wanted to cheat me out of my share of the money by keeping me ignorant."

Stuart affected a wounded look.

It occurred to Rachel that while Stuart's looks had gone to hell, his mind was still as sharp . . . and as devious, as ever. Getting the upper hand would require a bit more finesse than she had first supposed.

Raising her glass to her lips, she took a long draw of amber liquid then snaked her tongue out, running it along the rim of the snifter. "I've done my part."

While she spoke, she dipped the tip of a long, red lacquered finger into her drink and trailed the moisture over her bulging breasts and down into her cleavage.

Stuart's eyes were riveted to the moist, shiny skin. Unconsciously, he licked his lips.

Rachel grinned and continued in a husky voice, "I've seen to it that five of the loveliest girls in Georgia are

45

engaged to Glenn Crutchfield, including my own cousin. This was no easy feat considering that some of those girls have never even seen him." She raised a brow and paused allowing Stuart time to consider these accomplishments.

"I think it's high time I discovered what's to become of them . . . and how *we're* going to profit from it."

Stuart sat perfectly still. For so long, Rachel wondered if he intended to answer her. Finally, he did. "The plan is to sell the women into slavery."

"What?" Rachel asked incredulously. The notion was so shocking that she abandoned her seductive pose and leaned forward, imploring Stuart to continue.

"Beautiful white women bring a high price in the slave markets of the Middle East."

"You're not serious," she scoffed.

He shrugged negligently. "Syud Majid, the Sultan of Zanzibar, will pay a hundred thousand dollars for a beauty like Kathlyn. In return, he'll claim double that price when he sells her to the Sultan of Muscat, Baghdad, or one of the principalities of Turkey." Stuart rattled off the names of these impressive men as if they were his closest acquaintances. Rachel was clearly impressed.

Noting the look of pure amazement on her face, he chuckled. "Can you picture your virginal cousin in a harem?"

"She'll never stand for it," Rachel spat, disgusted as always at the thought of Kathlyn.

"Oh, I expect she'll behave. Those slave traders know how to handle women who resist."

"How?" She grinned, now obviously enjoying the conversation.

"They've been known to circumcise them, or they sometimes just mutilate their genitals and sew them up."

Rachel squeezed her legs tightly together. Dropping his head back, Stuart roared with laughter. "Perhaps you'd like to hear about the trip the lovelies will take.

You might not find it as painful."

Stuart was laughing at her, but at the moment Rachel didn't care. She had her own agenda.

And while the possibility of those atrocities happening to Kathlyn was gratifying, the thought of mutilated genitals *wasn't* arousing. And she wanted to be aroused. It was part of *her* plan.

"When Glenn's prospective brides arrive in Fort Smith, they'll find their groom strangely absent," he began dryly. "Naturally, they'll have to take the stage to Fort Gibson where he's stationed.

"Along the way they'll be kidnapped and taken by private coach through Indian Territory. It will travel along the old Butterfield line to El Paso, then Tucson, finally arriving in San Francisco. That's where we'll turn them over to the trader and be paid handsomely for our efforts."

Rachel rose and advanced on Stuart, swaying her hips as she approached him. Sensuously, she took his hand and slid it beneath the hem of her red taffeta gown. "I want to go to San Francisco with you."

"But what about your poor, crippled father?" Stuart's voice was anything but sympathetic. When his hand made contact with bare flesh, he smiled. "If you left him here alone, Kathlyn would be suspicious. And I don't want her to suspect anything. She's too valuable."

"You let me worry about my father . . . and Kathlyn too. On the fifteenth, she'll be on that train for Memphis. And if I work it right, she'll insist that her only *living* relative accompany her."

There was a hidden message in Rachel's reassurances, but when she sat on his lap and cradled his face with her breasts, Stuart was distracted.

"Take me with you," she entreated. "You'll be glad you did."

"Perhaps I should." A sinister smile crossed his face. "Yes, I'll take you with me."

Rachel stood and removed her clothes, hiding a smug smile, thinking she had won a great victory. Had

47

she known the thought uppermost in Stuart's mind, she would have had grave doubts.

As he surveyed her naked body, Stuart calculated how much Syud Majid would pay for Rachel.

she knew. The thought unnerved her. In the mind,
she would have had she known...
As he surveyed his ruined body, so she calculated
how much sympathy she would need...

Chapter Five

Kathlyn leaned her forehead against the rain-streaked
windowpane in her cousin's upstairs bedroom. The
moist breeze soughing through the partially opened
window cooled her arms as they clutched her slender
waist.

Her face flamed when she gazed at her bare hands.
Not until this very moment had she noticed her gloves
were missing. She had left them in Brad's office.

Well, he had a token of their afternoon together, she
thought facetiously. What did she have? Nothing.
Nothing but an incredible longing and a strange sense
of loss. She had to be crazy! Still desiring the man
who had broken her heart.

The tightening in her chest reminded Kathlyn she
had lost a lot more than her heart because of Brad
Hampton. She had lost her unborn child. And because
of complications following the miscarriage, she was
now sterile.

No one would ever know how that hurt. From the
day her younger brothers were born, she had wanted
nothing so much as a child of her own.

The boys had met her maternal needs for a while.
She had mothered them until they could be mothered
no more. But they were gone.

Still, she needed to hold her very own baby; her
heart longed to love her very own child.

She kept these maternal longings to herself. She had
long since locked them away in a tiny box . . . a box
small enough to conceal in her heart . . . a box much
smaller than a baby's casket.

Tears burned her eyes. She felt so alone. A soft coo-

49

ing sound touched her ear, almost as if to say, "You have us." Smiling, she crossed over to the delicate white cage. Swinging the door open with the tip of her finger, she whispered, "Yes, I have you."

With a soft flutter, two tiny, blue birds flew from the cage, calling continuously in flight. They lit on the gilt mirror above Rachel's dressing table.

"Ishta . . . Barta," Kathlyn called in a sing-song voice as she moved her face closer to her little friends. Responding trustingly, Ishta angled her tiny head toward Kathlyn. Barta rotated his head from side to side, keeping watch over his lady love.

"That's a sweet girl." Kathlyn kept her voice low so as not to startle the rare budgies.

All the while, she patted the drawers below. She ran her hands blindly across the bottles and jars, searching for something to cover them. Rachel would strangle her if her birds left their calling card on her vanity.

She didn't dare look away; any abrupt movement would frighten the birds. Ishta was so close now that even her low cooing sounded clearly in Kathlyn's ears. Just a little closer and Kathlyn would rub her face against the bird. All of a sudden, making physical contact with something warm and alive seemed very important to Kathlyn.

"Kathlyn McKinney!" Rachel screeched, banging the bedroom door open on its hinges. "Get those nasty birds away from my cosmetics!"

Kathlyn froze, but Ishta reacted instinctively. With all haste she made for a safe haven. Unfortunately, Kathlyn was directly in her path. Ishta's tiny beak cut Kathlyn's cheek with the force of her forward movement.

Kathlyn didn't notice the blood trickling down her face. She was too worried about her frightened birds.

"Get those flea-infested fowls back in their cage!" Rachel wielded her reticule like a hammer, attempting to knock Ishta from the air.

The violent attack only served to terrify and confuse the bird. Ishta headed for the cage, but Rachel blocked

50

the entrance. Flying blindly, Ishta was soon tangled in the false curls piled high atop Rachel's head. Barta watched from a safe distance, behind Kathlyn's shoulder.

"Please just be still, Rachel. I'll get her," Kathlyn implored.

Even at the best of times, parakeets were skittish. Ishta and Barta were no exception. Kathlyn reached for Ishta cautiously.

Finally, she was able to extract her from Rachel's fiery red hair and place her trembling body back in the cage. Giving Rachel a wide berth, Barta followed close behind. "Coward," Kathlyn scolded him quietly for leaving Ishta to brave Rachel's wrath alone.

If the birds could have spoken, Kathlyn was convinced they would have said they were just as pleased to hear the tiny gate swing shut as she. But the expression on Rachel's face told Kathlyn her cousin wasn't as content as the birds.

"I'm sorry about that," Kathlyn said weakly, her hands laying tensely over her chest, almost clutching at her throat.

She hated to distress her cousin. Rachel and her family had been so kind to take her in. She would do anything to repay them. But right now a weak response was all she could muster.

"You don't sound very sorry to me."

"I'm . . ."

"Yes, I know, you're sorry," Rachel broke in sarcastically. "I declare, Kathlyn, sometimes I believe you care more about those birds than you do about me and Daddy. And after all we've done for you," she finished, censure heavy in her tone.

Kathlyn stood silently beside the bird cage, knowing that Rachel was right, knowing that she should express her gratitude once again. But she just didn't seem to have the energy; seeing Brad had drained her.

Kathlyn's continued silence surprised Rachel. As she settled herself at her dressing table, she groused, "What's wrong with you tonight?"

51

"It's nothing really. I had that appointment at the bank today. You know how I was dreading that." Kathlyn stood at Rachel's back, meeting her eyes in the mirror.

Hairbrush in mid-air, Rachel twirled on the stool and fixed Kathlyn with an intense stare. "How much did you get for that worthless piece of land?"

Kathlyn winced at Rachel's unkind words. She was sure Rachel didn't mean to belittle her home. "Nothing yet."

"Oh," Rachel said, disappointed.

"You're sweet to be concerned. But you'll be glad to know that I'm going to get more for it than I had first thought."

"Oh?" Kathlyn had Rachel's undivided attention again.

Suddenly Kathlyn wished she had kept her mouth shut. She hated to admit she owed her good fortune to Brad. But Rachel obviously expected an explanation.

"Brad Hampton discovered that I was being cheated." She studied the floor between her slippers. "He convinced the buyer to make me a better offer."

I'll just bet he did. The thought of Brad and Kathlyn together still irritated Rachel, even though he had not so much as darkened the door of River's Edge since that night eleven years ago.

Further, she didn't like the tone of Kathlyn's voice, her reluctance to meet her eyes when she spoke of Brad. Apparently the silly twit was still carrying a torch for him.

Well she would have to take care of that! She would not have Kathlyn remaining behind in Georgia. The one hundred thousand dollar fee for her sale was Rachel's ticket west. Kathlyn damn well wasn't going to mess it up now. Not now that Stuart had agreed to take her to San Francisco with him. Not if Rachel had her way.

She could drive a wedge between Brad and Kathlyn again. Placing her hair brush on the table, she enthused, "That's so kind of him. You know what we ought to do? We ought to invite him to our Independence Day party tomorrow night so Daddy and I can thank him personally."

"You're going to have it then?" Kathlyn knew that the Independence Day Ball was a standing tradition in the Jackson household. But since the war, there was so little money. And her uncle was ill. She had expected the tradition to be ignored this year. Apparently, such was not the case.

"Of course we are. And for helping you, Brad will be an honored guest."

"That's very kind of you, Rachel. I'm sure he will appreciate it." Kathlyn's smile was stiff. She wanted nothing less than to attend the same Fourth of July party as Brad Hampton. It would be eleven years to the day since he had ruined her. But she certainly couldn't explain that to Rachel.

"You run write the invitation now," Rachel ordered, waving Kathlyn away. "I'll sign it and have Silas deliver it first thing in the morning."

Knowing she had to do as Rachel bid, Kathlyn nodded.

"And take those birds with you."

Kathlyn picked up her bird cage. As she left the room, she found herself wishing that tomorrow would never come.

Chapter Six

The next evening found Kathlyn standing at Rachel's window once again. Rachel was at her dressing table, applying cosmetics to her not-so-youthful face. Dabbing a hare's foot in a dish of soft red powder, she dusted color onto her cheeks, the lobes of her ears, and her slack chin.

Rachel leaned forward, resting her sagging bosom on the vanity, squinting into the mirror. Why in the world her face was a map of crow's feet and splotched skin, while Kathlyn—who was one year her senior—had the complexion of a downy-faced toddler, she'd never know. It just wasn't fair!

Rachel would give anything to know the beauty regimen her cousin had followed all her life. But she had not had the opportunity to observe her. Until Kathlyn had moved to River's Edge, during the final year of the war, the cousins had rarely seen each other. Actually, not at all, with the exception of that one summer. The summer Kathlyn had stolen Brad Hampton from her.

Rachel decided that it was not a regimen that made Kathlyn beautiful. Awash with paranoia, she imagined that Kathlyn had discovered some secret potion in the backwater town she hailed from. A potion that kept her looking like an adolescent, instead of the twenty-seven year old woman that she was. Perhaps Kathlyn even had a love potion that she'd used on Brad; that was how she'd stolen him from her.

Rachel lifted her head and stared into the mirror. Kathlyn's image was made smaller by the distance separating them. Still, Rachel could see her clearly. Her eyes were full of hatred.

Angling her lovely head toward the setting sun, Kathlyn watched the guests arrive. She was totally unaware of her cousin's intense scrutiny. In fact, she was oblivious to her cousin's presence altogether until Rachel spoke.

"You're sure Brad hasn't answered our invitation?" Rachel queried suspiciously.

"Not that I'm aware of. Maybe he had other plans. It was rather late notice, you know," she threw over her shoulder, careful to keep her voice unemotional.

Rachel wasn't certain if Kathlyn was disappointed by Brad's failure to respond or not. She was acting so strange, it was hard to tell. She just stood there, looking out that window. "What on earth are you looking for?"

"Nothing in particular." Kathlyn refused to admit— even to herself—that she was awaiting Brad's arrival.

"Well stop it. Do something else. You're getting on my nerves."

"I'm sorry." Kathlyn turned and began cleaning Rachel's room. One by one, she picked up a myriad of discarded gowns from the floor, painstakingly hanging them in the closet. She spoke from the closet interior, "I'm amazed that so many people would show up for a party, with the depressed state of the economy and the South in general."

Eventually she was drawn back to the window. She was mesmerized by the party-goers as they arrived, meandering up the winding lane toward the cavernous manor house. Dressed simply, some on horseback, others in wagons, they exhibited an air of excitement.

Social events were still scarce in the South. And though Southern gentry could no longer afford the fine silks and costly gems they wore before the war, they were obviously thrilled at the prospect of a party nonetheless. Resting her chin on the sill, Kathlyn caught their enthusiasm.

Then she jerked her head up. Her eyes widened. He

would have stood out from the crowd had he been dressed in rags. He wasn't. Far from it.

At first glance, he appeared dressed like the others. His clothing was simply cut, sedate in color, as if he didn't wish to flaunt his wealth. His sensitivity to those less fortunate warmed her heart.

The only outward sign that he was a wealthy member of Southern aristocracy was his ever-present silver-topped cane. It lent him an air of understated elegance. It was as much a part of him as his heart-stopping smile.

"He's gorgeous," Kathlyn whispered.

Sitting regally atop his spirited roan, Brad Hampton stood in stark contrast to mere mortals. Despite herself, the desire Kathlyn had once felt for him reared its head.

She was rooted to the spot, unable to tear her eyes away. He was riding alongside a gleaming carriage. Its occupants, an attractive couple also modestly dressed, were listening to him intently. The threesome was nearing the portico when Kathlyn heard the woman's soft drawl. Kathlyn recognized the speaker as Melinda Hampton, Brad's sister-in-law. She had aged well, and was still as lovely and vivacious as Kathlyn remembered.

Just then both men threw their heads back and laughed at Melinda's comment. What a pleasant picture they made. Though one man was dark and the other light, there was an unmistakable resemblance between Brad and his brother, Jared. And it was obvious this was a happy family.

"What must it feel like?" Kathlyn murmured wistfully, grieving for her parents and brothers.

"Did you say something?" Rachel asked from beneath a mound of faded red glacé silk.

Kathlyn tore her gaze and thoughts away from Brad and his companions. Crossing a well-worn carpet, she hurried to her cousin's side.

"Here, let me help you with that." Deftly, she tugged Rachel's ball gown into place, mindful to hold it away from her cousin's face lest she smear Rachel's make-up.

Kathlyn's eyes widened. She was a bit shocked to see the vast amount of blue-veined flesh pushed above Rachel's low bodice, but she tried to hide it. To no avail.

Rachel was not pleased with the look on Kathlyn's face. "It's a bit worn, I know, but it's the best I have," she said defensively. "I'll have you know this is a Charles Worth gown, and a Worth gown never goes out of fashion."

"You misunderstand; your gown is lovely."

"Well what then?"

"It's just that . . ."

A deep male voice sounded distinctly from below.

"That's him." Forgetting her displeasure, Rachel made for the window. "He *did* come."

Kathlyn joined her, following her line of vision. For a scant second, she wondered why Rachel was so pleased that Brad had accepted their invitation.

Then, as always, when confronted with Brad Hampton, rational thought was a passing shadow. "Yes, he *did* come," Kathlyn repeated softly, mindful that they could be heard below.

"Just look at him, he's so handsome, and single . . . and rich!" Rachel enthused. As if an afterthought, she said, "The two of you were close once, weren't you?" Something fierce flickered in her eyes.

"Not really. We were merely acquaintances." Unable to meet her eyes, Kathlyn looked over Rachel's head.

Rachel suppressed a grin. Her cousin lied so poorly. "Whatever," she dismissed, patting Kathlyn's hand as it rested on the window sash. "At any rate, you're an engaged woman now. Besides, Brad fought for the Confederacy, and I know how you feel about men who fought for the Confederacy.

"Why, I just had the most awful thought." Rachel cringed visibly. "Wouldn't it be horrible if Brad was the soldier who killed your brothers . . . or even your father? It's possible, you know."

As intended, Rachel hit a nerve. The thought was so repugnant, Kathlyn could hardly consider it. Her breathing grew labored; she dropped her gaze to the toes of her lavender slippers.

Satisfied for the moment, Rachel slipped from the room.

Inordinately distraught, Kathlyn was unaware of her departure. Was it possible? Had Brad wielded the weapon that destroyed her family? Had he been party to murdering her brothers and father? Did being a former Confederate make him guilty in principle if not in fact?

Seeking answers, she watched the scene below. Brad was still on the portico, talking with her Uncle Roth. He was so tall and muscular, his shadow covered Roth completely.

As always he seemed larger than life. Never had she seen another man so blatantly virile, so perfectly male. Never had she seen a man so incredibly handsome as this Adonis who had broken her heart. And who, if allowed, would surely break it again!

Her uncle's wheelchair barely reached his waist. He was so large. Yet the hand he laid on Roth's shoulder was gentle. Tanned, smooth, steady . . . and strong. It didn't look threatening at all.

Surely, Rachel's horrible thought was not true. Surely, those hands hadn't wielded the weapon that had destroyed her family.

A lock of his shiny hair, as black as the bowels of hell, fell across his brow, giving him a look of boyish vulnerability. She wished he would straighten so she could see his eyes. Would that vulnerability be evident in their depths? She wondered.

Mentally chastising herself, she dismissed the possibility. Brad Hampton may be many things, but vulnerable was not one of them. And definitely not boyish. The innate way he held himself, as though he were royalty, belied all semblance of that, and labeled him all man.

Sensing her eyes upon him, Brad straightened to his full height, tilted his head back, and raised his eyes to Rachel's bedroom window. Instinctively, Kathlyn wrapped her arms around her waist in a protective gesture.

This was not lost on Brad as he stood watching her intently. His breath stilled; he visually devoured her. Her eyes were soft—yet probing, her cheeks were luminous—yet flushed, and her full, pouting lips were neither curved upward in a smile, nor downward in a frown. They merely looked delicious.

But it wasn't her physical appearance alone that drew his attention. It was the inner fire burning in those iris eyes that held him spellbound. He wanted to look away; he needed to look away; though he couldn't look away. People flowed around him as if he were a boulder in the middle of a stream. He was wholly unaware of their presence. He had eyes for no one, save Kathlyn. His gaze pinned her to the spot.

Those velvety brown eyes exuded warmth. In spite of herself, Kathlyn's lips spread into a shy smile. Brad's answering smile was so seductive that her cheeks flamed. For a moment in time something passed between them, something indefinable, heretofore unknown. They both sensed it.

Standing on the porch out of sight, Rachel watched them. She sensed it too.

Chapter Seven

Slowly, Kathlyn descended the swaying staircase. Her gaze was fixed, unseeing, on the scarred treads below her feet. She didn't dare raise her eyes; he might be there.

"Kathlyn, sweetheart." Her Uncle Roth's voice claimed her attention. "Where have you been? The party's half over."

Kathlyn crossed the area between them. Bending at the waist, she buzzed her uncle's cheek with a kiss. "Don't you know that a young lady should always be fashionably late?" she teased, her soft laughter warming the old man's heart.

"Seems mighty cruel to me, making all these young bucks wait for a sight of that pretty face." He placed his hand alongside her jaw.

She covered his hand with her own. "You wouldn't be a little prejudiced now, would you? Just because I happen to be your niece . . . you might see things a more discriminating gentleman wouldn't."

"I'm mighty particular myself, but I'd have to agree with you, Roth," a deep, familiar voice caused her to jump. "She's just as pretty today, as she was at sixteen. Prettier."

Kathlyn's breath caught in her throat.

"Now there's a man with good taste." Roth smiled up at Brad. His failing eyesight didn't miss a thing: Kathlyn blushing from head to toes; Brad looking as if he could eat her alive, trembling lips and all.

The silence in the foyer grew heavy. "I was going to claim the first dance with this young lady myself, but since you're here, I reckon you might as well do the honors," Roth said, giving Brad a conspiratorial wink.

Roth would have liked nothing more than for Kathlyn and Brad to pick up their romance where they left off eleven years ago. His reasons were many. The Hamptons were rich as Croesus. If Kathlyn married the handsome banker, she would be well taken care of. Further, as Brad's wife, she wouldn't be able to marry that damn Yank. That in itself was sufficient motivation for Roth's matchmaking.

But Kathlyn didn't appreciate his efforts. Self-consciously, she attempted to make light of the situation. "I'd like to see you dance in that wheelchair." She tossed her head back in challenge. "Besides, I'm sure Mr. Hampton could find a more suitable partner."

The old man wasn't given time to object; Brad spoke for himself. "I can think of no one I'd rather have as a partner."

There were several ways Brad could mean that, but neither he nor Kathlyn were prepared to deal with any meaning other than the most obvious.

Casting her uncle a look that said clearly, "I'll deal with you later," Kathlyn accepted Brad's outstretched arm. Roth blew Kathlyn a kiss, obviously not worried about her nonverbal promise of retaliation.

Brad guided Kathlyn through the arched doors into the ballroom, both blissfully unaware of the venomous looks Rachel cast their way. "He's a kind old gentleman."

"If he tries to pawn me off on anybody else, he's not going to get any older," Kathlyn uttered. The love shining in her eyes, belied the threatening statement.

"Don't blame him. I put him up to it."

Kathlyn stared at Brad, wide-eyed. The quartet struck a waltz and he gathered her in his arms. "Why would you do that?" she asked.

"Let's just say I like to waltz." He whirled her about the floor, savoring the feel of her slight form in his arms.

She angled her head back, craning her neck to look into his face. "Why me?" She had to know.

"Is he very ill?" He ignored her question in favor of another subject.

Kathlyn was caught off guard momentarily. Though she shouldn't have been. As she recalled from their summer together, Brad often changed the subject at a moment's notice. Those with slower minds than his — which encompassed most of the civilized world — were left to catch up as they may. He didn't do it on purpose; he just did it.

"He seems a little weaker, tires a little easier, but other than that, I think he's all right," she explained.

A movement behind Brad's back caught her eye. It was Jared and Melinda, waltzing by in one another's arms. Suddenly, a chill of foreboding crept up her spine. "Has Dr. Hampton . . . has Jared told you something that I should know? Has he examined Uncle Roth?"

"Not that I know of."

Brad had not meant to upset Kathlyn, questioning her about Roth. She obviously loved her uncle a great deal. It was just that Roth looked so . . . defeated. Despite the old man's teasing nature, Brad could see that he had given up on life. Looking around him at the general disrepair of the once impressive manor house, Brad understood.

"And I doubt if he will," Kathlyn broke into Brad's thoughts. "I tried to get Uncle Roth to call for Jared, but he wouldn't. He doesn't have the money."

"That doesn't matter to Jared," Brad said automatically.

Kathlyn bristled. "It does to Uncle Roth. For some of us, our dignity is all we have left."

Brad took note of the fiery indignation glowing in Kathlyn's eyes. Righteous indignation wrapped around her like a sable cloak; she was the picture of stiff-necked pride in the extreme. And he had never seen her more beautiful than at that moment. Nor more compelling.

It had been so long since he had been with a woman who challenged him. This one would be a challenge to any man, he knew. Perversely, it excited him.

Deviling her on purpose, he asked, "So you agree he should ignore his health, as long as he preserves his dignity?"

"Well of course not! Didn't I just say that I tried to get him to contact Jared?" Kathlyn feared she might explode. Brad was purposefully misunderstanding her. The lout! The oh-so-handsome lout!

"So you did." Brad's lips stretched into a mocking grin. "Then if I ask you to, you'll let Jared take a look at your cheek?" He brought their clasped hands upward, toward her face. Tenderly, he traced the narrow cut Ishta had inflicted.

"It's just a scratch." Kathlyn was touched, confused, and discomfited by his concern.

"How did it happen?"

"It was an accident," Kathlyn evaded. She didn't want to tell him about Ishta and Barta. She feared he might think of her as a pitiful, long-in-the-tooth-spinster with only birds to love. Which was too close to the truth as far as she was concerned.

"You should let Jared have a look at it," he said more dictatorially than he intended.

Kathlyn affected a stubborn look.

"If you don't take care of it, it might scar. It would be a shame to mar such beauty." Lightly he brushed the backs of his fingers along her jaw, wondering why he was making such an issue of a little scratch—a little scratch on a woman he *should* dislike. She just brought out the protective nature in him, he decided. But then, she always had.

Kathlyn's cheeks grew warm. Hating herself for her vanity, she was inordinately pleased at Brad's unexpected flattery. She didn't trust herself to speak, so she just shrugged her shoulders.

Brad frowned his disapproval as the waltz ended. He tucked Kathlyn's hand through his arm, covering it lightly with his own. "You're a stubborn woman, Kathlyn McKinney. You know that, don't you?"

When they reached her uncle, Kathlyn looked up into Brad's face. "Thank you for the dance." Then without missing a beat, she added, "And I'm not stubborn, Brad Hampton, just independent."

Roth stifled a grin. "She's got you there, boy."

Brad rolled his eyes as if to say, "Women!" Gallantly, he inclined his head to Kathlyn. The warmth in his parting glance was not lost on Roth.

Brad didn't care to dance with anyone else at the moment. Moving a few feet away from Kathlyn and Roth, he leaned casually against the wall. They were unaware of his continued presence.

"Are you having a good time, honey?" Roth asked.

"Yes, sir. Though it seems strange to be having a good time when . . ." she couldn't finish the thought.

Roth knew what was left unsaid. Based on prior talks with his niece and the melancholy expression on her face he knew she was suffering with guilt. Guilt that she was alive, and her family was not. Guilt that she was dancing and enjoying herself, while her younger brothers were lying cold and lifeless in the McKinney family cemetery . . . the cemetery she was being forced to sell.

"Life has to go on." Roth reached for Kathlyn's hand. "We've all lost a lot, you more than most, but you can't hold onto the past, or blame yourself for surviving it. You're young and beautiful. Your whole life's ahead of you. Try to think of the future."

"I am thinking of the future, Uncle Roth. That's what's so scary."

Kathlyn spoke to Roth softly, though Brad heard every word. Had he not been so intent on the conversation taking place in front of him, he would have felt guilty for eavesdropping . . . again. But at Kathlyn's words, his heart was strangely warmed, his protective nature once again pricked.

"You're a brave woman, honey, with a great adventure ahead of you. Indian Territory is an untamed land and few women possess the strength to survive it. But you do! Don't fear your new life; look forward to it."

"I'll try. I really want to," Kathlyn vowed.

"Promise me that when you board the train to Memphis on the fifteenth, you'll leave your doubt and guilt behind. Promise me, you won't look back. That you'll look only to the future. Will you promise me that?"

Brad was so surprised to learn of Kathlyn's impending departure, he didn't hear her reply. She had just reentered his life, and now she was leaving again. It shouldn't matter so much, but it did.

Then he recalled Roth's exact words. "The train to Memphis on the fifteenth." It was the same day and the same train he and Dru were supposed to take. Surprising himself, he hoped Jared had not canceled their reservations.

With unseeing eyes, he stared at the dancers whirling past. He leaned more heavily on the wall and considered how Kathlyn's plans might affect him.

In all honesty he'd had many reasons to make the trip to Indian Territory, and only one to remain in Georgia. Kathlyn. Now that obstacle had been removed. Should he reconsider the trip?

That would depend on Kathlyn's reason for going to Indian Territory. What was out West for her? Or rather, whom? Brad's head jerked up as an unpleasant possibility occurred to him. His eyes sought Kathlyn. She was no longer seated with Roth. His gaze swept the room.

Just then she danced past him in the arms of John Dothan, a former Confederate officer who was looking at her as if she were a tender morsel. *Oh hell! She is a tender morsel,* Brad acknowledged, wondering what Dothan and Kathlyn were discussing so intently.

"I noticed you were dancing with Brad Hampton earlier," John said.

"Um hmm. He's a good dancer," Kathlyn remarked for lack of anything else to say.

"May I offer you a little friendly advice?"

The superior tone of John's voice set Kathlyn's teeth on edge. "Why of course. That's exactly what us poor, orphaned women need"—she offered him her best

65

Southern belle simper—"the advice of a man of superior intellect such as yourself."

If John noticed Kathlyn's sarcastic tone, he gave no sign. Actually, he deemed her smarter than most because she recognized her limitations. "Well"—he began conspiratorially—"if I were you, I wouldn't be seen with the likes of him. These days all we loyal Southerners have is our dignity and our good names. Women who are wise and want to keep their reputations intact avoid Brad like the plague." John was blissfully unaware that he was treading on dangerous ground.

"Oh I know, he's good looking and wealthy. And I know how money turns a woman's head." He smiled down at her indulgently, as if she were an empty headed dolt. "But I wonder . . . how did he get all that money?" he asked pointedly, elevating a sparsely populated eyebrow.

The only indication of Kathlyn's rising ire was the darkening of her iris eyes. As far as she could tell, her pompous partner was wrong on at least one very important point.

If he thought "women who are wise and want to keep their reputation intact try to avoid Brad," he should take a look around him. Nearly every woman in the room was looking cow-eyed at Brad, as if they would give their eyeteeth for one moment of his time. And Kathlyn suspected his wealth had little to do with it. Men like Brad didn't need money to attract women.

"Tell me, how *do* you think he got his money?" Kathlyn was the picture of innocence.

"I can't say for sure, but he was associated with the Treasury Department during the war." John's implication was obvious.

Although he didn't come right out and accuse Brad of absconding with the Confederate treasury, that was what he implied.

She was enraged. No matter how she felt about Brad personally, she knew he was no thief. "I appreciate your advice." Kathlyn gritted her teeth and looked duly

66

grateful. "I guess that goes for the other Hamptons as well. I suppose I shouldn't associate with Jared and Melinda either?"

"Well, no . . . I mean, yes."

Kathlyn batted her lashes, appearing quite confused. "Is it yes or no? I'm sorry Mr. Dothan, but I don't possess your superior intellect. You'll have to *advise* me more clearly. Should I or should I not associate with the other Hamptons?"

"Of course you should. Dr. Hampton has been kind enough to take care of our families; he has done nothing wrong."

Kathlyn was enjoying herself immensely. "But doesn't he have a lot of money too?"

"Well, yes."

"According to Rachel, the Hamptons have their finances consolidated." Kathlyn sniffed at nonexistent tears, appearing distressed not to understand the pearls of wisdom her partner so freely offered. "She says that Dr. Hampton doesn't charge patients nearly enough to support his family. If that's the case, wouldn't he have to be funded by Brad? And Dr. Hampton surely wouldn't take tainted money?"

When it was stated so plainly, even John Dothan could see the absurdity of his claim. He was rendered speechless.

"Never mind, Mr. Dothan. I guess there are just some things that are above female comprehension."

The music stopped, but Kathlyn had to get in one last dig. Cocking her head to the side, she widened her eyes, and exclaimed, "I just don't know what I would have done if you hadn't set me straight."

She tapped the rigid man's sleeve. "You're so wise, being able to figure out how there could be three members of the same family, living in the same house, sharing the same income. And one of them is a crook and the others aren't."

Placing her gloved hand under John's jaw, Kathlyn pushed upward. "Better close your mouth, Mr. Dothan. I wouldn't want you to catch a fly."

Kathlyn marched across the dance floor, back to where Brad stood, leaning casually against the wall. The top of her head barely reached his shoulder as she halted before him, feet planted, arms akimbo.

If he was surprised to see her, he gave no indication. His blank expression didn't alter. That same, self-assured mask that he had worn all evening was firmly in place. She'd hate to play poker with this one; his handsome face wouldn't reveal a single thought buzzing about in that keen mind of his.

Ever so slightly, he elevated a thick ebony brow. Coupled with the slight curving of his silken mustache, he almost seemed to be amused by her. This irritated Kathlyn to no end. She had just made a fool of herself for him, and this was the reception she got?

She wondered if the arrogant man was even aware that he was being gossiped about. Probably wouldn't care if he knew! But of course he knew. Nothing passed by Brad Hampton unnoticed.

To test her theory she asked, "Are you aware that people are talking about you?"

"No!" Brad feigned horror. The lazy smile that then arose on his handsome visage ruined the effect.

Tightening her jaw, Kathlyn tried to rein in her temper. How could he make light of this? "Yes! It seems that your neighbors think you're a thief. Not a common thief, mind you. But a full-scale embezzler who's absconded with the Confederate treasury."

Brad's smile faded. For a moment Kathlyn thought he might not speak. Then very softly, he asked, "And what does Kathlyn McKinney think?"

Now she *was* confused. It was almost as if her opinion mattered a great deal. But why? "I think you need a friend," she answered simply.

Brad's mask fell back into place.

"So, will you dance with me?" Kathlyn tried to tell herself that by asking Brad to dance she was making a statement to people like John Dothan. But she wasn't convinced. She feared she was just drawn to Brad like every other quixotic female in the room.

The muscle in Brad's jaw twitched suspiciously. "How charitable of you to ask," he drawled.

"You idiot!" There she was trying to help him, and he acted as if he were insulted. "Just forget it. But remember, I tried." She whirled about on her heel.

He grasped her hand, pulling her into his arms and out onto the dance floor in one fluid motion. "I thought you wanted to dance."

"You didn't seem too interested in the idea."

"I said I appreciated the invitation," Brad returned innocently. "Really! I've never been asked to dance by a woman before," he teased unmercifully.

Kathlyn groaned. She knew great frustration in that instant, for more reasons than one. "Well you should appreciate it."

"Mmm, I do." He pulled her closer into the circle of his arms.

"Well, you should," she whispered again.

Bodies aching, minds blissfully blank, Brad and Kathlyn were soon caught up in the romantic music. They whirled rapidly to an elegant Viennese waltz. Their young hearts beat to the strong propulsive impulse, then fluttered over the two lighter beats which followed, surging in their chests as the final beat pushed into the first, only to start the pattern again.

"Kat," Brad whispered.

His voice was so soft, so husky, that Kathlyn felt it, rather than heard it. She remembered when he had called her Kat during times of intense emotion eleven years ago. What was he feeling now? She looked questioningly into his eyes, holding her breath, frightened of the answer.

"Do you remember?" Brad asked.

Kathlyn expelled a breath of air. Of course she remembered.

It was during a waltz exactly like this that Brad had first confessed his love to her. Just before he led her through the garden doors, out into the night; just before he took her into the fragrant glasshouse and changed her life forever.

69

God help her, but she loved him as much now as she did then. And if she allowed her lonely heart to rule her head, she could interpret the warm look in his eyes as a reflection of that love.

But she wouldn't allow herself that luxury. She couldn't afford to. With a well-developed sense of will, she closed her eyes, shutting him out.

When she stiffened in his arms Brad sensed it instantly.

"Miss Kathlyn, may I have the next dance?" A male voice burst into their world.

Kathlyn and Brad broke apart. They had been so caught up in the past, they had failed to realize the dance was over.

Brad searched Kathlyn's flushed face, hoping to reach her again, but she wouldn't meet his gaze. Still holding her hand, he squeezed it lightly. "Thank you, Miss McKinney."

They both knew he was referring to more than the waltz.

The sound of merriment grew faint as Brad descended the sloped lawn and headed for the glasshouse . . . his and Kathlyn's special place. As soon as it arose, he dismissed the nostalgic thought.

In the distance, the refuge he sought stood as he remembered it beside the lazy Oconee. He hastened his step, drawn by the soothing sound of water brushing against the shore.

Roth Jackson's wife had loved every blossom and seedling that grew on River's Edge. Before the war — and her death — the Jackson lawns and gardens were well known for their beauty, but not now. Now, like everything else in the South, they were a pale imitation of their former state.

This did not deter his progress, however, for he wasn't seeking beauty, just solitude. Unbidden, thoughts of the treatment he'd received inside the mansion overwhelmed him. Balling his fist, he slammed it against his thigh.

Then he stood absolutely still. Stars overhead

dimmed as waves of agony washed over him. He had forgotten about his stab wound, but was reminded of it sharply. He sucked large amounts of sweet air through his mouth, willing the agony to cease.

Slowly the pain screaming in his forearm was over-shadowed by the hurt rising in his breast. His situation was worse than Kathlyn knew. This wasn't the first time he had been an object of scorn. Frankly he was damn tired of being treated like he was responsible for the war's atrocities. He wasn't certain how much more he could take, how many more times he could make excuses for the treatment his former friends meted out.

The pain in his arm subsided finally, and the world righted itself. The pain in his heart remained. As he moved down the path he wondered why he had even been invited to this gathering. And he wondered, not for the first time, why he had bothered to attend.

Inside, he knew the answer to both queries was the same. Kathlyn. Sighing heavily, he let himself into the greenhouse and walked over to a wrought-iron bench that was placed along the back wall.

He noted there wasn't a gardenia to be found. The aroma weighting the air wasn't sweet. The smell of earth and mold was strong in his nostrils. It was a pleasant smell, however. More pleasant than his mood, since Kathlyn had stiffened in his arms.

He seated himself, dislodging chunks of peeling paint from the metal bench. Then withdrew a cheroot from his frockcoat pocket. The scratch of a match against the sole of his boot sounded in the stillness, as did the rhythmic ticking of his pocket watch. He took a long draw off his cigar and shook the match, extinguishing its flame. The scent of sulphur remained in the air.

Shifting and leaning his head against the wall, he closed his eyes. The weight of indecision pressed hard on his shoulders. His once infinite fountain of energy was all but tapped out. When had he gotten so damn weary?

His tired mind wandered. Should he and Dru pack

71

up and leave Athens on the fifteenth? And if so, should the move to Oklahoma Territory be permanent, or just a visit to Chase and Lacy, as was earlier planned? And what about Jared and his family? Would they be safe in Georgia after he left?

"Oh hell." Finally he ceased thinking altogether; it took too much effort.

He allowed an angel's face to take shape in his mind, a face with fiery amethyst eyes, a face haloed by a wealth of glowing ebony hair. Kathlyn's face.

Bittersweet memories of eleven years past came to him and he warmed to the remembrance of possessing her for the first—and last—time in this building. He savored the passion of that night, reliving every kiss and caress they had shared.

They had been kids groping in the dark then. He wondered what would it be like to make love to Kathlyn—the woman. The fantasy quickened his blood. His lower body reacted instantly. Maybe he wasn't so weary after all. He smiled in the darkness.

Then, he remembered the morning of betrayal. The stark pain he had experienced when he received her note was almost as vivid now as it had been then. His smile hardened.

His pain had turned to rage that day. Tearing out of the house, he had ridden to the train station, punishing himself and his horse in his haste. He arrived just in time to see the train leave the station. With that train went his heart.

For months, he had tried to fill the emptiness. He vacillated between periods when his love for Kathlyn would almost smother him, and times when he would be overwhelmed by an emotion he called hate.

He had tried to replace her for a time. God knows how he tried. He courted every marriageable female within fifty miles, employed more than his share of fallen women. But nothing had exorcised her from his mind. No one had replaced her in his heart. He had yearned for her with all his being.

Finally, he traveled to Union Point. He was determined to see her, but her parents sent him away. They said she was ill, not that he believed them.

All he had wanted was an explanation. In his mind's eye, Brad stared questioningly into Kathlyn's lovely face. Hadn't he at least deserved an explanation? Face to face?

Physically and emotionally exhausted, he drifted into a numbing sleep. He wasn't sure how long he'd been in the greenhouse when something awakened him. His keen senses told him he was no longer alone. Instinctively, he tensed.

He opened his eyes slowly. There was someone to his right. Turning abruptly, he faced a most disconcerting sight. Rachel Jackson was standing within arm's length of him, as naked as the day she was born.

"Oh hell."

Chapter Eight

"That's not exactly the greeting I was expecting," Rachel purred.

"Where are your clothes?" Brad emphasized every word, surging to his feet.

Her low, seductive laughter told him she wasn't concerned with the whereabouts of her clothing. Before he knew what she was about, she moved forward and pressed her nude body against him.

Brad had always been a passionate man, enjoying sensual delights instinctively. But when Rachel rubbed against him, squeezing him as if he were a ripe melon, he was not aroused. He was repulsed.

Grabbing her bare shoulders, he thrust her from him. "What the hell are you up to, Rachel?"

"I thought we would have a party of our own," she enthused, untying his cravat.

He grabbed her wrists. "Stop it! For god's sake, you're supposed to be a lady."

In light of the current situation, they both knew that her maidenly virtue was questionable at best. Still, he had to appeal to the woman on some level. He had heard rumors about her lack of morality through the years, but had given them little credence. Shows how much he knew . . .

Still, to go to these lengths, she was up to something other than seduction. Whatever her agenda, everlasting love for him was not her motivation, he was certain. He had been around the fairer sex enough to know that females like Rachel—loose women—loved one person, themselves.

But his money . . . now that was a different matter.

The irony of her baring her all for his money, while the rest of the South begrudged his wealth . . . but he was too busy struggling with the avaricious female to appreciate the irony of the situation.

"It's best I take my leave now. Once you've dressed, you should return to your father." He spoke quite formally, not at all what one would expect of a man with a naked woman trying to wrap her arms and legs around him. He suspected that one day he'd see the humor in all this. But this wasn't that day.

Untangling himself from her clutches, he stepped back. "We'll just pretend none of this ever happened," he said, straightening his waistcoat and retying his neck wear.

Needing to detain Brad a bit longer, Rachel lunged for him. She caught him unaware. In a mass of intertwined arms and legs, they hit the floor. Breath rushed from their bodies with loud grunts.

Kathlyn tugged her short paletot more tightly about her shoulders, warding off the evening chill. She clutched Rachel's note in her black-gloved hand. The message sounded urgent. Concern for her troubled cousin hastened her step.

Hurrying across the verdant lawn she wondered why Rachel wanted to meet with her during the party. And why way out here? Had something distressing happened to her? Something so distressing Rachel didn't want to be overheard discussing it in the house? Something Kathlyn had failed to notice? It was entirely possible, for she had not spared Rachel a thought since Brad arrived.

Actually, she had felt like a frog on a hot rock all evening. Was it any wonder? Just being in his presence claimed her undivided attention . . . caused her untold confusion . . . gave rise to forbidden desires.

Even now, Rachel's problems fled her mind. Brad, only Brad, claimed her attention. Brad, and the painful result of indulging her desire for him.

75

She couldn't afford to be so foolish again.

"Maybe we can be friends," she whispered suddenly.

Yes, that was it. Just like she told Brad; he needed a friend. And since they were both older now, more mature, they could put the past behind them and be friends.

Besides, she was leaving the state in less than two weeks. No doubt they would never see one another again. And she didn't want to part on a bad note. Perhaps that was why they had been given a second chance. Undeniably they couldn't be lovers, but they didn't have to be enemies for the rest of their lives. They could make peace and look ahead unencumbered.

If she were to survive the future in an untamed land, she would need every ounce of strength she possessed; hating Brad took more energy than she could spare.

Squaring her slender shoulders resolutely, she vowed to take her life into her own hands, to control her emotions and not let them control her.

And she would begin with Brad Hampton. She would never allow him—or the thought of him—to upset her again! She would show him she could compartmentalize him, put him in his place. The thought made her smile.

As she reached for the latch on the glass-paneled garden doors, she heard a loud noise from within. "What on earth?" Her heart accelerated. Pushing the door open, she ran inside.

At first she saw nothing but great pools of shadow, relieved only where silver arrows of moonlight shot through the windows. Muffled noises, grunts, and groans came from the rear of the greenhouse. It sounded as if people were struggling. Panic advanced on her like the incoming tide.

Then a man's voice sounded clearly. "Dammit Rachel, be still."

"Brad?" Kathlyn ran in the direction of the voice. "Dear lord," she gasped.

Illumined by a pool of moonlight was her cousin's

bass drum rear, bare and shining for all the world to see. From her vantage point, Kathlyn could see that Rachel was sprawled on top of a man. And that man was Brad. It appeared that Rachel was trying valiantly to free herself from him. Kathlyn felt faint.

When Rachel heard Kathlyn's approach she maneuvered herself atop Brad. When Kathlyn reached their side, Rachel suddenly began struggling as if she were trying to free herself from him.

Instinctively, Brad grabbed her arms. He feared, that in her state of mind, she might try to assault him. And while he knew she could not hurt him—with the exception of causing his injured arm to throb like sin—she might do herself real damage. Though why he should care about the greedy slut was beyond him.

At present, still gripping her arms, Brad rolled Rachel to her back. Once on top, he arched his body, aiming to lurch away from the human octopus, lest she wrap her tentacles around him again. He paused, gasping for breath, trying to ignore the discomfort in his lower arm.

It was at this point that Kathlyn went into action. Pouncing upon him, she shoved him off her cousin, then scrambled to her feet. "Leave her alone!"

"I didn't . . ." Brad began, once he was free from Rachel. He rolled out of the darkness into a puddle of light.

His hair was tousled and his eyes flashed. Supposing Rachel had put the flame of passion in his eyes, Kathlyn dropped her gaze. Once again, she'd been utterly betrayed.

"Let me explain." The emotion in Brad's eyes had nothing to do with sensual passion. It was a reflection of anger, embarrassment, and regret that he had been discovered in such a compromising position.

Kathlyn forced herself to look at him. That was a mistake. Memories of a moonlit night, the sweet smell of gardenias, and the feel of his warm body covering hers flooded together and overwhelmed her. She closed her eyes.

"Kat," Brad implored, at a loss for words. Why did she look so stricken? He didn't expect that. Shouts, accusations, yes, but this look of sheer pain on her face, no.

After a moment, Kathlyn stiffened and visibly regained control. "In spite of all you've done to me, I thought we could be friends." She laughed ruefully. "Now we can never be anything but enemies. Not after this; not after you've hurt my cousin. Dear God, Brad, she's my cousin."

"I didn't hurt your cousin. And what do you mean, after all *I've* done?" Brad glared into Kathlyn's accusing gaze.

He was insulted and baffled by the statement, *"In spite of all you've done to me."* She obviously referred to their past relationship. But she acted as if she were the injured party. That's not how he remembered it.

Neither of them wondered that they were more concerned with their past than with the naked woman sprawled at their feet.

"Yes, he did; he hurt me," Rachel shouted, pounding the stone floor. "He molested me. He must have followed me in here and . . . and . . . he had his way with me." Rachel pretended horror.

Instinctively, Kathlyn stepped between her cousin and Brad, shielding the injured party with the skirts of her gown.

Brad flinched. "You don't believe this drivel, do you?" He wasn't particularly surprised to discover how much Kathlyn's opinion mattered to him.

"No, of course not," she spat sarcastically. Trying to cover her devastation, she knelt and clutched Rachel to her chest. "I'm sure my big, bad cousin just stripped off her clothes and jumped on top of you. You poor man!" Ripping off her paletot she draped it around Rachel's shoulders.

A muscle twitched in Brad's jaw. Suddenly, he was beyond angry, he was enraged, and more than a little insulted! Kathlyn's opinion of him must truly be low, if she thought he would wallow around on the floor

78

with Rachel Jackson. "Actually that's just what happened," he ground out.

This set Rachel off again. She howled indignantly. The message was something to the effect that now she was used goods and didn't know what would become of her.

Her tirade was lost on Brad. He was too aware of Kathlyn. Looking through a sea of rage, he found her breathtaking. Damn his eyes. The sight of her, coupled with the memory of possessing her in this very place, heightened his awareness. He was even attracted to the maternal way she was cradling the slut in her arms.

Mesmerized, he noticed little things. Like the glow of her complexion. He was sure he had never seen its equal. Bathed in silver, her skin resembled fine porcelain, eggshell thin, the color of sweet cream with just a hint of peach over her high cheekbones.

He longed to trace a single finger along her silken jaw. The moon-shaped cut on her face gave her a vulnerable look, bringing his protective instincts to the fore . . . as usual. There was just something about Kathlyn McKinney that made him want to wrap her in cotton and hide her close to his heart.

But the withering stare she flashed him at that moment brought him back to his senses. She was anything but vulnerable. He bristled under her unjust disapproval.

He went on the defensive. "Does it not occur to you as strange that I'm fully clothed while your cousin, this paragon of virtue"—he slashed his hand in the air, indicating Rachel—"is naked as the day she was born?" Grabbing Rachel's gown, he tossed it to her. "Please put this on. Apparently your plan has succeeded so there is no further need for you to lounge about like a Jezebel."

Rachel was more than insulted.

Kathlyn was puzzled. It did strike her as odd that Rachel was the only one naked. The fact that she was even considering listening to Brad's side of things irritated her. Yet even after all that had passed between

79

them, she had to admit this sordid situation seemed out of character for the man she knew. Or the man she thought she knew. She was so confused.

For what seemed an eternity, she considered the situation. *No.* She wouldn't allow herself to take Brad's side, no matter how much she wanted to. She shook her head as if to rid her mind of all doubt. "Men don't necessarily have to remove their clothing to do their ugly deed," she replied haughtily. Her cheeks flamed in spite of herself.

Brad knew that Kathlyn referred to the last time they had been in the glasshouse together. And it was as if Rachel had ceased to exist again.

Kathlyn's harsh words shook him. He was shocked not because she referred to something so indelicate as their moment of passion, but because of the bitter edge to her voice. Again, he wondered why she acted the injured party. What did she have to be bitter about?

"The deed isn't always ugly," he felt compelled to say.

"It is when love is absent." Kathlyn regretted the words as soon as they left her mouth. She didn't want to give him the satisfaction of knowing that she cared whether he had loved her or not. She studied him carefully, searching for a look of triumph.

He didn't so much as bat an eye. He assumed Kathlyn wanted him to know that although she had given herself to him, she had never loved him. Well she could have saved herself the trouble. Her terrible note had told him that much.

Why she wanted to make this point again, Brad couldn't fathom. Maybe it was because of Rachel. Maybe Kathlyn needed to thrust the knife in again as punishment for his supposed sins against the virtuous Rachel Jackson.

He suddenly experienced an overpowering wave of disappointment. He had thought more of Kathlyn than that.

Through the years he had decided she hadn't meant

to be cruel when she spurned him. He had virtually absolved her of guilt in his thoughts, if not in his heart. He reasoned that at the tender age of sixteen she didn't know her own mind, didn't know how much it would hurt a man to have his love rejected.

But now he wondered. If she could be cruel now, why not then? And if she was that callous, then why had she acted as if she cared that people were gossiping about him? *Damn*. Would he ever figure her out?

Shoving a hand through his unruly hair, he took a long look at Kathlyn. His face didn't reveal his tortured thoughts. "You're right. The deed is ugly when love is absent."

Her sharp intake of breath, the wounded kitten look in her eyes, confused him even more. *Oh hell*. What had he said now?

Suddenly, he just wanted to get away, to return to the refuge of Paradise Manor. Bowing his head slightly to Kathlyn, he turned on his heel and headed for the door.

"Well I never!" Rachel exclaimed.

Brad never broke his stride. "Sure you have," he said before disappearing into the night.

"Whoa! Where's the fire?" Jared questioned when Brad all but ran him over. He had been worried when he noticed Brad's absence from the party. Excusing himself from Melinda, so that he might find his volatile brother, Jared had come looking for him. He had not expected to find him looking as if he could commit murder.

"Just get out of my way, Jared." Brad's stride devoured the ground between the glasshouse and the barn at a rapid clip.

Brad had the horse half saddled before Jared reached his side. "What the hell's wrong with you?"

"Nothing is wrong with me. Everything is just fine. Couldn't be better," Brad raved like a lunatic. He was so frustrated that he feared he might explode. Four years of war had been easy compared to dealing with Kathlyn McKinney! Rachel's shenanigans he had already dismissed. But Kathlyn was getting under his skin again, and he didn't know what to do about it.

"I can see that everything is fine," Jared returned dryly. "That's why you've just saddled someone else's horse. Have you taken to stealing horses as well as the Confederate treasury?" he taunted.

"I wouldn't mess with me right now if I were you, Jared. It might not be too healthy." Brad turned on his heel and began searching the stalls for his horse.

"Has someone said something to upset you? Haven't you been treated well at the party?" The protective tone of Jared's voice cut through Brad's rage.

"Just great, if you don't mind being treated like Bloody Mary." Brad knew the reason he was so angry had nothing to do with the treatment he'd received at the party. But he didn't feel like explaining what really had him in a lather. Not that he understood it himself!

"All you have to do is take that train on the fifteenth." Jared busied himself unsaddling the strange horse.

Brad found an empty stall and leaned his arms over the sill of an open window. The lazy Oconee crawled by in the distance, just as it had eleven years ago. The smell of gardenias was overpowering in his nostrils though there wasn't a blossom within miles. It was all a memory.

But Kathlyn wasn't a memory; she was a flesh and blood pain in the neck. If he had a brain in his head, when she left for Memphis on the fifteenth, he would say good riddance to her and go back to living life as he knew it. But what did brains have to do with dealing with a woman? And what good was life without Kathlyn? *That* was the real question torturing him. Though he was loathe to admit it.

He heard the shuffle of Jared's feet in the straw. Without turning around he knew that his big brother was standing behind him now. The warm hand that grasped his shoulder was comforting. It was almost as if his father were with him again. Brad didn't realize how much he had missed his father, or how Jared had somehow taken his father's place. He hated to leave him.

"All you have to do is take the train to Memphis on the fifteenth," Jared repeated, softly this time.

Brad leaned into Jared's hand. The time to examine his motives was not now, but he knew he made the right decision when he said, "Okay, we'll go. Do you still have the tickets?"

Jared didn't answer, he merely squeezed his brother's shoulder.

Chapter Nine

"Uncle Roth, you wanted to see me?" Kathlyn asked softly, entering her uncle's study.

Though it was warm, Roth Jackson sat in his wheelchair before a blazing fire. He tucked a well-worn blanket more tightly about his useless legs, trying vainly to ignore the disrepair into which his home had fallen.

"Come closer child." He smiled warmly and beckoned Kathlyn forth with a gnarled, spotted hand. As he watched her approach, Roth prayed that what he was about to tell Kathlyn would not make her hate him.

She took a seat on the faded floral settee across from him, her skirts settling with a whisper. Roth noticed with admiration that her modest lilac gown was trimmed in black, indicating that she was in half-mourning—for her sainted mother.

Though the Thompson sisters—Kathlyn and Rachel's mothers—had both died in the same month, Rachel refused to observe the mourning dress code that proper etiquette required.

This grieved Roth, but it was the least of Rachel's improprieties. He felt a familiar crushing pain in his chest. His breathing grew shallow. His sagging jowls paled, and he slumped forward ever so slightly. He feared his wayward daughter would be the death of him yet.

"Uncle Roth," Kathlyn exclaimed, clearly alarmed.

Roth straightened in his chair and, with a trembling hand, waved her concern away. She was such a sweet child. Was it any wonder he loved her so? If only Rachel could be more like her . . .

"Rachel tells me that your young man has made arrangements for your trip to Fort Smith," he stated, physical and emotional pain rendering his voice weak.

"Yes sir." Kathlyn dropped her gaze to the folded hands she clutched in her lap, not wanting her uncle to see the wary look in her eyes. He had problems aplenty; he didn't need hers.

"What arrangements has he made beyond Memphis?" *You old chicken,* Roth accused himself. He was talking about travel plans when what he really needed to say was much more vital.

"I'll take the Overland Stage to Fort Smith. Glenn will meet me there. If the river permits, we'll catch a steamer to Fort Gibson; if not, we'll catch another stage."

Roth noticed Kathlyn's reticence, but attributed it to maidenly modesty and fear of the unknown. After all it's not every day a young lady marries a virtual stranger . . . and a Yankee at that.

He supposed marriage was frightening enough for gently reared young ladies who wed their own kind. Women who had mothers to counsel them. But for someone who had suffered the tragedies Kathlyn had, a fragile child orphaned by the war, it must be overwhelming indeed.

Overcome with emotion, Roth leaned forward gingerly, mindful of his constant pain, and covered her hands with his own. "Is there anything I can do to help, my dear? I have no money, but who has these days." This last wasn't a question, but merely an oft-repeated statement of fact in post-war Georgia. "Is there anything you would care to ask me?"

If Kathlyn had not been so apprehensive about her uncertain future, and so worried about her uncle's health, she would have laughed at the uneasy but determined expression on his face. The sweet old soul actually thought she might ask him about the birds and the bees. And he'd answer her too, she wagered.

"No, thank you." She stifled a grin.

"It's a shame your mother isn't here for you." He looked through the windows at the barren fields. "You can't know how I wish she were here on River's Edge, where she belongs," he finished softly.

Kathlyn thought that a strange statement. As far as she knew her mother had never been to River's Edge. And Kathlyn had been here only once, during her summer with Brad.

Obviously, theirs had not been a close family. Such a shame; they had missed so much. Especially her mother, Margie, and her Aunt Carolyn. Kathlyn didn't know why the sisters had been estranged all these years. Now, she supposed she never would. It just seemed such a waste to her.

Family was the most important thing in life. She knew that now. Maybe it's true that you don't value something until you lose it.

"I wish we had visited more often. I asked to, but mama always said no, except for that time when I was sixteen," Kathlyn remembered aloud.

Roth patted Kathlyn's cheek and changed the subject abruptly. He still didn't have the courage to say what needed saying. "Honey, do you want to marry this lieutenant? I mean, him being a Yankee and all."

Roth's derisive tone arrested Kathlyn's attention. It was obvious he hated Yankees. She weighed her words carefully. There was no way she could tell her Confederate uncle—who, thankfully, had been too old to fight for the rebellion—that her father and brothers had died fighting for the Union. How could she make this proud Southerner understand that she had no prejudice against Yankees, and conversely, that she held former Rebel soldiers in contempt? The answer was plain. She couldn't.

She had told Rachel about her family's Union sympathies, however. Glenn, a Union officer, had brought Kathlyn to River's Edge. When Rachel later saw her visiting with the Union officer, Kathlyn had felt it necessary to explain. She feared her cousin's reaction,

86

but she shouldn't have. Even though Glenn was a Yankee, Rachel had taken to him right off.

"Do you want to marry him?" Roth asked again when Kathlyn didn't answer.

She nodded her head affirmatively and brought forth a weak smile. It was an ineffective attempt to convince them both that she would be happy as the wife of this particular Yankee. But it didn't work.

"I'm glad," Roth murmured, unconvinced.

Kathlyn recognized that her uncle needed his rest; he was visibly weakened from their conversation. She rose to leave.

With a hand on her sleeve, Roth detained her. "Honey, sit here beside me. There's something else I need to tell you. Something that's going to be hard for you to understand." Roth noted the worried expression on Kathlyn's face and sympathized. He had made it sound earth-shattering . . . and it was.

"I want you to promise to hear me out. Will you promise me that?" Roth widened his eyes in question, and, unconsciously, massaged the area over his aching heart.

"Uncle Roth, you're scaring me. Are you all right? Has something happened? Is it Rachel? She's all right, isn't she?" she asked all at once.

Unbidden, the ordeal between Brad and Rachel came into Kathlyn's mind. *Oh please, don't let it be anything that Brad's done,* she prayed silently. Before she could question her loyalties, or examine her protective feelings for Brad, Roth reassured her.

"We're all right, honey. It's not about anything that's happened recently. All this happened a long time ago, before you were born." Roth passed a hand over his eyes in agitation. "I don't know where to start."

"I'm sure I'll understand." Kathlyn had never seen her uncle at such a loss for words. She didn't want to agitate him, but if he didn't explain his cryptic words soon, she was going to expire from fear of what was to come!

87

"A long time ago, a very long time ago, I came to work for your Grandfather Thompson. I had just been mustered out of the State Militia, had no family and no place to go. But I was strong and had worked on a farm before I enlisted, so getting a job at River's Edge seemed the right thing to do."

"I thought River's Edge belonged to your family, not to Mama and Aunt Carolyn's."

"No, the plantation had been in the Thompson family for four generations, passed from father to son, until your grandfather. Since he had no sons he divided River's Edge into equal shares and bequeathed it to his two daughters. When he died, Margie signed her half over to Carolyn and moved to Union Point."

Kathlyn was stunned. "Why did she do that? Why would she give up her home and move away?"

Roth still wasn't prepared to tell Kathlyn everything. "She had an old maiden aunt in Union Point. Ran a boarding house I'm told. Your mama moved in with her and a year later, met Herschel McKinney. They married and bought the farm where you were raised and your brothers were born."

There was a message in there somewhere, but it was lost on Kathlyn. She was puzzled by the strange way her uncle had said her daddy's name. It wasn't with malice; it was with rank envy. How could a man with a plantation the scope of River's Edge envy a small farm owner like her daddy?

"I didn't meet Carolyn until I had been at River's Edge for three months. But I met your mama the very first day."

A tender look came into Roth's faded eyes and his voice thickened with emotion. "I thought Margie was the prettiest little thing I'd ever seen. And she was just as sweet as she was pretty."

Roth turned his head and smiled at Kathlyn, tears magnifying his eyes. "You're so like her. That's one of the reasons I love you so much."

Overcome with familial emotion, Kathlyn knelt in front of Roth. He leaned forward and she circled his frail shoulders with her arms. "I love you too, Uncle Roth."

When Roth heard the word "uncle" he stiffened and pushed back in his chair.

"You loved her, didn't you?" Kathlyn asked simply, still kneeling in front of him.

"Yes, I loved her."

"You shouldn't have been afraid to tell me that. People fall in love . . . you couldn't help that." She smiled, returning to her chair.

"That's not all. That summer your mama and I spent every spare minute together. When I wasn't working in the fields, I was with Margie. The work was long and hard, but those were mighty happy days."

The loving expression on his face hardened. "Then Carolyn came home from a three month visit at a spa. It was real popular in those days for wealthy women to go away and get *rejuvenated.*" The disgust in his voice was fairly palpable.

"Carolyn was older than your mama, and pretty in her own way, though not soft and delicate like Margie. She had the kind of beauty — like Rachel — that excites a man physically."

Kathlyn's cheeks flamed with embarrassment and something else. She knew only too well how exciting men found Rachel, if Brad was any indication. She chided herself for being jealous of her cousin; last night had not been Rachel's fault.

Roth went on. "And she was Margie's older sister. It seemed that she wanted everything that belonged to Margie. And Margie was such a giving person, and Carolyn had always . . . I don't know . . . intimidated her, I guess you could say."

Kathlyn wondered why on earth her uncle was telling her all this. If his tone of voice was any indication, he had never loved his wife. But what did it matter now?

Was he trying to warn her about a loveless marriage? Was he astute enough to know that she didn't

89

love Glenn? Was he going to say she shouldn't marry him? How many times had she told herself just that? But she didn't have any choice in the matter.

She massaged her temples, attempting to ease the headache that was growing more intense by the minute. Now was not really the best time for her to hear about a loveless marriage. She doubted her decision to marry Glenn enough as it was. But the decision was made; the die was cast.

"Carolyn was very friendly to me, and since I didn't want to hurt her feelings, I dated both sisters. More and more Carolyn claimed my time. Before long, Margie just disappeared when I came around.

"Then, your grandfather died, your mother denied her inheritance, and left the same day. To my knowledge, your mother never set foot on this property again."

Obviously Roth was trying to tell her something important. She doubted he was enjoying his stroll down memory lane. But she was missing the point. Frustrated, she asked, "Why? Why would Mama give up her home like that? She never did anything on the spur of the moment. She was always the sensible one, so calm, and self assured." Her smile was bittersweet. "Daddy, with his Irish blood, was the precipitous one. I always thought I must take after Daddy."

"I don't think so," Roth said, so softly that Kathlyn barely caught his words. "It wasn't until a year later that I learned the reason your mother left. I was in Union Point on plantation business, and I saw Margie."

Abruptly, Roth stopped speaking. He cleared his throat and braced himself for what would occur in the next few seconds. "I saw Margie and our six-month-old baby girl."

Suddenly the blood rushed to Kathlyn's head, causing a roar in her ears. Her headache burst and shattered her mind into a million pieces. She couldn't believe what she had just heard.

When her mind could function again, she just

stared at her uncle. No, not her uncle. Her father. If what he said was true, Roth Jackson was not her uncle, and Herschel McKinney had not been her father. She clutched the arms of her chair as the room began to spin.

"I know this is a shock, and I never planned to tell you, especially not like this. I thought if Margie wanted you to know, she'd tell you," he spoke rapidly, frantically.

"That's what I told her that day. I told her if she promised to write and tell me about you, that I would never interfere in her life or in yours. I always kept my promise and she always kept hers. She wrote me twice a month—telling me all the important things in your life—until she fell sick at the end."

Kathlyn's face looked fuzzy through Roth's tears. But he could see clearly that she was panic stricken. Oh God, he wished Margie were here to help him explain.

"Did she know . . . about me . . . when she left home?"

"Yes. But it wasn't until years later that I found out she'd known. You were about four and I had gotten a letter from her, telling me about your first pony ride. Carolyn found the letter. She was enraged that Margie was corresponding with me and I guess she wanted to hurt me. So she told me that she had caused your mother to leave River's Edge.

"Before she left, Margie had confided in Carolyn that she was pregnant, hoping that Carolyn would help her break the news to their parents. But Carolyn talked her into keeping it a secret. She told Margie that if word got out, the whole family would be disgraced. And since their father was ill at the time, Carolyn convinced Margie that the truth would kill him."

"But why did she leave after he died?"

"I was away on business when your grandfather died. Apparently, Carolyn told Margie that I had found out about the baby, and that I had run off rather than accept responsibility. It was a lie. Still, when I came back, Margie was gone.

"When I asked Carolyn where Margie was, she told me that Margie had decided to marry an old flame of hers in Union Point. That, too, was a lie. But I didn't know it.

"I was angry and hurt. Still, I wanted to go after her. But I knew it wouldn't do any good. I knew if Margie had pledged herself to another man, whether she loved him or not, she would never break her vow. Margie was like that. So I just let her go."

Kathlyn sat still. Roth wasn't even sure she was breathing. He prayed that she wouldn't hate him for what he had told her. Most of all he didn't want to tarnish her mother's memory. But he had a reason for telling her.

"Did my father"—her voice broke—"did my father know it was you?"

"No, Margie didn't see the need to tell him. And he never asked. In both their minds, he was your father. She said he couldn't love you more if you had been from his own body. You were certainly in his heart!"

"Yes, I was that. And he was . . . is . . . in mine."

"I know, honey. And I don't want to change that. But I wouldn't change the fact that I'm your natural father either."

Stiffly, Kathlyn stood and walked over to the fireplace. She hadn't realized how tired she was. Leaning her head against the mantel, she asked, "Why did she let me visit, when I was sixteen? She had kept us apart for so long, why then?"

"I begged her," his voice broke. "I told her that you were almost a woman. That I deserved to see you, just once, before you were no longer a child." He wouldn't recount the battle he had had with Carolyn over Kathlyn's visit. It would serve no purpose.

Remembering her brief love affair with Brad, Kathlyn said, "I was already a woman." The anguish in her voice confused Roth.

92

"I discovered that. When I saw you and Brad together."

"Please, I don't even want to think about that. Not now." If her mother had remained firm, if she hadn't allowed her to spend the summer with the Jacksons, she and Brad would have never met. She would still be chaste, and she would still be able to have a baby. Oh Lord, she couldn't bear to think of that now. "Why did you tell me now, after all these years?"

"Because I want you to do something for me."

Breathing deeply, she turned to face him. "I don't know what I can do. If you want me to say that I love you as my daddy, I don't think I can do that. I love you, Uncle Roth, but as an uncle. In time . . ." Even as she said it, Kathlyn knew Roth Jackson would always be *Uncle Roth* to her.

"I know," he said quietly. "What I want you to do is promise me that you'll take care of your sister."

The word "sister" hit Kathlyn between the eyes like a sledge hammer. *Rachel!* Rachel was not her cousin; she was her sister. And Brad had been involved with her. Her knuckles turned white as she gripped the mantel to keep from falling.

"I'm not well, and I don't know how much longer I'll live. When I'm gone, Rachel will be all alone. Will you take her to Fort Gibson with you? Please?"

There was nothing more Roth could say. He knew Rachel was not the most pleasant person to be around, and left to her own devices, she would destroy herself. Kathlyn was his only hope. He prayed he wasn't destroying one daughter to save the other.

Kathlyn returned to his side on shaky legs. "Of course she can go with me. But what about you? If we both leave, there will be no one here to take care of you. Can't you go with us?"

He was touched by her concern. She truly was Margie's daughter. Even after the shock she had just suffered, she thought only of the welfare of others. "As long as I know my two girls are all right, I'll be fine."

"But . . ."

She started to object, but he halted her with an upraised hand. "There *is* one more thing I want you to do."

"Yes?"

Ignoring the fact that she didn't want to think about Brad, he said, "Forgive Brad Hampton . . . and yourself."

Chapter Ten

"I don't know what you mean," Kathlyn whispered, refusing to meet his gaze.

"I think you do. Margie told me what happened when you came home, after the summer you spent at River's Edge," he said pointedly.

Her cheeks flamed as she wondered if her mother had told Roth the *whole* story. Surely not. Her mother had not known the whole story.

"What you ask is impossible."

Roth tried another route. "Do you remember what you promised me last night?"

"That I would look to the future, and bury the past?" Kathlyn asked reluctantly.

"Yes. What about that?"

"I *will* do it. But I can never forgive . . ." The thought was too repugnant to finish.

Forgive what? And whom? Perhaps herself, for surrendering her virtue to a man who wasn't her husband? "Honey, do you think you're the first person to do something you're ashamed of? The first person to conceive a child out of wedlock?"

"Obviously not after what you've just told me about you and mother." Kathlyn sounded angry, but she wasn't. She just wanted to bring this painful conversation to a close.

Roth winced. This was going badly. He wanted to help Kathlyn come to grip with the tragedies in her life, not open an avenue whereby she could express her disapproval of his and Margie's actions. She hadn't been there; how could she know what they had felt?

95

But considering what had happened between her and Brad, maybe she could. Once the baby had been conceived, however, the similarity in their stories ended. Margie's baby had lived, while Kathlyn had lost the child of the man she loved. Also, Margie had found happiness in her life, while it appeared to him that Kathlyn had not. Nor had he.

"You're right. We made our mistakes, and, like you, we paid dearly. But your mother was able to do something that you haven't done. She was able to put the past behind her. That's why she was so happy with Herschel.

"And that's what I want for you, honey. I want you to make peace with your ghosts. If you don't, the past will always haunt you. I know. I wasn't as wise as your mother. I held onto the past and it ruined my chance for happiness."

Kathlyn felt terrible for snapping at her uncle. She sighed heavily. "I'm sorry." Her words sounded so inadequate. "I know you're trying to help, really I do. It's just that I haven't allowed myself to think about these things in a very long time. It still hurts."

"Margie said you lost the baby," Roth said, inviting Kathlyn to open up.

"I didn't lose it; I killed it," she confessed with a sob, wrapping her arms around her waist.

Roth knew that to show pity for Kathlyn now would be a mistake. She was struggling to maintain control and any show of sympathy on his part might push her over the edge. His arms ached to hold her, but he resisted. She needed his strength. Not his pity.

"Listen to me, honey," he began firmly. "You didn't kill your baby. You were young, little more than a child yourself. You had suffered a terrible blow. You were distraught. Margie said you couldn't even eat."

"You don't understand," she choked out.

"Margie thought you might die. If not from losing the baby, then from losing the man you love. Don't you think I can understand that?" he continued relentlessly.

96

"But I should have been stronger, for the baby. Brad shouldn't have mattered. I obviously hadn't mattered to him."

The tortured look in Kathlyn's eyes convinced Roth she was no longer speaking to him. She was reliving the pain of the past. Perhaps such catharsis was what she needed.

"I took the horse and ran off. If I hadn't fallen over that wall." She balled her fists in her lap. "Even then I might have kept the baby, but I had weakened myself so, refusing to eat, unable to sleep." She dropped her head into her hands and sobbed. She indulged herself. The walls she had erected sixteen years ago crumbled, leaving her raw and open to reexperience the tragedy of the past.

Roth stretched forth a trembling hand and touched her wet cheek.

After a long moment, she looked at him, pain deepening her eyes to the color purple. "Don't you see? I killed his baby. Brad killed something inside me, and I killed his baby."

It was obvious to him that the confession cost her a great deal. He suspected this was the first time she had voiced the notion, that somehow she had killed Brad's baby on purpose. "Did you want to kill Brad's baby? Did you really want your baby to die?"

She flattened her palms against her heaving chest. "No, heavens no! I never wanted to kill him. He was Brad's baby. I wanted Brad's baby; I love Brad." She was so distraught, she wasn't aware that she had used the term *love,* not *loved,* when speaking of her feelings for Brad.

Roth noticed. "Then how can you blame yourself for an accident? And why do you blame Brad?" he asked softly.

"Because, if he'd loved me like he said, our baby would be alive now. He betrayed both me and our baby. When he wrote that note, saying he didn't want me, I was carrying his child. If he didn't want me, then he didn't want my baby either."

97

"Did you tell him you were carrying his child?"

"No, but it wouldn't have mattered."

"I think it would." Roth identified with Brad from personal experience. "And, maybe he did want you. As I recall, I was the one who thought it was best for him to stay away from you that summer. It was an impossible task, keeping him away. I might as well have been trying to keep the sun from rising."

"Why?"

Roth narrowed his eyes, shaking his head in confusion.

"Why did you want to keep us apart?"

"Because you and Brad reminded me of Margie and myself when we were kids. Considering how that turned out, I wanted to spare you. You were only sixteen. And it was my one shot at being your father." This last was torn from the depths of his soul. "You have to know how sorry I am, if I finally drove him away."

"It wasn't your fault," Kathlyn said sadly. "If he had truly loved me, nothing could have driven him away."

"Maybe it's not too late." He remembered the hunger in Brad's eyes when he looked at Kathlyn at the party. Obviously, the young man wasn't free of the past either.

"Are you forgetting that I'm engaged?"

"Well, that can be remedied easily enough." Now that he knew she still loved Brad, he wanted her to break her engagement with her *Yankee* lieutenant. "If you would just give Brad a chance, I have a feeling the two of you could make a go of it this time."

"Have you forgotten what you said about mama keeping a vow? I am my mother's daughter." She smiled ruefully. "I've made a promise to Glenn, and I intend to keep that promise. Besides, even if I could forgive Brad for breaking my heart"—she paused—"I don't think I could forgive him for ruining my chance to have a family."

Once again Roth was at a loss.

98

"Of course, you don't know. I asked the doctor not to tell mama; I had put her through enough already.

"After I lost the baby, I had a terrible infection. The doctor said if I lived, I would never be able to have children. The baby I lost was the only one I'll ever conceive." Putting voice to the greatest disappointment of her life visibly drained Kathlyn.

Roth's eyes clouded with sympathy. "I'm so sorry, honey; I didn't know. But I still wish you could find a way to make peace with yourself, and with Brad."

"That might take a while," she whispered honestly, remembering not only the distant past. In her mind's eye, she saw Rachel and Brad as they had been last night. "We're both tired, Uncle Roth. Why don't you rest now. I'll see you at tea."

Roth nodded. Before he drifted off, he felt Kathlyn's lips on his weathered cheek.

"I love you," she whispered.

"And I love you, sweetheart." Silently, he breathed a prayer of thanksgiving that his firstborn daughter had been blessed with a forgiving heart. In spite of his emotional exhaustion, he fell asleep with a smile on his face.

That was the last time Kathlyn ever saw her *father* alive.

Rachel inched her way down the hall that separated her room from Kathlyn's. She clutched a small green bottle, filled with white powder, hidden in the folds of her gown. An ominous looking skull and cross bones decorated the label.

After checking both ends of the hall with a swift glance, she slipped inside Kathlyn's room. Silently, she closed the door behind her. To her relief, a soft cooing sound was all she heard; the room was empty.

Since she didn't know when Kathlyn would return, she worked quickly. With trembling hands, she withdrew the stopper from the vial, tapped the bottle against the edge of the birds' water cup, and poured

99

out a small amount of the mysterious powder. Carefully, she swirled the water, dissolving the powder. Then, she stood back and waited.

When the human entered the room, Ishta and Barta angled their heads toward the door. It wasn't the one they loved, so they remained on their perch, wary of the woman skulking about their cage. Four tiny eyes watched every move she made, pouring something into their water cup.

A blue blur, Ishta flew to the farthest corner of the cage. But Barta was curious. Bravely, he flew to the cup. He touched it with his dark blue beak. Nothing happened. Then he bumped the cup, sloshing a small amount of water onto the bottom of the cage. Still nothing. Becoming bored with it, he dipped his beak and drank.

Instantly the male parakeet keeled over, crashing into the cup as he fell. The contents emptied out into the cage, pooling water beneath the wire floor.

"Damn!" Rachel hissed. She would have to fill the cup again, but at least she had evidence the poison worked.

Just as she touched the gate, she heard a door downstairs bang open, followed by the sound of Kathlyn's voice. She couldn't run the risk that Kathlyn would come straight to her room; she had to leave with all haste.

"Double damn!" she cursed again. Glancing at the surviving bird, she whispered, "I'll be back for you." Like mother, like daughter. As Roth said, whatever had belonged to Margie, Carolyn wanted. And now whatever belonged to Kathlyn, Rachel wanted. Since the birds were Kathlyn's most prized possession, they had to die. It made perfect sense to Rachel. Smiling, she slipped out the door.

"I'll take Father his tea," Rachel offered stiffly, sailing into the kitchen from the back staircase.

Matty, the portly black woman holding the tray,

snorted and looked at Rachel suspiciously. That child had never offered to do anything for anybody in her whole life. She was up to no good. Matty knew it sure as the day she was born. But she was too busy to worry about it now. With a warning look, she handed Rachel the tray.

Uppity old woman, Rachel groused silently as she carried her father his tea. *She'd better watch herself or I'll take care of her too.* The weight of the small green bottle hidden in her waist pocket made her feel all powerful. She would teach people to defy her!

When Rachel handed Roth the cup of steaming liquid, her hands shook with excitement. "Here Daddy." She smiled sweetly, aping Kathlyn.

"Thank you, honey," Roth said, his heart warmed.

He was pleased that Rachel had brought him his tea, for more reasons than one. True, it was gratifying that his daughter wanted to do something nice for him. She wasn't known for selfless acts.

And it would provide him the opportunity to tell her she had a sister. He just hoped she took the news as well as Kathlyn. In fact, maybe Kathlyn could help him break the news to Rachel. She could soften it by offering to take Rachel west with her.

"Where's Kathlyn?"

Kathlyn, always Kathlyn, Rachel bristled. Why was it that everybody was so taken with Kathlyn? She'd brought the old fool his tea, hadn't she? Not his precious Kathlyn. The fact that it was laced with arsenic was beside the point. He didn't know that.

Rachel's lips spread in a smile that didn't quite reach her eyes. They were blue chunks of ice. "I imagine she'll be down shortly. She said not to wait on her. Go ahead, daddy, drink your tea. Before it gets cold."

Slowly, Roth lifted the chipped china cup to his lips. Rachel held her breath. She didn't so much as blink. It seemed to her as if he held the cup to his mouth for an eternity, when in reality it was a scant moment in time.

Then, many things occurred at once. Roth slumped forward, his cup falling from his lifeless hand. Two feminine voices split the warm summer air, one a mournful scream, the other a triumphant hiss.

Upstairs, Kathlyn clutched Barta's dead body to her chest and crumbled to the floor. Directly below her, in Roth Jackson's study, his second born pushed him aside and rifled through his desk, searching for the deed to River's Edge.

"What will I do now?" Rachel asked, seeming more inconvenienced than grief-stricken.

Kathlyn was taken aback at first. Then she decided her cousin was in shock. Just as she was herself; to learn that Roth was her father and then lose him the same day was a devastating blow.

But she knew the loss was even harder on Rachel, for she had known no father except Roth. Yes, Rachel was in shock. Trying to reassure her, Kathlyn spoke gently, "I'm sure Glenn won't mind if you come along with me." Overwhelmed by the thought that she and Rachel were truly sisters, the only family either of them had in the world, she embraced Rachel.

When Kathlyn released her, Rachel suppressed a smile. She didn't want to seem too anxious to accompany Kathlyn on her trip. "All right. I'll go with you. Maybe I can find a husband at Fort Gibson. I just hope there are some *officers* available." She turned away, not noticing the shocked expression on Kathlyn's face. "I'll show Brad Hampton yet!" she muttered irrelevantly, hastening away to make arrangements for the upcoming trip.

"Is that it? That's all you have to say?" Kathlyn called to her retreating figure, righteous indignation in behalf of Roth flaring.

"What?" Rachel asked from the top of the stairs. "No, there is one more thing. Do you think I could sell this place before we leave?"

"Rachel, no!" Kathlyn was shocked at her cousin's lack of sensitivity.

"Yes, you're probably right. There won't be time. But maybe I can get an advance from the bank, at least enough to cover my trip and buy a new wardrobe." She turned and stepped onto the gallery. "I plan to leave this place in style!"

"Wait! What about Uncle Roth's funeral?" Kathlyn tried to keep the exasperation out of her voice. Rachel *had* to be in shock; nobody could be that unfeeling.

Leaning against the railing, Rachel drawled, "Whatever you decide will be fine with me. I'm no good at such things, but you must be. You've had enough practice at it." Then she disappeared into her room.

Tears stung Kathlyn's eyes at Rachel's careless words. Surely Rachel didn't mean to be so cruel, referring to her family's deaths in such a cavalier fashion.

Wearily, she headed for Roth's office to make arrangements for his burial. She entered the study slowly, relieved to see that one of the workers had removed his body. When she sat behind his desk, her gaze circled the room. This was where the man who had been her father had run River's Edge. And no doubt, this was where he had mourned its ruin. Where he had yearned for her mother and even for herself.

Her gaze settled on the partially opened window, beyond which were acres and acres of some of the best farming land in the South. The rich earth lay barren now, as barren as she.

That thought brought to mind the conversation she and Roth had had earlier in the day. She hadn't really been aware that she blamed herself and Brad for the death of their child until Roth had pointed it out. She had buried those feelings, along with the innocent love she had possessed for Brad long ago.

Could she ever forgive herself for what she had done to her unborn child? And could she forgive Brad? Did it even matter how she felt about him, she asked herself. She would be leaving soon.

Rising to her feet, she crossed over to the window. The thought of never seeing Brad again hurt more than she cared to admit.

Absently, she ran her hand along the back of the wheelchair Roth would not be needing now. Tears filled her eyes and spilled over onto her pale cheeks. Was she crying for her uncle, or for Brad? She suspected both.

"Get a grip, Kat," she scolded herself, but to no avail. Stumbling back across the room, she threw herself into the high backed chair behind Roth's desk. Her heart aching for lost loved ones, she laid her head on her folded arms and wept.

She wasn't sure how long she had been in her uncle's study when she heard sounds of the house readying itself for night. Through the window she could see the sun disappearing over the horizon. The sky grew deep pink, tipped with purple, and finally turned black.

She had long since run out of tears, although her heart still wept. Rubbing her cheeks to erase the evidence of her weakness, she heard a knock at the door. "Come in," she called.

"Miss McKinney," Jared called, compassion evident in his deep tones, as he stepped into the semi-dark room.

"I'm over here."

He left the door ajar, allowing a golden pool of light to flow in from the hall. "Would you like me to light a lamp?"

"Thank you."

If Jared wondered why Kathlyn was sitting in the dark, in her dead uncle's study, he gave no notice. And if Kathlyn wondered what brought Jared to River's Edge, she didn't ask.

He supplied the information nonetheless. "The coroner couldn't come to check Roth, so he asked me to. I thought perhaps you or Miss Jackson might need something."

Just then, the lamp on Roth's desk burst into light,

chasing the murky shadows of night to the farthest corners of the room. Jared's doctor's bag rested on the seat of the chair fronting the desk. "I'm all right, thank you, Dr. Hampton. Please have a seat. Have you seen Rachel?" she asked.

Jared looked uncomfortable as he moved his bag to the floor and took a seat. He cleared his throat before he answered. "She's not in."

Kathlyn colored. How could her cousin go out on the very night her father died? Someone might come to the house when they heard of Roth's death. And if Rachel weren't here — well, she just wouldn't allow anyone to criticize Rachel.

"About your uncle," Jared said, breaking into Kathlyn's thoughts.

There was something about the way he spoke, the wary look in his eyes that alerted her. "Did he have a heart attack?"

"I don't think so." He paused. "Do you know what Roth ate today?"

Kathlyn found that a strange question. "He didn't eat breakfast. And for lunch, he had the same thing I did. Vegetables, buttermilk, and corn bread. Nothing unusual. Why?"

"I just thought he might have suffered an allergic reaction to something he ate," Jared hedged.

"He was drinking tea with Rachel when he" — her voice lowered — "collapsed. But I don't think he ate anything."

Jared eyes widened. He didn't want to alert Kathlyn to his suspicions until he examined Roth further. "Would you mind if I took him to my office." He kept his tone light.

"For an autopsy?" Kathlyn asked, aghast.

"It's really the only way I can determine the cause of death."

"No! You won't. I won't let you butcher my father!" Rachel shrieked from the doorway.

Kathlyn and Jared were on their feet in an instant. "Rachel, calm down." Kathlyn rushed across the

105

room. "I'm sure Dr. Hampton would do no such thing." Taking Rachel by the hand she brought her to Jared, imploring him with her eyes. "You'll have to forgive Rachel's outburst, Dr. Hampton. I'm sure you understand that we've had quite a shock today." She circled Rachel's waist with her arm.

"Of course." Jared stood stock-still, studying both girls intently. Kathlyn's lovely face was puffy from crying, her eyes dulled by grief. The only color in her otherwise pale complexion was the dark red half-moon on her cheek. He wondered inanely how the cut had occurred.

Then his attention was drawn to Rachel. Her eyes were blazing in a face heavy with cosmetics. Her look of resolve clearly dared him to challenge her. She showed not the least sign of grief.

"It was very kind of you to check on us, but I'm afraid we're both a bit the worse for wear. If you'll let yourself out, I really must see to Rachel."

Kathlyn's sincere expression touched Jared's heart. Suddenly, he wished he could get her away from her cousin. But how could he help her?

He sure as hell couldn't do anything for Roth. Not even determine how the man died. If his next-of-kin objected—as Rachel surely did—Jared couldn't call for a formal inquest without possessing overpowering evidence that the death was the result of foul play. And since he had no such evidence, there was nothing he could do.

Rachel must have known it as well. When she flashed him a smug smile, Jared's skin fairly crawled. That one was evil. He knew it as sure as the sun rose and set.

"I'm sorry if I distressed you and your cousin, Miss McKinney. Please remember, if you need any help at all, I'm at your service." Jared bowed gallantly to Kathlyn, scooping his medical bag from the floor.

Then just as his brother had done less than twenty-four hours before, he turned his back on Rachel and walked away. It was not very chivalrous of him, he

106

knew. But it was a sight better than what he wanted to do: see her strung up for the murder of her very own flesh and blood, of the man who gave her life, her father.

God, what a monster!

Chapter Eleven

The day Roth Jackson was buried seemed better
suited for a picnic than a funeral. The azure sky was
cloudless; the scent of honeysuckles was sweet on the
wind; and the flaming sun warmed the earth below.

But it didn't warm Kathlyn's grieving heart.

Descending the stair-steps of the manor house slowly,
she surveyed the crowded foyer. It was fairly bursting
with black garbed mourners. Her uncle's friends had
begun arriving at dawn, and still they came, crowding
into the house, spilling out onto the lawn. If the quality of a man's life could be judged by the number of
people attending his funeral, then it was obvious Roth
Jackson had been a good man.

A familiar, deep voice echoed Kathlyn's thoughts.
Her heart accelerated.

"My sympathies on your father's death," Brad said
formally, bowing low over Rachel's hand. "Roth was a
good man. The community will feel his loss."

Moving toward them, Kathlyn saw Rachel nod
weakly. Ever since Jared's visit, Rachel had seemed to
take her father's death badly. Kathlyn was worried
about her. Rachel demanded every moment of
Kathlyn's time, but Kathlyn didn't mind. It had been
far too long since she'd been needed. And caring for
Rachel in her time of grief took the sting out of her
own loneliness. For that she was grateful.

When Kathlyn reached Rachel's side, she said, "Rachel, the funeral will begin in an hour. Wouldn't you
like to rest?" She didn't look at Brad as she spoke to
Rachel, but she could feel his eyes upon her. Nervous

perspiration dotted her upper lip. She wished that he would move on. She wished that he had not come.

"Yes, I think I need to lie down. If you will excuse me Brad, I feel a trifle woozy," Rachel murmured. "Will you help me upstairs, Kathlyn?"

Kathlyn slipped her arm around Rachel's waist. "Lean on me," she instructed.

Rachel leaned heavily on the slight woman. For a moment Brad thought Kathlyn might buckle under her cousin's greater weight. But stiffening her spine, she managed to help Rachel mount the stairs and see her safely to her room.

Quite a woman, Brad thought of Kathlyn. Soft and sweet on the outside, with the strength and patience of Job on the inside.

"I'm concerned about her." A familiar voice broke into Brad's musings.

Turning, he looked into Jared's scowling face. "Rachel?"

"No, Miss McKinney," Jared answered, his eyes on the door through which the women had disappeared.

A frisson of foreboding skittered up Brad's spine. "Why? Is she ill?"

Jared caught the deep concern in Brad's tone. "Not that I know of."

"In danger?"

"Maybe."

"Good heavens, man, don't mince words. Tell me what you're talking about." Brad's voice was louder than he intended.

Jared flashed him a warning look and ushered him out onto the veranda, away from curious ears.

"I don't really know. It's just a feeling I have. When I look at those two together, it's like looking at a hungry shark and a tasty minnow. And Miss McKinney seems to be such a trusting minnow. She can't see her cousin for what she is." Jared couldn't tell Brad his suspicions concerning Roth's death, at least not now. What good would it do anyway? He had no proof.

"True, but you don't really think Rachel would hurt

109

Kathlyn, do you? After all, with Roth gone Kathlyn is Rachel's only living relative."

"Exactly," Jared remarked cryptically.

"Weeping may tarry for the night, but joy comes with the morning," the stoic reverend quoted the Psalm, completing the graveside service.

Kathlyn and Rachel stood together at the head of Roth's coffin. Kathlyn withdrew two blood red roses from a flower arrangement at her side. Handing one to Rachel and keeping one herself, she offered Rachel a bolstering smile.

As if in slow motion Rachel placed the flower on Roth's casket, allowing her fingertips to linger on the polished wood. Choking back a sob, it appeared for all the world as if she were reluctant to let her father go.

Kathlyn lay her flower on the casket; unlike Rachel, tears of grief slipped down her face.

Not noticing Rachel's dry eyes, Kathlyn reached over and took her free hand, squeezing it as the crowd approached them. One by one, the long line of mourners filed past the women, expressing their condolences.

Then, like the Red Sea, the assemblage parted. Like the haughtiest monarch, Judge Josiah Salt approached the women. "Miss Jackson, Miss McKinney, my sympathies." He bowed.

"Thank you," Kathlyn said.

Rachel was too overcome to speak.

"Whenever you like, I'll come out and go over Roth's will with you."

"Did you bring it with you today?" Rachel asked quickly.

Kathlyn marveled that her cousin's voice sounded stronger than it had since the night of Roth's death. She was relieved; she had been worried about Rachel.

"Why yes."

"Then I think we should do it now."

"Do you really think you're up to it, Rachel?"

Kathlyn asked, concern evident in her dulcet tones.

"I'll manage," she said bravely, slumping against Kathlyn's side.

"Very well." The judge turned to his assistant, whom neither woman had noticed until now. "Find Mr. Hampton and bring him to Mr. Jackson's study."

"Mr. Hampton?" Rachel and Kathlyn asked in unison.

"Yes. Didn't you know that Roth designated Brad Hampton as the executor of his estate?"

Rachel shook her head no. Kathlyn dropped her gaze, silently bemoaning the fact, if it had to be a Hampton, why couldn't it have been Jared?

"He did." The judge drew himself up, obviously insulted that mere females would question him. "And as the executor, Mr. Hampton must be present."

"Very well." Rachel didn't like the judge's demeanor one bit. She would, however, indulge the pompous windbag to learn of her inheritance. *Her inheritance.* "Why does Kathlyn have to be present for the reading? There's no reason for both of us to go through this." Rachel feigned concern for her cousin.

"It was your father's wish that you both be present." The judge's imperious tone implied, "and that's the end of this discussion."

Brad and Kathlyn were ill at ease, sitting beside each other in Roth's study. Whether Brad's discomfiture was from being the executor of her uncle's estate or from just being in her presence, Kathlyn couldn't tell.

But one thing she did know. From the way he watched Rachel's every move, he must be interested in the woman he'd "had his way with." Kathlyn gripped the arms of her chair, trying to tamp down her anger . . . and her jealousy.

As for Rachel, she was interested in nothing but the words of her father's last will and testament.

Thus far, it had sounded like a lot of legal jargon to Kathlyn, with meaning to no one except an attorney.

111

But the final bequeath in the document was clear—painfully clear.

". . . And all my worldly possessions, including my plantation, River's Edge, I leave equally to my two daughters, my firstborn, Kathlyn McKinney, and my last child, Rachel Jackson."

"Just like Grandpa Thompson," Kathlyn murmured, remembering that her grandfather had left River's Edge to his two daughters, just as Roth did now.

"What the hell?" Rachel shrieked, jumping to her feet. Then just as quickly, she remembered herself.

Kathlyn approached her. "He didn't tell you?"

"That he left the plantation to both of us?"

"No. That we're sisters."

Rachel was genuinely confused. "Would you please reread that last sentence." The words were barely discernible, slipping past frozen lips.

The judge did as instructed. "Perhaps you ladies would like to be alone," he finished, looking toward Brad. "Our work here is finished."

"Yes. I think that would be best," Kathlyn said.

Noting the threatening way Rachel towered over Kathlyn, Brad was reluctant to leave. But there was nothing else he could do.

Once they were alone, Rachel took a seat. She appeared quite calm.

Encouraged, Kathlyn related the story of her conception, just as Roth had revealed it to her. She omitted the poignant fact that it seemed Roth had loved her mother, not Rachel's. She ended, asking, "Are you all right?"

"Certainly. It's just that it's all such a shock. To find out that I have a sister, now, that Father's dead . . ." Rachel trailed off. She didn't care that Roth was Kathlyn's father. And it didn't matter to whom the old man left the plantation. Her *sister* wouldn't benefit from her inheritance anyway. Not if Rachel had anything to do with it!

The day before Annadru, Mammy Mae, and Brad

were to leave Georgia, Brad sauntered into the great parlor to take afternoon tea with his family one last time. Distracted, he moved over to the large window, pulling the curtains aside, gazing out over the only home he'd ever known.

His sister-in-law, Melinda, noted his rigid posture. He seemed to be carrying an incredible weight on those broad shoulders. Smiling, she remembered him when he was a young bachelor, carefree, almost sheltered.

When she first met him, a more heart-stealing rogue the South had never known. Little had changed in terms of his appearance. The passing years, a devastating war, and the death of his wife had not changed him one whit, physically. Once the answer to a maiden's prayer; always the answer to a maiden's prayer, she decided.

For as long as she could remember, females had fairly swooned when he cast his rakish glance in their direction. And he'd definitely cast his share of rakish glances.

His brothers had been known to say—with a note of pride in their voices—that Brad enjoyed women the way most men enjoyed fine brandy and cigars, exuberantly and often. All that was required of him to capture the hearts of blushing blondes, fiery redheads, or raven-haired beauties, was to bless them with a seductive smile. They fell into his lap like sweet Georgia peaches falling from a tree.

Personally, Melinda wondered if he hadn't hopped from woman to woman, trying to fill an emptiness. Perhaps he had loved someone once, someone who had not returned that love.

But surely not. What woman could be immune to Brad Hampton? Indeed, at thirty-two he was still irresistible. His polished good looks made women stop and stare whenever he crossed their line of vision. With hair as black as pitch, expressive brown eyes, and a broad shouldered, muscular physique, he was set apart from other Southern gentlemen.

113

But in Melinda's mind, his most winning characteristic was that he was at present and always had been totally unimpressed by his exceptional good looks and extraordinary talents. Just as her Jared was.

Crossing over to Brad, Melinda placed a hand on his arm. "Hello, handsome," she quipped.

The strain left his face. "Howdy, beautiful." He turned from the window, kissed Melinda's plump cheek, and winked at Jared across the room. "I think I'm going to take this lovely lady with me. You don't mind, do you?"

"Suits me, but you'll have to leave Mammy Mae here. I can't take care of all these kids by myself you know."

Pulling a face at her husband, Melinda sniffed, "You certainly are romantic. Surely I'm good at something besides being a nursemaid."

"I would say so," Jared returned suggestively, arching his brows.

"Jared, I withdraw the comment I made at Eagle Tavern." Brad laughed.

"What's this?" Melinda asked suspiciously.

"There was this barmaid . . ." Brad's eyes sparkled with mischief.

Jared threw him a scathing look and hastened to explain, "Your brother-in-law was charming another skirt, darling. He actually told the poor woman that I knew nothing of romance since I was married. I was simply an innocent bystander."

Melinda rolled her eyes heavenward. "I'll bet."

"Come over here and I'll show you where my loyalties lie." Jared grinned wolfishly.

"All right you two, enough of that. Where's Dru?" Brad queried.

"The last I saw of your little shadow, she and Tandy were picking a bunch of daisies," Melinda threw over her shoulder, hurrying back to her husband's side with a flushed look on her face.

Brad smiled at the thought of his daughter, dropping into a richly embroidered chair. For the first four years

114

of her life, he and Dru had been apart more than they were together. The damnable war was the culprit. Serving the South as the head of the Confederacy's Treasury Department, much of the time Brad was stationed in Richmond, Virginia with Jeff Davis.

He had viewed this position as the lesser of two evils. Being against slavery, as were all Hamptons since the time of Brad's grandfather, Jed Hampton, there was no way Brad could draw arms in its support. But in the tradition of Robert E. Lee—a Southerner born and bred—he, too, could never fight against his own people.

So he made what he hoped to be an acceptable compromise. Like Jared, who served the Confederacy as a physician, Brad served in his former profession. As a banker. Of the 364,000 Union soldiers who died in the War Between the States, none of them had perished at his hand. Granted that was small comfort; it was the best he could do in a country gone mad.

Brad was jerked back from his musings by the sound of little feet slapping against the hardwood floor. Jared's twins and their older sister, Linni, hurried into the parlor, the twins chattering like chipmunks.

Linni, the oldest, nodded demurely as she took her seat across from Brad. Sitting with her head held high and hands folded primly in her lap, she looked every inch the lady. It was an awesome responsibility being the eldest Hampton grandchild, but Linni more than met the challenge.

Brad winked at his niece just as Annadru burst into the room, crossing the floor like a tornado. When he opened his arms for his daughter, her eyes lit up in a special way that tugged unmercifully on his heartstrings.

All dressed in pale pink moiré taffeta; she looked as soft and sweet as cotton candy. Her shiny platinum hair was gathered at the nape of her neck by a matching satin ribbon; on her small hands she wore white mesh gloves. Surrounding her beauty was a celestial

115

kind of glow. She smelled of peppermint and peanut butter.

Throwing her arms around his neck, she bubbled, "I missed you today, Daddy!"

As always, whenever Brad looked into the mesmeric eyes of his five-year-old daughter, it was like looking into the eyes of Celia. He could hardly believe that his wife had been dead for two years. Yet at the same time, it seemed as if she'd been gone a lifetime. Still, if he lived to be a hundred, he'd never forget the absolute devastation he'd experienced upon reading Melinda's telegram saying Celia had died in childbirth.

Being positive by nature, he was surprised at his melancholy mood. He tightened his hold on Dru. It was damn hard leaving home. But he wouldn't be gone forever.

Pushing the painful thoughts aside, he smiled down into Dru's upturned face. "And I missed you, my little peanut. What have you been up to today? Have you driven Aunt Melinda and Mammy Mae completely around the bend?"

"Why no, Daddy! I've been ever so good!" Dru widened her eyes and cocked her head at her handsome father for emphasis. She knew quite well that he absolutely doted on her, but that was part of her charm.

"She's been an angel as usual," Melinda confirmed. "In fact, Brad, wouldn't you like to take the twins to Indian Territory and leave her here with us?" Melinda teased with adulatory merriment as she put her arms around her wide-eyed offspring. Everyone in the room, children included, knew that Melinda Hampton would kill for her children and that she was, most definitely, joking.

Brad grinned warmly. "As if you'd part with the little scamps! Though I expect their Aunt Lacy and Uncle Chase would welcome them."

"Daddy are we really and truly going to see Indians when we get to Aunt Lacy's?" Dru asked, barely able to contain her excitement.

Before Brad could answer, Linni spoke softly — as be-

116

fits a lady—but distinctly, "Of course, Dru. Don't you remember that I told you Uncle Chase is an Indian?"

"Yes, I guess so. But didn't you say that he has blue eyes?"

"Beautiful blue eyes," Linni murmured wistfully.

The adults smiled indulgently. Linni had met her half-breed uncle, Chase Tarleton, when she was the tender age of five. From the very first time she'd laid eyes on him she was totally captivated. As was he. And after six years of separation, Chase was still Linni's real life hero.

The adoring expression on Linni's face reminded Brad of his sister, Lacy. She and his wife, Celia, had been as thick as thieves and as inseparable as jelly on a biscuit. A tender smile touched his face. He pictured the petite pixies traipsing after him. Truth to tell, he'd enjoyed every minute of it. He was putty in their hands.

It was an awesome responsibility being their hero, although he'd found the fringe benefits well worth it. Not only had it been extremely good for his youthful male ego, it had provided him with a wife. After losing Kathlyn in '55, Brad had wondered if he would ever trust love again. He had.

Although his feelings for Celia had not been as passionate as what he had felt for Kathlyn, Brad had loved his wife with all the joy of his youth. Actually, he had loved her the way a person loves a close family member. She had been as much a second sister to him as a wife. And she had given him a child.

Thankful, he tightened his hold on Dru. As she snuggled closer to his heart, and his family conversed in comforting, familiar, tones around him, his mind wandered.

Chapter Twelve

Kathlyn. He had thought of little else since she walked into his bank. Daily, he relived their past, wondering if the love he had felt for her all those years ago had been real. It had surely felt so at the time. But that was so long ago. Still, when he had seen her again . . .

He had showed up at River's Edge early yesterday morning, unannounced, fearing that after the fiasco in the glass house, he wouldn't be welcome.

Nothing could have been further from the truth. As soon as Rachel had heard the amount of money he was willing to pay for River's Edge, all past grievances were forgiven. On her part, anyway. She had magnanimously apologized for the misunderstanding and suggested that they put it in the past and start over as friends. The woman's gall never ceased to amaze him.

Kathlyn was not as willing to forgive and forget, however. Being one of Roth's heirs, she was required to accompany Rachel to Brad's bank, to transfer ownership of River's Edge to him.

Later in the day, as the three of them sat in his office, the air was charged with energy. Rachel was giddy, flirting with him shamelessly. While Kathlyn seemed hell bent on ignoring him into oblivion. She was not very successful, he remembered smugly. All he had to do was touch her hand accidentally, or speak softly to her and she tensed.

He smiled in remembrance. The notion that he affected her so was immensely satisfying. True, he doubted his effect was of a positive nature. But for now, it was enough that she was moved by him.

He had heard somewhere that the opposite of love wasn't hate, but indifference. Well Miss Elora Kathlyn

118

McKinney wasn't indifferent to him. Not at all. She was quite moved and he would make sure she was moved in the right direction once they left on the trip.

". . . Uncle Jay," Linni giggled, as she finished relating something Brad had missed. Upon hearing his youngest brother's name, he turned his attention to the conversation.

"What's this about Jay? You haven't heard anything, have you?" Brad questioned Jared hopefully while Mammy Mae wheeled the tea cart into the room.

"No, I'm afraid not. Linni was just telling Dru about some of the mischief Jay and Lacy used to get into."

Jonathan Hampton, Jay to his family, had been a serious-minded professor of Classics at the University of Georgia. Before the war he had been a conductor on the famous Underground Railroad, helping slaves escape to freedom. When the war broke out in '61, he had traveled the only path he could, he joined the Union Army. Brad smiled wistfully, remembering his brother with pride.

While Jared and Brad served the Confederacy in noncombat positions, Jay served on the other side, as a trusted member of Lincoln's staff. The Hamptons had expected no less. They had understood his decision and given him their blessing, but had been saddened just the same.

Then the Hamptons had received word that Jay had been taken prisoner and was incarcerated at Libby Prison. It was when they received this tragic message that their father, Dr. Adam Hampton, had suffered a heart seizure and never recovered.

The family was shaken by the sudden loss of their patriarch and the imprisonment of Jay, but they survived. Try as they might, Jared and Brad were never able to discover further information on the fate of their missing brother, but they were sure he was still alive. As always, Brad comforted himself with the thought.

Brad leaned around Mammy Mae as she served Melinda a steaming cup of tea. "Jared, you'll get word to us if you hear anything at all, won't you?"

Jared nodded solemnly.

Melinda was purposefully evasive in front of the children. "Do you fellas really think there's hope after all this time?" The plea for an affirmative answer was evident in her soft Southern drawl.

Jared's crystal blue gaze met and held Brad's determined stare. "Yes, we do."

"Melinda, if he was gone, we'd know"—Brad tapped his well-muscled chest in the region of his heart—"in here."

After a moment of emotion-filled silence, Brad stuck his hand into his frock coat pocket and withdrew a legal document. Grinning sheepishly, he waved it toward Jared.

Jared was more than intrigued. "What's that?"

"A deed."

"A deed to what?"

"A plantation."

Jared knew that something was afoot when his articulate brother started answering questions in two word sentences. "Are you going to tell me which plantation, and why you have the deed, or do I have to guess."

Melinda laughed at the brothers; this was getting interesting.

"I bought River's Edge."

"You did what?" Jared roared.

"I bought River's Edge," Brad repeated slowly, enunciating distinctly.

"I heard you. What I want to know is why you bought a run down plantation the day before you leave the state? Surely you don't expect me to see to its restoration?"

Brad's raised brows and mischievous smile told Jared that he expected him to do just that. "I would do it myself except"—he paused—"my brother has convinced me to leave town."

"Brad Hampton, I oughta throttle you."

120

Annadru ceased her wiggling; her little body grew rigid. When she turned indignant blue eyes on her Uncle Jared, Melinda intervened, "Sweetheart, Uncle Jared didn't mean that. He's just being an older brother." She threw Jared a withering glare for upsetting Brad's child. Brad just sat back and grinned.

"I'm sorry, honey. I promise I won't throttle your daddy," Jared vowed. "No matter how much I want to," he muttered under his breath.

Dru relaxed against her father's broad chest. It was vibrating suspiciously, almost as if he were laughing. But when she looked into his face, he was smiling serenely.

"Now, would you mind telling me why you bought Rachel Jackson's extremely large, extremely run-down farm?" Jared asked with exaggerated politeness.

"It doesn't only belong to Rachel. It also belongs to Kathlyn McKinney. You remember Miss McKinney; the woman you're so worried about?" Brad answered pointedly.

"Ooooh," Jared drew out the single syllable. "I see. Rachel has to share her inheritance with her cousin."

"Yes and no," Brad began. "Yes, Rachel has to share her inheritance, but no, not with her cousin. She has to share it with her half-sister. I thought the money from the sale might make Kathlyn's trip more bearable."

Jared had had no idea that Kathlyn was leaving town so he just stared at Brad blankly. He knew that in his own good time, Brad would explain himself.

But Melinda was impatient by nature. "What trip?" she asked suspiciously, not wanting to discuss the particulars of Kathlyn's conception in front of the children. Further, she had noticed the way Brad had said Kathlyn's name and remembered the summer when they seemed more than friends. That's what interested her now.

"She's traveling west."

"Where?"

"To Fort Smith, I believe." Brad shrugged noncommittally.

"She wouldn't be leaving on the train for Memphis tomorrow, would she?" Jared queried.

"I believe so." Brad's soft words were drowned out by Jared's snicker.

"How convenient for you. And you were dreading this trip. I'm sure Miss McKinney and her sweetly turned half-sister will provide a great deal of amusement for you."

Brad's rigid posture told Annadru right well that her Uncle Jared was deviling her daddy. With all the wisdom of a five-year-old, she knew she had to be his champion. "Uncle Jared, go to your room," Dru said not unkindly.

She hated to do it, but it was necessary. Whenever her cousin, Turner, teased her, that's what Aunt Melinda made him do. And it always worked. After a few hours of solitude, Turner was always a much nicer young man. She had every confidence the same would be true of Uncle Jared.

Brad almost dumped his daughter on the floor when he burst into laughter. Once he'd righted her, Dru turned disappointed eyes on him. "Daddy, it's not nice to laugh at Uncle Jared."

"Yes, it's not nice to laugh at me," Jared huffed, his eyes fairly twinkling.

Dru turned back to him with a slightly reproachful look on her face. "Please go," she whispered.

"Can I take Aunt Melinda with me? I'll be lonely up in that big room all by myself." Melinda elbowed her unrepentant husband surreptitiously.

"No, I think Aunt Melinda needs to stay here and serve tea." Afraid that she had made her Uncle Jared unhappy, Dru hastened to add, "But if you promise to be very good, you may take Tandy with you."

The adults had been amused by Dru's attempt to bring her wayward uncle to task. But when she offered to part with Tandy, they sobered. It was a big step for her.

Brad was particularly impressed. Tandy was Dru's

122

porcelain doll. She had treated the doll as if she were alive ever since Celia's death, more often than not, speaking through the toy.

He had worried about it, but Jared assured him that children often clung to imaginary playmates after suffering a loss. Once Dru felt secure again, he said, she would cease the practice. Simple as it seemed, Brad hoped this silliness was some kind of breakthrough.

"I think she'd rather stay with you," Jared observed.

Now Dru was at a loss. She, too, didn't think Tandy wanted to be parted from her. But she couldn't let Uncle Jared be lonely. He was too sweet, even if he did tease her Daddy from time to time.

As usual, Aunt Melinda came to the rescue. "Sweetheart, I think if Uncle Jared agrees to be very good, we could give him another chance." At Dru's smile of relief, Melinda turned narrowed eyes on her husband. "But we'll be watching, and you must be very, very good."

Jared nodded soberly and Brad murmured, "This I gotta see."

Satisfied, the bundle of femininity wiggled on Brad's lap. "Are you and Mammy Mae all packed and ready to leave tomorrow, Peanut?" he asked.

"Yes, sir. Well, all except for Tandy, sir." Speaking so softly that her doting father had to lean down to decipher her words, Dru said, "But she told me she'd be packed in time."

She raised her tiny, gloved hand and stroked her father's cheek when he merely nodded.

It was a balmy, overcast morning, just before sunrise that found Brad making his way across the grounds of the sprawling plantation to the family cemetery. There, cradled in a grove of oak trees, was the final resting place of generations of Hamptons.

His quick-grab breakfast lying like a stone in his stomach, he bent at the waist, opened the gate, and stepped inside. In his hand he carried a nosegay of delicate, white violets; they were Celia's favorites.

His footsteps made deep, jade green impressions on

123

the dew-laden grass as he approached his wife's grave. The pink marble headstone was engraved to read: Celia Harrington Hampton, July 13, 1841-April 26, 1864, Beloved Wife and Mother. Beside her grave was a smaller headstone. Its inscription read: Christopher Bradley Hampton, Jr., April 26, 1864-April 26, 1864, Our Son.

This was an act that Brad had performed every day since returning from the war. As sure as the sun rose and set, he visited the graves of his wife and child. Today was different. Today he had come to say goodbye.

As was his habit, Brad knelt to talk to Celia. "Cee Cee, Dru, and I are leaving Georgia today." Brad had spoken to his wife's grave so often in the past year, he didn't feel self-conscious in the least. "I'm not sure when we'll return."

He looked at the gray sky overhead. "There are so many reasons to go. I've got to get Dru out of the South for a while. I don't want our daughter living in a state that's virtually under military occupation." Running a finger across the smooth surface of Celia's headstone, he said, "and I don't think you would either."

"It's just not the same here any more. It's not like it was when you and Lacy were pampered and adored by all of us. Life was so easy then . . . when the two of you were allowed to grow up in the beauty of innocence."

For a moment Brad's eyes took on a faraway look. Smiling wistfully, he allowed poignant memories of the past to wash over him.

Mentally shaking himself, he returned to the present. "I'm taking Dru to the Circle C, to meet her cousins."

"But Cee Cee, please know that you and little Brad will go with us in our hearts."

Brad's voice broke upon speaking of the son he'd never known. Stretching forth his hand, he traced *Christopher Bradley Hampton, Jr.* with a trembling finger. For a moment in time he mourned his namesake.

The eternal optimist, Brad then girded himself with

the knowledge that while he would never know his son, he had a daughter. A daughter who depended solely upon him.

Their future together was a blank page. Together, they would write a story. Whether it was a story of happiness or sorrow, they alone would determine.

It was time to move on.

The early morning sounds seemed to still around the cemetery. A bright spear of sunlight pierced the gray clouds, bringing a small blue bird in its wake. It settled on the headstone of Celia's grave. The heavy air lifted and a cool breeze blew, as if to sweep away the old and make way for the new.

Brad lifted his hand slowly. He scarcely breathed.

Brad had never believed in signs or omens, but even his doubter's heart couldn't deny that this bird carried a message. He felt Celia's presence all around him, and he sensed that when the bird left, she would leave too. But it would be all right.

Abruptly the bird flew away. The clouds moved together and the morning was overcast once more. Standing up beside the two pink marble graves, he smiled through his tears. His heart was strangely light; his painful past was behind him.

It was time to move on.

"Goodbye, honey," was all that was left to say. Then Brad turned on his heel and made his way back to his daughter.

To his daughter and their new life.

Part Two
The Journey

Who travels for love finds a thousand miles not longer than one.

— Japanese Proverb

Chapter Thirteen

Kathlyn's lilac and black mourning skirt swept along the floor of the train as she made her way down the narrow aisle to her seat. Bending, she peeked through the dusty windows every few steps. Each time, collectively, the male passengers sucked in their breath.

She was a study in sensuality. Her austere traveling suit of sturdy broadcloth was unable to hide the obvious curves straining against her flared jacket. Coupled with a white lace high-collared blouse, the outfit made it apparent to all who cared to look that she was not trying to appear physically enticing. Conversely, she had covered herself modestly from head to toe. Though to no avail.

Brad knew if she had been attired in sack cloth and ashes, the entire male population would have been compelled to gape in her direction. And he was no exception. Seated on a leather-covered seat, Mammy Mae and Dru had their backs to Kathlyn, but not Brad. Practically filling the seat across from the others, he watched the approaching vision. The tip of his silky mustache lifted in a satisfied smile. She had finally arrived.

He smelled the delightful fragrance of warm roses wafting across the aisle as she took her seat. Discretely, he observed the lady at his side.

She was unaware of his presence. But not for long.

"Daddy, Tandy wants to know how long we'll be away from home?" Dru asked Brad, drawing Kathlyn's attention.

"I don't . . ." Brad began.

Kathlyn turned in her seat and gaped in his direction. Incredulous, she jumped to her feet. "What are you doing on my train?" she asked accusingly, cutting off Brad's response to his daughter.

He knew he could play this scene many ways. He could turn on the Hampton charm and try to smooth Kathlyn's ruffled feathers, or he could act aloof as if he weren't concerned with her anger. Even better, he could ignore her snit and respond with humor.

The third option appealed to him. Probably because she would find it the most irritating. She was even more beautiful when she was irritated. He grinned devilishly.

"I wasn't told that you had purchased this train," he said as if impressed. "It's very nice." He looked about the interior of the car with an appreciative eye. "We had thought to buy one of our own, but this one was just sitting here, and I said, 'what the heck, girls, let's just take this one. We'll buy a train of our own on the return trip.' "

Dru and Mammy looked at Brad as if he had quite simply taken leave of his senses. Kathlyn's face reddened with anger and for a moment Brad feared she might burst into a ball of fire. He bit his lip to keep from laughing out loud.

"You know that's not what I meant! I demand to know where you are going, and why." Kathlyn strangled her reticule.

Brad rested a booted foot on his other knee and lazily tapped it with his silver-topped cane. Dramatically, he placed his other hand over his heart. "And I thought you didn't care." When Kathlyn looked as if she might do him physical harm, he continued bravely, "Actually, I figured since the train was going to Memphis, that would probably be our destination as well."

Kathlyn flopped back into her seat and presented him with her back. Bantering with the infuriating man was getting her nowhere. How she would dearly love to fling his carcass through an open window!

She felt the blood surging through her veins like white water rapids. Why, she moaned silently. Why did the sight of him unnerve her so? Was it because he was so blasted gorgeous? She knew other attractive men, albeit not as attractive as Brad. Yet they affected her not at all.

She had thought of him constantly, especially since the

130

day he bought River's Edge. And every waking moment she had chastised herself for it. Her only consolation had been that as soon as she boarded the train for Memphis she would be free of him. She would put a thousand miles between them and be free of his spell. To arrive and find him lounging across the aisle like a virile lion was more than she could bear.

Placing her possessions around her with short, jerky movements, she tried vainly to ignore him. If there had been any other seat on the train, she would have occupied it. Gladly. But this was the only vacant place she and Rachel could sit together.

Where is Rachel, anyhow? she thought peevishly. Ever since Rachel had so readily forgiven Brad, Kathlyn had been a little miffed at her. Rachel's tardiness now certainly wasn't improving the situation. The least she could do was board the train on time, and perhaps distract Brad for her. Was that too much to ask, Kathlyn fumed.

Pulling the hat pin from her wilted bonnet, she noticed that her hands were trembling. Searching for something that would make Brad less appealing to her, she seized the idea Rachel had suggested. Could it have been Brad who killed her father or her brothers? No. She had since learned that he was with the Treasury Department during the war. He was never involved in battle.

But did it matter whether he was the one who actually wielded the weapon or not? Didn't the fact that he was a Rebel make him guilty of their deaths in principle, if not in fact?

She glanced at Brad, then looked away. He didn't look like he could be guilty of such atrocities. Sitting there, proud and tall, smiling at his daughter, he was the picture of respectability. *And he's the most gorgeous man I've ever seen,* Kathlyn's traitorous heart reminded her.

Silence hung heavy in the air. Remembering himself, Brad rose to his feet in a show of respect. Kathlyn's hand still rested on her valise. He stepped across the aisle and bent to assist her. "Please allow me."

Discerning what he was about, Kathlyn jerked her head up. Angry at the quickening of her heart at the sight of his lazy smile, she snapped, "I am quite capable of seeing to my own things!"

Two sets of eyes flew open in shock as Mammy Mae and Dru heard the animosity crackling in Kathlyn's voice. She sounded even angrier than she had earlier. And she'd appeared nigh to exploding then, in Mammy's estimation.

For heaven's sake, Kathlyn complained wordlessly, even the doll is staring at me, as if I have corn stalks growing out of my ears. Didn't anybody ever refuse the chivalrous Mr. Hampton before?

Well, they would have to learn quickly that Elora Kathlyn McKinney doesn't need help from any man. Especially not Brad Hampton! Haughtily squaring her slight shoulders, she leveled her gaze on his adoring family.

Brad recovered his shredded dignity and folded himself into his seat. He scooted as far away from the tantalizing termagant as he could. Turning Kathlyn's negative feelings into positive ones would be a more difficult undertaking than he'd first thought. Looking across the aisle at her he wondered if it were even possible.

Kathlyn lifted her chin to a stubborn angle, hoping to appear confident. Her face colored slightly when she looked into the accusing gaze of the most precious child she'd ever beheld. Surely God had used Brad's blonde-haired offspring as the model for his host of angels.

The wounded way the child was looking at Kathlyn made it obvious that she belonged to Brad, though with her light coloring, Kathlyn surmised, she must resemble her mother. The woman he married after he threw her over! Kathlyn stoked the fires of her anger with this thought. Her nostrils twitched from the spicy scent of his cologne, denting her resolve.

Brad also noted Dru's displeased countenance and grinned in spite of himself. Though she was merely five years old, she was extremely protective of him. At least somebody liked him, he eased his wounded pride. Catching his daughter's eye, he beckoned her forward. The force of her blinding smile was like an entire forest set ablaze.

Dru slipped from her seat and climbed onto her father's waiting lap. Big, strong arms enfolded her as she snuggled against his warm body. She placed a wet kiss on his cheek to reassure him that most everybody in the world adored him, even if the cross newcomer didn't.

A woman's throaty laughter drifted through the open window.

"Thank goodness," Kathlyn murmured, rising to assist Rachel in boarding.

"Here, at last," Brad grumbled sarcastically.

Dru swiveled her head, recognizing the displeasure in her daddy's voice. "What's wrong?" she asked suspiciously.

"Nothing, Peanut," he lied, placing a kiss on the tip of her nose.

Satisfied, Dru turned her attention to the flamboyantly clothed woman making her way down the aisle. She squinted. The loud color of the lady's clothing was almost painful to the eye.

She was dressed in a Patti Dress of brilliant orange-colored silk in two shades, the dark above the light. The gown was trimmed with black lace appliqued leaves and flowers; small lace butterflies hovered around the bouquets. But it was the black Leghorn straw hat, adorned with its very own hummingbird, sitting atop her masses of red curls that captured Dru's eye.

"Daddy, that lady has a gold bird on her hat," Dru informed her bemused father in a stage whisper.

"Ishta!" Kathlyn exclaimed. Remembering that she had left her bird in her cage on the platform, she pushed past Rachel, all but knocking her over in her haste.

Brad kissed Dru's curls to hide his smile at Rachel's startled expression.

It was then that Rachel noticed his presence. For a split second, the look on her face was a combination of shock and menace. It disappeared so quickly, Brad wondered if he'd imagined it.

"Why Brad!" she enthused finally. "What on earth are you doing here? I didn't expect to see you. What a treat! Are you traveling west?" she gushed all at once.

"Rachel," Brad nodded. Rising to his feet, he depos-

ited Dru on the seat beside Mammy Mae. He didn't answer Rachel's questions; he was too occupied with the
irony of the situation. Who would have thought this
simpering woman was the same person who had accused
him of molesting her? It was amazing what a little
money could do to change a person's outlook. "Could I
help you with your luggage?" he offered without enthusiasm.

"Why, aren't you the sweetest thing," she declared,
stepping aside for him to edge his way between the seats.

He smelled Kathlyn's delicious fragrance and knew she
had returned. Once he stored Rachel's cases, he backed
out into the aisle. Bowing to Rachel, he took Dru into
his arms and the train lurched forward.

"Daddy, a bird," Dru breathed.

"I know," Brad whispered, thinking she was speaking
of Rachel's godawful hat again. Then, hearing a soft
chirp, he turned to see a tiny blue bird perched on a
wire in its cage, placed on the seat beside Kathlyn. It
strikingly resembled the bird he'd seen at Celia's grave.

Brad searched Kathlyn's face, almost as if he expected
her to know what he was thinking. She carefully avoided
his gaze, concentrating instead on settling her skirts
about her.

"Isn't it just wonderful that Brad is traveling with us?"
Rachel asked Kathlyn, dimpling at Brad.

"He's not traveling *with* us. He's merely occupying the
same train." Kathlyn tossed her head coolly.

"Why, of course, he's traveling with us. Brad's too
much of a gentleman to allow us to go unescorted.
Aren't you, Brad?" Rachel looked over at Brad. The
look in his eye compelled her not to push for an answer.

She knew he wasn't buying her helpless Southern belle
act a bit, but she didn't care. His trip west could prove a
definite threat to Kathlyn's engagement. She didn't intend to let anything interfere with that. She had to find
some way to keep her eye on him, until she could think
of a way to get rid of him—permanently.

"I confess, Brad, I've been worried about two helpless
women traveling alone. But now that you're here, so big
and strong—well, I just feel safer."

134

When she still received no response, she ceased her prattling—albeit temporarily. "Where are you headed?" she asked after a few minutes.

"To Fort Smith by way of Memphis," he answered finally.

Rachel sucked in a deep breath. Brad was going to Fort Smith? Not if she had her way about it. Looking across at the bird cage containing the lone parakeet, she patted the small bottle hidden in her pocket. If Brad got too close to Kathlyn, she would take care of him . . .

While Rachel schemed, Dru asked the question children cannot help but voice, "How much further, Daddy?"

Kathlyn smiled for the first time since she'd boarded the train.

Laughter rumbled deep in Brad's solid chest, tickling Dru's downy cheek with its vibration. "We're not even out of Clarke County yet, Peanut. It'll be quite some time before we even reach Memphis."

"When we get there will we really and truly go on a big boat?" Dru voiced over a tiny yawn.

Brad absently stroked his daughter's platinum curls, saying softly, "Really and truly."

"When will we come back home?"

"I don't know, sweetheart. You're not going to get homesick on me, are you?"

Barely awake now, Dru answered with the wisdom of a child, "You're where home is."

Brad pulled his precious bundle closer to his heart. And Tandy too.

Secure in her daddy's arms, Dru drifted off to sleep.

Chapter Fourteen

It was with a sense of loss that Kathlyn witnessed the tender scene between Brad and his daughter. Even though it had been over a year since her father, Herschel McKinney, had been killed by Confederate soldiers, she grieved for him as if it were yesterday.

Leaning her head against the vibrating window, she smiled wistfully. If she listened very carefully, she could still hear her Irish father's last words to her. "Me girl, whilst I'm away ye've got to take care of yer ma for me. Twill only be ye, yer ma has to depend on. Remember, yer da thinks ye're a bonnie lass, and he loves ye. And dinna ye worry, hinney. We'll be home soon as we whip the Rebs; and by God we'll whip the lot of them. Ye'll see."

She blotted the tears of remembrance from her eyes with a lace handkerchief her mother, Margie McKinney, had embroidered for her. She pressed the cloth against her trembling lips. Memories brought such pain!

Herschel was killed just before Lee signed the surrender at Appomattox Court House. Then, not long after that, her mother took ill. The doctor told Kathlyn there was nothing physically wrong with Margie; she was dying of a broken heart. She had died within the week. And with the exception of Rachel, her half-sister, Kathlyn was all alone now.

Well, that wasn't exactly true, she corrected herself. She raised her head wearily and looked through the dusty window at her side, not focusing on the countryside as it sped by at a rapid clip of twenty-five miles per hour.

Instead of blurred fields and farms, she saw a scene

from the past. The war was over; she and her mother were waiting anxiously for her father's return.

On his way north, Glenn had come by Kathlyn's home. It was he who had told her of her father's death. Naturally, she had been devastated by the news. But Glenn had helped her. So strong, so sympathetic, he had never been anything but completely kind to her. After her mother's death, he had taken her to River's Edge.

On leave from the Army, he had been able to remain in Athens for several months. He and Rachel became fast friends, spending a great deal of time together. Kathlyn had wondered if her cousin was falling in love with Glenn, but when she asked, Rachel denied it emphatically.

Not long after that, Glenn told Kathlyn he had been assigned to Fort Gibson. He soon left.

Rachel talked about him a great deal in his absence. It was as if she didn't want Kathlyn to forget him. When his letter arrived, asking Kathlyn to marry him, with Rachel's encouragement, she accepted.

I owe him, she acknowledged to the images flickering across the pane.

If she could have gone to be his bride without seeing Brad again, she might have found happiness with her new husband at Fort Gibson. If not happiness, at least contentment.

But not now. Now she could never be a good wife to Glenn, now that she knew her tender feelings for Brad had never died. What frightened her most was the certainty that they never would. But what was she to do about those feelings? she asked the countryside as it came into focus. She was so confused.

From the corner of his eye Brad watched the pain-filled expressions flit across Kathlyn's lovely face. The look of sadness and vulnerability tugged at his heart.

Upon further examination, his heart wasn't the only muscle that Kathlyn affected. Quite simply, he ached for her the way men had ached for women since the beginning of time! Why? Why in the world would he want her now, after all that had happened between them? Was it just unappeased desire?

137

Surely not. He certainly had not been abstinent lately, thanks to Lois. But these amorous excursions could never provide what he longed for now. Lois was nice, but she wasn't Kathlyn. Kathlyn was a lady.

Even though she was not a virgin, he knew she was innocent. If he was the only man she had been with—and he'd bet his life he was—she might as well have been untouched. They hadn't even undressed fully on their night of gardenias, he remembered with a measure of embarrassment and regret.

It dawned on him then that he had never seen all of Kathlyn's beautiful body. A sudden desire to see her completely unclothed flared up inside him with such force that he closed his eyes against its intensity.

The thought of unwrapping her like a prize of great price captivated him. The need to kiss and caress every inch of her smooth flesh caused his hands to tingle. From somewhere deep inside he longed to worship her with his love.

Love? he thought with a jolt. *God, I do love her!* The stark realization blocked out all reality. He could no longer think, only feel, only want, only need . . .

"I am appalled that we have to share a car with nigras," a man two seats back drawled in a cultured voice, as he cast a disdainful glare in Mammy Mae's direction.

Harsh reality intruded on Brad's fantasy. He was at a loss. While he didn't want to upset Dru by starting a fight, he hated to let the distasteful remark about his beloved nanny pass.

After smiling apologetically at Mammy, he glared at the rude man, hoping to intimidate him into silence. The bigot was obviously a former planter, and if his thread bare suit was any indication, he'd fallen on hard times since the war. Brad had dealt with his kind time and again. They were bitter, disillusioned, and hated virtually everyone. He suspected it would take more than an angry look to squelch the man.

Kathlyn was infuriated, and not just at the planter! She couldn't believe Brad would allow his servant to be spoken of in such a way.

For her part, Rachel agreed with the planter.

"And the odor . . ." The bigot's portly wife wrinkled her bulbous nose distastefully.

A muscle in Brad's jaw twitched with mounting rage. Mammy Mae smelled delicious; she smelled of vanilla extract, just as she had for as long as he could remember.

He laid Dru down across her own seat and started to rise, but Mammy patted his hand and shook her head in warning. Pointedly, she looked at Dru.

Brad sighed and sank back down into his seat. He held himself tense, his eyes darkening to the color of a starless night.

"Mother, do you see any other seats . . . around decent people?"

That did it! In unison, Kathlyn and Brad jumped to their feet. Shoving Kathlyn back into her seat, Brad closed the distance between himself and the startled couple. He grabbed the man by his worn lapels and jerked his face close.

"Listen, you sorry excuse for a human being! I tried to ignore your trashy mouth, but now you've sorely tested my patience," Brad ground out between clenched teeth. "If you or the lady"—he threw the corpulent woman a look of disgust—"malign anyone else, you won't have to worry about rubbing elbows with the other passengers on this train, because I'll personally throw you off."

Brad released the man so abruptly he fell into his wife's lap, unseating them both. "Do I make myself clear?"

In tandem, the twosome nodded their heads.

Brad turned to see three sets of widened eyes gazing at him, admiration evident in their depths. Only Rachel looked bored. "Sorry ladies," Brad said once he returned to his seat.

Dru was wide awake, all eyes and ears. "Daddy, those people were bad, weren't they?"

"Honey, what they said was bad. People aren't all bad or all good, they just do bad or good things." Though when it came to Rachel, he wasn't so certain he believed his own words.

139

In spite of her need to think badly of Brad, Kathlyn admired his actions. While she acknowledged he'd distinguished himself for the moment, she wasn't ready to nominate him for sainthood. Not just yet. Pulling the latch at her side, she pushed her seat into a reclining position and leaned back to rest.

"Thank you, Mistah Brad," Mammy Mae whispered, obviously pleased he had intervened despite her admonition.

Brad sketched a slight bow to his old nanny. Shortly thereafter, he heard Kathlyn's measured, deep breathing, assuring him that she had fallen asleep. Taking advantage of the situation, he angled in his seat to get a better look at her. His slow gaze began at the top of her head and traveled downward to her leather shod feet. His obsession grew.

He had never seen hair that color. It was almost black but a touch of fire ignited each silky strand. It shimmered with red highlights. Blazing next to her creamy ivory complexion, it proved quite an arresting contrast.

Thick dark lashes rested on her high cheek bones like fuzzy caterpillars floating in a dish of sweet cream. Burned in his mind was the vision of her almond-shaped eyes, a most unusual shade of lavender blue. Her nose was slim with a slight hump on its bridge; this tiny imperfection only served to exemplify the perfection of her other facial features.

Brad's gaze intensified, and he visually devoured her soft rosy lips. His mouth went dry when, at that very moment, her lips parted, emitting a breathy sigh.

The sound drew Rachel's gaze. After scowling at Kathlyn, she glanced at Brad. The look on his face verified that he was a grievous threat to her nefarious plans for Kathlyn.

But Brad was unaware he was being watched, so intense was his perusal of Kathlyn. Stifling a groan, he continued his visual journey.

The sight of her beautiful body was sensual torture for him. She was petite, the deprivation of war consuming what excess flesh she might have once had. Firm, ripe breasts caused her incredibly narrow waist to appear

140

even smaller. Though she was reclining, the lines of her slightly flared hips were well defined, leading into what he remembered as smooth, sleek legs.

When his body began to respond to the visual feast, he snapped his eyes shut and leaned his head back against the seat. "One, two, three," he counted sheep silently, trying not to notice their lavender-blue eyes—eyes a man could happily drown in. Almond-shaped, lavender-blue eyes, surrounded by dark lashes that rested on high cheekbones like fuzzy caterpillars . . .

Oh hell! It was hopeless.

Sometime later Brad awakened to a doublet of physical sensations. He felt a heaviness in his lap and a fluttering against his cheek. Forcing his eyes open, he was greeted by the sight of his daughter's strained smile. Sitting in his lap, she was patting his slightly bearded cheek.

The urgent look in Dru's eyes told him why she had awakened him. Her heart-felt whisper confirmed his suspicion. "Daddy, I gotta go!"

One of the marvels of train travel was the provision of a "convenience" in every car. He surmised it was to this "convenience" that Dru referred.

Gathering his daughter against his chest, he stepped into the aisle.

"I'll take her," Mammy Mae offered.

"You look tired, Mammy. Just rest. We'll be right back."

When Brad drew alongside Kathlyn the train lurched and he lost his footing. He bumped her shoulder with his hip.

Lazily, Kathlyn's eyelids parted, revealing slumber-softened, iris eyes. For a split second she gazed up into Brad's warm chocolate orbs with a disoriented smile on her face.

Their eyes met and held just long enough to provide him a glimpse of what it would be like to awaken with this beautiful lady every morning of his life. He was mightily unsettled by his body's response.

141

"Pardon me," he said abruptly. If he didn't hurry on his way, Kathlyn would see full well what her presence did to him.

Kathlyn misread his tone. Stiffening her spine, she retorted, "Consider yourself pardoned."

Brad cursed himself for pushing Kathlyn away when all he wanted was to hold her close. Vainly, he tried to smooth things over. "Kathlyn, I'm terribly sorry . . ."

Before he could finish his apology, she jerked her skirt aside as if she couldn't bear the thought of his touch. "Mr. Hampton, you had best see to your daughter and leave me alone!"

Brad shifted Dru in his arms and hurried down the aisle. He was so frustrated and aroused by Kathlyn that he feared he was going to howl at the moon. And it was still broad daylight.

Brad and Dru returned to their seats just after the train pulled into the station in Chattanooga, Tennessee.

"Daddy, I'm hungry," Dru declared.

"Me too. You stay here with Mammy and I'll run get us something to eat. Hungry, Mammy?"

"I reckon I could eat a little bite." Noticing Brad glance about the car, Mammy Mae grinned. She had felt the attraction between him and Miss McKinney since she had taken her seat. This was the first interest he had shown in a *decent* woman since Miss Celia, and Mammy reckoned it was about time! *Thank goodness he had the sense to be interested in Miss McKinney, not that red-headed woman who looks like she's fixin' to eat him.*

"That young miss just up and left soon as we pulled in," Mammy Mae answered his unasked question. "If you ask me, it ain't safe for a young'un as pretty as that one to be runnin' around all by herself!"

Rachel glared at Mammy behind Brad's back. Placing her hand on his arm, she stepped forward and drawled, "Do you mind if I tag along?" Rachel knew if she left Brad alone, he would sniff Kathlyn out like a hound in heat.

Brad stiffened. He had forgotten all about Rachel. But

142

the way she was pressing her bosom into his arm at the moment signaled she wasn't about to be ignored.

"I'll be right back," Brad informed Mammy Mae, not responding directly to Rachel's plea. He wanted to shake her off his arm, but sensed that would not be a wise move. Instead, he placed his free hand on Mammy Mae's shoulder and flashed her a pained smile. She handed him his cane, biting back the suggestion that he use it to beat Rachel off.

"Daddy, do you think I could watch the bird?" Dru narrowed her eyes at the woman who made her daddy frown.

"For all I care you can throw it out the window," Rachel interjected harshly.

Dru was shocked. The thought of hurting a living creature was so foreign to her innocent mind that she couldn't comprehend it. "I just wanna see it. I would never throw it away." Her lower lip trembled at the thought.

"Just look, Peanut. But don't touch the bird, not until we ask Miss McKinney's permission." Brad caressed Dru's cheek, stifling the urge to tell Rachel what he thought of her sharp tone toward his daughter, her unwanted presence, her catty attitude toward Kathlyn's bird, and her repugnant character in general. He started down the aisle as Dru rushed over to the cage.

"Tandy said she's hungry too," she called to her father's retreating figure.

Chapter Fifteen

Brad hopped from the train-step, landing lightly on the sun-bleached wood platform. Impatiently, he extended his hand to Rachel.

She stepped from the train, noting the way his gaze scanned the crowd. She didn't need to be told for whom he looked. The look of concern knitting his brow could only be caused by Kathlyn. It was sickening.

Brad was more than concerned, he was frantic. He feared if he didn't find Kathlyn posthaste she would fall prey to some unscrupulous lecher. His long stride accelerated. Fairly dragging Rachel along, he made his way down the platform.

He caught a glimpse of her fiery ebony hair as she stepped through an open doorway, disappearing into the dingy terminal. "There she is." He sighed relief.

Now, if he could just ford the river of bodies separating him from the building, he would . . . what? March up to her and tell her to get back on the train where he could act as her guardian angel? Now wouldn't she just love that? he thought, scoffing at himself. Still, his feet moved of their own volition, carrying him in her direction.

Rachel walked as slowly as possible, drawing Brad's attention. Exasperated, he stopped. She snuggled closer to his side, almost forcing him from the walkway. Her overpowering cologne filled his nostrils.

"Rachel, I'll be back in a moment." Before she could find her tongue, he withdrew his arm from her grasp and hurried off in the direction Kathlyn had taken.

Kathlyn wanted to put as much distance between herself and Brad as possible, even if only for a few minutes. Actually, she *needed* to put as much distance between them as possible. What she *wanted* was to be as close to him as possible, but alas that wasn't in her best interest.

Slowly, she ambled through the terminal. The dimly lit structure was crowded with hungry passengers in search of a hot meal. For each step she took, she was jostled and pushed backwards two. Claustrophobic, she made for the door leading to the back of the station. Soon, she was fleeing the mass of humanity, just as she was fleeing the dark-eyed Adonis teasing the corners of her mind.

When she awakened earlier and gazed into Brad's warm brown eyes, she'd experienced a moment of incredible longing, unlike anything she'd ever known. For the space of a second, she could have sworn she saw her need reflected in his eyes. But before she could gather her wits, he had brusquely rebuffed her, rendering her numb with shame.

I should have been the one to rebuff him. This time I should have rejected him. She shoved through the screened door, bursting into brilliant sunlight.

You would think a man would grow up in eleven years, she groused, squinting her eyes against the light. That after all that time he would no longer act one way, then affect a complete reversal. Years ago he had been loving; and then unceremoniously, he'd dumped her. Was history repeating itself?

Since she'd come in contact with him again, there were times when he seemed so warm, so concerned with her well-being. Then just when she let her guard down, he put on his haughty mask and acted as if she were of no more import to him than a bucket of horse manure.

Oh forget it! Why should I care if he's changed? He's nothing to me. He never was! she lied. *I'm engaged to a fine Union officer. I have no need of a rich man—a man who fought for the South. After all, Glenn fought for something noble; the preservation of the Union and the dissolution of slavery. What did people like Brad fight for?*

She suspected she was searching far afield if she had

to appeal to Brad's political leanings to malign him. After all, the war *was* over. Not to mention that there was more than enough in their romantic past to show her the futility of mooning over what might have been — enough to keep her from longing for what would never be.

Kathlyn stomped behind a pile of wood, asking herself why in the world she had given Brad the look she had when she awoke on the train. Truly the answer was beyond her. But there was one thing she *did* know: Satan would be wearing snow shoes before it happened again! She intended to treat Brad Hampton as a stranger from here on out.

On that note, she whipped around, determined to make her way back to the train and ignore the man into oblivion.

Her plan was rudely thwarted. Before she took three steps, she was confronted by two of the most horrendous looking brigands she could imagine. One was a slender man with rheumy, watery eyes; the other looked more like a buffalo than a man. Their clothes were filthy and torn; their shaggy hair dripped with oil. She smelled their unwashed bodies from ten feet away, making the very thought of their touch nauseating.

From the looks on their faces, touching her was what they had in mind; they certainly weren't collecting for charity. Suddenly the thought of Brad's company didn't sound half bad.

She turned to run, but it was too late. The men were upon her. She was thrown to the rock-hard ground. The breath was knocked from her lungs, as a huge, foul body pinned her down. She tried to scream, but a large calloused hand mashed her lips into her teeth. Gasping, she felt her own blood run down her throat.

She heard the sound of male laughter in the distance. With a sickening dread, she realized that the thin man was keeping watch, while the buffalo prepared to rape her. A hysterical cough burst from her throat as she wondered what Glenn would think if he saw his intended rolling around on the ground with a life form as low as this.

146

Abruptly, the distant laughter ceased; the stifling weight disappeared from her body. Kathlyn attempted to sit up, but the pain of a bruised rib caused her to crumble back with a sob. She distinctly identified the sounds of a struggle as darkness advanced from the nether world and took her pain away.

When Brad failed to locate Kathlyn at the lunch counter, his unease grew. Almost frantic, he continued his search. She was not inside the terminal. He headed toward the back door.

He couldn't believe that any woman with the sense God gave a goose would wander off alone behind a train terminal, but that was the only place left to look. Besides, if Kathlyn's association with Simon Percy was any indication, Brad knew she was very trusting. She might not realize the danger she was courting.

With a terrible foreboding, he exited the dimly lit terminal. The afternoon sunlight blinded him for a moment. Squinting, he stood very still. Then slowly his eyes adjusted, and the scene before him grew clear.

"Dear God," he hissed.

He saw Kathlyn lying on the ground with her skirt hiked up around her waist, writhing and whimpering beneath a ravenous beast. The sight of the would-be rapist's filthy hands against Kathlyn's pale skin sent Brad into a murderous rage.

A sound to his left penetrated the red haze. The lookout was so enthralled with the scene on the ground he never saw Brad coming. He gained the man's attention with a swing of his cane. It connected with his lower back. Before the gasping goon hit the ground, Brad tossed the cane aside, swung a rock-hard fist, and landed a solid punch to his jaw. Now unconscious, the look-out posed no threat.

Such could not be said of the man who was tearing at Kathlyn's underclothes. With one hand Brad jerked the meaty brute to his feet. Anxious to see to Kathlyn's needs, Brad quickly beat the startled man senseless, not even feeling the few punches the buffalo landed.

When the dust settled, Kathlyn's assailant had blood running from his nose and mouth, a broken jaw and

147

wrist, and numerous cracked ribs. If his unconscious state was any indication, he had suffered a concussion as well. Brad's barely healed knife wound throbbed. Other than that he was unharmed. It occurred to him that for a peace-loving man he had certainly had more than his share of fights lately.

Nonetheless, when he looked down into Kathlyn's beautiful face, he wanted to beat her attackers again. The faint smear of blood around her mouth caused his heart to ache physically.

He withdrew his handkerchief and gently wiped the blood from her cheek. She was so pale. Remembering her helplessness against the brigands, he felt a strong desire to coddle her. His arms trembled with the need to hold her.

Further, the need to reacquaint himself with her took root in his heart and blossomed . . . not just to experience the joys of her beautiful body again, but to learn what made her happy, what made her sad, what made her eyes shine with tears of loss or sparkle with the promise of love.

He tried to swallow, but his mouth had gone bone dry. To learn these things about Kathlyn, he would have to risk being hurt again. He would have to be willing to offer a portion of himself with no reassurance that she would accept him. He wondered if he was ready for that risk. With a shaky finger he touched the satiny smooth skin covering her high cheek bones. Some risks were worth taking.

"Kat, honey," Brad said quietly.

She fought her way through the black haze of unconsciousness, aware of a soft voice calling from faraway. For some unknown reason she was reluctant to embrace consciousness. It was as if she were afraid of something, something that wished her ill.

Then the heavy clouds of numbness evaporated. She found herself drowning in the most tender brown eyes she had ever beheld. Her heart pounded against her ribs and her eyes filled with tears as she relived her horrible ordeal in the span of a moment.

Brad was pleased that she had regained consciousness,

but the sheen in her eyes tore at his heart. "Everything's all right, sweetheart. They can't hurt you now," he soothed, caressing her brow.

Kathlyn's lower lip trembled pitifully before she could turn away from his intense gaze. She hated being helpless, almost as much as she hated being indebted to Brad. And he had he called her sweetheart!

"Can you sit up?"

Not raising her vision, she lifted her shoulders, only to slump back in pain over the strong arm he had placed at her back.

"My rib," she whispered through clenched teeth.

Just then the train's whistle pierced the air, signaling the passengers to return.

"I'll carry you."

The thought of being held in Brad's arms loosened Kathlyn's tongue. "That's not necessary. I appreciate your efforts on my behalf, but really, I'm quite capable of . . ."

"I know"—Brad began with forced patience—"you're quite capable of seeing to your own things." He was becoming irritated with this headstrong female. He'd risked life and limb for her and now she acted as if she found his touch offensive. It damaged his male ego more than a little.

The whistle sounded again. "It is necessary. Unless you feel up to walking to Memphis."

He didn't intend to let the train, carrying his daughter and Mammy Mae, leave without him, and he sure as hell didn't intend to leave this little ingrate behind. No matter that he did want to ring her lovely neck at the moment. Quickly, he reached for her.

"There is no way I'm going to allow you to carry me!" Her voice broke the moment he touched her.

Pleased that she was affected by his touch, he gathered her into his arms and stood. "There's no way you can stop me so just be quiet and enjoy the ride." His voice sounded more amused than angry now.

She spat and sputtered, gritting her teeth against the pain in her side. "Just what do you think you're doing? Unhand me, you arrogant lout. I've been pawed enough

149

for one day, thank you very much."

Walking at a fast clip toward the train, he struggled to maintain his grip on the reluctant damsel. "Perhaps you should recall that it was I who rescued you from being pawed. As you so naively put it. Believe me, Madame, those men had a sight more than pawing on their minds!"

Kathlyn sucked a massive amount of air through her clenched teeth. Whether it was a reaction to his pointed reminder or to a sharp pain in her side, he wasn't certain. Nevertheless, it put an end to her objections. Though Brad could feel the heat of indignation emanating from her cheeks.

He looked down at her and just for the joy of watching her blush, brushed her lips lightly with his. "Not that I blame them." His voice husky, his legs a bit unstable, he kicked the backdoor open with his booted foot, and disappeared into the cool darkness of the train station.

Satisfied that he wouldn't be seen by the couple, a huge, rough-bearded man stepped out into the sunlight from behind the outhouse. Crossing over to the would-be rapists, he kicked their unconscious bodies in disgust.

"Damn your worthless hides!" he hissed. "First the fools in Athens and now you."

Less than an hour later, Kathlyn's assailants regained consciousness. They were out in the middle of nowhere, trussed up like Christmas turkeys, leaning against a hardwood tree. If this wasn't the end of the earth, the largest of the men decided, you could see it from here. What were they doing so far from civilization, he wondered. And who had tied them up?

"I was waiting for you to come around before I killed you," a cultured voice spoke from behind them. Stepping around the tree, the stranger who had hired them that morning leveled a lethal-looking weapon on them.

"Wait," Skinny began.

"Shut up!" Their boss's voice was like a rifle shot in the still countryside. "Would you please repeat to me the exact instructions I gave you regarding Brad Hampton."

Sobbing with fright now, Skinny whispered, "You said to grab the girl and draw Hampton out. Then let her go and kill him."

"Did I ask you to rape her?"

With the word *no* forming on their trembling lips, they watched their rough-bearded captor raise his gun. Two shots in rapid succession cut off their response.

Chapter Sixteen

Brad and Kathlyn provided a curious sight as he effortlessly strode down the aisle of car eight, clutching the fuming woman to his chest. When they reached their seats, he noticed Mammy Mae attempting to hide a grin. Sitting beside Mammy, his unflappable daughter gazed at him mildly, then looked away, as if her daddy walked around carrying irate women in his arms all the time.

Rachel's expression was a bit more intense. She glowered at Kathlyn when Brad bent at the waist and gently positioned her in the seat. Then she swiveled her head and glowered at him. Then back again at Kathlyn.

If the woman didn't quit jerking her head from side to side, she was going to get dizzy, Brad chuckled silently. Perversely, Rachel's ill humor lifted his spirits almost as much as having Kathlyn in his arms. He stood, hands on his hips, grinning cheekily at the women. It was obvious to all that he was quite pleased with the turn of events.

Actually, pleased was not the word for it. Brad's smile faltered. He was more relieved than he could say. When he had seen Kathlyn in danger, his heart had all but stopped. He would die, absolutely die, if anything happened to her. He knew that now. His hands trembled slightly as they lay on his waist. *She's all right. Nobody can hurt her. Everything turned out for the best.*

And it had. He had rebuffed Rachel, rescued a damsel in distress, stolen a kiss, and held the lovely Miss McKinney in his arms, all in less than an hour. Not a bad way to start the journey, he revived his good humor with the thought.

Maybe the rescue would even make Kathlyn feel more kindly toward him — one day. Who knows, she might discover she liked him. That is, when she stopped trying to hate him.

"Really, there's no need to thank me," he said, winking at Kathlyn when she glared at him. Smiling, he settled in across from Dru and Mammy Mae.

"Daddy, why were you carrying that lady? Was she tired?" Dru asked as if it all made perfect sense to her.

Kathlyn gasped in shock that Brad's daughter would think a lady would permit a man to hold her in such an improper manner simply because she was too tired to walk! But looking furtively at Brad, she could well imagine women claiming fatigue to get those strong arms around them.

The thought of his muscular arms, rock hard beneath her fingers, set her heart to pounding. Her reaction irritated her. For goodness sake, one would think she'd never been held by a handsome man before!

She squirmed. Even though she was sitting on the leather seat away from Brad, she could still feel his touch across her derriere and around her torso. And the feeling was playing havoc with her self-control.

Mindful of her injured rib, he had gripped her just above the waist. She swore he had placed his hand close to her breast on purpose. With the slightest shift of his fingers, he could have caressed her intimately.

Such musings caused her breasts to tingle, their tips to tighten. Her cheeks burned. *Stop it!* she ordered herself. She'd never be able to hide her feelings if just remembering the blackguard's touch inflamed her senses. And she wouldn't dare acknowledge that her lips still burned from his kiss. Unconsciously, she slid her tongue across her lips, trying to taste him.

A low satisfied chuckle rumbled in Brad's chest. He recognized a look of blossoming desire on a woman's face when he saw it, and the ice maiden across from him was definitely blossoming.

When Dru repeated her question, he answered, "No, Peanut, the lady wasn't tired. She fell and injured herself, so I helped her back to her seat." But then, leaning forward with a disgustingly attractive smirk on his face, he added in a loud whisper, "Really, I just think she likes me and wanted to attract my attention. You know how women are . . ."

Again, it made perfect sense to Dru. Who wouldn't want her daddy's attention?

Kathlyn, who was listening for Brad's answer, fairly choked. "Of all the conceited, arrogant, black-hearted bast . . ."

"Now, now, now, Madame," Brad interrupted just in time. "Need I remind you that there are tender ears among us?" He elevated a black eyebrow and cocked his head in Dru's direction.

Clamping her mouth shut so rapidly that she practically bit her tongue off, Kathlyn jerked her snapping eyes away from him. For once in her life, she was truly speechless.

Dru's clear azure eyes regarded Kathlyn with amazement. She had never heard a lady talk to her daddy like that. What on earth was wrong with the woman, she wondered, shifting her gaze back to Brad. "Daddy, why is the lady so cross with you?"

Innocently, he shrugged a thick shoulder. "I'm not sure, Peanut, unless she's playing hard to get."

Before Kathlyn could attack Brad physically, Mammy Mae came to the rescue. She admonished him good-naturedly, "Mistah Brad you behave yourself. You've deviled this poor youngun enough—and her hurt and all—you oughta be ashamed of yourself!"

Brad looked not the least repentant as understanding dawned on Dru. Her daddy was just teasing the lady, though the lady obviously wasn't aware of it. Well, she would just have to enlighten her. She couldn't have anyone thinking unkind thoughts about her father. Sliding from her seat, she walked over to Kathlyn and placed a chubby mitt on her slender hand.

"I'm sorry you're hurt. But you mustn't be angry. Daddy's just teasing you." Her face lit up with an indulgent smile when she looked back at her father.

Cocking her head to one side Dru studied Kathlyn's softened lavender-blue eyes. "He does that to me all the time when I fall out of my tree-swing. He just wants to make you laugh so you won't cry."

Then fixing a serious gaze on Kathlyn, she implored her with her eyes. "You're not really angry with Daddy, are you?"

Kathlyn was hopelessly lost. Without a doubt, the human being had not been created who could resist this little cherub. Her heart melted and ran down her insides as she looked into the gaze of Brad's precious child.

Remembering the soft brown eyes she had awakened to, Kathlyn knew all too well where Dru got her charm. And she feared the father would prove as difficult to resist as the daughter.

Raising her hand to touch Dru's silken, platinum curls, she responded, "No, sweetie, I'm not really angry with your daddy. I guess my hurt side has made me a mite touchy." Then over Dru's head, she softly informed Brad, "You have quite a goodwill ambassador."

Brad nodded like the proud father he was.

Satisfied that all was well, Dru turned to her daddy. "What did you bring us to eat?"

Brad groaned. "I'm sorry, Peanut. I didn't have time to buy any food after I stopped to . . . uh . . . help Miss McKinney . . ."

"Rachel and I would be pleased to share our food."

"You didn't really bring food along, did you?" Rachel asked with disgust. She had watched the sickening scene between Brad's brat and Kathlyn and she was spoiling for a fight. "People will think we're poverty-stricken hicks."

"I thought home-cooked food would be better for us than what we could buy in a train station," Kathlyn answered, somewhat embarrassed. "And we might need the money we'll save."

"Thanks to Brad, we don't have to pinch pennies anymore."

The look Rachel turned on Brad was so sweet it made his teeth hurt. What *was* her game, he wondered? One minute she glowered at him and the next she looked at him as if he were the answer to all her prayers.

"Thanks," Brad said to Kathlyn, ignoring Rachel altogether. "We haven't had a picnic in a long time, have we, Peanut? Could I help you get the basket, Kathlyn?"

It happened again. The moment Brad turned those big, brown, velvety eyes of his on her and spoke her name, Kathlyn's body reacted: her heart raced, her breathing accelerated, her hands trembled. If she didn't know better, she'd swear her corset was laced too tight. What was happening to her? She couldn't even remember his question.

To cover her unease, she bent over to pull the picnic basket from under her seat. When it caught on something, Brad rolled to his feet, reached around Kathlyn, and pulled it forward.

His breath was warm on her cheek, and his familiar, spicy scent caused her arms to lose their strength. She slumped back into her seat. Brad placed the basket beside her. Their hands remained on the handle, scant inches apart.

She sat gazing into sultry brown eyes. Reasons why she should resist Brad scattered through her brain like tumbleweed in a windstorm. Struggling to pin one down she wondered if other women were more immune to his sensual charisma than she?

If so, she couldn't imagine how. He was so devastatingly attractive, he no doubt made all women feel as if they were about go up in flames. Dadburn his hide! Her hand dropped heavily into her lap. She'd bet Uncle Joe's nose the rake did it on purpose! No man could affect a woman like that without trying.

Not privy to Kathlyn's thoughts, Brad opened the picnic basket. He didn't so much as look inside. Instead, he studied her face. Lost in her eyes, his senses caught fire. The sparks flying between them were fairly tangible. He knew he had to regain control of himself or he would embarrass them both. In a passion thickened Southern drawl, he said, "Looks delicious." He didn't mean the food.

Almost in a daze, Kathlyn's gaze slid to his lips. "Umm," she agreed, not referring to the food either.

"I'll provide the meal at our next stop." He made the innocent offer in a very seductive tone, while looking at her as if she were the only meal he desired.

Kathlyn swallowed deeply. He would be quite a meal.

Mammy Mae took pity on them. Gently, she placed her hand on Brad's forearm and stepped around him. "Here Miz Kathlyn, I'll have that food laid out in a jiffy."

Reluctantly, he moved back into his seat. "Peanut," he said, opening his arms.

While Dru crawled up into his lap, Mammy Mae set about emptying the picnic basket.

We might need the money . . .

Kathlyn's words popped into Brad's mind. Why would she need to hoard her money? Surely the sale of River's Edge was sufficient to provide for her trip and a new wardrobe. He calculated the cost mentally.

He watched as Kathlyn helped Mammy with the food. For the first time he noticed Kathlyn looked a bit down on her luck. Her clothing was slightly outdated; the lace on her collar was frayed; her lilac and black traveling suit was faded.

Some banker he was! Men who made their livelihood as money lenders were trained to notice everything about a person, particularly signs indicating their financial status. How could he have overlooked her obvious poverty?

He knew how! She was so beautiful — inside and out — the slightly outdated style of her attire had escaped his notice. Her hair was so rich and lustrous, it had drawn his eye away from the worn lace of her collar. And her gentle curves were so arousing he hadn't noticed the faded condition of the suit jacket that covered them.

But now that he did notice, he wanted to help her. Smiling wistfully, he imagined dressing her in the latest fashions, adorning her with the finest jewelry, and lavishing on her the finest French perfumes money could buy.

Sobering, he looked out the window. Would he always strive to be Kathlyn's knight in shining armor? And more to the point, would she always refuse him?

He sincerely hoped not. Whether she knew it or not, she needed him. Who else did she have? Rachel? If Rachel Jackson was all that stood between Kathlyn and disaster, she was in poor shape indeed.

But was Rachel all she had. It occurred to him then

157

that he still had no idea why Kathlyn was going west. All he knew was her destination: Fort Smith. But what was waiting in Fort Smith for her? Or whom?

He looked at Kathlyn as if to discover the answer. She was smiling over at Dru and Dru was smiling back at her.

Feeling his eyes upon them, they both smiled at him. His heart warmed instantly. Kat's attitude toward him had certainly changed for the better since she had been charmed by Dru. Silently, he blessed his daughter for that. He suspected he would need all the help he could get, if someone special was waiting for Kathlyn at the end of her journey.

Surely she wouldn't look at him that way if she had someone waiting for her. Would she?

that he will be ...
All by ...
was smothering ...
The world in ...
uncertain ...

He knew ...

Chapter Seventeen

Kathlyn writhed beneath the oppressive weight of her attackers. Gasping for air, she struggled, desperately seeking freedom. A faceless apparition of evil pinned her to the hard ground, slamming his body against hers, cutting off the air her bursting lungs craved.

Panic gripped her heart like steel fingers slicing through the quivering muscle. A terrified scream was trapped deep inside her throat. She had never felt so helpless. Something awful was about to happen, and she was powerless to prevent it.

Brad awakened abruptly. Looking out the window, he saw that the sun had fallen behind the mountains; he'd been asleep for some time.

Stretching and yawning, he glanced over at the peacefully sleeping forms of his daughter and Mammy Mae. Satisfied that all was well with them he looked in Kathlyn's direction. Although she was dozing, a tortured look clouded her face.

He slid across the seat and leaned over, closing the distance between them. Very gently, he touched her shoulder. "Kathlyn . . . Kat," he whispered.

Kathlyn's eyes flew open. Disoriented, she jerked her head up and stared blindly into his face.

He straightened and opened his mouth to speak. Before he could utter a word, she threw herself across the aisle, sailing into his arms, pushing him backwards, flush with the window. She lay half over him, clutching his shoulders in a death grip. "Please don't let them hurt me," she whimpered into his neck.

"Shh now, nobody will hurt you. It was just a dream. You're safe now," he crooned, as if he were comforting Dru after a nightmare.

For a long while he ran his hands down the length of her slender back, soothing her, a strange sense of longing swelling in his breast. His nostrils filled with her light floral scent. She felt so soft and warm pressed against his solid length that he was reluctant to release her.

He rocked slowly, angling his head to see if they were being observed. As far as he could tell, the other passengers were asleep.

His desire grew. Overcome, he almost forgot she had reached out to him for comfort and protection, not passion. When he couldn't stand the exquisite torture a moment longer, he leaned back ever so slightly and hooked a long tanned finger beneath her chin, lifting her face. "Are you all right now?" he asked thickly.

It had been so long since Kathlyn had been held and comforted that she was momentarily stunned. She hadn't realized how hungry she was for security, not until then. Tears clouded her eyes. Just for that moment in time, she didn't care that she was reclining with a man in public, clutching him to her lest he slip away.

The war had been hell for her, and if possible, Reconstruction had proven worse. Then Roth had died, leaving her all alone except for Rachel. Was it any wonder that she took to Brad's comfort like a flower opening to the sun's rays?

She was afraid and she was tired of being alone. She just wanted to cuddle deeper in his arms and have him hold the cruel world at bay.

She should be ashamed of her weakness, she knew. She should be stronger, more self-sufficient. Lately, whenever the wind blew, she turned into a veritable watering pot. And Brad was always there to witness her loss of control.

Well it had to stop! Stiffening her spine, she pulled away from him. "I'm fine."

"Would you like to step outside on the platform for a breath of fresh air?" he asked hopefully, feeling empty now that she was no longer in his arms.

Despite her determination to be a lone heroine, she

160

placed her hand in his and rose. They made their way down the aisle.

Mammy Mae opened one eye. Her lips spread in a satisfied smile. Playing possum, she had witnessed the scene between Brad and Kathlyn. "Baby, Ol' Mammy thinks your daddy's gonna get you a mama yet," she whispered into the sleeping child's blond curls.

Rachel overheard Mammy's prediction and flashed the old woman a venomous look. "Not if I can help it," she hissed.

Mammy drew a cross over her heart with a shaky finger. At the look of pure evil in Rachel's eyes, she pulled Dru more tightly against her bosom.

The night was clear and the stars overhead twinkled to the rhythm of Kathlyn's rapid heartbeat. She felt unaccountably self-conscious in Brad's presence now. That struck her as odd considering she had thrown herself into his arms moments before.

She had to stop being so silly. He wouldn't bite. He was just an ordinary man. No. If there was one thing Brad Hampton was not, it was ordinary. Perhaps that was why she reacted so strongly to him.

Drawing a deep breath to slow her heart, she grasped the rail with trembling hands. Blindly, she stared out into the darkness; the countryside whizzed by. With the heat from Brad's body warming her back, and the cool night air flowing across her in front, she was achingly aware of his presence. Vainly, she sought a sense of control.

He was equally affected by her nearness. Standing close behind her, he circled her waist with his hands. She was so small, so soft, so pliable; he knew the exact moment she lost the battle to keep her distance from him.

An overwhelming sense of pleasure flooded him when she leaned back against his chest. Once again her scent stimulated his senses, not just the fragrance of summer roses, but her woman's scent, the delicious smell that was uniquely Kathlyn. He stifled a moan. Not wanting to frighten her away, he stood still.

The feel of her heated his blood, causing an exquisite

161

arousal to swell inside him. It felt so good, it was almost painful. Nevertheless, he exercised great control, dropping only a light kiss beneath her ear.

Together, they shuddered. Whether it was he who trembled, or she, or perhaps the train shimmied, he wasn't sure. The way she made him feel, it might have been an earthquake. He tightened his arms around her waist, shifting to fit their bodies together.

A force drew her to him like a magnet. His nearness caused the blood in her veins to burn hot as molten lava. Swirling pressure gathered in a pool in her lower abdomen, causing her to expect a volcanic eruption of sensation at any moment.

The explosion occurred when he turned her in his arms. Their bodies were tight against one another, chest to chest, thighs to thighs, hips to hips.

She dropped her head back and looked up into his face—the same devastatingly handsome face that had haunted her every waking moment for the past two weeks. Try as she might she couldn't keep him at bay, physically or emotionally. Her eyes fixed on his sensuous mouth. Unwittingly, she moistened her lips in anticipation of his kiss.

Accepting the invitation, he slowly lowered his head. With his lips poised over hers he breathed, "You're so beautiful." Hungrily, he captured her lips. He deepened the kiss. His tongue caressed the soft interior of her mouth. Boldly, she rolled her tongue over his, sending a white-hot wave of desire through his body.

He groaned with need, drawing her ever closer. All at once, his hands had a mind of their own. Gently, yet purposefully, they mapped the contours of her willowy frame.

Absently, she scolded herself for giving into the desire generated by his touch. But she was powerless to resist him. His kisses were as sweet as ripe peaches, his nearness more drugging than fine wine. And those hands! Everywhere his butterfly touch lingered she flamed with pleasurable sensation.

"Oh Brad," she moaned as his fingertips lightly massaged her sensitive breasts.

Gingerly, she slid her hands up his arms, slowly encircling his neck. Despite the resulting twinge in her side, she wanted to enjoy all of him, all six foot two inches of raw sensual power. She came alive wherever their bodies met.

He kissed her until their legs grew weak with need. Neither could stand alone. In their intimacy, the heat of their passion blazed out of control: hearts pounded, hands wandered, lips melded, and bodies burst into flames.

"Oh Kat, I want to make love to you," he whispered.

Something broke loose inside her at his bold confession. Rational thought left her as surely as water rushing down a mountainside.

He sensed her final capitulation. He stepped even closer to her, capturing her between his thighs, pressing her against the rail. Of their own accord, his hands wandered down her slender back until they stilled, finally resting on the gentle swell of her bottom.

Alternately kneading and caressing, he was driven by an overwhelming need to possess her. The intensity of his feelings set the pace as he rained kisses on her eyes, cheeks, and neck. Slowing his raging assault, he captured her lips.

He tore his mouth from hers, burying his face in her neck, leaning against her for support. His breathing was rapid and labored, sounding loud in the darkness. If he didn't stop now, he wouldn't be able to. And he just couldn't see making love to Kathlyn on the platform of a moving train. No matter how badly he wanted to.

"Brad?" she whispered throatily. Moving her head to the side, she attempted to look up into his face.

He groaned as the light scent of roses floated from her hair. Mindless with need, he clutched her to him, sensually rotating the evidence of his desire against her softness.

A seductive sound, part surprise, part longing, escaped her throat. For a moment she mimicked his movement, thrilling to the feel of his warm member grinding against her belly. Then, she grew rigid in his arms.

163

Chapter Eighteen

He didn't notice the change at first. Finally, however,
he realized his advances weren't being returned. With his
arms still encircling her waist, he stepped back and
looked down into her face. Silver rays from the moon
washed over her, illuminating the hesitancy in her eyes.
"Sweetheart, is something wrong?"

Something wrong, indeed. How could she explain why
she had stopped responding to a man she wanted more
than life itself? How could she explain her reservations
to him when she didn't truly understand them herself?
How could she tell him she had never stopped loving
him, not even when he had broken her heart, not even
when she had lost his baby?

And how could she tell him about Glenn—about the
man she was honor bound to wed? The thought of her
future with Glenn—actually the thought of a future
without Brad—caused an aching pit to form in her stomach. She moaned softly.

"Honey, what's wrong?" His voice trailed off as he
gently pulled her to his chest. Cupping her head with his
hand, he settled her cheek against the rapid beat of his
heart.

Her answer was muffled in the navy superfine of his
coat. "It's nothing, really."

He placed his free hand under her chin, tilting it upward. "Tell me."

"I'm just so confused."

"About what?"

"The past." She looked into his eyes. "The present."
She touched his kiss-reddened lips. "The future," she
whispered, looking over his shoulder in the distance.

For a long moment, he said nothing. His passion

164

cooled slightly now, he wasn't a great deal more confident about their relationship than she. Finally, he said, "The past is over, it's best forgotten. As for the present, maybe we should just go slow and see what happens. And the future—the future can be anything we make it."

"You don't understand," she began.

Gently, he ran the backs of his fingers along her jaw. "I understand that you and I are drawn to each other. That what we had eleven years ago isn't dead. Not by a long shot. Beyond that, what is there to understand?"

She grabbed his hand, squeezing his fingers, willing him to understand. "If only it were that simple," she whispered, fervently. "What's wrong?" she asked when he winced.

"My hand's just a little sore."

Kathlyn turned his hand toward the light streaming from inside the train. His knuckles were purple and swollen. "Brad, you're hurt."

"That big guy I fought at the station had a hard head." He chuckled.

Tenderly, one by one, Kathlyn kissed each injured knuckle. Then at his low moan she touched each injury with the tip of her tongue. "Better?" she asked, kissing them again.

"Oh Lord, what are you doing to me?" he groaned. Hungrily, he dipped his head, kissing her deeply.

She responded in kind, drawing closer to his warmth. Her hands grasped his upper arms. She squeezed his rock-hard muscles and began a sensuous assault of her own.

"Kathlyn—my dear sister—what would your fiancé think?" A harsh voice brought the world crashing in on them. Rachel stepped out onto the platform, a strange fire flashing in her eyes.

"Fiancé?" Brad asked quietly.

"I am sorry," Rachel said in a tone that all but curdled the stomach with its sweetness. "I thought you knew that Kathlyn was going to Fort Smith to join her fiancé."

"No, I didn't know," he answered, his eyes never leaving Kathlyn's face. "Rachel, if you'll excuse us, I'd like to talk with Kathlyn alone."

Rachel cast Brad a smug smile. "I'm sure you would." She backed through the doorway.

He stood quietly. Kathlyn was still near him, though they weren't touching now. The chasm between them seemed very wide. Finally, he asked as nonchalantly as he could, "What's this about a fiancé?"

She stepped back so she could see his face. The indifferent expression he used when he didn't want to share his thoughts with the world was firmly in place. "I'm engaged to an officer who's stationed at Fort Gibson. It's close to Fort Smith."

Brad withdrew a cheroot from his waistcoat pocket and struck a match to it. He drew on it deeply. After exhaling the blue-white smoke, he tipped the thin cigar toward his face and blew on the lighted end. The red tip flamed almost as brightly as the rage burning in his heart. He stared out into the night, cursing himself for being a fool. He should have known there was someone else. God, he should have known.

After a long while, he said flatly, "I know where Fort Gibson is. Is he from Union Point?" The slight inflection Brad put on the word *he* was not pleasant.

"No, I believe he's from Pennsylvania."

"You believe?" he asked dryly, another plume of smoke swirling upward in front of his carefully schooled face.

Kathlyn was becoming flustered. What did Brad care where Glenn was from? And why was he so angry? She had tried to warn him, to tell him things weren't as simple as they seemed. "No. I mean, yes. He is from Pennsylvania. I think."

"Well which is it, dear? Is the love of your life from Pennsylvania or not?" His facade was beginning to crack. And sounding like a snippy spinster wasn't good for his male ego.

Kathlyn resented his tone. "Since he fought for the Union, in the Pennsylvania militia, I imagine he is from Pennsylvania," she explained coolly.

"Oh, a Yankee?" Brad observed noncommittally. Why he said that he wasn't sure. He had nothing against Yankees in general, just Yankees engaged to Kathlyn.

"Yes, what of it?" she challenged.

It occurred to Brad that they were having a rather civil argument considering the passionate embrace they had shared before Rachel so rudely interrupted. The sudden remembrance of Kathlyn's enthusiastic response to him raised a very important question in his mind. He hated to ask it, but he did. "And is he the love of your life, Kat?"

She hardly needed to consider the question, though she paused before answering. In the lull, he raised a finger to trace the pale evidence of Ishta's cut on her cheek. The tender gesture touched a spot in her she preferred to leave undisturbed. Finally, she whispered, "He's my fiancé."

His hand dropped to his side like a lead weight. "You're right, it's not as simple as I thought." On that somewhat cryptic note, he returned to his seat . . . alone.

Left behind on the platform, Kathlyn raised her tear streaked face to the sky. For a long moment, she allowed herself to wonder what life would have been like if the past eleven years had not occurred. She allowed her yearning heart to transport her back to a glasshouse filled with gardenias, where she lay cradled in the arms of a man who owned her heart and soul. A man who had pledged his love to her.

Closing her eyes, she pictured becoming Brad's bride, bearing his children, rearing a family with him on Paradise Manor, growing old together . . . and falling deeper in love everyday.

Why? Why couldn't life cooperate? Would she always have happiness at her fingertips but never in her grasp? Tears slid down her cheeks.

Mentally shaking herself, she turned toward the door. She had made a promise to Glenn and she would keep that promise. Even if happiness eluded her for the rest of her life, she would have the satisfaction of knowing that when Kathlyn McKinney gave her word she kept it.

She prayed that it would be enough.

Two days later, the morning sky shone pink with the first rays of sunrise. It was a beautiful sight to behold, but Brad stared at it with unseeing eyes. Standing outside on the gently rocking platform, he willed this disturbing trip to come to an end. He was more distraught than he cared to admit — about many things.

First, there was Kathlyn. He just couldn't believe that after eleven years he had opened his heart to her again, and again she had trampled it. She was engaged for God's sake! How could he have been so blind?

Even amid her icy rejoinders he had imagined a spark of warmth. But was it just wishful thinking? Had he seen only what he hoped to see? Felt, only what he hoped to feel?

Sure, she lusted after him. He could feel that whenever they were within touching distance. But that was no longer enough for him. If lust was all he wanted, he could stick with women like Lois.

He wanted more; he needed more; he needed love. And he had almost despaired of ever finding it again. Then Kathlyn came back into his life, and for the first time in a very long time, hope had lived in him. And it had felt so good.

But now, with the single utterance, *fiancé,* he had been robbed of that hope. He felt empty and confused. He didn't want to abandon all hope, yet he couldn't imagine going forward in a relationship with an engaged woman. No matter how strongly he felt about her.

For the past two days he and Kathlyn had not spoken a word to each other. Their dark moods had permeated the group — the adults at least. But not Dru. She was the only bright spot in his life now.

He smiled, remembering his daughter's antics on the trip. She considered it all a great adventure. The fact that they hadn't bathed, eaten a decent meal, or slept in a bed for three days had obviously escaped her notice. And though the adults were a bit the worse for wear, she was positively blossoming, with energy to spare.

Much to Mammy's dismay. When he thought of Mammy Mae, Brad's smile was replaced by a look of distress. She was another concern. Each day his old nanny seemed to grow weaker, less able to corral and care for his very active daughter.

Kathlyn had apparently noticed this as well. With every passing hour she had claimed more of Dru's attention, talking with her, reading to her. Naturally, Dru was quite taken with Kathlyn. Brad groaned . . . like father, like daughter.

Turning his back to the rail, he looked through the dusty, glass-paned door. He couldn't see her, but he wondered if Kathlyn was feeling as lost as he.

Inside the train, Kathlyn was miserable. Rachel reached over and patted her hand. Kathlyn smiled weakly. It was obvious Rachel felt bad about the scene of two nights ago. But she shouldn't have. Kathlyn didn't blame her for her misery.

Rachel had apologized more than once for her abruptness. She had told Kathlyn that she believed Glenn—not Brad—was the best choice for her. Whether Kathlyn agreed with Rachel's assessment or not, she couldn't blame her half-sister for trying to protect her. In fact, she should be pleased that someone cared.

So why did she feel so alone, Kathlyn wondered as she pulled Ishta's cage into her lap. Cooing to her little friend, she sought the sweet feeling that always came when she was with the bird. This time it didn't come. Kathlyn knew why.

She was grieving for Brad, for what would never be. He had touched her tender heart again and awakened her sleeping passion in a way she had thought lost forever. And now, it was over. With a sense of despair she knew no other man would ever reach her. Not like Brad. Not even Glenn.

As the train rolled into the Memphis station yard Brad made his way down the aisle. For a split second his eyes met Kathlyn's. Then he turned his distracted mind to the task of preparing his family for disembarkation.

Kathlyn stood and began collecting her things.

"Daddy, where have you been?"

"Just outside getting some air, Peanut." Brad touched his daughter's cheek, hoping his voice didn't sound as husky to the others as it did to him.

The train lurched to a halt beside the terminal, throwing his massive frame against Kathlyn. He heard her gasp with pain ever so softly upon impact. Overcome with concern and remorse, he forgot the problems between them and reacted instinctively, enfolding her in his arms. She moaned in agony.

"Kat, I'm so sorry. I lost my balance. Did I hurt you?"

Kathlyn, visibly pale with pain, whispered, "It's all right."

Even through the pain she was affected by his nearness. Why did she have to feel so good in his arms? It was unfair! She tried to draw away from him, but he held on tight.

"It's not all right, you stubborn woman. If you don't have enough sense to take care of yourself, somebody has to. As soon as we reach the hotel, you're going to let a doctor look at that rib!" His hand, gently hooked around the nape of her neck, massaging just below her hairline, took the sting out of his words.

"I don't need your help. If I choose to see a doctor, I will see one on my own," she feigned indignation.

"Frankly, Kathlyn McKinney, I don't trust your judgment. If I thought you would see a doctor, I would be thrilled for you to go alone. But I don't trust you, and no matter what you say, I am taking you to the doctor." Brad employed the dictatorial tone Kathlyn was beginning to resent.

"You pig-headed man," she muttered, a bit ashamed to resort to name-calling.

Mammy Mae attempted to keep Dru occupied while Brad and Kathlyn debated the issue. Knowing how protective Dru was of her daddy, Mammy feared she would take issue with Miss McKinney's label for Brad. But she shouldn't. It was obvious neither of them were really angry. They were crazy in love, or she missed her guess.

They sure looked crazy, she chuckled to herself. Mistah Brad, standing there, holding the fuming girl in his arms, telling her he knew best. And her, calling him names, looking at up at him with her heart in her eyes. It was sweet. That's what it was. Sweet.

"I'll see a doctor before we board the stage," Kathlyn said.

"You're traveling by coach?" Brad asked.

"Of course. How else would we get to Fort Smith?" Rachel answered for her.

Brad slanted Rachel a hard look. *Bound and gagged, if I had my way.*

"I wish you could go on our big boat. I wanted to help you take care of Ishta," Dru said, poking her bottom lip out pitifully.

Brad smiled at his daughter's pout and winked at her, attempting to restore her customary good nature. Then he furrowed his brow. He wondered when Kathlyn's stage would leave Memphis. Actually he wondered how much longer he would have before she waltzed out of his life again. Determination sculpting his face, a devious idea forming in his mind, he released her.

She bent to retrieve Ishta's cage from the floor. Her hands were trembling. She was loath to admit that her reaction was due to Brad's nearness, but she knew it was. Whenever she was near him she acted like a fool. How on earth would she manage to say goodbye to him? She couldn't bear to think of it; she needed a distraction. Anything that would keep her mind off Brad Hampton.

"Will you stop standing there like a ninny and go on," Rachel complained, pushing Kathlyn down the aisle.

The words that came to Brad and Kathlyn at that moment were both apt descriptions of Rachel. They weren't the same word, however.

Kathlyn looked at Rachel and sighed, *distraction*. Brad scowled at Rachel and thought a word less benign: *bitch*.

Chapter Nineteen

Brad led Mammy Mae and Dru out of the bustling train station to the covered carriage that would transport them to their hotel. After settling them inside, he spoke to the lad helping with their luggage. Then he and the boy returned to the terminal and found Kathlyn and Rachel, standing apart from the crowd. "Where are you ladies staying until your stage leaves?"

"We don't have a place yet. Where are you staying?" Rachel asked, hoping he would suggest they accompany him to his hotel. After witnessing Kathlyn and Brad's moonlight embrace, Rachel wasn't about to let him out of her sight. Otherwise, he would make contact with Kathlyn on his own, there was no doubt about that. Keeping him close, she could monitor his comings and goings. Who knows, she might even convince him to return to Georgia.

And he had to go back to Georgia. Rather, he couldn't be permitted to go to Fort Smith. It would never do for him and Kathlyn to be in the same state, let alone the same town. Since they had once been lovers, it would be far too easy for them to fall in love again . . . if they hadn't already.

While Rachel grew nauseated at the thought of the twosome falling in love, their amorous relationship was not her main concern. Her primary reasons were many — 100,000 to be exact. 100,000 dollars. That's what Kathlyn was worth to her and Stuart.

And she and Stuart would not permit Brad to interfere with their plan. They would be rid of him even if they had to resort to murder. Rachel imagined Stuart had killed men for a lot less. She knew she would. She had thought as much when they boarded the train in Athens.

"Don't worry. We'll find one," Kathlyn said, jerking her head away from Brad in a nonverbal hint to her "sister" that they should leave.

"Nonsense," Brad said with an indulgent smile. Taking Rachel's luggage, he spoke to the lad beside him. "Please take Miss Jackson's valise to the carriage, and then come back for her trunks and Miss McKinney's valise."

"This really isn't necessary . . ." Kathlyn began.

"No, but it is awfully kind of you," Rachel interjected, stepping between Brad and Kathlyn.

"Would you like for me to have your bird taken to the hotel? I'll see that she's well taken care of," Brad asked.

"That's thoughtful, but I'd prefer to keep her with me."

Rachel pulled on Brad's arm. "Well, shall we go?"

Brad tore his eyes from Kathlyn. "By all means," he spoke through clenched teeth. As usual, he had the strongest urge to shake his arm, as if to dislodge a very large, red-headed leech. But suppressing the inclination, he escorted Rachel to the carriage. Reluctantly, Kathlyn followed behind.

When Kathlyn stepped up into the carriage, Dru squealed with delight. "Oh Daddy, the pretty blue bird is coming with us."

Brad nodded, settling himself on the seat beside Kathlyn.

Kathlyn warmed to the little girl's excitement. "You really like birds, don't you, honey?" She thought she heard Dru mutter, *"Not on hats."* Surely not.

"Yes, ma'am. Tandy does too." Trancelike, Dru reached her hand toward the cage, stopping just short of the bars.

"Would you and Tandy like to pet Ishta?"

Dru looked to her daddy for permission. Brad smiled his approval.

Cautiously, Kathlyn opened the tiny white gate. "Come here, Ishta," she cooed.

Brad watched enraptured as the beautiful blue bird edged toward Kathlyn's slim finger.

"Oh," Dru breathed in awe.

173

Kathlyn smiled at the innocent wonder lighting the child's face.

Just as Ishta passed through the doorway, the spell was broken. "Kathlyn, surely you're not going to let that nasty bird loose in this carriage!" Rachel shrieked.

Dru scampered back to the safety of Mammy's arms.

"I'm sorry, Rachel. I forgot how frightened you are of birds," Kathlyn said sincerely, gently closing Ishta's cage.

Bitch, Brad hissed silently. Rachel Jackson was frightened of birds about as much as he was frightened of pretty women. Not at all.

It was becoming clear to him that Rachel was obsessed with the need to control Kathlyn. And Kathlyn was so kind and loving, she was blind to Rachel's intentions.

He could see that Kathlyn held her family sacred. And she would never do anything to harm her half-sister, assuming that Rachel felt the same way.

But Rachel felt nothing for Kathlyn. Brad was convinced of that. Nothing positive, anyway. In fact, he was beginning to believe her feelings were quite negative where Kathlyn was concerned! He remembered Jared's warning about Rachel's threat to Kathlyn; the woman would bear watching.

Now he had another reason to keep Kathlyn close, in addition to his reluctance to say goodbye to her. He turned to Dru. "Perhaps Miss McKinney could bring Ishta to your room later at the hotel, Peanut."

"Pleeeze?" Dru turned pleading eyes on Kathlyn.

"I would be happy to."

Rachel glowered.

"Here we are." Brad announced when the carriage drew to a halt. Throwing open the door he dropped down onto the cobblestone street. One by one, he lifted his female companions from the carriage. He planted a loud kiss on Dru's downy cheek as he swung her through the air, groaned comically when he helped his portly mammy through the door, and covered his handsome face with a stoic mask when he presented his hand to Rachel.

Then it was Kathlyn's turn. With Ishta's cage filling her right arm, she held out her left hand to Brad. He recalled the sincere look of regret on her face when she had angered Rachel. Instead of pulling her through the door as she expected, he brought her gloved fingers to his mouth and touched them lightly with his lips. The act quite frankly took her breath away.

Then, looking over his head, she gasped, "Oh my dear, it's exquisite."

Knowing quite well that Kathlyn was speaking of the elegant hotel at his back, he helped her from the carriage. When she was on sound footing, he tucked her arm under his. "Thank you. I don't usually receive such high praise for kissing a lady's hand," he whispered close to her ear.

"I didn't mean . . ." Kathlyn began. When she saw the teasing glint in his eyes, she couldn't help but smile. "You really are a scoundrel. You know that, don't you?"

Brad winked ever so slightly. "One tries."

Kathlyn blushed shamelessly and looked about for something to interrupt the intimate moment. Her gaze settled on the magnificent structure before her. "It really is beautiful."

The Kaleidoscope Hotel was named properly, she decided. It was predominantly white, with various pastel hues of the finest marble providing relief here and there. It brought to her mind a piece of Islamic sculpture she had seen in a book.

The blocks of azure blue and rosy pink intersected with strips of incandescent foam green. With the sun shining on it, the hotel resembled nothing so much as the view through a giant kaleidoscope.

Brad barely noticed the hotel he had purchased only a few months before. His eyes were only for the woman on his arm.

"Mr. Hampton," a chubby man fawned, rushing over to Brad's party. "We have been waiting for you."

"Will." Brad nodded cordially.

Will reached for Brad's hand with his chubby paws.

Reluctantly, Brad allowed the desk clerk to pump his hand. The man shook Brad's hand with such vigor he feared water might pour from his arm at any moment. His fingertips began to feel numb. Bringing a halt to

Will's exuberant greeting, Brad said, "I have two extra guests in my party. Would you see to their comfort?"

"Brad, I don't think we should," Kathlyn said.

She knew that she and Rachel could not afford to stay in a hotel like the Kaleidoscope. Their stage wasn't due for a few days, and while she didn't know the room rate, she knew they didn't have the funds to cover it. Establishments like this were not for the likes of her; they were for the privileged, like Brad Hampton and his little princess.

"Nonsense," Will enthused. "Of course, you are welcome at Mr. Hampton's hotel."

"Your hotel?" Rachel and Kathlyn asked.

Brad merely nodded his head, yes. He wanted Kathlyn to stay, but was wise enough not to push her. Help came from an unexpected source.

"Of course, we'll stay. If you will, show me to my room," Rachel said in the haughty voice she reserved for servants. Obviously, Brad planned to provide lodging for them at no cost. That suited her fine. It would give her additional funds to purchase clothing for her trip to Los Angeles.

Will looked to Brad. When he nodded his approval, Rachel swept away, her ample hips swaying like a pealing bell. A host of hotel employees rushed forward. Along with their baggage, Brad, Kathlyn, and Mammy Mae followed in silence.

No one noticed as Dru tucked Tandy beneath her arm, cocked her head to one side, and drew her lips into an unpleasant grimace. Sniffing, she pranced across the floor behind the adults, mocking the bad woman with the bird hat.

Later that afternoon, Kathlyn stood at her window overlooking a beautiful flower garden. She turned in surprise when a knock came at her door.

"Yes?" She opened the door.

Standing in the hallway, Brad grinned at her cheekily. When he stepped uninvited into her room, he was followed by a dapper gentleman who bestowed upon her a gentle smile.

176

"To what do I owe this honor?" Kathlyn asked Brad dryly.

The gentleman standing between Brad and Kathlyn explained. "I'm the hotel doctor, Miss McKinney. Mr. Hampton tells me you were injured on your trip from Athens."

Brad's brow furrowed at the doctor's solicitous tone of voice.

"Slightly," Kathlyn allowed. She was smiling at the doctor in a way that made Brad decidedly uncomfortable. Which was as it should be, for that was her intention.

"How terribly dreadful for a woman as lovely as yourself to experience pain."

"You're too kind," Kathlyn answered softly, revelling in Brad's glowering expression. Stepping forward, she lay her hand on the physician's sleeve.

As he stared down into Kathlyn's smiling face, the doctor stammered, "N . . . not at all." A veil of crimson crept up his face.

Brad was beginning to lose his patience, both with his employee's bedside manner and Kathlyn's friendly response. "Just examine her, Doc. We wouldn't want to keep you from your other patients."

"I'm sure he would examine me, if you would excuse us." Kathlyn widened her eyes in mock innocence.

She had no intention of letting the good doctor get his hands on her, but Brad didn't have to know that. She was enjoying his display of jealousy too much. He was obviously discomfited, but it served him right, bringing a man into her room without her permission.

"Yes, Mr. Hampton. If you *will,* please excuse us. Miss McKinney will need to disrobe if I'm to examine her properly."

"Maybe we should just forget it," Brad gritted.

"Maybe we better," she agreed smugly, crossing to the door.

"Are you sure?" The doctor cast a wistful glance at Kathlyn.

"She's sure," Brad growled, pushing the doctor from the room more forcefully than necessary. When the door

177

shut behind them, Brad heard peals of laughter coming from the other side. Little wench, he smiled inwardly. She'd certainly gotten the best of him that time.

After taking a relaxing bath, Kathlyn dressed in the same clothes she had worn since she left Athens. Her valise had not been brought up yet. Making a mental note to check at the front desk, she left her room. First, she would look in on Rachel and visit Dru.

"Rachel," she called softly, tapping on the door.

"Come in."

Kathlyn stepped into the suite. Rose and ivory drapes were drawn against the afternoon sun, casting the elegantly appointed room in semidarkness. She stood in the doorway until her eyes adjusted to the dim interior.

"Rachel, are you all right?"

A figure on the bed rolled over onto her back. "Yes. I'm just tired."

Kathlyn was concerned with the weakness of Rachel's reply. She crossed the room for a closer look.

Against Rachel's pale skin, her forehead cloth and dog-skin gloves appeared almost black. The leather beauty treatments were messy, impregnated with oil. Usually Rachel donned them only at night. Why was she wearing them in the middle of the afternoon, Kathlyn wondered.

"Aren't you going down to dinner tonight? You need to eat to keep up your strength."

"Yes, I'm going to take these things off after I rest." Rachel lifted her hands off the mattress. "The air on the train was so dry I needed an extra application. After all, *dear sister,* we can't all have perfectly smooth skin like you." Rachel regretted the catty remark as soon as it passed her lips. She didn't want to show her true feelings to Kathlyn; it wasn't part of the plan. She smiled to soften her words.

Kathlyn noted the resentment in Rachel's tone when she said the word *sister* nonetheless. She was surprised by her vehemence. "Do you want to talk about it?"

"Our sisterhood, you mean?" Rachel tried to keep the

178

sneer out of her voice. She shifted to her side and the strong smell of orrisroot floated upward, causing Kathlyn's nose to twitch.

"Yes."

"No. I just want to rest. Wake me an hour before dinner so that I can prepare myself to be seen," Rachel dismissed, flopping over onto her side.

"Oh, by the way," she threw over her shoulder. "Have the desk clerk send the items on that list to my room." She pointed to a piece of the hotel's thick ivory stationary with a leather covered paw.

"Certainly." Taking the note with her, Kathlyn quietly left the room.

She had never really noticed how much attention Rachel paid to her beauty regimen before. But now that she thought of it, Rachel was always applying some sort of lotion or paste to her face and body.

She must be awfully insecure about her appearance, Kathlyn mused, halting beside a gaslight that hung over a huge potted plant. Squinting in the dimly lit hall, she perused Rachel's list.

Most of Rachel's requests were quite common. She had asked for burnt matchsticks to darken her lashes, geranium and poppy petals to stain her lips, and rice powder to pale her face. There was a final item Kathlyn could hardly believe. *Raw meat.*

Sure, Kathlyn knew the old wives' tale. But rubbing tiny pieces of uncooked cow across one's face was strange, even for Rachel! It would take a lot more than the promise of a beautiful complexion for Kathlyn to do it.

Yes, Rachel definitely was concerned with her appearance! If she didn't watch her, Rachel would be rolling naked in the dew to enhance the alabaster quality of her skin.

Kathlyn chuckled at the mental picture.

Chapter Twenty

"Is it a private joke, or would you care to let me in on it?"

Kathlyn jerked her head upward and looked into Brad's laughing brown eyes. "You startled me." Her voice sounded low and shaky. "What are you doing wandering the halls? Do you have another doctor for me to see?" she returned, widening her eyes.

"Hardly. The next doctor you see will be related to me. That scamp I brought to you earlier had more on his mind than your health."

She laughed softly. "You may be right."

Pointing to the sheet of paper she held in her hand, he asked, "That wouldn't be from the lecher, would it?"

She shook her head. "Afraid not," she sighed.

"Very funny," he deadpanned.

"I thought so."

"You're certainly in a good mood today." Brad stepped closer. "Could that note be the reason? Tell me, who's it from?"

Kathlyn elevated her eyebrows. "I'll never tell."

"Come on. Is it a secret admirer?" he prodded.

"Maybe." She smiled impishly, placing the note into her waist pocket, covering the pocket with her hand.

Stepping forward, he dwarfed her slight stature. He trapped her hand against her pocket, pressing his palm against her slightly, his fingers cupping her waist. "Since you're in my hotel . . ."

"Yes?" she interrupted.

"You're my responsibility. Therefore, you must let me see that note," he whispered in her ear, massaging her hand with his palm, his forearm dangerously close to her breast.

"Is that right?" she challenged weakly. His responsibility, indeed. If he'd just step back a bit and take his hands off her, she'd tell him what she thought of his responsibility! But honestly, with him standing so close, caressing her waist, her mind was like fog in the face of the morning sun. It just disappeared.

"Mmm hmm. My responsibility," he drawled. He knew full well what his touch did to Kathlyn. His chest swelled with the knowledge.

He moved even closer, so close he could smell the scent of her hair. Oh hell, it was gardenia! The little imp had washed her hair with gardenia scented soap.

With a less than steady hand, he raised her face. Staring down into her eyes, he searched for the answer. Did she remember their night of gardenias? The night when she gave him her most precious gift, lying on the floor of the glasshouse, surrounded by a scent as sweet as her kiss. "Umm, you smell of gardenias," he whispered against her cheek.

The door at the end of the hall banged open. "I'll be back," Dru called over her shoulder to Mammy Mae. "Miss McKinney, where's your bird?"

Dru rushed down the hall, watching her daddy and the nice lady jump apart. She'd have to ask Tandy about that later. They acted like *she* did when Aunt Melinda caught her doing something naughty. But surely her Daddy would never do anything naughty. He was perfect, just like the angels Mammy had told her about.

Dru sailed into Brad's waiting arms and turned the full force of her charm on Kathlyn. "Where's Ishta?"

"She's in my room, dying to see you. I was just coming for you and Tandy when I met your daddy in the hall." Kathlyn's voice was a bit too breathy to suit her pride.

"Goodie," Dru chortled, squeezing Brad around the neck.

Sheepishly, Brad looked into his daughter's face.

181

"Peanut, I'm afraid I have to borrow Miss McKinney for a couple of hours before she can play with you."

Kathlyn and Dru said, *No,* in unison. Kathlyn was thinking that she shouldn't be alone with Brad, and Dru was thinking that her daddy was more perfect sometimes than he was at other times, and this was certainly one of those other times.

Brad surveyed the two scowling females. He could see into their minds as if they were made of clear glass. "I'm afraid Miss McKinney's luggage has been stolen."

"Oh my," Kathlyn gasped, placing her hand on the wall for support.

Quickly, Brad set Dru down. For some reason the loss of a banged-up valise, filled with a few well-worn mourning gowns was causing Kathlyn undue distress. All the color had drained from her face. He placed his hand under her arm so she wouldn't slide to the floor.

"I'm sorry. But surely it wasn't that great a loss. I'll replace your things," he offered.

His sympathy was appreciated, but he didn't have the full picture. Everything she owned, except Ishta and the clothes on her back, was in that valise. Even her money.

Now what would she do? She had her stage ticket to Fort Smith in her reticule. But what if things didn't work out once she arrived? What if Glenn learned that she couldn't give him children and decided not to marry her? What would she do then? With no money, and nowhere to go, she'd be trapped.

With the loss of her luggage, she had lost her freedom. "My money," she said simply.

"You mean to tell me that the money you made on the sale of River's Edge was in that valise?" Brad was looking into Kathlyn's eyes, but that was not the picture in his mind. Instead he saw a young boy—the one he paid to throw Kathlyn's bag into the Mississippi River.

With one arrogant gesture, he had taken from Kathlyn everything she owned in the world. And all because he had wanted to provide her with a new wardrobe. Something he was sure she hadn't had since

182

before the war. Well, so much for good intentions. He would replace everything, if only he could find a way to get her to accept it.

"I'd say we have some shopping to do," he said suddenly.

"But I couldn't."

"Nonsense. What you *couldn't,* is travel all the way to Fort Smith with only one dress."

Kathlyn saw the wisdom of his words. "Maybe I could borrow some of Rachel's things." She dismissed the thought immediately.

Even if she had been willing to wear Rachel's outrageous clothes, which she wasn't, and they could be taken in to fit her, which they couldn't, she feared Rachel would not be willing to share. As concerned as she was with her appearance, Rachel was very possessive of her new wardrobe. Wresting so much as a garter from her would take Herculean effort. So where did that leave Kathlyn?

"You don't need Rachel's things. You need things of your own."

Kathlyn sighed in resignation. "You're a banker, are you not Mr. Hampton?"

Brad nodded.

"Then I fear I must apply for a loan."

Brad's lips spread in a relieved smile.

"But I insist that we do this in a businesslike manner. I will repay you . . . somehow," she said firmly.

In an attempt to ease the tension, he leaned forward, raised one ebony brow, and whispered for her ears only, "I'll think of something."

"Ooff."

"Please excuse me, Mr. Hampton," Kathlyn apologized innocently.

Dru stood aside, observing the adults who had obviously forgotten she was there. She didn't know what her daddy had whispered to Miss McKinney, but whatever it was, it seemed to make her nervous. At least Dru assumed that was why the lady's arm had jerked. *Boy, it must hurt to be hit in the stomach like that.*

183

Now they just stood there, looking at each other with big eyes. *Grown-ups sure are strange.* "Can I go shopping too?" Dru's voice reminded Brad and Kathlyn of her continued presence.

There they went again, jumping like frogs. At least they looked like frogs to Dru. Hitching Tandy over her shoulder, she whispered into the doll's ear, "They're weird."

"Of course you can go, darling." Relieved, Kathlyn smiled sweetly at the little girl. Surely she could control herself with Brad's daughter along. And who knows, maybe he could control himself too.

Nah, she thought. The woman or child has not been born who can make Brad Hampton be anything other than what he is, the sexiest man alive. *That* she might be able to resist; but combine all that raw sensuality with his old world chivalry and she feared she was a goner . . . every time.

"Daddy, what's a porte-jupe?" Dru whispered loudly.

Brad shrugged and murmured wryly, "I don't know, Peanut. Just listen, and I'm sure it will be explained shortly . . . and in great detail."

Sitting beside Brad and Dru on the sofa, Kathlyn had to bite her lower lip to keep from giggling. Standing in front of them, with enough false hair to build a french poodle, and wearing a peplum so covered in jet that a tornado couldn't budge her, Miss Scarlet Garibaldi was in her element.

If her animated lecture on Gothic versus Classical fashion hadn't been enough to amuse Kathlyn, Miss Garibaldi's name would have. Kathlyn remembered the *Garibaldi Jacket,* touted as "the gem of the season," when it first hit the fashion scene.

The fact that the much admired article of clothing had been scarlet cashmere with military trimmings of gold braid, caused her to wonder about the origin of the proprietress's name. Her name was Scarlet and her demeanor was not unlike that of the staunchest general.

"Now with your vivid complexion, my dear, you could wear any color. But in my professional opinion, I think you would be all the rage in the latest shade, bismarck."

With great flourish, Scarlet Garibaldi swept an elegant gown made of plum colored silk into her arms and spread it across Brad's lap. Pulling on the hem of the skirt, she held it next to Kathlyn's flushed face. "Don't you think Miss McKinney would be just too too in bismarck, Mr. Hampton?"

Brad's eyes teared with the control he exerted to keep from laughing aloud. Not trusting his voice, he merely nodded his head. Though she never made a sound, Brad could feel Kathlyn shaking with laughter at his side. They both would have been able to maintain control had it not been for Dru, who chose that moment to sniff royally and say, "Yes, too too."

When the laughter died down, Kathlyn realized that she and Brad obviously misunderstood each other in terms of her wardrobe. It appeared she hadn't made it clear that all she intended to purchase was a few mourning costumes.

As long as Scarlet had been chattering on about the purely Classical weapon, the peplum, becoming a Gothic addition to a dress with a few alterations, Kathlyn was comfortable. According to the verbose shopkeeper, with the addition of more points to the peplum, it becomes glorified vandyking, then if one bunches out the back garment, it becomes a polonaise. And of course, once it becomes a polonaise the Classical appearance is destroyed, and the garment is truly Gothic.

Kathlyn never doubted it.

All that was fine. Kathlyn didn't care if her gowns were Classic or Gothic, whether the garments sported vandyking or a polonaise . . . as long as they were black.

Naturally when Scarlet mentioned bismarck and produced that lovely gown, Kathlyn knew there had been a misunderstanding.

185

"Miss Garibaldi, if you would give us a moment, I need to speak with Mr. Hampton alone."

Scarlet gasped at the impropriety of Kathlyn's request. If word spread that two such attractive young people were left alone in the back room of her shop, well, she'd just never live it down.

Having no such reservations, Dru rose to her feet and pulled on the elaborate peplum that covered the woman's dress. "Come on Miss Baldy, me and Tandy want to see a porte-jupe."

The thought of having such an outmoded devise as a porte-jupe in her shop was far more abhorrent to the owner of the boutique than the possibility of a scandal in her back room. "My dear, I wouldn't have one in my shop. They are *passé* . . ."

Miss Garibaldi's lecture trailed off as she and Dru made their way to the front of the shop.

"What's the problem?" Brad questioned, though he already knew.

Kathlyn confirmed his suspicion. "Brad, you know I'll be in mourning for the next year. My uncle has just died. I can't wear bismarck, or any other color. For the next six months I'm required to wear black paramatta trimmed in crape, the three after that I'll be in black, and the final three, I might add violet or gray, but like the dress I have on, everything will be trimmed in black.

"The only reason I'm not in formal mourning now is that there wasn't time to have proper clothes made before we left Athens."

Brad looked at the agitated woman at his side, and realized once again the depth of love she possessed for her family. He could identify with that; he loved his family fiercely. But in his estimation love of family wasn't at issue here.

Really, whether Kathlyn chose black or vibrant colors wasn't uppermost in Brad's mind. Putting the painful past behind her was what he was trying to help her do. He just thought if she could abandon her mourning attire, it might be easier for her to

186

look ahead.

"Roth wouldn't want you in mourning," he began simply. When she would have objected, he held up his hand. "No, let me finish. The night of the party, I overheard a conversation between you and Roth. In that conversation, he told you to look to the future, not to the past."

"This was not what he was talking about." Kathlyn swept her hand forward, indicating the mounds of exquisite cloth all around her.

"I know. But I think his words apply, nonetheless. To wear mourning in memory of Roth, you have to look back. He wouldn't want you to do that."

Since their talk the day Roth died, Kathlyn knew her uncle had not been talking about looking back in general. He had been talking about the painful memories she had of her baby's death, her inability to forgive herself and Brad for that death. "You don't understand," she whispered softly.

Brad noted the tortured look in Kathlyn's eyes, the tears that sprang unbidden to the surface. The clothes were forgotten. "Explain it to me, Kat. Maybe I can help."

"You're the last person who can help." As soon as Kathlyn said the words, she knew they were untrue. In fact, the opposite was the case. Brad was the only person who could free her from the past, the only person who could heal her pain over the loss of their child. But at what risk?

"I don't suppose you want to explain that remark." Her unwillingness to open up to him caused more pain than he cared to admit. He bet she'd open up to her fiancé.

Kathlyn didn't see the jealousy in Brad's eyes as she looked down at the black-gloved hands clenched in her lap. After much soul searching, she realized she was not ready to deal with the distant past, but she had to make a decision about the present.

He was right. Roth would not want her in mourning any longer. He would want her to start her new life without negative trappings. Suddenly, her heart felt lighter than it had in ages.

"No, I don't want to explain that remark." Then she smiled and said, "You're right, though. Uncle Roth wouldn't want me to remain in mourning. If your kind offer of a loan still stands, I'll purchase a suitable wardrobe."

She winked impishly. "But I might need your advice."

At Brad's questioning look, she whispered, "The last thing I bought was a new Garibaldi jacket in '59."

"Need I ask the color?"

"Why scarlet, what else?"

The sound of laughter coming from the back room attracted Dru magnetically. Running from the front of the store, she flashed and sparkled, a dimpling, gilt genie. All over her dress she had pinned filigree silver and gold brooches of fantastic designs; ladders, saddles, bridles, birds, beetles, fish, flies, and croquet mallets.

The large gold bracelets that encircled her chubby arms jangled as she jumped into the midst of the two amused adults. Her daddy leaned over and planted a kiss on her cheek, barely avoiding being poked in the eye by a dangling earring. Instinctively, Dru passed the kiss on to Miss McKinney.

After a slight hesitation, the sweet-smelling lady hugged her close . . . just like her mama used to do.

188

Chapter Twenty-one

The pink wrapped packages began arriving about an hour before Kathlyn and Rachel were scheduled to join Brad in the hotel dining room for dinner. First the runners delivered the modest — but colorful — wardrobe Kathlyn had chosen.

Although the packages were yet unwrapped, she could well imagine what treasure each box contained. After giving the men a generous tip from the spending money Brad had pressed on her, she closed the door and began ripping the pink paper from the packages, not seeing the strange looks the men exchanged as the door slammed in their faces.

Moments later, a sharp rap on the door halted her progress. "Just a minute." It must be Brad, checking to see if everything arrived, she thought. Her heart began to beat a little faster.

She threw the door open wide. In addition to the two workers she had just dismissed, two others stood in the hallway. All four of Miss Garibaldi's delivery men were fairly weighted down with the now familiar packages. "What on earth?"

"The rest of your order, ma'am," the self-appointed spokesman of the group answered.

"There must be some mistake. I didn't order all that." Kathlyn gestured frantically.

"You'll have to take that up with Mr. Hampton, Miss McKinney. If you don't mind, we'd like to bring these things on in so that we can get the rest of your order."

"I've already told you, I have received all my purchases!" Kathlyn enunciated distinctly, but the men paid

189

her no mind. Instead, they pushed past her and deposited the merchandise wherever they could find an empty spot.

"There must be an error," Kathlyn repeated to herself, for all the good it did her. Obviously, the men just wanted to empty their wagon into her bedchamber, whether the things belonged to her or not.

Flopping down on the edge of the bed, she sat with her mouth agape. She had never seen so much merchandise at one time in her life. A princess wouldn't need a wardrobe of this magnitude.

As if to underscore the thought, the men returned, still laden with more. Then once more, until a very overwhelmed Kathlyn was all but lost in a sea of pink. This was how Brad found her.

Cautiously, he stepped through the open door. "Kathlyn," he called, not seeing her at first.

"Over here." Her voice was muffled. "On the bed."

Brad wound his way through the haphazardly stacked packages. Finally arriving at the bed, he mounted the dais upon which it sat. Nestled among the multi-sized boxes, Kathlyn peeked up at him. She looked so small, so bewildered. "Hope you're not allergic to pink," he teased, his thick voice betraying his emotion.

Kathlyn raised both hands, palms up. "Who could possibly wear all this?"

"You."

"Right!" she scoffed. "Even if I could afford it, I wouldn't need it. I doubt it would even fit on the stagecoach. Guess I'll have to open all these packages to discover what belongs to me and return the rest."

"It all belongs to you, so let's get started. Once everything is opened, I'll have a maid sent up to get you out of that mourning gown.

"You have to try everything on before you leave Memphis. That is, if you want Miss Garibaldi to make the necessary alterations." Turning away, Brad began ripping the paper and ribbon from the boxes closest to him.

Coming up on her knees, Kathlyn grabbed his arm.

190

As she whirled him toward her, she lost her balance and plopped over onto her back, maintaining her grip on his arm.

Surprised, he lost his footing. "What the hell!" With a loud thud, he fell on top of her. The mattress creaked and pink paper flew high into the air, returning to the bed in a flutter.

With great effort, she filled her lungs with air. "Brad Hampton, did you buy all this stuff?" She wheezed.

He angled up on his elbows and peered down into her face. Casting a meaningful glance at their intimate position, he raised a rakish brow. "A simple thank you would have sufficed. Not that I'm complaining." He smiled suggestively.

"You overbearing oaf. Get off of me!"

He didn't budge. "First you pull me into your bed, then you tell me to get off. Kat darlin', you're gonna have to make up your mind."

The murderous look in Kathlyn's eyes told Brad clearly he didn't want to hear what she had to say next. So he occupied her mouth.

Just as she parted her rosy lips to spit what no doubt would have been a fiery curse, he lowered his head, capturing her mouth. He placed his hands on either side of her head, holding her face still as he sipped lightly, then drank deeply of her sweet nectar. Risking grave injury, he slipped his tongue between her lips. Her sharp intake of breath reminded him she wasn't immune to his kiss.

But she hadn't surrendered completely yet. She thrashed her hips from side to side, attempting to dislodge him.

Her body brushing against his had a devastating effect. Brad moaned. "You've got to be still." Gritting his teeth, he fumbled with the clothes around his waist.

"Please get off, Brad. We can't do this," she whispered weakly. Kathlyn was frightened; her control was faltering and Brad's was obviously gone. Bucking her hips, she said again, "Please, don't. Please, get off of me."

"Just be still," he grunted, pulling at the front of her bodice now. "Dammit, Kathlyn, be still. I'm not going to hurt you." Brad raised his head. His expression was rigid with desire and something else. It looked as if he were angry with her. Pressing his lower body into Kathlyn, he arched his back, pulling first at his clothes, then at hers.

Kathlyn's eyes darkened with desire. The heat of Brad's tumescent member burned through her gown; his scalding gaze held her captive. This couldn't be happening. She couldn't give in to him. But she wanted him so desperately. Oh, why not? They were adults. And it wasn't like she was a virgin . . .

Groaning, she raised her head and pulled his face close to hers. Just before she captured his lips, she heard, "Miss Kathlyn, are you in here?"

Brad jumped as if he'd been shot. "We're over here, honey," he called hoarsely. Without looking at Kathlyn, he fumbled between their bodies. This time, he was successful; he unwound his watch chain from the last button on her bodice.

"I can't see you for the pink," Dru said, closer now.

"Up here, Peanut." Brad heard Kathlyn slip off the bed.

Dru edged her way toward the bed. Finally, she saw Miss McKinney's face peeking above a pile of boxes. Dru wondered why Kathlyn's cheeks were so red just as Kathlyn noticed that Dru's cheeks were so wet.

"Honey, you've been crying," Kathlyn exclaimed.

Brad met Dru at the edge of the dais. Kneeling to her eye level, he asked, "What's wrong, sweetlin'?"

Dru sniffed loudly. "Mammy's lying down." She wiped her runny nose with the back of her hand. "I think she's sick."

Drying her eyes with his handkerchief, Brad appeared completely calm. "I'm sure she's just fine."

He walked over to a velvet-covered chair and retrieved a large package. When he turned to Kathlyn her cheeks flamed again. He pretended not to notice. While all the other packages were tied with white ribbon, the box

192

O GET YOUR
4 FREE BOOKS
MAIL THE COUPON BELOW.

FREE BOOK CERTIFICATE

GET 4 FREE BOOKS

Yes! I want to subscribe to Zebra's HEARTFIRE HOME SUBSCRIPTION SERVICE. Please send me my 4 FREE books. Then each month I'll receive the four newest Heartfire Romances as soon as they are published to preview Free for ten days. If I decide to keep them I'll pay the special discounted price of just $3.50 each; a total of $14.00. This is a savings of $3.00 off the regular publishers price. There are no shipping, handling or other hidden charges. There is no minimum number of books to buy and I may cancel this subscription at any time. In any case the 4 FREE Books are mine to keep regardless.

NAME

ADDRESS

CITY _____ STATE _____ ZIP

TELEPHONE

SIGNATURE
(If under 18 parent or guardian must sign)
Terms and prices subject to change.
Orders subject to acceptance.

HF 107

GET 4 FREE BOOKS

HEARTFIRE HOME SUBSCRIPTION
SERVICE
P.O. BOX 5214
120 BRIGHTON ROAD
CLIFTON, NEW JERSEY 07015

Brad offered her was tied in lavender. "Go ahead. Take it. It won't explode."

He spoke softly, calmly to Dru, "We'd best run check on Mammy." Hand-in-hand, father and daughter left the room.

Once she was alone, Kathlyn regarded the present suspiciously. It was obviously something special. Brad's expression as he handed it to her told her that.

But suddenly the gift was unimportant. She fell heavily onto the velvet-covered chair. She was concerned about Mammy's health, Dru's tears, and Brad's distress over both. Without her knowledge, he and his family had become very important to her. That frightened her as nothing else could. Except perhaps her willingness to make love to him just before Dru interrupted them.

And he had only been trying to untangle his watch chain, she groaned aloud.

Chapter Twenty-two

When Dru and Brad returned to th
shared with Mammy Mae, the child's fa
awaited her. A tray of silver dishes fill
chicken, mashed potatoes, green beans,
two big pieces of coconut cake sat up
table beside the window. The table was se
Mammy Mae.

Dru ignored her dinner. She ran across
knocked on the closed door to Mamm
snuffling quietly. Brad's heart ached.

"Come in child."

Brad was alarmed. Never in his thirty-o
he heard his nanny's voice sound so we
the sitting room in two long strides, h
Mammy's open door and followed Dru in

Dru sat on the bed beside Mammy
wrong, Mammy? Are you sleepy?"

His daughter looked incredibly small
frightened. Although the room was dim,
that Mammy was ill. "Sweetheart, why
eat your dinner. I need to talk with Mam

Reluctantly, Dru walked from the room

"What's wrong, Mammy?" Brad asked
filled the kind old woman's eyes he w
alarmed; Mammy Mae had been the Ham
anchor as far back as he could remembe

"I'm just tuckered out is all. Don't yo
self. Soon as I rest up a minute, I'll go
eats all her supper."

"You'll do no such thing." The com

Brad's eyes softened his directive. "You're to stay right where you are. I'm going to get Miss McKinney to sit with Dru. Then I'll go get Alan."

Weakly, Mammy tried to rise from the bed. Gently, Brad prevented her from doing so. "Now you stay right there. You hear?" When Brad kissed his nanny's cheek, his tears mingled with her own.

Brad wiped his face with the back of his hand and walked from Mammy's room. He cleared his throat and smiled at his daughter. "I'll be back in a minute, Peanut. Will you listen out for Mammy while I'm gone?"

"I'll take care of her," Dru promised solemnly.

"Peanut, Miss McKinney is going to stay with you and Mammy while I go after the doctor."

Dru's pale blue eyes looked far too serious for a five year old, but Brad didn't have time to allay her fears. Not knowing how ill Mammy Mae was, he felt a sense of urgency.

"Don't worry, we'll be fine." Kathlyn handed him his hat and cane.

Brad nodded. "Thanks. I've just checked on Mammy and she's sleeping. I'll have to leave the hotel, but I won't be long." He dropped a kiss on Dru's tousled curls, settled his hat upon his head, and with a final look at Kathlyn, walked out the door.

Kathlyn was touched by the deep concern she had seen in Brad's eyes. It was obvious to her he was more than a little worried about Mammy Mae's health and his daughter's emotional state as well.

As was she. She latched the door behind Brad as Dru seated herself on one of the settees in the large suite. Crossing through the cavernous room, Kathlyn knelt in front of Dru. "What would you like to do, angel?" She smiled into Dru's upturned face, marveling again how like an ethereal being Brad's child truly appeared.

Dru shrugged. Her thoughts weren't entirely different

195

from Kathlyn's. She thought Miss Kathlyn looked pretty, dressed in the new gown she bought from Miss Baldy, like a beautiful angel, sitting on a plum-colored cloud. If she hadn't been so frightened for Mammy, she would have told her so.

"Did you finish your dinner?"

Dru nodded, yes.

"Are you sleepy?"

Dru shook her head, no.

Kathlyn wished she could get the child to talk. She recognized the look of fear and sadness on Dru's face all to well. Seeing such emotions on one of such tender years disturbed her.

Absently, Kathlyn wondered how many times in the past few years she herself had looked like that. She felt a great affinity with Dru. All of a sudden, helping the little girl grew into a need so intense Kathlyn had to grip the material of the settee to remain steady. Her voice didn't betray the depth of her emotion, however, when she asked mildly, "Would you like to tell me what's bothering you?"

Dru studied her seriously. Maybe if she told Miss Kathlyn her feelings, she wouldn't feel so afraid.

Pulling Tandy into her lap, Dru said hesitantly, "Tandy says Mammy's going to go to heaven like Mama and baby brother did."

"May I?" Kathlyn asked before she took Tandy into her arms. "Tandy, I know you must be very worried about Mammy Mae and I'm sorry." She smoothed Tandy's silky hair. "Why do you think she's going to heaven? Maybe she's just tired and needs to rest."

"Tandy says that when Aunt Melinda sent for the doctor, Mama and brother went to heaven. Then, when Papa got sick and the doctor came to see him, Papa went to heaven too." Dru turned imploring eyes on Kathlyn.

"Please don't let the doctor see Mammy. I know Daddy thinks the doctor can make Mammy well, but he wasn't home when they went to heaven." Tears welled in her eyes. "He doesn't know she'll go to

196

heaven if the doctor comes. I don't want Mammy to go away."

Kathlyn reached out and took Dru into her arms, Tandy trapped between their bodies. As she held the crying child, Kathlyn tried to make sense of what Dru had said.

She recalled from a conversation with Rachel that Dru's mother, infant brother, and grandfather had all died during the war while Jared was away. She surmised that with these exceptions, Dru had known of no one to care for her family when they were ill but Jared or her Papa. And to Dru, Jared was not a doctor, he was an uncle. And her grandfather was just that, a grandfather. In her childlike reasoning she thought people went to heaven when doctors came to see them, but they got well when Uncle Jared and Papa took care of them.

How could she comfort the child? Kathlyn wondered. Then she remembered a smitten doctor who had been fetched by a certain jealous man and smiled. Angling back on her heels, Kathlyn held Dru away from her by the shoulders. Though she addressed Tandy, she smiled into Dru's eyes. "Tandy, did you know that Dru's daddy brought a doctor to look at my sore side this afternoon?"

"Tandy didn't know." Dru was wide-eyed.

"Well he did. And I feel fine. I have no intention of going to heaven right now. I'm going to stay around and take care of Ishta and get to know you and Dru better."

Dru studied Kathlyn carefully. Satisfied that she looked healthy enough, she said honestly, "Tandy and I sure hope you don't go to heaven. You're nice." Then after a shy smile, she concluded, "You make Daddy smile a lot."

Kathlyn's heart warmed as she considered Dru's last words.

Dru yawned hugely. With the innocence of a child, she had accepted Kathlyn's reassurances without reservation. Now that she was calm, the long day had caught up with her. "Tandy's tired," she declared.

"Do you think she would like us to rock her to sleep?"

"Yes, ma'am. She said she'd like that." Dru slid off the sofa, tucked Tandy under her arm, grasped Kathlyn's hand, and led her to a bentwood rocker placed in front of the marble fireplace.

With pale pink organdy whispering against bismarck silk, the sleepy little girl and her rosy-cheeked doll settled into Kathlyn's lap. Dru was asleep before the chair had rocked three times.

Kathlyn's soft voice filled the room in song:

On a hill faraway, stood an old rugged cross, the emblem of suffering and shame. But I love that old cross, where the dearest and best, for a world of lost sinners was slain. I will cherish the old rugged cr . . .

"Mama," Kathlyn whispered brokenly. How many times had her mother held her in her arms, rocking her to sleep, singing that hymn with a pure, clear voice? Too many to count.

"Mama," she uttered again. Something she would never be. She would never sing the old hymns to her baby like her mother had sung to her. The old, familiar pain rose in her breast. Unconsciously, she tightened her grip on the child in her arms.

Dru shifted and snuggled closer. Tandy fell to the floor, but she didn't notice.

Kathlyn kissed Dru's forehead. She noted her action and wondered at it.

She had mixed emotions concerning Brad's child. Remembering that she could never have a baby of her own, she felt the need to withdraw from Dru, from the maternal feelings she brought out. For self preservation, she wanted to run as far and as fast as she could.

But it felt so good to hold her. To pretend for a moment that Dru belonged to her, as surely as if she had been born from her own body. Part of her wanted to stay right where she was, holding Brad's child for eternity. She was confused.

198

Beset by a myriad of emotions, one thing was clear. She realized how important both father and daughter were to her. They eased the void left by the passing of her own mother, softened the loss of her father and brothers. In a strange way they had become her family. And in such a short time . . .

A light rap on the door jolted Kathlyn from her poignant musings. Rising carefully, so as not to awaken Dru, she hurried over to the door. "Who is it?" she asked softly.

"Brad," a deep, masculine voice responded.

Half-holding, half-balancing Dru, she unlatched the door and stepped back for the men to enter.

Brad tossed his hat and cane on the glossy, cherry-wood secretary. "Here, she's almost as big as you are," he scolded softly, taking his daughter from Kathlyn's arms.

"Shh," she cautioned. Her arms and heart felt strangely empty when she surrendered the child to Brad. "Which one's her room?" Kathlyn gestured toward the three closed doors off the sitting room.

"The one on the right." Brad held Dru as if she weighed no more than a feather. "Be right back, Alan," he threw over his shoulder to the attractive man who had entered with him.

Kathlyn scarcely noticed the doctor, though she did wonder why Brad had not employed the hotel physician. She rushed ahead of him and opened the door he had indicated. Crossing over to the canopied bed, she pulled down the mint green counterpane and sheet. When Brad placed Dru in the center of the bed, they worked together in silence, unclothing her down to her blue-ribboned combination undergarments.

Kathlyn rushed to the front room and scooped Tandy up in her arms. When she returned to Dru's room, Brad was sitting on the edge of the bed, dwarfing it with his size. She bent around him to place the doll in the crook of Dru's arm. Ostensibly to accommodate her, he arched his back and braced himself with a warm hand placed firmly on her hip.

Kathlyn gasped and angled her head, staring into laughing brown eyes. She wondered at his playful mood, considering Mammy was lying in the next room, God knows how sick. She had no way of knowing that Brad had explained Mammy's symptoms to the doctor, and the excellent physician—his first-cousin, Alan Turner—had reassured him that Mammy's condition wasn't serious.

"Daddy." Dru rubbed her eyes with her fists as she came awake.

Brad chuckled when Kathlyn blushed. Throwing Kathlyn a sideways glance when she scampered away from the bed, he questioned Dru, "Were you playing possum?"

"No sir, but I think Tandy was."

Brad considered Tandy with mock seriousness. "I have no doubt that she was."

Dru squinted her eyes and searched the room for Kathlyn. Finding her, she smiled. "Daddy, did you bring the doctor?"

"Yes. And I'd better take him in to see Mammy." He leaned over and kissed Dru on both of her chubby cheeks. Automatically, he dropped a kiss on Tandy's cold face.

Kathlyn smiled.

"Night, night, Peanut. I love you."

Kathlyn's smile faded. The soft, husky way Brad said those last three words pierced her heart. It was more than she could gracefully witness, so she headed for the door.

"I love you, daddy. Miss Kathlyn," Dru called before Kathlyn could pass the threshold.

Kathlyn turned hesitantly. "Yes, sweetie?"

"You really won't go away? Will you?"

Kathlyn knew Dru referred to an untimely trip to heaven.

"No, I won't go away. You tell Tandy everything will be just fine."

Dru whispered into Tandy's ear, "Stop worrying. Miss Kathlyn said everything'll be fine."

200

Brad was more than intrigued. He turned to question Kathlyn, but she was gone.

"Would you like for me to leave the light turned low?"

"Please, sir. You know how scared Tandy is of the dark." Dru showed relief at her daddy's offer.

Brad's eyes swept the sitting room. Alan was standing patiently beside Mammy's door, his black doctor's bag in his hand. Kathlyn had taken her position beside the door to the outside hall, just waiting until Brad settled Dru to take her leave.

"Good night," she said to Brad.

"Please don't leave. I'll need to talk with you after Alan has seen Mammy."

Kathlyn nodded.

"What did he say? Is Mammy Mae all right?" Kathlyn asked Brad once they were alone.

"Would you mind stepping out onto the patio with me? I could use a smoke."

Kathlyn preceded Brad through the double glass door. The patio column felt cool against her back as she leaned on it in the shadows. Instinctively, she wrapped her arms around her waist in a self-protective gesture.

Brad propped a hip against the half-wall enclosing the patio, stretching his long legs in front of him. When he struck a match against the column within inches of Kathlyn's shoulder, she tensed.

"Bit skittish tonight, aren't you?" The hint of amusement in his tone was meant to be deceptive. The light flooding through the open door lit his face. A night-black lock of hair fell across his brow, making him appear almost young and carefree, but not quite. "About earlier, in your room . . ."

"Please, let's not speak of that," she interrupted him. "It was a misunderstanding. That's all."

Kathlyn was so embarrassed she could barely speak. He had been trying to untangle his watch chain, and she had assumed he was molesting her. And how had she reacted? She had tried to kiss him, for heaven's sake. She stifled a groan. It was a blessing she was standing in the shadows, so Brad couldn't see the color staining her cheeks.

"Why did you fight me so? Did you really think I would hurt you, Kat?"

"Fight you? As I recall, I didn't fight you nearly enough."

Brad's lips spread into a satisfied grin. The memory of Kathlyn's pitiful pleas had hurt his pride. They had almost made him forget her final capitulation.

"Well you needn't look so pleased with yourself," Kathlyn snapped.

"Sorry." He chuckled. Brad tossed his cheroot over the balcony, then stepped forward and laid his hand alongside her jaw.

"No you're not," she whispered, leaning toward him instinctively.

"Well, maybe not too much." He grinned.

"It's just a good thing that we'll be saying goodbye soon, Brad Hampton. Or else I'd make a fool of myself good and proper."

Kathlyn surprised both herself and Brad with her honesty.

"That's what I wanted to talk with you about."

"What? Making a fool of myself?" she quipped, hoping to cool the romantic moment.

"No"—he paused—"about saying goodbye."

Kathlyn stiffened. Had the riverboat arrived to take Brad and his daughter away? Or perhaps he'd received word on the Butterfield stage. Would she and Rachel be leaving soon? Now that the time had come she hoped she had the courage to bid Brad goodbye without embarrassing them both.

"The *Robert E. Lee* docked tonight. We'll be leaving Memphis the day after tomorrow. And . . ."

Kathlyn closed her eyes. So it was goodbye. In less

202

than forty-eight hours Brad would walk out of her life again. With white-knuckled fists clenched at her sides, she was determined to handle this well.

"And?" she invited him to continue.

"And . . . I want you to come with me."

Chapter Twenty-three

"You what?"

Was Brad saying what she thought, what she desperately hoped? Despite their past association, with all its pain and disappointment, in that instant, Kathlyn knew if Brad asked her to go with him—anywhere, anytime, for as long as he wanted—she would not turn him down.

Strange musings perhaps for an engaged woman; but Glenn Crutchfield was as far away from Kathlyn's mind as the stars shining in the black velvet above.

Such was not the case with Brad; Kathlyn's fiancé was a grave concern to him. As much as he wanted to ask Kathlyn to go with him—to stay with him, forever—he couldn't get past the fact that she was promised to another. Not just yet.

Oh hell! Maybe if he could keep her with him a while longer, he would find a way to satisfy his inconvenient sense of honor. He sincerely hoped so.

"Will you and Rachel travel with me and Dru on the *Robert E. Lee* instead of going by stage?" He modified his request for the time being.

Kathlyn's face fell. To be offered her heart's desire, only to have it snatched from her grasp hurt more than she wanted Brad to know. More than she cared to admit, even to herself.

"Why would we want to do that?" she asked coolly.

Her change of mood was fairly tangible. Supposing she was reluctant to spend more time with him than necessary, Brad launched his sales-pitch. "Mammy will be staying behind with my cousin here in Memphis. I need someone on the boat to help me take care of Dru, and she *is* fond of you.

"Also, traveling by steamboat is a sight more comfortable than bouncing around in a coach for hundreds of miles. I thought Rachel would appreciate that," he said this last wryly, slipping his hands in his front pockets.

"And you won't need to reimburse me for the clothes. If you'll accept the position as Dru's governess, we'll call it even when we reach Fort Smith. I figured you'd rather have a job than a loan. A loan that size would take forever to repay." He rocked back on his heels, waiting for her response. Her expression revealed nothing; she appeared completely composed. Like a porcelain doll. Untouched.

Nothing could be further from the truth. She was crushed. It was a business deal, pure and simple. Brad didn't really care for her, not like she cared for him; his impersonal offer told her that.

If she had listened to his anxious tone rather than his actual words, however, she would have been encouraged. But she didn't; all she heard was a man offering her employment, not the love she so desperately craved.

She drew a deep, cleansing breath. If not for Dru, Kathlyn would turn him down flat; her pride demanded it. But Dru had become very important to her.

"I don't think I should commit myself without talking to Rachel first. But I can assure you of one thing, Mr. Hampton; if I decide to forego your generous offer of a job"—she drawled sarcastically—"I *will* repay your loan. And it *won't* take me forever." Her face no longer blank, she was the picture of stiff-necked pride in the extreme.

Oh hell! Couldn't the woman see that hiring her as Dru's governess was just an excuse to keep her with him? Did he have to spell it out for her? Maybe he should just show her. Honor be damned. Kissing her was a lot easier than talking to her. And it was a hell of a lot more fun.

Sensing his intent, Kathlyn stepped back. "I'd best return to my room now."

"Wait." He grabbed her arm as she rushed past him. "I thought you wanted a report on Mammy Mae."

The slow heat of embarrassment began at her toes and traveled upward to her hairline, dragging a telling red veil with it. She had been so distracted by her own problems, she'd forgotten that Mammy was sick. "Is she very ill?" Her arm trembled in his grasp.

"No, thank God. Alan said she's just worn out. Nobody knows for sure how old Mammy is. She's suffering from old age and a wicked case of rheumatism. Her blood pressure is sky high, her heart rate isn't the best either." Giving the report on Mammy sobered Brad.

"Oh Brad, I'm so sorry." Kathlyn covered the hand still holding her forearm with her own. Her genuine concern for Mammy Mae chased her maudlin musings away.

"Yes, me too," he said huskily, releasing her and turning away.

Not wanting her to see the depth of his emotion, he walked over to the edge of the patio. To have to admit that Mammy could no longer care for the Hamptons was hard on him. She had been a part of his family for as long as he could remember.

His mother, Lysette, had died when he was very young. The night his sister, Lacy, was born, his father, Adam, had delivered the squalling child and placed her into Mammy's waiting arms. Tears from Mammy's big black eyes had fallen onto Lacy's slick curls as Mammy stood and watched Lysette's life drain away.

It was Mammy who had told him and his brothers their mother was gone; their father had been too overcome with grief. As a frightened little boy, it was only natural that Brad had sought what Mammy Mae so readily offered—herself as a surrogate mother. And now he had to leave her behind. For the time being . . .

"Does she know she'll be staying in Memphis?" Kathlyn asked.

Still standing with his back to her, Brad answered softly, "Yes."

"Is she terribly upset?"

Brad shook his head. "She understands."

"Why can't she return to Georgia?"

"Alan said the trip would be too hard on her. At least for a while. But she'll be well cared for. Until she's able to go home." He was silent for a moment.

"Alan's mother, my Aunt Jean, will be with her. Mammy Mae has been with my mother's family since mother and Aunt Jean were children. Aunt Jean and Alan's wife, Lindsey, will take good care of her," his voice trailed off.

Kathlyn wished Brad would turn around so she could see his expression. She knew it hurt to say goodbye to someone you loved, and Brad obviously loved Mammy Mae very much. She wanted to comfort him. Cautiously, she reached out and placed her hand on his shoulder. "Is there anything I can do?"

Slowly, he turned and took her hand in his. "There is something. I'll need to be out all day tomorrow, getting Mammy settled and taking care of some business. I hate to ask it . . . since you haven't decided if you're going to accept the position as Dru's governess or not . . . but do you think you could keep her occupied for the day?" He ran his unoccupied hand through his hair, then touched her cheek lightly. "Leaving Mammy behind is going to be hard on her."

She grasped his hand and squeezed. "Of course I'll take care of Dru."

"I would really appreciate it. I'll bring her to your room in the morning around eight?"

Kathlyn nodded.

Together, they stood, beneath the summer sky,

hands clasped, eyes locked, mesmerized by each other and the quiet moment.

"It's late," she said finally, breaking the spell. "I suppose I should say good-night." She stood for another moment, staring up into his shadowed face. When he didn't respond, she whispered, "And Brad, I'd be honored to accept the job as Dru's governess." Standing on her tiptoes, she touched her lips to the dimple in his cheek. Then she dropped his hand and hurried away.

Touching the slight indentation where Kathlyn's lips had been, Brad breathed deeply.

"Where have you been?"

"Rachel," Kathlyn gasped, her hand at her throat. "You frightened the life out of me. I didn't expect you." Moving further into the darkened room, she searched the side table for the lamp and matches. Hands still trembling from her interlude with Brad, she was unable to strike the match.

"Here, let me do that," Rachel snapped, jerking the matches from Kathlyn's hands.

"Thank you," Kathlyn murmured, hurt by Rachel's tone.

The bedchamber burst to light.

"I asked you where you've been."

"Mammy Mae took sick and Brad asked me to come sit with Dru while he went for the doctor. Then I had to wait until after the examination because Brad needed to talk with me after the doctor left," she explained quietly.

"I'll just bet he did."

Kathlyn heard the bitterness in Rachel's voice. "What's wrong, Rachel? Are you angry with me?" Then, she remembered.

"Oh goodness, we were supposed to meet you for dinner, weren't we? I'm terribly sorry. We were so worried about Mammy Mae, we just forgot all about it."

"You were so worried about that old black woman that you left me sitting in a drafty dining room for hours?" Rachel affected a wounded look.

Actually, she had not waited in the dining room for seconds, let alone hours. She hadn't even gone down to dinner. She was just playing on Kathlyn's guilt to maintain control of her. And she, had to have absolute control of Kathlyn; otherwise Brad would get the upper hand to the tune of one hundred thousand dollars. Rachel's eyes darkened at the prospect.

Kathlyn wasn't certain if it was hurt or disgust written on Rachel's face. Whatever the cause, she was in a lather. But Kathlyn was getting tired of buckling under. One could only make excuses for a person for so long, then it got tiresome, very tiresome indeed. "You mustn't be unkind about Mammy. She's very ill, you know. In fact, she won't be going on with us to Fort Smith."

"With *us?*" Rachel asked suspiciously, not missing the independent tone of Kathlyn's voice and not liking it a bit.

Kathlyn could have bitten off her runaway tongue. Given Rachel's odd mood, she didn't relish the idea of telling her there had been a change in plans. Well, there was no help for it. "Brad has asked us to accompany him and Dru on the steamboat to Fort Smith. I would be going as Dru's governess, of course."

"Do you mean to tell me we're going to have to baby-sit that brat all the way through Arkansas? No thank you! You can just count me out."

Kathlyn stiffened at the slur on Dru. "Not we . . . me," she repeated. "Brad has asked *me* to be Dru's governess. All you have to do is come along. It will be a lot more comfortable traveling by steamboat than by stage."

When Kathlyn unwittingly repeated Brad's most effective argument, her voice lost its uncharacteristic edge. Now was not the time to assert her independence, not if she wanted Rachel to come along. If

Rachel refused, she would have to say goodbye to Brad, and she couldn't bear to do that.

Yet, she couldn't abandon Rachel either. No matter how tedious she could be.

Rachel suspected that Kathlyn would follow Brad to the ends of the earth if need be. Well, she would have to follow along with her. Stuart would no doubt have apoplexy when he learned of the change in plans, but that was his problem. Although after the sexual acrobatics she had planned for him tomorrow night, he should be more malleable. She'd just wait 'til their carnal deed was done — at least once — before she told him that she and Kathlyn weren't taking the stage as planned.

"All right," Rachel said begrudgingly.

"Wonderful," Kathlyn enthused. Crossing over to a massive armoire, she opened the door.

When Rachel saw the exquisite wardrobe Brad had purchased for Kathlyn, she all but choked. "Where did that come from?"

Kathlyn pulled a white lawn nightdress from the back of the chest. It was so delicate, it looked as if it were made of angels' wings. Rachel burned with envy.

"From Miss Scarlet Garibaldi's boutique," she answered. "My valise was stolen, with all my clothes. My money, too. Brad was kind enough to advance me the cost of a proper wardrobe.

"So you see, I have to be Dru's governess now. I could never repay him otherwise." Stepping behind a white lacquered screen she began undressing.

"I imagine he could think of something," Rachel muttered. Brad was putting out a great deal of money for Kathlyn. It would be up to her to see that he got nothing in return for his investment.

"Did you say something?" Kathlyn pulled the gown over her head.

"I said I'll be out tomorrow evening." Rachel paused at the door to the hallway.

"Well, don't stay out too late. The boat leaves

210

bright and early the next morning. We wouldn't want to miss it."

Kathlyn was a little too cheerful to suit Rachel's taste. She hadn't even balked at the idea of Rachel going out unescorted. She really must be smitten.

Enjoy it while you can. Because when Stuart and I finish with lover-boy, there won't be enough of him left to enjoy.

When Kathlyn circled the screen, Rachel was gone.

Chapter Twenty-four

Brad leaned against the doorjamb to Kathlyn's room, enjoying the sight before him. Lying side by side on their stomachs, a book open in front of them, Kathlyn and Dru were giggling to beat the band. Kathlyn could hardly read, she was laughing so hard.

You are old Father William, the young man said,
And your hair has become very white;
And yet you incessantly stand on your head—
Do you think, at your age, it is right?

Dru gathered her legs beneath her, balancing on all fours. Then she placed the top of her cap covered head on the floor and attempted to mimic Father William. Kathlyn cast her a sideways glance, propped her up with a hand to the rear, and continued to read.

In my youth, Father William replied to his son,
I feared it might injure the brain;
But, now that I'm perfectly sure I have none,
Why, I do it again and again.

Dru toppled over onto her back as their laughter rang out. Kathlyn leaned over her and tickled Dru until they were both breathless. Tears of mirth magnified their eyes and hung precariously on their damp lashes.

"Who has no brain?"

"Daddy!" Dru squealed, running over to Brad. "Come see the book Miss Kathlyn bought me."

Dru dragged her daddy into the room by the hand. "Alice is talking to a caterpillar and he talks back. Can you find me a caterpillar like that, Daddy?"

"Kathlyn." Brad nodded and smiled down into Kathlyn's face.

Kathlyn smiled her welcome and smoothed her new skirts nervously. Earlier when she'd dressed in her new lavender day gown, she had imagined just how she would pose when Brad saw her in it for the first time.

Perhaps she would stand in front of the window, she had thought, with the sunlight creating a glow around her. Or maybe she would lounge in a chair, with a copy of Shakespeare's love sonnets lying open on her lap, allowing her apple green petticoat to peek from beneath the braided hem of her dress.

Of all the poses she had imagined, however, lying on the floor on her stomach, giggling like a mindless ninny was not one of them. Her cheeks warmed.

"What have you got there?" Brad asked when Kathlyn didn't speak.

"Alice's Adventures in Wonderland! By Lewis Carroll." She was almost shy. Why she felt so self-conscious in Brad's presence all of a sudden, Kathlyn didn't know. Maybe it was the way he was looking at her, as if he were reliving their tender moment on the balcony.

"It has a little girl in it, with yellow hair. Just like me," Dru interjected excitedly, pulling on her daddy's hand. "And a white rabbit with pink eyes. And he talks, and he wears clothes, and he has a watch." She giggled and held her side. "Do you think you could find me a rabbit like that, Daddy? And a talking caterpillar. Please don't forget the caterpillar."

"Whoa, Peanut. If you don't calm down, you're going to take flight."

"Daddy, little girls can't fly," she scoffed, covering a giggle with her dimpled hand.

213

Brad arched a brow at Kathlyn. "But caterpillars and rabbits can talk?"

"Of course they can." Kathlyn held the leather-covered volume out to Brad. "It says so, right here."

Dru smiled at Kathlyn conspiratorially.

"Yes, well, guess I'm like Father William. I don't have a brain. But I do have presents for both of you in our suite."

"Goodie, let's go." Dru was out the door in an instant, headed for her room.

"Shall we?" he asked, offering Kathlyn his arm.

"By all means . . . Father William." Kathlyn smiled as she placed her hand in the crook of Brad's arm.

He laughed. "Maybe I shouldn't give you your present after all," he threatened, standing very still, very close.

"Oh no you don't. You can't get a woman's hopes up and then disappoint her."

The intimate turn of the conversation was as stimulating to Brad as the sweet scent of gardenias rising from Kathlyn's hair. "I would never want to disappoint you."

"I know you wouldn't. Just as I want very much to please you."

Brad lowered his head toward Kathlyn's. She parted her lips slightly in anticipation of the kiss to come.

"Daddy, hurry. I can't find my surprise!" Dru called from down the hallway.

"Remind me to strangle that child," he groaned facetiously.

"Daddy," Dru called again.

"Lord, the other guests are gonna call the footpads to me if she keeps yelling like that." With Kathlyn in tow, Brad quit the room. Both were still warmed by their brief, yet promising encounter.

Darkness had fallen when Rachel slipped out of the hotel and made her way down Union Street toward Stuart's hotel. A heavy fog hovered in the air, making

214

the street lanterns mere smudges of gold in the thick gray soup.

A mournful whistle from a barge sounded in the distance. A movement to her left caught Rachel's attention. She pulled her Norwich shawl tight across her bosom and jerked her head in that direction.

"Damn cat," she hissed, kicking at a rail-thin tabby as it ran across her magenta satin slippers.

She hurried on her way and cursed Stuart in her mind. Why in heavens name he couldn't take a room in a decent part of town, she didn't know. Once he left Georgia, he seemed to flourish in seedy, out of the way dives like the Memphis Bell.

Well, if he intended to take her to California with him—which he had promised—he would have to change his habits. She liked traveling first class, like she did when she was with Brad. And she wasn't about to shed her newly acquired addiction for the finer things of life now.

By the time she finished her silent declaration, Rachel had gone three blocks down Union Street, crossed to South Street, and finally turned right on River Front Street.

When she arrived at the Memphis Bell it was worse than she'd expected. The outside of the hotel looked as if it hadn't seen a coat of paint since the Revolutionary War; inside was just as bad. The foyer was grimy, leading to a set of batwing doors beyond which was a noisy saloon, and, no doubt, the obligatory bordello.

Sitting behind a scarred wooden counter, the clerk looked as if he hadn't seen a bar of soap or a razor since Christmas. When he leered at Rachel his scum-coated teeth told her he was acquainted with tooth powder and brush even less than he was with soap and water.

Tilting her nose skyward, Rachel flounced toward the stairs leading to the private rooms. Perched on the bottom step she turned on the clerk to find him still staring at her. "What are you looking at, imbecile? Haven't you ever seen a lady in this dump before?"

"Nope. And still ain't."

Rachel muttered an oath, then continued her climb. The hallway upstairs was dimly lit by a lantern at each end. Faded paper was all but falling from the walls, she noted with disgust as she found room 207.

She pulled her watch from her waist pocket. It was 8:15, a quarter of an hour later than Stuart's missive had instructed her to arrive. Not wanting to be subservient to him in any way, she was purposefully late. After a moment's hesitation, during which time she caught her breath, Rachel knocked on the door.

Stuart cracked the door and peered out into the dimly lit hall. When he saw Rachel, he swung the door wide. "You're late," he growled.

"I'm a busy woman," Rachel said haughtily, sweeping into the room. "I can't jump every time you say frog." She crossed over to the bed in the center of the room and jerked her mantle from her shoulders, tossing it over the headboard.

Stuart stood and gaped at Rachel. "Dear God, you make a man pray for cataracts. Those colors you're wearing and that red hair of yours is enough to blind me."

"What's wrong with these colors?" Rachel drew herself up, smoothing her hand down the front of her striped magenta and bois de rose gown. "And you're one to talk about a person's appearance," she huffed, pointing to his long, bushy hair and dark, tattered clothes.

"What have you got on your head?" he continued as if she hadn't spoken.

"Are you referring to my bonnet or my coiffure?" She leveled her indignant gaze on him.

"A bonnet. So that's what you call it?"

Rachel was incensed. She had paid good money for her headgear. Actually, she'd paid good money for her coiffure too, but Stuart didn't have to know that.

She was sensitive that her hair was thinning. She had hoped the neat row of false curls that she'd fastened on her head, creating a chignon à martreaux, looked

216

natural. She also hoped they stayed attached, when she thrashed about in Stuart's disheveled bed with him.

As for her bonnet, it was very chic. It sported a spray of briar and small dog roses, with gold leaves trailing behind her left ear; she wouldn't lower herself to defend it. "Did you call me here to criticize my appearance, or was there another reason?" she asked sarcastically.

Stuart was distracted as Rachel intended. "There's been a change in plan," he said unceremoniously, throwing himself down on the end of the bed.

Rachel searched Stuart's face suspiciously.

"Since you don't seem to be able to get rid of Brad Hampton, I've decided not to wait 'til we reach Fort Smith. I'm going to overtake the Butterfield tomorrow and kidnap Kathlyn early."

Actually, Stuart's plan had changed more than he let on. He would kidnap Kathlyn early all right, but he had no intentions of turning her over to slave traders. He intended to keep her for himself. His plans for Rachel were different too. He dropped his gaze, concealing a predatory look.

"You what?" Rachel ground out. And she had worried that Stuart would be angry when she told him of *their* change in plans . . .

"I have changed my plans. I am kidnapping Kathlyn early," he enunciated.

Rachel was furious that Stuart had made such a weighty decision without consulting her. And she was more than a little suspicious of his refusal to meet her eyes. "Well, you had best change them again because Kathlyn and I are not taking the Butterfield stage tomorrow. We're sailing with Brad on the *Robert E. Lee*," Rachel threw in his face.

Stuart came uncoiled. All he could think of was Kathlyn in Brad's arms, the Hamptons besting him again. Crossing the room in two long strides, he backhanded Rachel across the face.

She tasted blood in her mouth, causing a hot, heavy, surge of sensation to rush to her loins.

Through a red sea of rage, Stuart saw desire flashing in her eyes. His body reacted instinctively. Grabbing her low bodice in his fist, he slung her in an arc, tossing her onto his bed like a doll of rags. A huge man, he mashed her into the mattress as he fell full length upon her.

Looking into Stuart's visage was like staring into the face of hell. His hair was wild around his massive shoulders. Fire flashed from his pale blue eyes; rage in them giving him the appearance of a madman. Fear and the desire for violence rose high in Rachel's breast, arousing her to the point of agony.

Snarling and ripping, Stuart divested Rachel of the costume she had so carefully donned an hour earlier. Once she was bare, he reached between their bodies and freed his angry member. Making an animal sound low in his throat he thrust into her. The sound of flesh pounding flesh, coupled with vile curses filled the tiny cubicle of room 207.

It was over as quickly as it began. Once dressed, Stuart crossed over to a broken table that was propped against the wall. He opened the bottle of bourbon atop the table, poured himself a glassful, and tossed it off in one long gulp.

"We have to get rid of Brad," Rachel said as she dressed.

Stuart turned on her. "Tell me something I don't know."

She ignored his sarcasm. "The boat's first stop, after leaving Memphis, is a small town called Arkansas Post. If I can arrange for Brad to leave the boat and go into town alone, do you think you can go ahead of him and arrange a fatal accident?"

"I don't see any problem. But how are you going to get him off the boat and into town?"

"That's my concern. You just do your job; and I'll do mine."

Stuart's analytical mind rushed ahead. With Brad out of the way he would allow Kathlyn and Rachel to travel on to Fort Smith. Once there, he would appear

218

to follow the original plan to the letter. The only change would be that, once they reached California, he would sell Rachel along with the girls Glenn and the others had kidnapped. And he would leave, Kathlyn in tow.

Shrugging at his continued silence, Rachel rose to take her leave. "Since you didn't offer me a drink, I'll take mine with me." She picked up the bottle of bourbon.

"My humble pardon, your royal highness." Stuart sketched a mocking bow.

Without another word, Rachel slipped out the door, closing it firmly behind her. Before she descended the stairs, she removed a small green bottle from her reticule and poured some of its contents into the whiskey. Her nose wrinkled at the unpleasant smell of garlic. She swirled the liquid until the white powder was dissolved and the garlic smell was overcome by the pungent scent of Kentucky bourbon.

Replacing the cork, she descended the stairs and approached the counter. "I think I was a little rude to you when I came in," she drawled to the clerk, batting her lashes. "Here's a peace offering, to show you how a real lady comports herself." She handed him the bottle of liquor.

He grabbed the bottle from her hand and hooted, "How would you know how a real lady acts?"

Clenching her teeth so hard her jaw ached, Rachel headed for the exit. Just before she pushed through the door, she looked over her shoulder. The clerk already had the cork off the bottle and was guzzling its contents.

A genuine smile lit Rachel's face as she stepped out into the still, gray night.

Chapter Twenty-five

Brad and Dru were waiting for Kathlyn in the lobby just outside the dining room. Dru was engaged in animated conversation with a dark-haired child named Millie Shelby. Brad was becoming acquainted with Millie's father, Jacob.

The Shelbys would also be traveling on the *Robert E. Lee* to Fort Smith; Dru and Millie were thrilled. The energetic twosome wiggled and squirmed on the sofa beside Brad, all the while trying to behave like the proper young ladies their parents had reared them to be. It was a losing proposition. They were just too excited, thinking of all the fun they would have on their exciting journey.

Brad lounged on the wine velvet sofa; Jacob perched in a mauve and cream striped wing chair at his side. Both men talked softly, sipped tall, frosty drinks, occasionally gave their respective daughters an indulgent look, and awaited their female dinner companions.

Millie's mother, Hannah, was a sturdy young woman with a kind face. She arrived ahead of Kathlyn. After introductions were made, the Shelbys went in to dinner, the children promising to share dessert later.

"Daddy, where is Miss Kathlyn?" Dru asked impatiently.

"She'll be down in a minute, Peanut. It takes ladies a bit longer to dress than it does men."

"But I'm a lady, and I'm already dressed."

Brad's dimple deepened. "I know, but Miss Kathlyn helped you dress before she went back to her room. Remember?"

"Oh yes. I forgot." Absently, she kicked her feet

back and forth, banging her black patent leathers on the sofa.

The long day was taking its toll on Dru and Brad feared his daughter might well fall asleep in her mashed potatoes. "Do you like your new locket?" he asked, hoping to distract her until Kathlyn arrived.

"It's wonderful, daddy." She fingered the tiny filigree pendant circling her neck. "What does the writing say?"

Brad took the piece of jewelry between his thumb and forefinger and turned it over so he could see the back. For the third time since he'd given the gift to Dru, he read: " 'I love you, Peanut. Daddy' "

Dru smiled as if she had never heard the inscription before. Brad returned her smile. It didn't take a great deal to please his daughter. That was one of her traits he found most endearing. Remembering Kathlyn's exuberant reaction when he presented her a locket of her own, his smile widened.

"Does Miss Kathlyn's necklace have writing too?"

"Uh huh." Brad nodded.

"What does it say?"

The sound in the room grew hushed and Brad raised his gaze. His heart accelerated.

Like a vision come to life, Kathlyn floated down the staircase. She was dressed in an Isabeau-style gown of white glacé, the overskirt of spangled net, flounced and ruched, a simple gold locket nestled between her breasts. Looking like nothing so much as a fairy princess, she captured every eye in the room as she walked toward Brad.

Brad rose and met her halfway across the lobby. "You're beautiful," he whispered honestly, bringing her hand to his lips.

"Hello, Miss Kathlyn," Dru greeted, joining them.

"Hello, sweetie."

As if given a second wind, Dru launched into a long discourse, telling Kathlyn about her newfound friend. Brad stood to the side, enjoying the enthusiastic sound of his daughter's voice, yet mesmerized by Kathlyn.

Surreptitiously, Kathlyn drank in the sight of him. She hoped she nodded and smiled in all the right places, but truth to tell she could scarcely concentrate on Dru's monologue when confronted by Brad Hampton in formal wear. He looked just as he had long ago, on their night of gardenias.

In his well-tailored black evening suit, blindingly white shirt, pearl-gray waistcoat and matching cravat, he was absolutely devastating. From the top of his neatly combed hair to the toes of his shiny black slippers, he was male perfection. Succumb-to-the-vapors-gorgeous. With shoulders as wide as the horizon, he all but blocked the world from Kathlyn's view.

Almost, but not quite. Her brow furrowed. Peeking around his right shoulder, she saw a breathtaking child-woman standing beside a distinguished looking gentleman in a white military uniform. It was obvious the girl shared her glowing assessment of Brad. Much to Kathlyn's dismay.

Bristling, she wondered who they were. As if her thoughts drew them, the couple bore down upon them.

"Mr. Hampton," the officer greeted Brad when Dru finally stopped for a breath of air.

"Sir?" Brad turned.

"Good evening. I'm Jake Spivey, captain of the *Robert E. Lee*. I understand that you and your family will be traveling with us."

"Yes." Brad shook the beefy paw Captain Spivey presented him. The man certainly didn't look like a riverboat man to Brad. He looked more like a pastry chef. A pastry chef who was his own best customer.

Though short and dumpy, the captain held himself in just such a way, giving the appearance of one born to lead. He sported a thick beard of salt and pepper whiskers below wire-rimmed glasses. His eyes were accented with fine lines, no doubt the result of squinting against the sunlight that reflected off the Mississippi.

The gold buttons that fastened his coat in front were pulled slightly to one side, in order to reach their sockets. Brad swore he could almost hear the shiny discs and stretched holes groan with the effort.

In the few seconds it took Brad to measure the captain, Kathlyn did the same with the beautiful young woman at his side. The girl appeared to be in her late teens or perhaps just the other side of twenty. She wore the single most revealing gown Kathlyn had ever seen. Made of scarlet watered-silk, it hugged her curvaceous form like a glove. The decolletage was so daring that Kathlyn feared the girl would spill forth in their faces if she weren't careful.

And the enraptured look on the girl's face as she stared at Brad wasn't lost on Kathlyn either. Given her own quixotic musings about Brad, however, Kathlyn understood. Still, she didn't like it.

Placing his hand on the girl's bare shoulder, Captain Spivey said proudly, "This is my daughter, Jill. She's traveling with me for the first time in three years."

Brad nodded politely. When he bowed over Jill's extended hand, her eyelashes fluttered wildly.

"Mr. Hampton," she greeted in a low, husky voice, stepping closer to Brad than Kathlyn thought necessary.

Brad felt Kathlyn stiffen at his side. Slipping a finger inside his collar, he cleared his throat. "May I introduce my daughter, Dru, and Miss Kathlyn McKinney."

Dru curtsied to the newcomers, and Kathlyn extended her hand for the captain to bow over. "Your companions are lovely, Mr. Hampton." The ruddyfaced man winked at Dru and Kathlyn.

"I certainly think so."

Dru's stomach rumbled. "Pardon me, daddy. But I am ever so hungry." She was striving to act like a lady, but all this standing around was getting tiresome.

"Me too, Peanut. If you'll excuse us Captain, I believe our table is ready. A pleasure, Miss Spivey." He inclined his head in a slight bow.

"Mind if we join you?" Jill asked brazenly.

"Marvelous idea," the Captain boomed. "And on the *Lee* you all will dine at my table."

Brad nodded graciously. "Lead the way." He gestured. His strained smile turned genuine when he heard Kathlyn mutter, "Oh goodie."

The formal dining room was awe-inspiring. The floor was pastel marble; the walls were covered with matching silk paper. The ceiling was decked with exquisite chandeliers, all cocoon-shaped fixtures formed by hundreds of crystal tear drops. Suspended by brass chains, each one was a different pastel hue; violet, mauve, peach, lemon, azure, and pink.

The colored light cast dancing shadows on sheer curtains that fluttered in front of a dozen pairs of open French doors. At the far end of the room, elegantly clad belles and beaux mimicked the movement of the light as they whirled on a raised dance floor to the strains of a Viennese waltz.

To Kathlyn the entire effect was like a scene from a *romantic* novel. And all this beauty belonged to Brad. Walking proudly at his side, it took conscious effort to keep from gaping like a thunderstruck bumpkin. Somehow she managed.

As for Brad and Dru, they barely noticed their opulent surroundings. That much was obvious to Kathlyn. She could see that they were at home here. It was as if a life of wealth and privilege was all they had ever known, as if it had been served to them on a silver platter. But Kathlyn knew that wasn't the case. Brad had worked hard for everything he had, and she admired him for it.

There was a time when she would have despised him for the ease with which he went through life, never wanting for anything. But no more. Now she could no more despise Brad and his family for their wealth, than she could despise others for their poverty. Quite a change in attitude since that day in the bank, when Simon and Dunn tried to cheat her.

"Your place is here beside me," Brad murmured to Kathlyn, stopping at the head of a linen-covered table. Once he'd seated her on his right, he allowed his hand to brush the nape of her neck. A hot flow of sensation skittered down her spine. When she trembled,

Brad motioned to a liveried servant. "Please close the doors. Miss McKinney is chilled."

Kathlyn wanted to tell Brad she was enjoying the light breeze, but to do so she would have to reveal that she'd trembled at his touch. *That* she couldn't do. Instead, she dropped her gaze to the table. She trembled anew; placed beside the fine boned china was a small crystal bowl, filled with floating gardenias.

Brad was seating Dru, but Kathlyn felt his eyes upon her. He was no doubt watching for her reaction to his fragrant offering and the memories it would invoke. The heat that had skittered down her spine now warmed her heart.

"Look at the pretty flowers," Dru exclaimed.

Kathlyn's breath lodged in her throat.

"Pink roses—my favorite." Dru breathed deeply, appreciating the fragrance. "Thank you, Daddy."

Kathlyn eyes popped up, locking with chocolate brown orbs. She looked from Brad to Dru. Placed beside the child's plate was a crystal vase, filled with a bouquet of pink sweetheart roses.

"You're welcome, Peanut."

"Yours are pretty too, Miss Kathlyn," Dru said.

"Yes, they are," Kathlyn said softly. When she looked back at Brad she noticed the dimple in his smooth-shaved cheek had become more prominent, and his silken mustache twitched slightly. Then, he winked at her. Despite her best efforts, she blushed. "Thank you."

With the scent of gardenias teasing their nostrils, Brad and Kathlyn locked gazes. As if with one mind they realized the implication of their actions. She had worn gardenia scent on the trip, and now he was presenting her with the actual blooms.

They wondered if they were trying to tell each other something.

Chapter Twenty-six

The food arrived. The sweet scent of roses and gardenias mingled with the aromas of expertly prepared beefsteaks, golden baked turkey with stuffing, blackened duck with orange sauce, and roasted chicken.

Kathlyn's mouth watered at the sight of hot yeast rolls and steaming vegetables being placed on the table. Dishes of fresh creamery butter, and thick cream clinked against pots of golden honey. Various types of wine were available for those who indulged in alcoholic beverages; water, tea, and coffee were provided for the others.

Dru was served a large glass of cold milk just as Kathlyn's stomach reminded her she hadn't eaten all day. As if on cue, Dru's stomach answered. Sheepishly, they began filling their plates.

Brad was pleased to see Kathlyn's hearty appetite, for her thin frame—a result of wartime deprivation—gave him cause for worry. He smiled at the purely proprietary thought of fattening her up.

Everyone ate quietly for a time.

"Mr. Hampton, will your wife be traveling with you?" Jill broke the silence.

A muscle in Brad's jaw tightened when he noticed Dru halt her fork in mid-air. As he considered his answer, Kathlyn leaned over and whispered something in Dru's ear.

Dru looked toward the ceiling, smiled, then continued eating.

"My wife passed away during the war," he said simply.

Although Captain Spivey doted on his daughter, he

could see she had offended Brad. Anxious to smooth things over, he escorted her to the dance floor.

When the dessert tray was rolled to the table, Dru's little friend, Millie, joined those remaining. Brad took this opportunity to lean over and ask Kathlyn what she had said to Dru.

"Just that our mamas were watching us from heaven," she answered softly.

Brad propped an elbow on the table and rested his chin on a fisted hand. He stared appreciatively into Kathlyn's eyes, but said nothing.

"I know it may sound simple to an adult, but it obviously worked." She shrugged her shoulders.

The movement appeared so self-conscious, so vulnerable to Brad that his heart warmed. "You're really something, you know that?"

Kathlyn was inordinately pleased at Brad's praise. "And you're quite charming—when you want to be." Mischief and intense satisfaction chased each other in her lavender gaze like friendly specters.

Reaching over, Brad covered her hand with his own. His touch ignited a fire that shimmered just beneath her skin.

Her hand felt soft and small beneath his. He traced its fine bones with his thumb. She was so fragile, so frail. Her bones shifted easily under gentle pressure.

Her gaze dropped to his mouth; her tongue peeked out and slid slowly across her upper lip. Where the smooth pad of Brad's thumb made contact with her skin, Kathlyn could clearly feel the thud of his heart. He increased the pressure on her hand. Smiling, she felt his heart rate accelerate.

But her smile died an ugly death when Jill walked up behind him and leaned over his shoulder.

"Would you care to dance, Mr. Hampton?"

Brad looked from Kathlyn to Jill and winced. There was no graceful way to refuse. He squeezed Kathlyn's hand then stood.

"Please excuse me, Kathlyn," he murmured, presenting his arm to Jill.

Kathlyn nodded and the twosome walked away. She would remain calm. Just because Brad had a scarlet-draped siren dripping off his arm was no reason for her to turn into a screaming harridan. No matter how great the desire.

And that walk! If the floozy didn't cease undulating her hips, she was going to throw her back out. Why stop with her back, Kathlyn plotted. Why not throw her whole body out, or rather in . . . down into the cold, dark depths of the mighty Mississippi. Way down deep, where all manner of creatures roamed, waiting to eat the eyeballs of flirtatious . . .

"Miss Kathlyn, are you all right," Dru interrupted Kathlyn's grisly thoughts. "You look like you have a tummy ache."

"I'm fine, sweetie. Just a little tired is all," Kathlyn answered stiffly.

"Are you going to sleep in Mammy Mae's room tonight?"

The answer, no, sprang to Kathlyn's lips, but she couldn't quite call it forth. Surely, she wasn't entertaining the idea of sharing a suite with Brad? After all, she was a single woman—a very betrothed single woman. And while Dru would be there, a five year old did not make a very effective chaperone.

"I'm not sure that your daddy wants that," she hedged.

"But you're taking Mammy's place. Daddy said so."

"What did Daddy say?" Brad asked, ruffling Dru's curls.

Kathlyn was surprised to see Brad and Jill standing behind Dru's chair. Had their dance ended so soon?

Brad answered Kathlyn's unasked question. "I noticed that Dru was practically falling asleep in her chocolate mousse. Miss Spivey graciously agreed to give me a rain check on our dance so I could take Dru up to bed."

When Brad smiled at Jill, she moved closer to him and cast Kathlyn a smug look.

"Don't concern yourself, Mr. Hampton." Kathlyn's

tone was harsh. "Since I'm Dru's governess, it's my job to take Dru up to *our* suite. We won't wait up."

Brad's mouth fell open. *Our suite?*

"But I thought . . ." Dru began.

"Tell Millie good night, sweetie. You can see her on the boat tomorrow," Kathlyn interrupted Dru, feeling triumphant at the narrowing of Jill's eyes. Her victory was short-lived.

"That's wonderful, Brad!" Jill emphasized the familiar address. "Now you can escort me to the docks. I'll give you that tour of the *Robert E. Lee* we discussed," she oozed. Her expression said she would give him a great deal more.

Brad regarded Jill with a bemused expression. She may be young, but she knew exactly what she was doing. She obviously wanted to rattle Kathlyn's chain and she was succeeding famously. For his part, he thought her a kid. A beautiful kid, but a kid nonetheless.

Most men would have been flattered to have two beautiful women scrapping over them, but Brad wasn't. When he turned his gaze in Kathlyn's direction, the look of betrayal in her eyes gave rise to guilt.

But he hadn't done anything to feel guilty about. *Oh hell!* Guilt turned into righteous indignation. Did she believe he would pursue a kid like Jill? For God's sake, she didn't appear much older than Dru. He was more than a little insulted. He might be guilty of many things, but cradle-robbing was not one of them.

As if on cue, Jill chose that precise moment to press her all-but-exposed bosom against his arm. *Well, maybe she's not a child,* he amended. *But she's still too young.*

"Kiss your daddy good night, Dru. He has a *pressing* engagement."

Brad muffled a laugh.

Dru looked suspiciously at Miss Kathlyn. She had never heard her use such an abrupt tone. Was she angry with her? If so, what had she done? Maybe it was like she'd said earlier. Maybe Miss Kathlyn was just tired.

Brad knelt in front of Dru. "Good night, sweetheart." He noticed the puzzled look on her face as she encircled his neck with her arms.

"Everything's all right. I'll check on you when I come up," he whispered into her ear, placing a light kiss on her cheek.

"The key, please." Kathlyn held her hand out to Brad, refusing to meet his eyes.

He fished into his waistcoat pocket and withdrew the key, cradling it in his fingers. When he transferred the key from his hand to hers, his fingers brushed her palm. The brief contact with her bare skin rocked him to his toes. Delicious heat surged through his fingers, up his arm, across his chest, down his stomach, slamming pleasurably into his lower regions. How he could become aroused by just touching her hand was beyond his understanding.

The heightening color in Kathlyn's cheeks, her rapid intake of breath, told him she was affected as well. "Good night, Kathlyn," he drawled softly.

"Mr. Hampton." She jerked her head, refusing to meet his gaze. She grasped Dru's hand, and quickly hustled her charge off to bed.

Kathlyn jumped when the mantel clock struck twice. It was 2 A.M. and she had yet to go to bed.

Pacing from one side of Mammy Mae's vacated room to the other, she flattened her hand over her heart. Her floor length gown brushed her bare ankles while the soft glow from her bedside lamp caught the fiery highlights in her ebony hair. The silken tresses flashed and swayed in concert with the bolts of lightning emanating from her stormy eyes. She was in quite a state.

And she absolutely refused to admit it was because Brad was still out. What did she care if he was ensconced in some secluded stateroom enjoying a midnight romp with a certain garrulous nymph, she asked the ceiling, clenching her teeth?

"Not midnight," she corrected herself. "Two A.M."

Suddenly the walls seemed to close in on her. Grabbing a light shawl to cover her sheer, batiste nightclothes, she opened her door and bolted into the outer suite.

The room was cast in total darkness. Funny, she thought she had left a lamp burning when she went to bed, but maybe not. Her muffled curse sounded loud in the cavernous room when she stubbed her toe against the rocking chair.

Limping slightly, she made her way to Dru's bedchamber. Quietly, she eased the door open and peeked inside. Lying on her canopied bed, Dru resembled a slumbering angel. The poor baby was so tired a twenty-one gun salute wouldn't awaken her.

"Curses," Kathlyn hissed, tripping over a lump on the floor beside Dru's bed. It was Tandy. Kathlyn retrieved the doll from the floor and placed her on the pillow beside Dru.

Pulling the covers up around the child's chin she dropped a kiss on her forehead. Dru never stirred. Not even when Kathlyn lost her balance and closed the door a bit more forcefully than she'd intended.

Returning to the suite, she crossed to the Tiffany lamp, lit it, and turned the flame low. Then she slipped through the French doors, out into the night air where she hoped to find some semblance of peace.

Once outside, she leaned against the half wall surrounding the balcony and filled her lungs with cool night air. The blowing breeze whipped her gown, molding the diaphanous material to her slender legs. Her unbound hair mimicked the whipping motion and the silken strands swirled around her waist. Throwing her head back, she sighed with contentment. She felt better already.

Brad's breath lodged in his throat as he stood just outside the partially opened French doors. Silhouetted by the moon, Kathlyn presented a picture more provocative than if she had been totally nude. The glow of

231

the lamp inside the suite bathed her form in golden beams, washing away the pale yellow fabric that hugged her delicate curves.

In the span of a moment, he was a mass of aching need. "Kat." He spoke her name softly so as not to startle her.

the faint beating of the beams, watching every file hugged her densely carved. In the form of a miniature head, "No," He took her smile set.

Chapter Twenty-seven

Kathlyn wheeled in surprise.

Brad swayed slightly, whether from drink or desire he wasn't sure. Despite the fact that he had consumed enough brandy to float the *Robert E. Lee,* his mouth felt dry. His hand trembled where it rested against the wall. He hadn't expected to encounter Kathlyn alone in the moonlight. He was mesmerized by her beauty and the innate sensuality she exhibited.

Her gown was nearly transparent. The lamplight in front of her and the moonlight at her back, revealed every delicious inch of her body: her breasts were firm, the dusky circles of her areolas perfectly round, her abdomen, flat and firm, led down to a dark vee. Brad's desire caught flame.

The look in his eyes spoke more clearly to Kathlyn than words. She was moved by the sight of him. He was magnificent, standing across from her, wearing only tight-fitting breeches, partially unfastened. His broad chest was bare except for a thick mat of ebony hair that tapered downward in a fine line, until it finally disappeared into his pants.

His skin was smooth and shiny in the silver light. Not pale, like that of most gentlemen of his standing. But bronzed, as if he were used to physical labor or cavorting out of doors partially clothed.

Her hands tingled with the need to touch his satiny skin. Involuntarily, she took a step toward him. Simultaneously, he advanced on her. From his tousled hair to his bare feet, a thread of tension was running the length of him. With heady excitement she thought he looked as if he had just come from a woman's bed. With that thought came the image of Brad and Jill as she'd last seen them.

The breath left her body in a rush; her stomach lurched at the thought. Pulling her shawl more tightly about her slender shoulders she tried to appear composed. "Good evening, Mr. Hampton. I didn't expect you back tonight." Her voice wavered.

"You didn't," he began, confused for a moment. He had been back for some time, but apparently Kathlyn had not heard him come in. Obviously not, or else she wouldn't be standing on the balcony half naked.

So, she had thought he was with Jill all this time, doing Lord knows what. And the green-eyed monster had reared her ugly head. Brad tamped down a smile.

Kathlyn's jealousy pleased him. Almost as much as the sight of her coral nipples straining against the fabric of her gown. Almost, but not quite. Groaning inwardly, he ran his finger along his mustache. "Good evening, Kat." He bowed formally, if a little bit off balance.

But Kathlyn didn't notice his poor equilibrium. When he said her name like a caress, she blushed instantly, helplessly. Her eyes locked with his. She breathed in deeply and her nostrils were tantalized by a fragrance that was indefinably male, uniquely Brad. Then she smelled the liquor.

"You've been drinking. A lot." It wasn't just the smell of brandy on his breath that revealed this fact to Kathlyn. It was the look in his eyes. A predatory look that warned her of an absence of inhibitions. She knew then she wasn't dealing with Brad Hampton, quintessential gentleman. She was dealing with an aroused man who had had too much to drink.

When he blessed her with a lazy, half smile, he reinforced the notion that he was a bit deep in his cups, a bit out of control. She had to be wary; she had never dealt with this side of Brad. Instinctively, she knew he would play his hand, he would pursue her, even more vigorously than he had on the train platform. It would be up to her to fight their undeniable attraction.

234

But did she really want to?

Brad closed the distance between them.

"I should say good night." She halted him by placing her hands on his chest.

"No." He burned beneath her palms.

"No?" she whispered. Her nose twitched at the smell of brandy and mint. It was a pleasant smell, a heady smell. If she didn't make a quick exit she would be drunk as well. But not drunk on spirits as Brad was. Rather she would be drunk on the irresistibly charming man who was tracing her jaw lightly with his finger.

Instead of retreating, she moved closer to him. His face above hers was only a hairsbreadth away. Heat radiated from his body and penetrated her thin nightgown as the night air cooled her back. The resulting contrast only served to intensify her awareness of him. They touched, then shared a deep, shuddering breath.

Kathlyn's presence was playing havoc on Brad's composure as well. With each shallow inhalation, he could feel her warm breath on his cheek. She looked so soft, smelled so sweet. Her innocent sensuality was more drugging than all the brandy in the world.

Taking one of her hands into his own, he whispered, "I've been in for hours." Slowly, he raised it to his lips.

Kathlyn's cheeks flamed. Was her jealousy that apparent? "Oh? I thought you had plans."

"No, I had no plans. Perhaps someone had plans for me, but I had no plans. Other than to share a few drinks with the captain. Which I did. Right before I came upstairs—alone."

"What you do is none of my affair, Brad. I'm sure I couldn't care less." The desire in her eyes belied her weak denial.

"Well, at least we're back on a first name basis. And I don't believe you, Kat. I think you care a great deal."

"I don't have the right to care," she reminded him fervently.

Quickly, desperately, he covered her lips with his own. She gasped in surprise, and he thrust his tongue into her mouth. Their senses swam; their breathing grew sweetly

235

uneven. Despite Kathlyn's earlier admonition, they shared a mutually ravenous kiss.

Finally, Brad halted his delicious assault. "Whether you have the right or not is immaterial." His mouth hovered scant inches away. "What is important is that we stop lying to and pretending with each other. I can't do it any longer. I won't do it any longer."

Brad placed a strong hand at the nape of Kathlyn's neck and pulled her close. Tangling his fingers in her hair, he anchored her head to his naked chest. The rapid beat of his heart fluttered against her cheek.

Made uninhibited by his alcohol consumption and drugged by Kathlyn's nearness, he whispered honestly, "I care for you more than I ever thought possible. I want to make love with you so damn much I hurt. That's the truth and if you can't handle it, then you'd better stay the hell away from me." But even as he warned her to stay away, he tightened his grip.

Kathlyn's mouth dropped open. She had seldom heard Brad curse, and certainly never at her. It must be the alcohol, she reasoned.

"For God's sake, Kat, I had to get drunk before I could bring myself to come up here. Just the thought of sleeping in the room next to yours aroused me to the point of embarrassment."

His eyes fixed on the darkness above her head. He described the scene being played out in his mind. "I was afraid I'd burst into your room and gather you into my arms. Then carry you to my bed, and make love to you all night, until the sun rose on our hot, wet, writhing bodies."

"Oh Brad," she moaned. His erotic word picture and the husky timbre of his voice caused her heart to thunder in her chest.

He felt it against the hard planes of his stomach. "Can't you see you're a fever in my blood? Don't you know I could never want anyone like Jill Spivey? Sweetheart, I don't want anyone. Not anyone but you."

Slowly lowering his lips to hers, Brad initiated a passionate kiss. When she opened to receive his kiss he delved his tongue deeply into her mouth, then thrust again, over and over. The provocative movement of his tongue reflected the pulsing ache below his waist and the slight, instinctive movement of his lean hips.

"Oh, Brad," she breathed again, throwing her arms around his bare shoulders. Her firm, young breasts flattened against his hair-roughened chest. Feeling his muscles ripple against her taut nipples, a delicious warmth spread down past her abdomen. It settled into her moist center.

The stiff fabric hugging Brad's thighs felt strangely erotic pressing against her, and she unthinkingly rotated her hips against him. Tilting her head back she gave his lips greater access to travel down her bare, slender throat.

When she opened her eyes the stars overhead seemed to burst into a blaze of sensation. Her low moan of pleasure was like adding fuel to Brad's already raging fire.

He pulled the laces at the front of her gown, exposing her breasts to his heated touch. He was drawn to the sweet nectar of her dusky-tipped globes like a bee drawn to honey. Nipping, kissing, laving, and suckling, he paid homage to the sensitive peaks. He smiled against her bare flesh at her gasps of pleasure.

With eager hands, he untied her gown all the way to her feet. He slipped his fingers beneath the voluminous material at chest level and widened the opening. Pulling her into his embrace, he rubbed his hair-roughened chest against her breasts. Groaning low in his throat at the delicious sensation, he captured her lips again.

Kathlyn was beside herself as she strained toward his body. The tactile sensations she experienced overwhelmed her, burning rational thought from her mind. His kisses snatched from her mind the hateful fact that she was promised to another.

When Brad's fingers dipped to test her readiness, Kathlyn moaned into his mouth. Her abdomen grew rigid with immediate release. "Brad," she gasped in surprise.

237

Raising up on tiptoes at the unfamiliar sensation, she fought for breath, dropping kisses over his eyelids, cheeks, jaw, and mouth. After the shock waves abated, she breathed deeply and lowered her heels to the patio.

The seductive innocence of her response cleared Brad's alcohol-dulled brain, but set his senses reeling. With a tenderness born of deep feelings, he kissed and caressed her willing flesh. He couldn't get enough of her.

In the back of his mind, the voice of reason shouted for him to retreat. While his body screamed for him to advance. For the time being, he listened to his love-starved body.

With hearts pounding in unison the two young lovers shared a white-hot passion that neither had known before. In the heat of the moment, the past was forgotten, and the future was of no consequence.

All that mattered was the present: the kisses they shared, the caresses they bestowed. It was a prelude to greater passion.

"I need you," he confessed again.

Her whole body ached in response to his skillful seduction. She was emboldened by his heartfelt confession. The silver moonlight washed over them, standing like two intertwined statues as she became the aggressor, exploring his hot, aching body. Her touch was light as dew, rippling over the rise and fall of his corded muscles.

Below his collarbone, she massaged his nipples, making tiny circles, feeling the pebbles rise against her fingertips. Then she sifted her fingers through the bush of hair covering his chest. She smiled into the darkness; his midnight curls felt soft yet crisp between her fingers.

His breathing grew harsh when her hand traveled lower, halting and fingering the button at his waistband. He held his breath.

Instead of dipping her hand to caress the bulge below his waistline as she desired, she placed her thumb in the indentation of his navel and massaged it with slow, deep rotations. Her fingers splayed over his hard abdomen, learning the feel of him.

238

He groaned and slipped his arms under her gown, circling her waist, finally resting his hands on her bare buttocks. He dug his fingers into her tender flesh. In one swift movement, he lifted her to the half wall, leaning her back against the smooth column.

The tail of her gown shielded her tender flesh from the scratchy concrete beneath her, but nothing could shield her from the man intent on devouring her. He was out of control now. From neck to knee, not one sensitive, aching, inch of Kathlyn's bare body was spared his loving attention. All the while, he returned and drank from her lips, as if he were a man dying of thirst.

Suddenly the desire to see all of her overwhelmed him. The moonlight was quite an aphrodisiac, but he needed lamplight. Eleven years ago he had been denied the sight of her. Tonight would be different. Or so he thought.

Sliding an arm around her waist and one under her bottom, he lifted her into his arms. He turned toward the suite, but met with resistance.

Kathlyn hooked an arm around the pillar and held tight. "Wait. Please. This is going too fast for me." She knew if she went through those doors with him, she would be lost. Her sense of self-preservation was just too strong for that.

He stood very still, holding her stiffly in his arms. His face was clearly illumined by the moon. His eyes were dark, turbulent. His breathing was harsh in the stillness.

"I'm sorry, Brad, I'm just not ready for this."

Was Kathlyn's fiancé the reason for her reluctance to finish what they had begun, Brad wondered. His jealousy grew to enormous proportions. "If I recall, you felt ready to me." He slid his hand below her waist, cupping her intimately.

Kathlyn's cheeks flamed. His implication was obvious. "Please put me down." Her quiet voice broke through the red sea of his indignation.

Instinctively, his arms tightened around her. Then slowly he slid her down his body until she was standing, unsteadily, between his legs.

The hem of her gown caught on his open trousers,

baring one perfectly formed hip. He trailed his fingers across her naked bottom. Then reluctantly, he untangled her gown and dropped the fabric.

He regretted throwing her arousal in her face. Bowing his head, he placed his damp forehead against her own. "I'm sorry, doll." He straightened his spine. With trembling hands he retied her gown, shielding her from his view.

Her heart lurched. "I know," she whispered honestly, her heart aching, her body throbbing with unappeased desire.

He drew a shuddering breath. "I want to kiss you good night."

He told himself he would steal one more kiss, then he would send her to bed . . . alone. So quickly—before she could object—he twined his fingers through her hair and brought her face to his. Just one kiss. But one kiss turned into two, and two turned into three, and before long he stopped counting.

Finally, he raised his head. "Go to bed. Now!" he ordered her in a harsh whisper.

She stepped around his frozen form. When she reached the threshold, his soft voice stopped her.

"Do you love him?"

It was as if nature was suspended. The night sounds ceased, the summer air stilled, the stars overhead dulled. He held his breath.

She turned toward his broad, bare back. Staring out into the Tennessee night, he looked so rigid, so powerful, larger than life. But with that simple question, he bared himself to her, allowing her to see his vulnerability. She was so moved all she could manage was a husky whisper, "No."

When he turned toward the door, she was gone.

Chapter Twenty-eight

A single ray of sunlight broke through the drapes in Kathlyn's bedchamber, penetrating her tightly closed lids. Groaning, she opened her eyes. The night had taken its toll on her; the world looked absolutely ghastly.

Grabbing the closest pillow, she covered her head against the morning glow. Still, the events of the previous evening haunted her.

After she had retreated to her room, she had thrown herself across her four-poster bed and indulged in a self-serving pity party. Then, she had pulled herself to a sitting position and engaged in a bit of soul searching.

Ever since the war and the loss of her family, she had felt as if she were marking time. Not really living — just existing.

And always lurking beneath the surface of her emotions was a nagging sense of guilt. Not the piddling kind of guilt one experiences from eating too much tapioca pudding, or killing a fly, or placing another book on top of the Bible. But a debilitating sense of guilt. Remorse that forms a pit in your stomach and awakens you at night, shivering and covered in perspiration.

She recognized the focus of this guilt now. She had been given something her parents, her brothers, and countless others had been denied. LIFE. She was alive, while so many were dead.

Why? Why had she been allowed to live through the war? Was there something monumental she was supposed to achieve in her lifetime? Was she supposed to bring about world peace, or maybe annihilate famine and pestilence on the earth?

Or was she simply supposed to wander through life,

achieving nothing more than becoming Mrs. Glenn Crutchfield? With this precious gift of life, was she to be content marrying a man she didn't love, not even able to give him a family. Was she to accept the inevitable, settle for less than her heart's desire? Never feel the exhilaration of loving a man like Brad. But never experience the devastation of loving and losing either, she reminded herself.

After all, it was easier to drift along, allowing the winds of circumstance to take her where they would. Safer, less risky than taking control of her life, than reaching for her dreams. She gripped the pillow tighter.

It was so much easier to exist, than to live. To live was to leave one's self open to pain. In Brad's arms she had felt alive last night. No doubt about it. What they had done would definitely be categorized as living. Not merely existing there.

But where had it led? Now with the pain of uncertainty plaguing her in the light of day, she wondered if the fleeting moments of bliss in the moonlight were worth the hurt.

She pulled the pillow off her face and stared at the canopy above her. *Do you love him?* Brad had asked. Had she imagined the sound of vulnerability, or was it the effect of too much brandy she had heard in his husky voice? Was his interest in her caused by lust and alcohol, or did he feel something deeper for her?

He seemed to care for her at times, and she was quite simply mad about him. If she didn't watch herself, she would become lost in him. She could ill afford to exist merely as a plaything for a rich man. Even if his slightest touch made her heart pound, her body tremble, and her passion burn.

Her head threatened to burst. She had no answers. Slipping out of bed, she crossed on trembling legs to the armoire. She withdrew a voluminous housecoat the same delicate lemon hue as the gown Brad had practically divested her of in the moonlight. Blushing at the memory, she pulled the wrapper around her shoulders and stepped into matching slippers.

"Stop it!" she ordered herself, taking a deep, cleansing breath, squaring her shoulders. She had a lot to accomplish before they left for the *Robert E. Lee*. And wool gathering about life and love wasn't getting the job done.

Dru sat in the bentwood rocker, a frown marring her otherwise cherubic face. "I think Daddy needs a nap," she groused into Tandy's ear. "He's ill as a sore-tailed cat," she repeated one of Mammy Mae's favorite sayings.

"I wish Aunt Melinda was here. She'd straighten him out right quick." She looked around the room to see if she and Tandy were truly alone. "She'd fix his wagon," she whispered another Mammyism confidently.

Dru didn't know what was wrong with her daddy. He was usually so kind to her. He hadn't really been unkind this morning, she allowed.

He'd just ignored her. Fact is, he'd ignored everybody—even Miss Kathlyn. Maybe he didn't like the way his face looked today, green as a butter pea.

"When I offered Daddy a bite of my poached egg, he didn't even say 'no thank you.' He just grabbed his stomach, jumped up from the table, and ran away. I don't think that was very polite. Do you?" Dru questioned her porcelain friend. "Me either," she reiterated as if Tandy had agreed with her.

"It's time to go, sweetie," Kathlyn said, entering the parlor and standing beside the mountain of luggage that was to be taken to the docks.

"Where's Daddy?"

"I believe he's already gone to the wharf." Kathlyn forced a smile. "We better get a move on. We wouldn't want to miss the boat; it's a long swim to Arkansas," she teased halfheartedly, turning to check the room for their belongings one last time.

Kathlyn's musings were much the same as Dru's had been moments before. Brad had been so reserved with her; he'd barely said two words at breakfast. When he left to get their tickets, he didn't even say goodbye.

It was quite a departure from his behavior in the moonlight. The memory brought a flush to her cheeks. She halted in front of an open window and leaned her hip against the sill. Pushing the fluttering curtains aside, she welcomed the cool breeze that blew across her blazing cheeks.

Dru noticed Kathlyn's flushed appearance and became concerned. Was Miss Kathlyn sick? she wondered. Involuntarily, she tightened her grip on Tandy.

Kathlyn was so involved in her thoughts, she didn't notice Dru's unease. She was preoccupied with thoughts of a brown eyed, dimpled Adonis who caused her heart to pound whenever he flashed his gallant smile.

Brad stood on the dock below the *Robert E. Lee*, gripping the rails with white-knuckled fists, suffering from a hangover the likes of which he'd never known.

He cursed his foolishness each time a wave of nausea assailed him. Drinking half the brandy in Memphis had seemed like a good idea last night, but today he felt as if he would die from it. Which would serve him right. What was he thinking of, devouring Kathlyn like that? If only he had had a clearer head.

Rubbing his churning stomach, he was reminded of the first time he'd gotten drunk. He was fourteen. He and Jared had found Mammy's stash of scuppernong wine. The tart taste brought tears to their eyes, but they had drained the jug nonetheless.

Early evening, their father had returned from delivering a baby only to find his sons retching their insides out. He took one good look at their pea green faces and wisely decided their punishment would be complete when they sobered up.

He was right. They awakened the next morning with what Brad had been sure was a terminal hangover. It was the longest day of his life.

He had only gotten drunk one other time. His second episode of over-indulgence had been with none other than William T. Sherman. It was the night Celia announced her engagement to Beau Patton. If memory served him correctly, he'd over-indulged every night for a week.

When he sobered up, he discovered that the engagement had been forced on Celia and that Beau had been physically abusing her. Beau almost killed Celia. If Stuart Shephard had not put a bullet through Beau's head, Brad would have.

But that was a lifetime ago . . .

"Brad," Jill squealed, bounding down the dock.

Automatically, his hands rose to shield his pounding head. When Jill reached his side, he took her offered hand and bowed slightly at the waist. The sky and dock changed places. His world swirled around him. To maintain his equilibrium, he grasped the nearest solid object — Jill.

It was at this precise moment that the carriage carrying Dru, Kathlyn, and Rachel arrived. Brad was unaware of their arrival, but Jill saw them immediately. Noting the shocked look on Kathlyn's face, she snuggled closer to Brad and whispered loudly enough for the women to hear, "Tonight, then."

The loud buzzing in Brad's ears drowned out Jill's voice. "What?" he asked, confused. He was further confused when she planted her lips firmly on his.

"Daddy," Dru squealed, jumping down from the carriage. "Is that our big boat?" She, unlike Kathlyn, had been too impressed with the *Robert E. Lee* to notice Jill's theatrics.

"Have you purchased our tickets yet? Or have you been too busy?" Rachel asked cattily, her implication obvious.

Brad set Jill aside and turned his attention to the new arrivals. Dru smiled sweetly at him, having forgiven his strange behavior due to her excitement over the impending trip. He returned her sweet smile.

His smile faded when his eyes met Rachel's. Standing next to Kathlyn, Rachel was dressed to the teeth. The bright colors of her costume did little to help his headache.

Squinting, he perused Kathlyn. Her expression was that of an angel whose favorite harp had just been stolen. Flashing him a sharp look, she then fixed her gaze on the toes of her purple kid slippers.

She was a vision, dressed in a short maize gown, topped with a purple paletot and matching petticoat peeking from beneath. The locket he had given her less than twenty-four hours before was conspicuously absent. Her only jewelry was a simple amethyst pin.

He wondered if the absence of his locket was a message of sorts. Was she angry because he had mauled her in the moonlight? She hadn't really seemed angry last night. She had just changed her mind at the last minute. It was a woman's prerogative.

"Do you have our tickets?" Rachel asked again, enunciating each word as if he were an idiot.

Brad tore his gaze and thoughts from Kathlyn, and scowled at Rachel. "I was on my way to the ticket desk when you arrived," he informed her with exaggerated politeness.

"I'll go with you," Jill offered, grabbing his arm.

Brad pleaded for divine patience. He'd been walking alone for more than three decades and he didn't need Jill's assistance. "Suit yourself." He was too much a gentleman to rebuff her, and too hungover to be chivalrous.

A number of people were at the ticket desk buying passage on the packet when Brad and Jill reached the area. Despite Jill's urging to push ahead, Brad waited his turn on line.

Ignoring her chatter, he gave full attention to the *Robert E. Lee*. It was a magnificent sight, rising up out of the murky water of the Mississippi. Although he had heard about the beauty of riverboats, to see a three hundred foot, 1,467 ton service vessel that looked like nothing so much as a giant birthday cake up close was awe inspiring. Even through bloodshot eyes.

He was a bit surprised to find a vessel of such opulence anchored in a Southern port so close on the heels of the Civil War. He had heard Reconstruction in Tennessee was worse than it was in Georgia. Apparently not.

"Brad, I'll see you later," Jill broke into his musings, eyeing the half naked roustabouts who were loading her father's boat. Without waiting for a reply, she sashayed past the men, casting them what could only be described as a come-hither look.

Brad narrowed his eyes. He was glad to be rid of her, but she was too young to be prancing about like that. Nonetheless, she wasn't his responsibility. He had three females awaiting him; one he planned to be rid of straightaway.

"May I help you, sir?"

"I certainly hope so," Brad said.

The riverboat employee smiled up at him, cocking his head.

"I'm traveling with my family so I'd like cabin tickets to Fort Smith for four passengers in the ladies' cabin, please. Two adjacent rooms—a single and a double family room—and another single, as far away from the other cabins as possible."

The ticket seller chuckled, raised a brow at Brad's strange request, and handed him the appropriate receipt form. Brad offered no explanation. He scrawled his signature across the bottom and paid the rather exorbitant fare, completing the transaction. With tickets in hand, he made his way back to Dru and the ladies.

"We're all set." He reached down and lifted Dru into his arms. Then he led Kathlyn and Rachel aboard.

The boat's second officer, Mate Gunn, a spare, bearded man dressed neck to ankle in white, took their tickets and escorted them up a flight of stairs to the texas deck. He halted before two adjoining staterooms located in the ladies' section of the cabin.

Brad gestured to Rachel's ticket clutched in Mate Gunn's hand. "Would you have someone show Miss Jackson to her cabin?"

With a quick nod, Mate Gunn summoned a cabin boy, relating Brad's request. Leaving a scowling Rachel in competent hands, Gunn bid the others a pleasant trip

247

and hurried off. Brad flipped a coin to the boy for his trouble.

"Thank you, sir. If you will, ma'am, it's this way." The boy headed toward the far end of the ladies' cabin. After staring daggers into Kathlyn, Rachel said, "I'll see you at dinner." It sounded quite like a threat.

Kathlyn and Brad breathed a collective sigh of relief as Rachel followed the retreating cabin boy. Chattering like a chipmunk, Dru rushed into the double room.

"Kathlyn." Brad placed his hand under Kathlyn's elbow.

"I really must get Dru settled." Kathlyn wanted to talk to Brad, but she couldn't get the image of Jill kissing him—kissing the lips that had tasted so sweet to her only the night before—out of her mind. Fearing she would make noises like a jealous harpy, she disappeared into her cabin.

Shaking his head—then groaning from the resulting sensation—Brad stepped next door to his own cabin. Absently, he surveyed the room he was to use on the long trip. It was nicely decorated, adequate, he decided with a nonchalance reserved for the wealthy.

About ten-feet square, it was actually rather elegantly furnished with tufted-velvet chairs, fronted by low hassocks. The French bed, wardrobe, and washstand were fashioned of glistening rosewood.

Overhead, Gothic tracery drew his eye. The morning sun was bright, shining through the painted-glass skylight, casting streams of color on the tesselated floor and rich Brussel's carpet underfoot. A chandelier provided additional illumination, mirrors a sense of space.

There were doors on three of the four walls. One leading to Dru and Kathlyn's room, one to the deck, and one directly into the saloon. The door to the gallery was heavy mahogany, embellished with a handsome oil painting of the Tennessee countryside in spring.

A knock on the saloon door sounded.

"Surprise." Dru giggled when Brad opened the door.

Brad smiled down at his incorrigible daughter.

248

"Isn't it beee-yu-tee-ful, Daddy?" Dru referred to the spacious saloon.

"It's certainly ornate." He leaned negligently against the door jamb, impressed in spite of himself.

With burgundy carpeted floors, the saloon was decorated in steamboat Gothic. On the walls hung ornamental paintings of naked women and flying cherubs, along with bevel-edged gilt mirrors.

The furniture was upholstered in matching velvet. Several chandeliers with over thirty oil lamps and numerous glass pendants were suspended from the high ceiling.

The bustling room was long and narrow. Brad squinted, judging the size to be approximately two-hundred-feet long and fourteen-feet wide. It was unbroken by columns, tie rods, or engines. Long tables for dining dominated the center of the room.

Other than the upholstery, paintings and carpeting there was very little color. The walls were white paneling with florid carving. Sun shone through painted skylights on each side, providing a breathtaking contrast of light and shadow.

The ladies' parlor was situated in a secluded part of the cabin, a grand piano on a dais providing the focus. Pale, floral sofas and rocking chairs dotted the carpeted area. The soft clamor of feminine voices caused Brad's lips to tilt upward at the edges.

For the gentlemen there were barrooms on either end. The gaming tables were already occupied by brightly clothed gentlemen, playing poker, whist, and brag. They sipped such pick-me-ups as brandy smashes, gin slings, whisky cocktails, even mint juleps. Despite the unobtrusive sign on the wall reading, *"Games for money strictly forbidden,"* there seemed to be a great deal of cash interspersed with tall, frosty glasses.

One man in particular caught Brad's eye. He was what Melinda would call a *handsome devil*. Brad suspected the tall, expensively dressed gambler was the kind of man who could charm a woman right out of her chemise. Possessive as always, he wondered what Kathlyn would think of the man.

"Brad," Jacob Shelby called, crossing through the dining area to Brad's side. "Can I interest you in an eye-opener?" He held out a pale green drink.

Brad's stomach grew queasy. Swallowing, he straightened away from the door. "No thanks. Just coffee."

Immediately a liveried waiter handed Brad a cup of the warm, fragrant brew.

"Do I have to ask Daddy?" Dru's voice drifted into the saloon from the cabin she shared with Kathlyn. Kathlyn's soft response was drowned out by the patter of little girls' feet.

Brad and Jacob knew what was coming. They tightened their grips on their drinks and braced themselves. Their daughters rushed into the saloon. Hannah Shelby and Kathlyn followed close on Dru and Millie's heels.

"Can I please, Daddy? Can I please stay overnight in Millie's cabin?"

Kathlyn's cheeks flamed, but she met Brad's penetrating gaze nonetheless. The thought of spending the night in a room adjoining his, without Dru's presence, was unsettling to say the least. Just about anything could happen.

An unmarried woman who proved indiscreet might well be put off the boat. But lying in Brad's arms all night could be worth the risk. The color in her cheeks deepened. She wondered if anyone knew what she was thinking.

Brad had a good idea and it was having an arousing effect on him. An effect that could prove embarrassing if he didn't occupy his thoughts elsewhere. "What's all this?" he asked, dropping onto one knee in front of his daughter.

"Millie's mama said I can stay all night with Millie, if you let me. Please say yes, Daddy."

Kathlyn held her breath.

"Will you promise to be a good girl?" Brad asked.

"Oh yes, sir," Dru enthused, hugging Brad around the neck.

Brad raised his gaze to Kathlyn. She avoided his eyes.

"Come along, Dru. Millie and I will help you find

your nightgown. Then you girls can play together this afternoon, and later the three of us can have our dinner in the cabin." Hannah smiled into Dru's face.

"No," Kathlyn said, more forcefully than she intended. "What I mean to say is that Millie can stay overnight with me and Dru. That way you can go to dinner with your husband."

"Mama's too tired to go anywhere at dark. She's gonna have me a baby brother. She needs me and Dru to stay with her and take care of her. Don't you, Mama?" Millie turned her innocent gaze on her mother.

"Millie," Hannah admonished gently. "Ladies don't talk about babies being born around gentlemen."

The adults had to bite back grins at the crestfallen look on Millie's face.

"I'm sorry, Mama. But don't you need me and Dru to take care of you? Don't you?"

"Yes sweetlin', I do."

Brad winced at Kathlyn's overt attempt to avoid him. Perhaps she no longer trusted him to act the gentleman. Well, he would redeem himself. When they were alone tonight he would be on his best behavior. He would show Kathlyn that he could control himself, even if he did want to rip her clothes off with his teeth.

Right Hampton! If you buy that best behavior drivel, I'll sell you swamp land in Florida at a good price.

Dru took Brad's silence as an affirmative answer. "Thank you, Daddy."

"You mind Mrs. Shelby now," he said.

"Yes, sir," she answered automatically before she and Millie disappeared through the doorway of Dru's cabin. Hannah excused herself and followed after the girls. When Jacob headed for the bar, Brad and Kathlyn were left alone.

Brad's stomach chose that moment to remind him of his overindulgence. "Captain Spivey expects us at seven. I'll knock on your door at five 'til," he said politely, his lips white around the edges. "Now if you will excuse me." He turned quickly and disappeared into his cabin.

Staring after Brad, Kathlyn was visually devoured by

251

the *handsome devil* fanning cards at the corner table. She felt his eyes upon her. Tearing her gaze away from Brad's stateroom, she looked in the direction of the gambler.

The hair on the nape of her neck stood on end. But it wasn't the gambler who caused her reaction. It was the lustful gaze of the tattered giant lounging behind him.

Kathlyn looked away. Scolding herself for being cowardly, she jerked her head in the direction of the two men, boldly seeking the gaze of the huge man.

He was gone.

Chapter Twenty-nine

Two hours later the great boat's paddle wheel came to life, forcing the vessel out into the Mississippi currents. Brad, Dru, and the Shelbys stood at the railing which surrounded the texas deck, watching the shoreline fall away with each mighty stroke of the wheel.

In the distance, vegetation of every sort was evident; flowering crab trees, pink and white dogwood, wild honeysuckle, sweet shrub, Cherokee roses. All growing smaller by the second.

The air on the upper deck was festive. Impeccably groomed gentlemen stood proudly beside their exquisitely clothed ladies, while their children squirmed under the watchful eyes of their nannies. When the locals, peppering the shore, waved to these well-to-do cabin passengers, they gained a rousing response.

"Where's Miss McKinney?" Jacob asked Brad over the sound of the noisy crowd.

Brad shrugged.

"She's in her cabin," Hannah offered. The twinkle in her eye told both men that Hannah knew more than she was telling.

Hannah and Jacob returned their gazes to the shore, but not Brad. He looked down. The poor unfortunates who were traveling on the lower level were provided no beds, chairs, drinking water, or even bathroom facilities. Unlike the men, women, and children surrounding him, deck passengers had little time for gaiety. They were too busy searching for a place to rest.

A few, tired, disheartened, men sat on the bare deck, leaning back against the side railing, while others reclined on haphazardly stacked cargo. All manner of animals roamed the deck, spreading a stench in their wake.

The deck noise was even more deafening than the festive shouts from above. Babies cried for lack of food, mothers shrieked at unruly children, fathers bemoaned their lot in life and cursed the wealthy passengers above them. They cursed the men, women, and children who had no more to concern themselves with than to shout inane farewells to shoreline strangers.

Brad's heart went out to them. When he had watched them board earlier, he had noticed that some of them looked as if it had been a while since they'd had a decent meal. Especially some of the children. One little girl in particular had caught his eye. She was about Dru's age. But where Dru was pink and chubby, this child was pale and gaunt. Her eyes were old beyond their years.

Brad swallowed against the lump forming in his throat. He knew he couldn't save the world, but perhaps he could provide the little girl and her fellow passengers with something to eat. He would speak to the captain.

"Do you know what our first stop is?" Brad leaned over and asked Jacob.

"Arkansas Post."

Brad nodded his thanks. *Arkansas Post it is.* He would leave the boat at Arkansas Post, buy all the food he could in the limited amount of time he had, and have the captain and his crew distribute it among the deck passengers.

That settled, his thoughts returned to Kathlyn. He wondered where she was, what she was doing, and, most importantly, what would happen between them tonight?

Kathlyn's nervous gaze settled on the Chippendale shelf clock sitting on her dressing table. The delicate hearts and curling flames carved in the rich mahogany surface reminded her of Brad. *Hearts and flames.* She waxed poetic. Whenever he drew near, her heart went up in flames.

Stretching forth her finger, she traced the ornate roman numerals on the surface of the clock. *6:25.*

Brad would arrive in thirty minutes and here she sat, clothed only in her convent-made underwear, silk stockings, boned corset, and satin corset cover. Her chair was surrounded by pastel puffs of material, each colorful cloud a gown she had tried on then cast aside.

A mass of indecision, she dropped her hands into her lap like lead weights. She sighed deeply, her slim fingers moving of their own free will, stroking the fine embroidery, pressing the delicate tucks that had been painstakingly fashioned into her filmy petticoats by faceless, nameless nuns.

What should she wear? She wanted it to be something very special. The near-transparent garments that covered her bare flesh now would not be sufficient, she mused wryly. Though last night her transparent nightgown had been quite effective. Too effective.

"Are you warm?" Josie, Hannah's personal maid, asked Kathlyn when she noticed the rosy blush on Kathlyn's cheeks.

She shook her head, no, the abrupt movement pulling an ebony wisp from Josie's grasp.

"Move over there," Josie instructed.

Kathlyn settled herself on the white oak footstool Josie indicated. With long, sure strokes the maid brushed Kathlyn's hair. Crackling with electricity, the silken curls shone. Dropping her head back on her shoulders, Kathlyn shook the shiny curtain, glistening curls winding their way around the knees and brackets of her oval shaped perch.

When she raised her head, she met Josie's eyes in the mirror and gestured to the colorful gowns littering the Brussels rug. "I'm usually not this indecisive. Or this clumsy." She fingered the slightly scorched curl at the nape of her neck.

It was a blessing that Hannah had insisted Kathlyn

use her maid for the evening. If not, there's no telling what she would have done to herself. She had been all thumbs and butterflies before Josie had taken her in hand.

With no nonsense, the competent woman had bathed, powdered, perfumed, and soothed her. It had taken Josie two hours, but Kathlyn was almost ready.

"Such pretty hair. I don't know why on earth you were trying to crimp it. Hair this full and rich don't need such as that," Josie scolded around the hairpins protruding from her mouth. With determination, she took great handsful of the silken mass. "Look down," she instructed Kathlyn, not unlike a commanding general.

Obediently, Kathlyn did as she was told. She hadn't really wanted to crimp her hair; the heat was uncomfortable against her tender scalp. It was just that she wanted everything to be perfect. She had to look her very best. It had become a fever in her blood, this desire to look just right.

When she looked down, she noticed the discarded clothing all around her again. Had she really gone through that many gowns?

They were all beautiful, but somehow they weren't quite right.

The peach organdie with its long bronze sash made her hair look brassy; the jade green taffeta frock seemed too youthful. *What about the delicate moiré?* It was a breath-taking blue-green, the color of a robin's egg. *What was wrong with it?* She didn't remember why she'd rejected it; she just had. And the cherry watered-silk with the white satin bow lying alongside the rustling brocades in a rainbow of colors, none of them were quite what she had in mind.

"All done," Josie announced proudly.

"Thank you." Kathlyn raised her gaze. She smiled with pleasure when she saw her image in the mirror. "Nice."

Nice. Josie stared skeptically at the vision in the mirror. Nice didn't cover it. Kathlyn was too modest

256

by half; the girl was absolutely breathtaking.

Her hair was her crowning glory, Josie decided. A cloud of fire kissed curls fashioned in a large chignon, placed high on the crown of her head. With airy wisps surrounding her face like a halo, it made her creamy skin glow. And it smelled delicious. After shampooing it twice, Josie had rinsed it in cologne.

Eyes the pale purple of wild violets were round in her lovely face. Never had Josie seen anything quite that color. They weren't lavender, more light purple, but not really, with just a touch of blue. The unusual hue had caught her attention as soon as the maid entered the room. And since then they had changed many times, each color more striking than the last.

She suspected the color of Kathlyn's eyes changed in tandem with her emotions. A noise sounded from the adjoining stateroom, like someone dropping a shoe. Kathlyn cocked an ear. The color washed from her eyes, becoming an almost transparent iris. While Josie had never seen eyes that remarkable color, she recognized the expression. The young woman bore the unmistakable look of a woman in love.

Perhaps that was why her beauty was beyond anything Josie had ever seen. It was obvious that Kathlyn was wholly unaware of her beauty; that in itself made her even more lovely.

"Well, Missy, what are you going to wear? You can't go like that," Josie grinned, unknowingly putting voice to Kathlyn's previous sentiments.

"I don't know," Kathlyn agonized. Then she remembered the pale pink box with the lavender ribbon, the special gown Brad had chosen for her. She jumped to her feet.

"What?" Josie asked, intrigued by the lights flashing in Kathlyn's eyes.

"I know it's here somewhere." She crossed to the wardrobe on stockinged feet. Her head disappearing through the doors, she rooted through a wealth of gowns she'd not yet tried on.

"Here it is!" she exclaimed, pulling the long, shiny

257

box from the top shelf. As excited as a kid on Christmas morning, she brought the large, rectangular box over to the bed.

Josie noticed Kathlyn's hands tremble as she untied the lavender ribbon. "Oh my lord," she breathed when Kathlyn jerked off the lid and pulled back the pink tissue paper. "That's it. That's the color."

Kathlyn was so enthralled with the lovely gown she scarcely heard Josie's declaration.

The exquisite gown was the exact color of Kathlyn's eyes, the color Josie recognized as expressing the emotion of a woman in love. Obviously someone else had noticed that color and been mightily impressed by it. Impressed enough to buy the single most costly piece of clothing Josie had ever seen. She would give a years wages to know who bought the dress, but servants didn't ask such things, even servants who spoke their mind as freely as she.

"Oh, isn't it absolutely perfect?" Kathlyn echoed Josie's thoughts.

The latest in French fashion, the gown was a pale lavender-blue robe Gabriellé. Modest in a seductive way.

Kathlyn held the one-piece dress to her and twirled around. It was made of twenty yards of the finest silk, closed with mother-of-pearl buttons in front from neck to waist, accented with three buttons at waist level in back. It was covered from neck to hem with fragile, handmade *point de gaze* needlepoint lace.

"Well don't stand there gaping at it. Give it here and let me get those wrinkles out. Your young man'll be here before you know it, and there you'll be, standing in nothing but your fripperies."

Handing the dress over, Kathlyn giggled like a school girl at Josie's good-natured scolding. When she shoved the box off the bed making room for the dress, she heard a muffled thump. Disappearing in a mountain of petticoats, Kathlyn knelt beside the box.

"Oh, Josie look. Slippers to match." Plopping down on her bottom, Kathlyn lifted her stocking clad feet one at a time, sliding the satin shoes on. "What's this?" she asked, on her knees again.

"What's what?" Josie asked.

Kathlyn produced a large, flat, jewelry box. The velvet covering felt soft beneath her fingers, crushed, as if it were very, very old. She crossed over to the footstool and dropped down onto it. Capturing a full, rosy lip between her teeth, she slowly opened the lid. The breath left her body in a rush.

Now it was her turn to exclaim, "Oh my Lord!"

Chapter Thirty

"What on earth?"

Too stunned to speak, Kathlyn handed the jewelry box to Josie.

"God's eyebrows! Reckon how much they cost?"

It wasn't the monetary value of the exquisite diamond and amethyst earrings and choker that had stolen Kathlyn's breath. It was the delicately embroidered name on the cloth beneath them that had sent her into a tailspin.

Lysette Hampton. These beautiful gems had belonged to Brad's mother. Why would he give them to her? What was going through his mind to do such a thing?

He should save them for Dru, or give them to his sister, Lacy, or—an incredibly painful thought—keep them for his future wife. Anything, but give them to her. She didn't have a right to accept the precious offering; she was still engaged to Glenn.

The tiny bit of blood coloring Kathlyn's face drained out when there came a soft rap on the outer door.

"It's him," Josie hissed, snapping the lid closed and grabbing Kathlyn's gown all in one motion. "Get behind that screen." She pushed the voluminous dress into Kathlyn's waiting arms.

As Kathlyn dove for cover, the maid hurried to the door and jerked it open.

"Good evening." Brad bowed to the thunderstruck maid. "Is Miss McKinney ready?"

God's eyebrows, Josie repeated silently. *He's gorgeous.* The only time she had seen a man this handsome was in Europe before the war. She and the

260

Shelbys had taken a holiday to Paris. In a museum called the Louvre, she had seen paintings of men like the one standing before her. Like him, they possessed an aura of aristocratic grace coupled with a devilishly handsome face and a physique fit to make a girl forget her raising.

But even they paled in comparison to this one. This one had the smile of an angel with eyes that promised wicked delights. If she were ten years younger, she would give Miss Kathlyn a run for her money.

Finally finding her voice, Josie said, "Ten more minutes." Then she slammed the door in Brad's face.

"Josie, could you help me?" Kathlyn rounded the screen, half in her gown, half out.

"Child, why didn't you tell me he looked like that? Now that's what I call a man. Bet that one can crunch pecans between his bare toes. And those brown eyes of his looked soft as summer butter."

"Why Josie," Kathlyn teased, "I didn't know you were such a poet."

"Not hardly. But if he was waiting on me, Missy, I wouldn't be in such an all fired rush to get my clothes on."

"Josie," Kathlyn gasped. "You should be ashamed of yourself." Actually her own thinking was along the same line, but she would die before admitting it.

"Hmmff!" Josie snorted, fastening Kathlyn into her gown with nimble fingers. "Just call 'em as I see 'em."

"Isn't it beautiful?" Kathlyn pirouetted in front of a gilt-edged looking glass, anxious to change the subject.

"Aren't you going to wear the jewelry?" Josie gestured to the box containing Lysette Hampton's glittering stones.

"No," Kathlyn said simply. She didn't deserve the jewelry and she wouldn't wear it.

The vulnerable yet stubborn expression on Kathlyn's face convinced Josie—just this once—to keep her advice to herself. "Well, are you going to wear any jewelry?" Like any good lady's maid, Josie knew that to be fashionable one had to wear jewelry, classically heavy jewelry, and lots of it.

The look on Kathlyn's face softened. Her eyes lit, reflecting an inner glow. Almost reverently she fastened the plain gold locket Brad had given her around her neck, caressing it as it lay between her breasts. She finished with amethyst drop earrings that had once belonged to her mother.

Josie approved. The jewels were unremarkable, but on a woman with Kathlyn's beauty they seemed exquisite.

"Now you sit over there in that chair. No not that one, the one under the window." With a gesture Josie indicated the Chippendale easy chair covered with Italian red silk damask. The iris lace of Kathlyn's gown and the crimson chair made for a dramatic contrast.

"What are you up to?" Kathlyn was suspicious of the expression on Josie's face. Nonetheless, she settled into the stately chair, resting her wrists daintily on the rolled armrests.

Kneeling in front of her, Josie fluffed Kathlyn's gown, curving the train around the ornately carved chair legs. She rose to her full height and studied the picture the lovely young woman presented.

Lounging elegantly in the beautiful chair, with the partially opened window at her side, a light breeze off the Mississippi blowing across her, lifting and playing with a wayward strand of hair, Kathlyn looked too fragile for this world. The pale bluish-purple of twilight bathed her, accenting the swells and indentations of her form. Liquid moonlight limned her profile, giving her an ethereal quality that couldn't be denied.

"He'll drop his roebucks," was Josie's heartfelt assessment.

The thought of Brad with false teeth made Kathlyn smile. It had not fully formed before *he* rapped on the door again.

"You stay right there," Josie ordered.

"Josie, this is silly." She made to rise.

"No back jawin', Missy. I mean it . . . right there." She shook her finger at Kathlyn.

262

Then Brad was virtually filling Kathlyn's cabin, and Josie was gone.

He was dressed meticulously as always. Attired in rags the man would be devastating, but in traditional black evening clothes he was beyond handsome. There wasn't a woman aboard the *Robert E. Lee* who could resist this gorgeous package, Kathlyn decided. Her included.

But it wasn't the clothes that caught the eye; it was the man inside. The black of his expertly tailored suit dulled in comparison to the rich color of his ebony hair. The blinding white of his shirt didn't quite equal the beautiful shine of his smile. And nothing . . . absolutely nothing, could surpass the masculine beauty of his body. *He probably* could *crack pecans with his toes.*

Slowly, gracefully, as if in a ballet, he closed the distance between them. He stood before her, the knife-sharp pleats of his trousers brushing the voluminous folds of her gown. She dropped her gaze. The sight of fine black cassimere touching lavender-blue lace seemed incredibly intimate to her. Her breath stilled.

"What's this?" he asked, pulling her to her feet.

She felt the warmth of his hand radiating on the surface of her breasts when he lifted her locket. Stroking it sensuously with the pad of his thumb, he compelled her to raise her eyes to his.

"A lovely gift," she answered.

For how long neither of them knew, iris orbs drowned in chocolate brown pools. He lowered the locket to its original position then, the backs of his fingers lightly touching her sensitized breasts. He was pleased she had worn his locket, even if she hadn't worn his mother's jewels. Maybe diamonds weren't to her taste, he reasoned.

"Hungry?" His voice was the merest hint of a whisper.

Kathlyn's mouth went dry. She was starving. She had been for eleven years.

Brad muffled a curse silently when the dinner bell

pierced the night air, breaking the seductive spell he had unwittingly woven.

"Shall we go?" Kathlyn asked a bit too breathlessly to suit her pride.

Brad restrained her with a hand to her shoulder. "About last night," he paused, "I'm sorry, Kat. I was a bit under the influence."

"A bit?" she questioned, raising her perfectly arched brows.

Brad had the grace to look chagrinned. "I guess I got a little carried away."

Kathlyn's eyes lost their teasing glint. "And carried me right along with you."

"I had heard that Tennessee moonlight was dangerous." He brushed a curl off her forehead.

"Treacherous," she agreed, trembling from his slightest touch.

"Maybe we'd better steer clear of it." His words sent one message, his eyes another. Brad didn't want to stay out of the moonlight with Kathlyn. In fact, he didn't want to stay out of Kathlyn. The provocative admission cost him his composure. "Why do you have to be so damn beautiful?" he groaned. "Please pardon my language." He remembered himself.

Kathlyn suppressed a smile. "Why do *you* have to be so damn beautiful?"

Brad's eyes widened. He chuckled then. "Why Flora Kathlyn McKinney, I'm shocked. A lady like yourself using such language." He tapped the end of her nose. "Besides, men aren't beautiful."

"What then?"

Slanting a glance at his reflection in the gilded mirror, he pretended to consider the matter. He swiveled his head from side to side, stroked his mustache thoughtfully, then ran a flattened hand down the front of his white satin waistcoat.

"Gorgeous?" Kathlyn offered.

"I think not."

"Lovely?"

"I hope not."

"Fair, comely, radiant, pretty?" She laughed at the increasing horror on his face.

"Don't you know any masculine adjectives?"

"What then?" she asked again, enjoying their moment of silliness.

He struck a regal pose and answered with all the aplomb of a monarch, "Dashingly handsome."

She shook her head, feigning disgust. "And modest. Don't forget modest," she deadpanned.

"That goes without saying."

"If your head will fit through the door, shouldn't we go to dinner now?"

He offered her his arm. "By all means."

As previously planned, Brad and Kathlyn dined with Captain Spivey and Jill. The riverboat cuisine was extensive, offering such culinary delights as gumbo and shrimp creole, doves in wine sauce, crumbly oyster patties covered with cream, fish baked in oiled paper flavored by limes. It was wasted on Kathlyn and Brad. They were far too interested in each other to notice the food.

Their good-natured bantering earlier had heightened the sexual tension that invariably crackled whenever they were within arms' length of each other. All it took to set their hearts pounding was the sound of the other's voice, a stolen glance. They were off and running. Everyone seated in their proximity was aware of this. Some found it charming; others had a different opinion.

Jill was to Brad's right, while the handsome gambler, Lucky Diamond, filled the vacant position beside Kathlyn. Rachel was seated to the gambler's left.

For a full hour, Jill and Rachel flirted with both Brad and Lucky. The women tried to outdo each other, not-so-subtly pointing out their attributes, bragging about the hearts they had broken, leaning over at every opportunity, displaying their bare bosoms like crafts at a county fair.

Brad was poised as always, his polite dinner conversation not revealing how little their presence affected him. Lucky was unaffected by them as well. Both men were only too aware of Kathlyn, who sat quietly, speaking only when spoken to.

"Miss McKinney, what takes you to Fort Smith?" Lucky asked.

It was the moment Rachel had been waiting for. "She's going to join her fiancé at Fort Gibson."

Kathlyn dropped her gaze to her lap. Brad's body tensed, though his face remained expressionless.

His eyes fixed on Kathlyn's face, Lucky realized he had caused her distress. That had not been his intention.

"That's interesting," the captain spoke as if he didn't notice the tension permeating the air.

"How so?"

"Why?" Brad and Lucky questioned simultaneously.

"In the past month we've had five beautiful young ladies traveling to Fort Gibson to be married." With that seemingly innocuous statement, the captain seized Brad and Lucky's undivided attention. "They were all marrying officers," he added.

Feigning nonchalance, Lucky asked, "Did you catch the names of the lucky men, Captain?"

"No, come to think of it, I didn't. Just that they were officers stationed at Fort Gibson."

"Six officers married in one month?" Brad said.

The tension around his mouth didn't bode well for Rachel and Stuart's plan. Rachel's heart threatened to beat her to death. *Damn*. Brad Hampton was too smart for his own good. Shifting her eyes to Kathlyn, she was pleased to see that her cousin seemed unaware of the significance of the conversation taking place around her. The silly chit was just looking down in her lap, with that distressed calf look on her face that men found irresistible.

As if to add credence to Rachel's thought, Lucky spoke softly to Kathlyn, "Miss McKinney, do you think your fiancé would care if you joined me for a breath of air?"

Lucky felt Brad's displeasure from across the table. Kathlyn's longing glance in her handsome employer's direction was not lost on him either. *So that's the way the wind blows.* He had thought Brad's interrogation of the captain merely the concern of an employer for his employee. Obviously not.

"A walk around the deck would be lovely, Brad," Jill hinted shamelessly, laying a possessive hand on his sleeve.

Rachel rolled her eyes heavenward.

"I'm sorry, I can't." Brad eased his arm away from Jill's grasp. "Miss McKinney and I have business to attend to."

Rachel's eyes hardened. But she held her tongue.

"Perhaps another time." Lucky stood and smiled down at Kathlyn. He turned his back on Brad, bent at the waist, kissed Kathlyn's hand lightly, and winked into her bemused face.

She stifled a grin. Was that jealousy she heard in Brad's voice? Possessiveness, at least. Her heart accelerated when Lucky moved away, and Brad assumed his place.

"Mr. Hampton, we'll reach Arkansas Post in the morning," Captain Spivey said.

Rachel tensed. She had to see that Brad left the boat tomorrow. But how?

"Thank you, Captain," Brad said. "I'll be ready to go ashore first thing. Now, if you will, please excuse us."

"You're going into town tomorrow?" Rachel asked before Brad was out of earshot.

He turned slowly. "Yes," he said, his voice bland, his eyes alert.

"Just wondered." She shrugged dismissively, turning away so he might not see the triumphant gleam in her eyes.

Lucky watched the exchange with more than passing interest.

267

* * *

"Business to attend to?" Kathlyn grinned at Brad's profile as they walked along the texas deck.

"I merely wanted to rescue you from that lecherous gambler." Brad kept his eyes averted, feigning great interest in the stars overhead.

"And I appreciate it." There was an unmistakable note of wry humor in her tone.

He stiffened slightly. "Perhaps you'd like to go back inside. I'm sure his offer still stands." He continued to walk away from the dining area. Faster now.

She stole a peek at his face. She cleared her throat to hide a chuckle. Brad Hampton—gorgeous, wealthy, powerful—had the unmistakable look of a man whose favorite horse was being coveted. "I said I appreciate your efforts on my behalf. Wait, we just passed our staterooms."

"Obviously you want to walk in the moonlight. Since I came between you and your handsome gambler, the least I can do is take a turn around the deck with you." Brad winced. He could only hope he didn't sound as jealous to Kathlyn as he did to himself.

"He's not my gambler. Besides, didn't you say Tennessee moonlight is dangerous?" Her voice was light, airy, breathless. She *did* want to walk in the moonlight, and *not* with the gambler.

Brad swiveled, grasped Kathlyn's hand, and pulled her into a darkened alcove. Placing both his thumbs beneath her chin, he angled her head, cradling her face in his palms, his lips mere inches from hers.

"We're in Arkansas," he whispered before his open mouth claimed hers.

268

Chapter Thirty-one

His solid body pinned her to the wall. Hungrily, he plumbed the warm, moist depths of her mouth with his tongue, breathing life from his lungs into hers. Over and over he drank from her sweetness until they both ached with need.

When he felt her hands twine in his hair, he flattened his palms against the wall over her head. Still he continued to kiss her, revelling in her uninhibited response.

Her hands skimmed his back, coming to rest on his hips. He groaned low in his throat and ground himself against her belly. A hot bolt of lightning tore through his life-giving member. It shocked him with its force, returning him to his senses.

Wrenching his lips from hers, he uttered against her forehead, "I'm sorry. I didn't mean for this to happen again. But God help me, Kat, you're driving me crazy. I want to make love to you. Is that so terrible?" He asked of himself as well as Kathlyn.

Her voice strained and throaty, she answered, "No. It's not terrible. It's just not right. Under other circumstances, it would be wonderful. I thought it was right eleven years ago." She balled her fists in frustration.

"But everything's so complicated now," she continued. "I'm not sixteen anymore. We're not young and irresponsible with only our own lives to consider. We both have responsibilities, obligations."

The mention of responsibilities and obligations brought Glenn to Brad's mind again. He couldn't bear

269

to hear any more. Gently, he placed his fingers over her lips. They were warm, swollen, moist from his kiss. "Shh, let's not talk of that tonight."

The vulnerable look in Brad's eyes tore at Kathlyn's heart. She wondered if perhaps he was as hurt by the past as she, as uncertain about the future, and maybe . . . just maybe . . . a little frightened by it all. Her stomach knotted at the thought. She leaned her head against his chest.

For a poignant moment they stood like that. Him holding her in the moonlight, her listening to the strong, propulsive beat of his heart. Then gently he dropped a kiss behind her ear. "I wonder," he whispered.

"What?"

He nipped her earlobe. "If it was as wonderful as I remember."

There was no doubt in her mind to what he was referring. Their night of gardenias.

How many times had she wondered the same thing? How often had she relived every delicious moment of that night, trembling at the memory of his heated touch, tasting his kisses again, feeling him warm and alive, moving inside of her. Raising up on tiptoes, she rested her hands on his shoulders and pressed her lips to his.

"Attending to business?" an amused voice queried.

Brad whirled around and shielded Kathlyn from the gambler's view.

She buried her face between his shoulder blades, embarrassed at being discovered in such a way.

"What we are doing is none of your concern, Mr. Diamond. You had better move on." Brad's warning struck like a whiplash in the night.

"Pardon me, ma'am." Lucky sounded sincere. "Actually, I wanted to speak to you, Mr. Hampton. Perhaps later." He bowed and backed away.

Brad felt foolish, barking at Lucky like that. It was just that his emotions were running rampant. Turning and pulling Kathlyn into his embrace, he dropped his head back and looked skyward. Once more, he felt like howling.

The full moon hung in the sky like a shiny silver dollar. The liquid rays streaming from it washed over the deck. A light breeze wafted over the shimmering river, cooling their heated bodies.

"Let's walk, please," Kathlyn requested once she regained a measure of control.

Brad nodded. Placing his arm around her tiny waist, he pulled her loosely against his side and moved deeper into the night. He felt her shiver. "Are you chilled?"

She was trembling, but not from cold. She was trembling with unappeased desire.

Halting in another secluded spot, Brad removed his coat and placed it around her shoulders.

She stared up into his passion-darkened eyes. "Thank you."

Ever so slowly he lowered his lips to hers. As she opened to receive his tender kiss, he slid his hand behind her neck. Time and time again he sipped from the sweet nectar of her mouth, massaging her neck lightly.

Never had he wanted a woman as badly as he wanted Kathlyn. And he didn't just want to have sex. He wanted to love her. To love her both physically and emotionally, to drink from her sweetness and feel her passion flow, to make her desire him as much as he desired her, to capture her completely, body, soul, and spirit.

Kathlyn felt Brad's need and responded. His worshipful kisses were more erotic to her than anything she'd ever experienced. Each time his warm lips brushed over hers, each time his smooth tongue dipped lightly into her mouth, her heart threatened to pound her to death.

Twining her arms around his neck, she pulled him closer and, breathlessly, deepened their kiss. His passionate groan excited her all the more. Boldly she plundered his moist cavern while brushing against his

271

solid, warm body. As light as a butterfly in flight, his hands fluttered over her soft curves, searching for and pleasuring every sensitive point.

Together, they shook with need.

While continuing to hold her close his voice sounded husky in her ear. "Sweetheart, we've got to stop." He knew in another moment he would be lost.

Kathlyn was lost already, but she didn't have the words to tell him. "Oh Brad," was all she could manage.

A lump formed in his throat. His name was like a caress on her lips. He felt like a lovesick fool, about to burst into flames. "Oh Kat." Another wave of longing swept over him. He *had* to explain what he was feeling. Had to make her understand. "I want you, but not just your beautiful body. Sweetheart, I want all of you. Do you understand what I'm saying?"

Kathlyn heard the yearning in Brad's voice and hurt for them both.

A noise alerted them that someone was walking their way. Reluctantly, they pulled apart. Some moments later they found themselves standing outside their staterooms, knowing nothing had been settled between them, but feeling powerless to do anything about it. Brad leaned around Kathlyn, pushing her door open. "I guess this is good night then." Gently, he brushed his lips against hers.

Staring into his eyes, she stepped inside the room.

He took a deep breath and closed the door, remaining on the gallery outside.

Inside her cabin, Kathlyn collapsed in the red silk chair. She held her breath, listening to Brad open his door and step into his room. The swish of fabric told her he was removing his coat. The sound continued. He must be shedding his shirt by now. Remembrance of him, bare chested on the hotel balcony, caused perspiration to form on her upper lip. A squeak then a plop and she visualized him dropping into a chair and taking off his boots.

The next sound proved her undoing. On quiet feet,

Brad crossed over to the door joining their rooms and turned the key. Metal scratching metal, he unlocked his door. With that simple act, Brad told her that if she wanted an intimate relationship, she would have to come to him.

It would have to be her decision. A decision that took her all of two seconds to make. She would give herself to Brad for as long as he wanted her.

And this decision did not involve her relationship with Glenn, she reasoned. It was about her and Brad, spending what few moments they had left, loving one another with all their hearts. If in the end they went their separate ways, then so be it. At least they would have beautiful memories. That was a sight more than most people had.

Jumping to her feet, she shed her gown. Pins flew as trembling hands loosened her elaborate coiffure. She brushed her long mane exactly one hundred strokes until it cascaded down her back, shining like a river of liquid diamonds.

Barefooted, dressed in a pale periwinkle gown, she moved to the door. Gingerly, she placed her hand on the door knob. As if it were red hot, she jerked her hand back and wiped her moist palm down her thigh. She drew a steadying breath. Then quickly, before she lost her nerve, she threw the door open.

He was standing with his back to her, looking out the window, the moon visible through the opening. He seemed relaxed, as if half naked women rush into his room every night. Eyeing him from head to toe, she could well imagine that they did.

When she moved to his side he slowly turned. The look of naked desire flashing in his eyes shook her. Her fear must have shown on her face, for his next words were meant to tease.

"What took you so long?"

Throwing her arms around his bare shoulders, she nipped at his chin. "Chew glass, Mr. Hampton."

"I'd rather chew you, Kat," he growled. Then he feasted on her like a starved animal.

273

Scant moments later they were lying side-by-side on Brad's bed with only the moonlight as their cover. They had undressed each other with eager hands while sharing kisses so passionate they were rendered breathless.

Brad gently pushed Kathlyn onto her back. His loving gaze absorbed her incredible beauty. He was quite certain he'd never seen a woman as beautiful and desirable as the one lying before him.

"I didn't get to see all of you before. I want to look my fill." His virile body stiffened as he allowed one long finger to trail along after his gaze. It required all the self-discipline he could muster not to take her as she lay. But looking into her liquid iris eyes he fought for self-control and fanned the flames of her desire.

Kathlyn was surprised that she felt no shame lying naked before Brad. The look of pure adoration in his eyes turned her bones to molten lava; his gentle touch left a trail of fire in its wake.

Shifting slightly toward him, she was afforded her first unimpeded look at a completely naked man. He was glorious! His tanned shoulders seemed a yard wide; his stomach hard and rippled as a washboard. And below . . .

Shyly, she reached forth her small, white hand, sifting slender fingers through the coarse black hair covering his chest. When she allowed her hand to drift lower along the tapering hair line he sucked in his breath.

Before Kathlyn could dip her inquisitive hand below his waist Brad grasped it and placed it over his thundering heart. "Not yet," he moaned, kissing her desperately.

Exquisite sensations burned throughout her body, coming together to pool in a throbbing ache in her moist center. Deep inside she was swollen and hungry. She knew that Brad alone could satisfy her need. And it certainly felt like he was giving it his best effort.

He was everywhere at once. His tongue, lips, and hands worshipped every inch of her body, tuning it to

274

a fevered pitch. He couldn't seem to get enough of the taste and feel of her.

She was so fresh and uninhibited in her passionate responses. The little moans slipping past her kiss-reddened lips caused him to quiver with need. The feel of her swollen, throbbing breasts burning against his bare chest stole his breath, and the trembling of her hands as she sought to pleasure him raised goose bumps along his heated flesh.

"My beautiful, beautiful Kat," he murmured passionately as he sought the center of her desire with an intimate caress. Lovingly he stroked her where no other person had ever touched. Her world tipped precariously.

He nuzzled her long slender neck. Kissing his way up to her shell-like ear, he dipped his tongue inside, swirling it sensuously.

"Can you feel how much I want you?" he whispered hoarsely.

Kathlyn shuddered as Brad labored to bring her desire to full bloom. The throbbing ache in her womanhood was punctuated by her rapid inhalations.

When she was certain she was about to burst into a fiery flame, Brad slid between her quivering thighs. Instinctively, she opened up to him like a beautiful flower. Then, for a split second, she tensed.

He recognized her hesitation and crooned lovingly into her ear. When he felt her relax he reached between them to position the tip of his huge, aching need at the mouth of her soft flesh. Gazing into her dazed eyes he slowly slid his most intimate part inside of her and stilled. He shuddered from the sensation.

It had taken them eleven years to get here. But now that they had, it wasn't enough. The erotic sensation of warm fullness felt wonderful, but Kathlyn knew there had to be more. But what? Wordlessly, she questioned Brad with her eyes as he remained poised—still—above her.

"Tell me what you want," he instructed softly, mingling his breath with her own.

"Move." It was more a moan than a word.

He gladly obeyed. In the space of an instant he thrust forward. Resting his forearms on either side of her head, he set the pace. She was so warm and so tight. He feared he might lose control. Tenderly, he dropped tiny kisses over her eyes and cheeks, along her jaw, and down her neck. With his breath hot on her mouth, his full lips barely touching hers, his body quaked with need.

He carried them to the mountain top of sensual fulfillment time and again. They were overwhelmed with the fierceness of their passion. Her hoarse cries mingled with his deep moans.

Grasping her close, he ground himself against the core of her womanhood. Then he raised his head, looked intently into her passion-brightened eyes, and watched her plunge over the cliff, gasping from the power of her completion. He kissed her passionately, as earth-shattering tremors racked his body with his own glorious release.

Drifting slowly back to earth, he continued to caress her silky flesh. Although his passion was momentarily sated, the need to love her was greater than ever.

He bent to her heaving breasts capturing first one rosy peak and then the other between his lips. He remained warm and cradled inside her love nest.

She tangled her hands in his thick hair, pulling his face ever closer to her chest. Moaning his name, she felt his maleness swell and fill her once more. With growing desire she writhed beneath him, clutching the rumpled covers in her fists.

Then they exploded once more . . . crying out in unison with the joy of shared passion.

He slid to her side and wrapped her in his arms. "That was wonderful, my love," he whispered in a tremulous voice.

Her eyes were wide, dazed with wonder. "Is love always so . . . so moving?"

Angling up on one elbow, he smiled down into her face, lazily tracing the outline of her sensual mouth. "I don't know . . . I've never experienced anything like it before." He noticed she was fading fast. "My poor darling, I've exhausted you."

"I'm not complaining."

Gathering her naked body against him, he chuckled roguishly.

She cuddled against him. When her heavy lids closed, he thought she was asleep.

Bending low to place a feather light kiss on her lips, he confessed softly, "I love you, my precious Kat."

Her heart ached.

Kathlyn awakened abruptly with an overwhelming sense of anxiety. It was not yet daylight, though the mauve shadows cast about her room signaled that dawn was near. She was alone in her own bed.

Instantly, helplessly, she burned from ebony roots to manicured toenails as she recalled the moving events that transpired in Brad's bed throughout the night. It all seemed like a beautiful dream.

Twice more during the night he carried her on a long sensual journey and each time she lost a bit more of her heart to him. Then, after loving her soundly, he carried her to her own bed.

Her emotions were mixed. Just the thought of Brad's potent lovemaking set her heart to pounding. He was the most exciting, virile, tender, loving man she'd ever known.

Truth to tell, she wouldn't trade anything on earth for the pleasure they'd shared. And even though they'd been apart but a short while, she felt empty without him. It was more than obvious to her that the handsome man from Georgia had captured her heart.

But that didn't change the fact that she was promised to another. *Glenn.* She owed him, yet she hadn't a ghost of a notion what to do about it.

Somehow she couldn't imagine herself married to an aristocrat like Brad. Yet how could she go to Glenn soiled. *Soiled* . . . such an ugly word for such a beautiful experience!

After much soul searching, she remembered the plan she had formulated last night. It would have to do. She would enjoy the time she and Brad had left, love him for the moment, and not worry about the future.

Throwing her legs over the edge of the bed, she rose to her feet. She was humming pleasantly and tying on a wrapper when she heard a quiet knock on the door that separated her room from Brad's. "Just a minute."

A deep, familiar voice ordered, "Open up sleepy head."

Just the sound of Brad's voice caused Kathlyn's legs to go weak. She steadied herself with a hand on the wardrobe, stole a peek in the mirror, then hurried across the room and opened the door.

He leaned against the door jamb, smiling seductively, looking like she had never seen him before: from Stetson hat to cowboy boots he was a tribute to the Western male.

"Where's your horse, Tex?" she teased.

His sensual smile spread at the sight of her slightly disheveled appearance. Seeing her with her wrapper half on and her fiery hair tangled about her shoulders was strangely erotic. Her lips were still swollen from his kisses; a beard burn reddened her skin. He knew without a doubt he'd never seen a more desirable woman.

Snaking an arm around her waist, he pulled her into his room and against his body. Absently, she registered that he left the door open as he cupped his other hand around her nape. He guided her face to his own.

"Good morning," he whispered.

She expected the kiss to be gentle, but was pleasantly surprised. Though his outward composure appeared intact, his kiss spoke of barely restrained desire. Her response was mutually ravenous.

After kissing her breathless, he gazed down into her upturned face. "We need to talk."

"About what?" she asked, feigning ignorance.

"Us. The future."

Raising a delicate hand to stroke his cheek, her eyes filled with love, she responded, "I don't know if I'm ready for this."

Momentarily, his own fears flashed across his handsome face.

She grew uneasy. "How about some coffee first?"

"Laced with brandy?" he deadpanned.

"Arsenic?" she teased.

Just then an excited voice came from Kathlyn's room. "Daddy, Miss Kathlyn, where are you?"

In unison Brad and Kathlyn breathed, "Dru."

Dru sailed through the doorway just as Brad and Kathlyn jumped apart. "Daddy," Dru greeted enthusiastically, planting a big kiss on her daddy's cheek. He scooped her up in his arms, tossing her into the air, petticoats and platinum curls fluttering madly. Her childish laughter filled the room.

"Did you have fun with Millie?" he asked breathlessly.

"Yes sir. Did you know the boat's gonna stop today?"

"I sure did." Brad looked over Dru's head into Kathlyn's eyes. "We're docking in a few minutes. I'll be back before dinner."

"Can I play with Millie while you're gone?" Dru scratched her daddy's shoulder, gaining his attention.

"Whatever Miss Kathlyn says." He placed Dru on the floor.

"Okeedokee," she chirped, hurrying back into the other cabin to greet Ishta.

"Okeedokee?" Brad raised a questioning brow. He moved over to the bed and picked up a gun and holster. "Do you suppose that means yes?"

"I guess." Kathlyn's eyes narrowed on the weapon Brad was buckling around his hips.

He turned toward her, noting her unease. "It's just a precaution." When she didn't look convinced, he leaned down and kissed her. "We'll talk tonight."

She nodded and brought forth a weak smile. "Is that a promise or a threat?"

"Come here."

She stepped into his arms.

Eyes bright, he whispered something into her ear.

Her cheeks flamed; the pulse in her throat beat rapidly. "Brad Hampton!"

He chuckled. "And that's a promise!"

Still blushing, she whispered, "Hurry back."

His dimple deepened. "Okeedokee."

Part Three
The West

Love shouts, clamors, pierces the heart.
Then falls silent.
To be rediscovered in the quiet, still, sound
of a lover's voice.
To be seen in the tender shadows of a lover's eyes.
Love is fragile.
Love is priceless.

Love is forever . . .

— Teresa Howard

Chapter Thirty-two

Captain Spivey stood on the hurricane deck, squinting against the summer sun, and guided the *Robert E. Lee* into port. He had taken the cut-off to White River, entering the state of Arkansas some twenty-five miles north of the mouth of the Arkansas River. He saw Arkansas Post in the distance.

It was a small settlement where boats docked in order to load and unload cargo, and where passengers changed from packets headed south to New Orleans to those headed west for Fort Smith and Fort Gibson.

A typical western town, the streets and boardwalks were full of roughnecks, roustabouts, farmers, stable hands, cowboys, and hard-case gunslicks. Its few buildings, constructed of weathered clapboard, lined both sides of its main street like belles and beaux assembled for the Virginia reel. From his vantage point the captain identified three saloons, a general store, a blacksmith shop, a livery stable, and the town jail.

A hard rain the night before had turned the street into a trough of black gumbo. Wagons, pulled by heavy-hooved work horses, bogged down to their axles. Men, wearing tall work boots, forded the quagmire as if such an inconvenience was their lot in life.

Suddenly, two cursing drunks burst from one of the saloons. Flesh pounding flesh, punctuated by vile oaths, drew the riverboatman's gaze. He watched as the combatants' momentum carried them into the street where both were soon covered with mud, streaked with blood. A few onlookers watched from the boardwalks, cheering the roughnecks on.

Before either man could do the other significant

harm, a tough-looking man with a tin star pinned to his vest rushed from the saloon, fired a couple of warning shots into the air, and hustled the brawlers off to jail. All of this with an air of boredom that testified to the town's violent nature.

During the altercation, two young boys raced down the street, slipping and sliding in the mud, chasing several pigs which had escaped from their pens. Amidst the squealing and grunting of the pigs and the laughter of the frolicking boys, Spivey couldn't decide whether the brawlers or the pig brigade had offered a more entertaining sight.

But he was certain of one thing. Arkansas Post was not a town for the faint-hearted. The hard cases in this uncivilized settlement had to be approached on their own terms. That's why he was concerned that Brad Hampton wanted to go into town. He hoped the sophisticated banker wasn't biting off more than he could chew.

When Captain Spivey dropped his gaze to the texas deck and saw Brad by the railing, he was suitably impressed. "Well, I'll be damned," Spivey said.

Dressed in well-worn denim breeches, plainly tooled Western boots, shirt, vest, and dusty John B. Stetson, Brad looked like anything but an aristocrat. His .45 Navy Colt tied to his thigh gave no evidence of the genteel businessman Spivey knew him to be.

As the Captain took Brad's measure, Brad patted the hunting knife and scabbard that were tied to his bare leg beneath his Levi's. In addition to his other weapons, he had a .41 two-shot derringer, resting inside his vest pocket.

Brad rarely wore a handgun in Georgia, but he knew how to use one. He had almost always won the local shooting contests held on the Fourth of July. Just as he had that Independence Day long ago, when he and Kathlyn had first made love.

Smiling from the memory, he could hardly wait to return to her. He missed her already. As if his thoughts had conjured her up, a small, white hand rested on his shoulder. He turned, drowning in iris eyes.

Squealing, Dru clapped her hands in delight. "Daddy, with your gun you look just like the cowboys in my picture books."

Brad smiled at Dru's excitement, then turned his gaze back to Kathlyn. In that instant they relived the hours they had spent in each others' arms, remembered the passionate promise he made just moments before.

And it was written all over their faces. Standing behind Kathlyn, Rachel saw that at once. Brad couldn't get into Arkansas Post soon enough to suit her. "I thought you were going into town. What are you doing here?"

As usual, Brad ignored her. He was getting good at that. Kneeling, he kissed Dru on the cheek. "You stay with Miss Kathlyn." He spoke Kat's name like a caress. "I'll be back before you know it."

Dru returned her daddy's kiss. "Bring me and Tandy something."

He nodded. Anxious to complete his business and return to a certain violet-eyed angel, he winked at Kathlyn. "See you tonight."

"Tonight," she whispered.

Smiling, he descended the steps and made his way to the gangplank.

"You be back here in two hours, Mr. Hampton, or the boat's liable to leave without you," Mate Gunn warned from his post by the exit gate. "I don't know why city folks always go ashore. Not safe no matter how many guns they wear."

Gunn's low grumble reached Brad's ears, but did nothing to dampen his spirit. Visions of the coming evening with Kathlyn had put a grin on his face. And it was there to stay.

Or so he thought . . .

Pushing his way through the batwings of the Blue Hog Wallow Saloon, Brad's gaze traveled throughout

285

the room. The establishment certainly lived up to its name. It was a filthy dive, and heavy, miasmic smoke hung in the air. The stench of unwashed bodies and spittle-coated floors was stifling.

He was surprised by the large number of customers so early in the day. Men crowded the bar or sat around tables, drinking, playing cards, and otherwise passing time. A heavily bearded septuagenarian, spare as a skeleton, sat in the corner of the hall, tickling the ivories of a broken-down piano. Torturing the ivories was more accurate, Brad decided.

He stepped up to the bar. A dark-eyed saloon girl looped her hand through his arm. As he turned his head slightly, his nostrils twitched. The strong smell of her cheap perfume caused his eyes to tear.

"How 'bout something cool to drink, cowboy?" she purred.

Brad shook his head. "Thanks, but no."

"Something hot then?"

The falsely seductive look on her face left Brad cold. His expression remained carefully blank. "Sorry, miss. I don't have the time."

Something fierce flickered in her eyes. Her brittle smile remained in place.

"I need to hire a couple of men," he said.

She gestured around her. "You're in the right place. Who do they have to kill?"

Several men within hearing laughed.

Brad wasn't altogether sure she was teasing. "I just need them to transport supplies to the *Robert E. Lee.* Should take about an hour."

"Folks round here are picky 'bout who they work for." She shrugged, purposefully allowing the strap to slide off her left shoulder. "I might be able to help you though. You know, put in a good word. But you'll have to buy me a drink first."

Brad's smile was false. All he could think about was getting back to Kathlyn. He suspected the saloon girl could make his task easier, however, by pointing him in the right direction.

286

"Certainly," he said finally, catching the bartender's eye. "Two whiskeys." He pitched a silver dollar on the counter.

"You sure that's all you need." She placed her hand on Brad's chest. "I've got a room upstairs."

This was getting tiresome. Tossing off his drink in one gulp, he gently wrapped his fingers around her wrist. Removing the girl's hand from his chest, he held it between their bodies a moment. "Sorry, another time. I've got a boat to catch."

"Hey, mister, that's my girl you're pawing," a rough voice boomed from the back of the saloon.

The noise level was such that Brad didn't hear him.

"Hey, mister, I'm talking to you," the voice thundered again, louder this time. "Take your filthy hands off my girl."

Turning, Brad saw a tall, heavy-set man moving his way. He wore homespun range clothes and sported a big Colt, tied low on his leg. His red-rimmed eyes were blazing. His hand rested on the butt of his gun.

"Sorry, friend," Brad said, releasing the girl. He stepped away from the bar. Brad and the man squared off. Brad's expression was pleasant; the drunk was scowling. The saloon girl rubbed her wrist as if Brad had hurt her.

"Bastard," the drunk yelled. "I'm going to kill you for touching her."

"Look, I'm sure we can . . ." Brad began.

Foolishly, the man went for his gun.

Brad drew his Navy and shot his assailant through the hand before he cleared leather. The wounded man bellowed in pain, sinking to the floor.

"Oh hell," Brad muttered. Disgusted at the turn of events, he turned to leave. Before he could take a step, the barkeep hit him in the back of the head with the butt end of a sawed-off shotgun. Barely conscious, he sank to his knees.

Above him, the saloon girl's blurred face contorted into a smug grin. A large man appeared at her side.

Brad was unable to focus on his face. His field of

vision was obscured by the whiskey bottle in the big man's hand. It grew larger as it moved toward to Brad's head. A devastating pain exploded in his skull. Glass showered his face. Then a heavy black curtain fell.

Marshal Henry Rhodes stepped around Stuart Shephard, a bag of money clutched in his left hand. "Damn near killed the son of a bitch," the lawman observed. Bending low over Brad's inert form, he placed a calloused finger at the base of Brad's throat. "He's still alive. Colt, you and Rod drag him out back and take him to the shack. Tell Doon I'll be along tonight and deal with him."

They did as they were told.

Stuart's money had talked effectively and quickly. The marshal was more than obliging. As usual. "I didn't pay you to take him for a ride. I want the son of a bitch dead and buried by sundown," Stuart hissed, tossing the neck of the broken whiskey bottle aside.

Recognizing the light of insanity in Stuart's eyes, the marshal held up placating hands. "I've never let you down before," he reminded Stuart. "And I won't let you down now."

Stuart glowered. "See that you don't!"

The bartender moved over beside the marshal after Stuart disappeared through the batwings. "Wonder why he didn't kill the stranger himself. Why he hired you to do it?"

" 'Cause he's a chicken shit," the marshal answered correctly. Hefting the bulging bag, he grinned. "But he's a rich chicken shit."

The men laughed lustily then went about their business, as if nothing untoward had happened.

"You're gonna wear a hole in the deck," Jacob Shelby spoke from behind Kathlyn.

Kathlyn started at the unexpected voice. For the past thirty minutes she had stood on the texas deck, watching for some sign of Brad. Rachel hovered at her side.

288

"Mr. Shelby! Thank goodness. I'm worried about Br . . . about Mr. Hampton. He hasn't come back from town yet." Worried was putting it lightly; Kathlyn was frantic. The boat whistle had already sounded twice, signaling the passengers to board. The *Robert E. Lee* would leave soon.

"Don't worry, Miss McKinney. Brad strikes me as the kind of man who can take care of himself. Besides, you know how conscientious he is about Dru. He'll be back," Jacob sought to reassure her.

To no avail. "I don't like this. He should be back by now. He wouldn't wait until the last minute. Something has happened. I know it has."

"Have you checked with Captain Spivey? Perhaps he'll send someone into town," Jacob offered.

"I hadn't thought of that." Crossing over to the stairs leading to the captain's perch, she found him preparing for departure. Immediately, she voiced her fears.

"Now don't you worry your pretty little head, Miss," Spivey soothed, pulling the chain at his side. Another round of loud blasts belched into the air. "That oughta do it. There's no way he could have missed that. He'll be along any minute now."

"You won't leave without him, will you?" Kathlyn's throat constricted.

"Of course not. If he's not back in five minutes, I'll send one of the men after him."

"Thank you," Kathlyn said sheepishly. She was relieved by his assurances and a bit embarrassed to have carried on so. She returned to the cabin deck and resumed her vigil. Jacob was nowhere in sight.

"Feel better?"

She colored slightly as she turned around and looked up into the friendly eyes of Lucky Diamond. "As a matter of fact, I do," she admitted, smiling slightly.

"He'll be along in a few minutes." He winked and flashed her what might have been a heart-stopping grin, if she had been paying him any mind. "I know I would."

Suddenly, the great paddle wheel of the *Robert E. Lee* began to churn the water.

"Oh my God, we're moving," Kathlyn gasped.

"What the hell?" this, from Lucky.

Rachel stood a short distance away, enjoying the look of pure terror on Kathlyn's face. She knew by now that Stuart was in the perch, holding a gun to Captain Spivey's head. Her smile faded. She didn't like what she saw in Kathlyn's eyes. "Kathlyn." Rachel stepped forward, grabbing Kathlyn's arm.

"Ask Mrs. Shelby to see after Dru," Kathlyn told Rachel, ripping her arm from Rachel's grasp. Stumbling as she ran, she made her way down to the lower deck, arriving at the exit gate as it was being closed by Mate Gunn.

He was shocked to see the slight Southern belle barreling toward him like a runaway freight. "You can't leave, Miss McKinney. We're already moving. It's too late to get off."

"Move out of my way," Kathlyn shouted. She rushed past him, hiking her skirts to her knees, and leaping the short distance to the dock, landing safely on the weathered planks.

"Damn," Lucky cursed. By the time he reached the gate, it was too late to pursue her. Kathlyn and Arkansas Post had grown small in the distance.

Colt Chandler and Rod Hawkins dragged Brad out of the Blue Hog Wallow Saloon and tied him belly-down across a saddled mare. Mounting their own horses, they led him away from town. They traveled some seven miles, crossing prairies and forest, arriving at a shack by mid-afternoon.

"Doon!" Colt shouted, reining in.

"Hold it right there." A hoarse warning sounded from a thicket behind them. It was accompanied by the ominous click of a rifle. "One false move and you're dead as buzzard guts."

"Doon, what the hell's got into you? It's Colt and Rod. Get your sorry ass over here and help us with his prisoner," Rod said.

Now conscious, Brad listened intently. Visions of Kathlyn and Dru—at Rachel's mercy—caused his heart to quicken in his chest. Damn it all, he had to get away from these imbeciles before the boat sailed.

"Not so quick, you oily snake," Doon sneered. "Maybe you're Colt and Rod and maybe you ain't. Drop your guns and hold your hands up."

Oh for heaven's sake! Brad was losing his patience. He knew the sheriff meant to kill him and he planned on being long gone before the man arrived. But if this Doon didn't cease his theatrics, he wouldn't have sufficient time for an escape.

The brigands' patience was running thin as well. Yet they had no choice but to do as Doon said. Dropping their guns, they held their hands high in the air.

From the corner of one eye, Brad saw Doon emerge from the woods. The man looked two days older than dirt; he was ninety if he was a day. His beard, white as the new fallen snow, hung down to his waist. A head full of white hair glistened from under a tall, rounded mountaineer's hat. He carried a huge .60 caliber Kentucky rifle that must have been as old as he was. And it was aimed dead-center at Colt and Rod.

"Now get down off them bones of soap slow and easy." Without turning his head, he spit a long stream of tobacco juice on the ground.

"Damn fool," Rod muttered, exasperated. "He's lost what little mind he had." He spoke to his partner who agreed wholeheartedly.

Undaunted by Rod's harsh words, Doon approached Brad's abductors and peered into their faces. Then he smiled, revealing a mouth full of tobacco stained snags. "I'll be damned. It is you. A man can't be too careful these days. Whatcha waitin' for? Come on in and have a drink."

Relieved to see Doon lower his Kentucky, the two men retrieved their guns and turned their attention to Brad.

Doon paused on the top step, pointing to Brad with

291

the barrel end of his rifle. "What's he done?"

"Hell if I know, but whatever it is, he'll be dead by nightfall," Colt answered.

Doon spit out another stream of brown liquid. "Why wait? One shot from my Kentucky and he'll be deader'n vomited maggots."

"Rhodes said to wait until he got here. So we'll wait." Rod spoke with such authority that Doon didn' question him further.

The cold metal of Colt's pistol pressed against Brad's temple as he untied him. "One wrong move and we'll give the old man the nod. That'll be the end of you. Now get into that shack." He shoved Brad forward.

Brad's knees almost buckled under his full weight. The two blows to his head had left him weak. With great effort he placed one foot in front of the other, finally stepping into the dimly lit cabin.

"Sit down," Colt growled, shoving Brad toward a cane-backed chair.

Brad gladly complied. The cabin consisted of one room about twelve-feet square. A fireplace took up most of one wall. A filthy cot lay up against another wall. The only light in the shack came through the door and one small window. A plank table stood in the middle of the room, surrounded by four cane-back chairs.

His gaze flickered to the door, judging the distance he would have to cross when he made his escape.

"I don't like what I see in your eyes, mister." Doon startled Brad with his rough voice. "If you're thinking about runnin', forget it. Nobody gets away from Door Handle. That's why the marshal sends hard cases like you out here."

Brad's eyes bounced off Doon's. There was cruelty in their depths, like a boar pig's; he would do well to be wary of the man.

"I'll fix it where he can't escape," Rod said, producing a length of piggin string from his pocket and tying Brad to the chair.

"Leave his left hand free," Doon ordered, cryptically. The evil smile on his face raised the hair on Brad's nape.

"Hold his hand flat down on the table," Doon instructed Rod. "Hold him tight 'cause he ain't gonna like this."

Brad knew full well what Doon intended. And he wasn't about to sit passively by while a nail was hammered through the back of his hand. Balling his fist, he backhanded Rod, driving him against the wall. Rod's nose was reduced to bloody pulp.

"Whoopee!" Doon yelled. "This one's got balls o' brass. I don't think you younguns can handle him."

Colt's face turned red. Grabbing a thick hickory stick, he clubbed Brad about the face and upper body.

Brad defended himself with his free arm. He was oblivious to the pain. All that mattered was that he break free. Determined, he wrested the stick from Colt. Then, as much as he was able, he returned the punishment.

Seeing that things had gotten out of hand, Doon retrieved his Kentucky, cocked it, and pointed it straight at Brad's head. "Go ahead, mister, give me a reason to blow your brains out."

Slowly, Brad lowered the hickory and dropped it to the floor.

"Colt, you and Rod hold his hand flat on the table," Doon repeated, disgusted.

Rod, wary of Brad's backhand, wrapped his arms around Brad's chest and squeezed, cutting off his breath. Colt grabbed Brad's hand and slammed it against the table. Brad fought both men, breaking loose, upsetting his chair. After significant injury to themselves, the brigands subdued Brad, righted the chair, and managed to flatten his hand on the table.

Suddenly, Brad relaxed, letting his free arm go limp. Feeling him relax, Colt nodded for Doon to proceed.

Doon laid his rifle against the doorjamb, picked up a ball peen hammer and sixteen penny nail. "Now we'll see how tough he is." Holding the nail just above

Brad's hand, he drew back the hammer to strike.

Before the steel hit its mark, Brad jerked his arm back and in the process pulled Colt's hand beneath the point of the nail. The hammer struck home and drove the tip through Colt's flesh, anchoring his hand to the table.

All hell broke loose in the tiny cabin. Colt bellowed at the top of his lungs and let out a string of oaths that would have singed the most hardened sailor's ears.

Brad reached down, pulled his knife from its scabbard, cut the piggin string that held him bound to the chair, and, with a backward flip of his wrist, buried the weapon in Doon's throat. The old man gurgled and fell facedown on the floor.

Rod drew alongside Brad, making for the door as if the breath of Satan were on his neck. Brad swung his right fist. He struck the fleeing man in the rib cage under his right arm. Stunned by the power of the blow, Rod bent over, gasping for air. A second blow rendered him unconscious.

Colt was writhing in agony, attempting to remove the nail from his hand. Without a claw hammer, it would be some time before he accomplished that feat.

Brad stepped to his side and retrieved his Navy from Colt's belt. His eyes glacial, he yanked the knife free of Doon's throat, then he wiped the bloody blade on the old man's trousers. He strode toward the door, not sparing his captors a backward glance. Mounting the best of the horses, he raced back toward town, trying not to think of the carnage he left behind.

When he reached Arkansas Post, the sun had just disappeared over the horizon. The western sky glowed with a beautiful pink sunset. Ominous thunderheads, having built up during the heat of the day, displayed silver linings above their dark and foreboding interior. The dark side of nature mirrored Brad's mood.

He looked toward the dock and saw what he feared. "Hell!" The *Robert E. Lee* was gone. His only consolation was that Dru was with Kathlyn. They would be safe until he could be reunited with them. They had to e, for they comprised the center of his universe.

He was anxious to see them, but first he had a
core to settle with Marshal Rhodes. He had no idea
why the man had had him abducted. But he sure as
nell intended to find out. Since his problems began at
he Blue Hog Wallow, he began his search there.

Checking his Navy, he let it rest loose in its holster.
He replaced his knife in the scabbard tied to his leg.
He had lost his derringer when it had fallen from his
vest pocket on the bumpy ride from town.

Stepping up on the boardwalk, he peered into the
window of the saloon. Through a smoky haze he saw
men playing cards at the tables. Rhodes was at the far
end of the bar, engaged in animated conversation with
one of the saloon girls.

Brad ran his hand through his hair. Pulling his hat
ow on his forehead, he slipped down the side of the
building. He made for the rear entrance. Cautiously
opening the door, he saw the marshal not ten feet in
front of him.

The lawman was still busy charming the floozy. Si-
ently, Brad drew his gun, slipped through the door,
tepped up to the marshal, and pressed the barrel to
his head.

Rhodes froze.

Brad removed the marshal's pistol and stuck it into
his belt. "Now let's back out of here nice and easy,"
he instructed, softly. "Miss, if you want to keep your
friend alive, you'll just pretend nothing happened."

"Do what he says, Angela," the marshal whispered
harshly.

Angela nodded her consent.

Brad and Rhodes backed out the door into the alley.
After closing the door, Brad spun the marshal around
and shoved him against the building. He pushed the
barrel of his gun into Rhodes' mouth. The lawman's
eyes grew wide with terror.

"All right, marshal. I'm in a hurry and not in the
best of moods. I won't mind blowing your head off.
So if you know what's good for you, you won't give

295

me any trouble. Do you understand?"

Rhodes nodded his head like a puppet on a string.

"Why was I kidnapped? You've got one chance to come up with the right answer." Brad's icy demeanor frightened Rhodes more than the Colt he slipped from the marshal's mouth.

"Talk."

"A big man, dressed in black, gave me five thousand dollars to get rid of you. But, I swear, I wasn't going to kill you."

"Why did he want me dead?"

"He didn't say, and I didn't ask. He flashed the money and I took it. I knew he would be leaving on the boat, so I didn't think it would hurt to get you out of town for a while. I would have turned you loose. I swear. I'm a lawman. I wouldn't break the law."

"Now why do I doubt that?" Sarcasm was heavy in Brad's voice.

"Drop it, or I'll drill you where you stand," came a loud voice from the side of the saloon.

"Oh hell!" Brad turned and saw three men at the far end of the building, their guns drawn and trained on him. Two were wearing deputy marshal badges.

Irritated more than anything else, he cocked his Navy. "Go ahead and shoot. But before I die I'll blow the marshal's head off."

Rhodes stared into Brad's icy eyes. "Don't shoot. He means what he says. Leather your guns."

Reluctantly, the men replaced their guns in their holsters.

Brad turned to Rhodes. "Let's take a walk. Slow. If anyone makes a false move, you'll be the first to go."

Again the marshal nodded his consent.

One of the deputies went for his gun. Brad saw the movement and whirled around. Instinctively he used the marshal for a shield. The deputy's gun spit fire and Rhodes went down with a bullet in his chest.

Brad returned fire then darted down the alley.

296

Wheeling and firing, he turned the corner. Bullets whizzed past his head. When he reached Main Street, the town was in an uproar. Men were running in all directions, shouting that the marshal had been shot. One old man rang a bell attached to the livery stable, alerting the town of a crisis. Brad cast about for a place to hide.

Just then someone shouted, "There he is."

A mob of angry men palmed their guns and started in Brad's direction.

His heart sank; he saw no means of escape. The loving faces of Kathlyn and Dru flashed before his eyes for a scant second. He closed his eyes against the pain. Breathing deeply, he held his gun and waited for the inevitable.

Chapter Thirty-three

From the safety of the dock, Kathlyn turned and watched the *Robert E. Lee* approach a bend in the river. Rachel stood on the texas, a look of rage and hatred clouding her face. She was screaming, but the words were drowned out by the churning of the giant paddle wheel.

Kathlyn stood, watching the *Robert E. Lee* disappear around the bend, trying not to have second thoughts about her impulsive act. *This is not the time to go missish,* she scolded herself. *Brad needs you. Use your head, find him, then y'all can get the heck out of town.*

Purposefully, she lifted her skirts and headed toward town. She entered Arkansas Post, making her way down the main street.

If she weren't so worried about Brad, she would have been scared spitless. The raucous western town reminded her of Sodom and Gomorrah. The roughneck sodbusters and range-hardened cowboys milling around her made the red-necks of Georgia look like choirboys.

"Come here, sweet thing," a drunken farmer spoke from beside her.

"Chew glass," she muttered, jerking her chin in dismissal.

Crossing over to the other side of the street, she trudged through the mud, his threatening shouts following her. Finally she reached the boardwalk. Her hem was heavy with black gumbo. Leaning against a hitching post, she tried to shake the worst of the mud from her dress.

Why had Brad come to such an awful place? Head

high, chin firm, reticule strangled in a death hold, she moved down the boardwalk. The center of activity seemed to be the long line of saloons stretched before her. It was as good a place as any to begin her search. She came first to the Blue Hog Wallow. Charming place, she thought facetiously when she peered through the window.

A few men, playing cards at tables covered with green felt tops, drank whiskey from small thick glasses. Most of the crowd, though, just sat leering at the scantily clothed saloon girls who circulated among them, filling their drinks, stroking their heads — and anywhere else their adventurous hands chose to roam.

Kathlyn's cheeks warmed. *Soiled doves* she had heard them called. The expressions on their heavily painted faces reminded her more of vultures than doves.

This assessment was reinforced as she proceeded down the walk to the next building, the Razorback Saloon, and peered through its window. Plenty of painted women and leering men, but no Brad.

She continued her search until finally she was standing before the Last Chance Saloon, aptly named since it was the last saloon in town. She leaned toward the window, wiping the dust from the pane with the flat of her hand. As in all the other saloons, she came up empty. Brad was nowhere to be seen. Where could he possibly be?

"Nobody turns me down," the drunk she had rebuffed earlier growled, grabbing her from behind. "Stop it, damn you," he grunted, trying to dodge the blows she rained down upon his face and shoulders as he dragged her into the alley beside the saloon.

Her shrieks were incoherent, but Kathlyn's message was clear. She wanted to be left alone. Desperately!

She was frightened to death. At the very least, she suspected the animal pulling at her clothes, the fiend pressing her up against the building, had rape in mind . . . if not murder. Hysterically, she wondered if she would die before she could *rescue* Brad.

"Hold still, dammit. All I want is a poke."

299

The sound that issued forth from Kathlyn was primal, guttural. Remembering the tenderness with which Brad had made love to her, mere hours before, she became even more determined to fight off this groping, rutting, piece of filth.

Where she was terrified before, she was enraged now. Curving her fingers like claws, she raked her nails down both sides of her attacker's face, leaving furrowed trails of raw flesh and pooling blood from eyebrow to jaw.

He lost all semblance of sanity then. Yelling vile oaths at her he swung one powerful fist, clipping her under the jaw, knocking her onto her back in the mud.

He fell upon her, unaware that he had rendered her unconscious with the force of his blow. Panting from rage and exertion, he placed his hands around her neck and squeezed. He shook her like a mongrel dog would a dead rat, growling low in his throat.

Then he slumped over.

Standing beside Kathlyn and her unconscious attacker, a metal pipe clutched in her hand, Arkansas Post's most sought-after whore, Candy Wells, smiled. True, she was a soiled dove; she had no illusions about her place in society. But she would be damned if she would allow a lady, like the child at her feet, to be defiled.

Kathlyn groaned hoarsely, slowly climbing back from the depths of oblivion. She hurt from crown to sole, particularly her head and throat. She felt as if she had been run over by a team of mules.

"Just lie still, honey," a soft, sweet voice floated to her, accompanied by a soothing touch to her brow.

"I can't." Kathlyn grabbed her throat in agony, squeezing her eyes shut. "Why does it hurt to talk?" she whispered roughly.

"Shh, you just rest now. We'll talk later. Just try to go back to sleep."

"I can't," Kathlyn repeated. She sat up in bed, setting free a million fiery demons in her head. Clenching her teeth, she held perfectly still.

"Where am I?" Kathlyn whispered.

"The Painted Lady. I'm Candy Wells, the owner." Candy placed a gentle hand on her patient's shoulder.

"I can't stay here."

Candy dropped her hand to her side. "Nobody's gonna bother you, if that's what you think. I don't need to recruit my girls off the street."

The hurt in Candy's voice sounded over the roar in Kathlyn's ears. "You misunderstand. I know you wouldn't let anyone hurt me" — Candy smiled at Kathlyn's trusting statement — "And I would be honored to stay and visit with you, but Brad needs my help."

How could Kathlyn convince anyone she had a rescue mission in progress while lying helpless, flat on her back? She didn't look like she could save a cat, much less a flesh and blood man. And she sounded so damned naive. But it was hard to exude worldly wisdom when you felt like you were about to pass out.

"You can't go," was all Candy said.

Slowly, Kathlyn opened her eyes, blinking from the glare of dozens of lit candles set about the reddest room she had ever seen. Everything around her was red: pillows, chairs, sofas, rugs, drapes. Even the sheets she lay upon. Carefully, she moved her head to the side, searching for the woman who had spoken to her. The world faded in and out of focus.

The provocative color scheme was broken by a white lace wrapper worn by the angel of mercy at her side. "You've had a tough time, sugar. Now you lie back down. I'll get you some honey and lemon for your throat."

"I can't. I've got to go."

"Not now," her savior said forcefully. She moved across the room with an unconscious grace that belied her profession. Standing before a cherrywood commode, she shook a bottle of honey in Kathlyn's direction. "You've been knocked unconscious, beaten, and strangled. You're in my place now, young lady. The doctor told me nothing is broken, but you need to rest. And as long as Candy's in charge around here, rest is what you'll get."

Her concern surprised Kathlyn. She was no fool. She knew Candy was a prostitute—she had all but told her as much. And while she was no authority on prostitutes, she never expected one to be so kind. Obviously, the woman had saved her life and was now trying to take care of her. But Brad needed her.

"I appreciate it, Candy. But I don't have time to lie about."

"Who is this man that you would climb out of your sickbed for?" Candy asked over her shoulder, mixing the soothing potion.

"A friend. Perhaps you've seen him." Kathlyn described Brad in a whiskey-roughened voice. Her words were cut off by the sound of gunshots in the street below.

When the warning bell clanged, Candy pushed the portieres aside. Turning, with a smile on her painted lips, she said, "Your description didn't do him justice, but I think I know where you can find your man."

Kathlyn stumbled outside and saw Brad at the far end of the street, being approached by a mob of bloodthirsty men. Looking about frantically, she spotted two horses tied to the post in front of the general store.

She had no idea to whom the animals belonged and, frankly, she didn't care. She and Brad needed a means of escape and fate had provided them one. Fear for Brad clearing her head, she jumped onto the smaller mount, wrapped the reins of the other around her saddle horn, kicked her horse in the flanks, and galloped down the street toward Brad.

The look of surprise on his face would have been comical had the bullets whizzing past her head not

302

frightened Kathlyn out of ten years of her life. Tossing the spare mount's reins to Brad, she croaked, "Let's get out of here."

"Where's Dru?" he shouted.

"On the boat with Hannah."

He nodded, pointing toward the woods. "I'm right behind you." He fired cover shots as Kathlyn took off. Seconds later, she burst into a thicket of woods, with Brad close behind. He passed her. "Follow me!" Single file, they raced through the forest, fleeing the angry posse that would soon follow.

The going was tough. Branches blocked their way at every turn, and the rocky terrain made the trail hazardous for the horses.

Soon the sky opened up, releasing torrents of rain. They were soaked to the skin.

After an hour of hard riding, Brad reined to a stop. Dismounting, he pulled Kathlyn from her horse and into his embrace. His mouth slanted over hers hungrily.

"God, you'll never know how glad I was to see you." His breathing was harsh, his voice rough with emotion. "I had about run out of options."

Kathlyn smiled into the darkness.

Tilting his head down, he placed his hand under her chin. Tenderly, he sipped the raindrops from her mouth, licking the small streams of water running down her cheeks with his tongue.

She felt his body swell and moved against it. They both knew what they wanted more than life itself.

The clouds shifted then and a shaft of moonlight illuminated them. Brad muttered a curse. Rage was evident in his stance. "What happened to you?"

She had been so worried about him, she had forgotten her own brush with danger. "A gentleman in town got a bit too amorous," she said lightly.

He grabbed her arm, pulling her toward the horses.

"What are you doing?" she asked.

"We're going back to that cesspool and I'm going to kill the bastard who touched you."

Kathlyn dug her heels into the soggy earth. "Have you lost your mind?" she shouted, wincing at the pain in her throat. "We can't go back there. We've been running away from a posse half the night. Do you plan to waltz through them and stroll up to the bad guy, unseen?"

He glared down at her while affectionately tracing small circles on her upper arm.

"Besides, we've got to get back to Dru. She's more important than taking vengeance on some low-life who dared to touch your woman." She tried to shake some sense into him, but couldn't budge him. He was too big. It was like shaking a marble statue.

He chuckled. She was right. "My woman, huh?" Not giving her time to respond, he kissed her lightly. "Did he hurt you, honey?" Gently, he skimmed her body with trembling hands. "Anywhere else?"

The pain in his voice was evident. She placed her hand alongside his cheek. "No, I'm fine. Hadn't we better ride?"

He nodded, then helped her mount, handling her as if she were made of glass.

The rest of the night they rode hard. Coming down as it was, the rain obliterated their trail. By morning they would be safe from discovery.

Kathlyn was certain the night would never end. She had not been on horseback since the day she galloped away from her Union Point home at sixteen, the day she had fallen and lost her baby. The wear on her unused muscles was excruciating. She desperately needed to rest. But she didn't complain.

The rain was blinding much of the time and a bad situation grew steadily worse. After a couple of hours in the saddle her sodden gown weighted her down, pulling on her shoulders, causing a throbbing pain in her neck. She kept her own counsel, determined not to slow their pace.

Brad felt like hell pushing her as he was. He stopped occasionally to see how she was faring. On one such stop, he motioned her to his side. Pulling her

304

off her mount, he settled her on his lap, to ride with him.

Gently, he kissed her. "Are you sure you're all right?"

"Will you stop worrying?" She smiled, covering a yawn with her hand.

"Never." He pulled her close to his chest and tucked her head beneath his chin. "Get some sleep, sweetheart."

She fell asleep instantly.

"What do you want?" Rachel barked at Dru as the child cowered in the doorway to Kathlyn's stateroom.

Limned by a heavy curtain of rain at her back, Dru's face had gone as white as the nightgown she wore. All she wanted to do was get Ishta and sneak back to Millie's cabin without being missed.

But the angry lady was standing in front of the cage. She would have to get past her first.

"Are you deaf? I asked you what you want in here?" Rachel gripped the green bottle hidden in the folds of her gown tightly.

Finally, Dru found her voice. "I came to get Ishta." She squared her shoulders and lifted her chin, aping the confident demeanor Miss Kathlyn adopted when confronted by her mean cousin.

With great flourish, Rachel stepped aside. Dru's brave facade crumbled.

"As you can see, Ishta does not need you."

A tortured sob escaping her throat, Dru rushed over to Ishta's cage. Her finger trembled when she stretched it forth and touched her tiny friend. Just as she feared, Ishta was not asleep. She was dead.

Dru's next reaction caught Rachel by surprise. Turning on her, the child flailed her with her fists.

"You killed her. You killed her," Dru shrieked.

Grasping a handful of Dru's curls, Rachel wrenched her head back. She would teach Kathlyn to defy her, to leave the boat after she told her not to. There were

305

three things her dim-witted cousin cherished most in the world: Brad, Dru, and her damn bird. Well, Stuart had taken care of Brad, she had poisoned the bird, and now she would do something about the kid.

Leaning down into Dru's tearstained face, Rachel growled, "You know what you are, brat? You're too smart for your own good. But I'm sure glad you're here. You saved me the trouble of coming after you."

All the fight left Dru then. Still, she whimpered, "I'm gonna tell my daddy on you." She flinched at Rachel's harsh laugh and cringed at her menacing words.

"Oh no, you're not."

By early morning the rain had stopped. Kathlyn opened her eyes. There was a faint light in the eastern sky. After a rosy pink glow, the panorama burst forth in brilliant rays of gold. The terrain was flat as far as the eye could see. Occasionally the prairie was interrupted by woodlands; then it opened up again into endless fields of green grass and running brooks.

Her bed was rocking. When heavily muscled arms tightened around her waist, she remembered that she was on horseback, safe in Brad's embrace.

"Good morning." His husky whisper fluttered a curl beside her brow. Tenderly, very tenderly, he kissed her awake.

"Good morning," she returned, lifting her face for another taste of paradise.

He gladly obliged. While dropping light kisses on her lips and cheeks, he guided their horses into a thickly wooded area.

"We'll stop to rest the horses." Sliding easily out of the saddle, with Kat clutched tightly against his chest, he carried her over to a large oak.

"It's not necessary to carry me, but I could certainly get used to it," she purred.

"Me too." He kissed her deeply, seducing her mouth with his tongue, taking all the time in the world. Finally, he halted his delicious assault. Her stomach

306

growled at that moment and they both laughed.

"Alas, we must eat. I'll try to scare up something. Be right back." Just once more, as if he couldn't help himself, he kissed her. Finally, he set her on her feet.

Kathlyn smiled, watching him walk away. Actually he didn't walk, she decided. He sauntered. The kind of loose-hipped ambulation that was just shy of a strut, a slow rolling movement that drew a woman's eye, a provocative action that fanned the flames of her desire.

And she didn't smile, she allowed. She leered. Leered like a sailor who had been at sea for a month.

And was it any wonder? Brad Hampton, aristocratic gentleman from Georgia, as gallant and protective as ever, became more virile with every mile. He had become as tough as the land he traversed. And the sight of him, no, the very thought of him, caused delicious feelings to burst inside her.

She was standing in the same spot, thinking about this *new* Brad, when he topped a small rise in the ground. He carried bunches of muscadines in his hands; his pockets bulged with pecans.

Winking at her as if he divined her appreciative thoughts, he dropped a light kiss to her lips. "Let's eat." He tossed the tart fruit on a pile of leaves and emptied his pockets. Tugging her down with him, he settled beside their quick-grab breakfast.

Greedily, they devoured the fruit and nuts. He retrieved the canteen he'd found on his horse and offered her a drink. She washed her last bite of food down with the lukewarm water, then returned the vessel to him. Positioning the canteen so that his lips touched the rim exactly where hers had, he slaked his thirst, never breaking eye contact with her.

Slightly embarrassed by the desire burning in his eyes, and a bit overwhelmed by his new rugged persona, she looked away. "Where are we?" she asked.

"Not far from the stage line that runs from Memphis to Fort Smith." Provocatively, he traced her jaw with a water-dampened finger. "Come here, gorgeous." With just the slightest pressure, he turned her head toward him. His lips brushed hers lightly. "If we head due north, we'll probably cross the line in a day or two." His touch snaked down her bare neck.

"From there we'll follow the road to one of the Butterfield relay stations where we can get something *hot* to eat." His eyes and fingertip caressed the fullness of her breasts. His breath felt hot on her cheek. Holding her in his lap for the past few hours had built a fire in him the likes of which he'd never known.

It showed in the timbre of his husky voice. "Then we'll catch the stage to Fort Smith." Slowly, very slowly, he circled the tip of one breast, almost groaning aloud when it pebbled against the bodice of her dress.

"We should get there not too long after the *Robert E. Lee.*" His words sounded more like a lover's litany than those of a man imparting travel information.

"What about the posse?" She colored at the squeak in her voice. "Do you think they're still trailing us?" That was better. She hadn't sounded like a mouse that time. She sounded in control now.

The desire he had kindled in her had made her bold. Closing her eyes, she leaned forward and flicked the underside of his jaw with her tongue. His sharp intake of breath did her feminine ego good.

With a graceful move, he rose and pulled her to her feet. "They probably are, but the rain erased our trail. I doubt they would count on us coming this far north." His hands were on her shoulders now. Applying slight pressure, he diminished the space between them.

"I hope they think we followed the river west. But I can't be sure. We'll have to travel in the woods as much as possible." When his hands dropped to the small of her back and he pressed her against his throbbing body, it became clear that he wanted to do a sight more in the woods than travel.

He kissed her then. Soft, hard, soft again. His tongue made a desperate foray into her mouth, thrusting, sweeping, skimming, tasting. Their breaths mingled

308

in the dewy air, their moans and gasps broke the early morning stillness.

Finally, he pulled away from her. Lacing his hands at her waist, he placed his brow against hers. When he could trust his voice, he whispered, "We'd best put some miles behind us."

Reluctantly, she agreed.

"Tonight," he whispered, grinding his mouth against hers, giving her a taste of what they would share later.

"Promises, promises," she sighed seductively.

He laughed, turned her toward her horse, and gave her a saucy slap on the rear. "Don't get fresh with me young lady."

Swaying her hips provocatively, she walked away from him.

Brad groaned aloud. "It's going to be a long, haaard day," he drew out. Her step faltered at the implication of his words. "Something wrong, sweetheart?" he laughed.

Chapter Thirty-four

Still in all, the ride that day was more pleasant than the night before. The sun overhead burned hot, warming them through, drying their clothes.

Just before the breath of evening soughed over the land, they passed a stream, bubbling with crystal clear water. It shifted and shimmered, its beauty drawing the weary travelers like a siren's song.

"We'll camp here tonight," Brad said, hopping down.

Kathlyn slid from the saddle. While Brad watered the horses, she walked around a clump of trees for a moment of privacy. "Brad," she called.

He circled the bushes. About one hundred feet down the embankment the stream had overflowed its banks, forming a small lake.

"Isn't it beautiful? It looks so cool." She coveted every drop.

"Ummm," he agreed. "Be right back." Whistling happily, he tethered and unsaddled their horses. He picked up their blankets and headed back toward the lake. As an afterthought, he shed his shirt, tossed it over their saddlebags, then hurried to Kathlyn's side.

Her eyes widened at the sight of his naked torso. His physique was gorgeous, absolute perfection. Her heart threatened to break her ribs it pounded so.

All she could do was stare at him. The thick carpet of hair that matted his chest appeared more enticing now than it had in the moonlight on the balcony or in the low lamplight of his stateroom. She just *had* to reach out and touch it. She just had to.

"That feels good," he said, moving closer.

She smiled seductively. "Does it?"

"Oh," he exhaled his appreciation.

"Feels good from this side too," she said.

He chuckled. "Help yourself."

She used both hands now, her fingers drifting to his shoulders. Bronzed and broad, the muscles rippled beneath her caress. Her hand trailed lower, cupping the corded muscles of his upper arms, measuring, squeezing. "You're big."

He groaned and she giggled. "Oops, I didn't mean that how it sounded." She dropped her gaze. "Buutttt," she drew out.

"Flatterer," he whispered.

Her hands never stopped mapping his torso. "Ummm, I like this." As if she were blind, she lightly grazed his skin, memorizing the slow swelling peaks and shadowed valleys of his hard, washboard stomach. His rapid breathing caused his abdomen to rise and fall beneath her touch. His skin was soft and warm. "Like satin soaked in sunlight," she murmured.

Her cheeks flamed and her mouth grew dry when she imagined her tongue trailing along after her hands. She closed her eyes, savoring the image. Taking the corner of her lower lip in her teeth, she drew ever widening circles on his belly.

His muscles tensed. He was inordinately pleased at the look of rapture on her face. She was driving him mad. Without conscious thought, he stretched, inviting her to explore him further, giving her freer access to his lower body.

She accepted his invitation. "Oh," she whispered, squeezing her eyes shut. Gently, very gently, she traced the line above his breeches. Her hand slipped lower. When her fingers met the evidence of his desire, her eyes jerked open. Her breath stilled. Desire pounded her like waves against the shore. Her hand had a mind of its own.

A spark of passion sharp and quick as summer lightning streaked through his loins. He covered her hand with his own, pressing down involuntarily.

311

God, he ached for her. But damn it all, he smelled like a horse. With a strength of will he was unaware he possessed, he twined his fingers through hers, pulling her hand away and bringing it to his lips. They both stood and stared into each others eyes until their breathing returned to normal.

"How about a bath?" Brad asked. "I'll even wash your back."

He placed tiny kisses in her palm and waited for her response. His fingers tingled with the need to caress her. Just imagining how she would feel, her naked, slick flesh rubbing against his as they cavorted about in the water, made his heart quicken. "Kat?" he prodded with a husky whisper.

Smiling gently, she nodded her head.

A heavy, warm feeling engulfed his heart . . . and spread lower. Hand-in-hand they walked down the hill to the lake. She was scarcely breathing. He dropped her hand and strode over to a large boulder at the edge of the water. "Come here, sweetheart." Now *he* was scarcely breathing.

Slowly, she crossed the distance between them. She was so near to him her gown brushed his boots. He pulled her onto his lap. Leaning back slightly, he perched precariously and aligned her body to his.

She leaned into him, initiating a mutually ravenous kiss. His hands and lips roamed constantly, adoring, igniting fires that shimmered on the surface of her skin. His arousal was warm and solid beneath her. Instinctively, she massaged it with her hips. But that wasn't enough. She wanted to feel him inside of her.

Apparently he was of like mind. He growled with impatience.

Together, they struggled to remove her voluminous skirts. Panting, mouths fused, they tugged at her clothing. Just as she felt the cool afternoon air stir against her legs, he tore his lips from hers.

"Oh, oooh," he yelled. Cushioning her body, he fell backwards, landing in the lake with a gasp.

After a moment of icy shock, he regained his footing and pulled her back into his arms. The frigid water did nothing to cool his ardor. It would take the run-off from a glacier to douse the fire raging in him. He expected steam to rise from the surface of the water when he continued his amorous assault.

Her dress grew heavy with water, dragging them down. Lifting her, he carried her to shore and lay her on the grass.

She tightened her grip on his neck. He covered her body with his own. They embraced from shoulder to ankle. Lips met, hands caressed, bodies strained. They were a mass of explosive energy, a body of aching need, writhing against the rising tide of desire. She trembled in his arms.

"Cold?" He nuzzled her neck, pulling her closer to the heat of his body.

"Not hardly," she moaned. Her voice was thick, convincing.

A slow chuckle rumbled low in his chest as he took her mouth beneath his own. Kissing and caressing, his lips and tongue made love to her mouth while he massaged her softness. He ached for her with all his being. Out of control, he made no effort to restrain himself. His breathing was labored, his body on fire.

Instinctively, she tried to part her legs for him but her movement was restricted by the heavy skirts pinned beneath her. She whimpered in frustration and shook with unfulfilled desire.

"Let me," he whispered. He undressed her then, pausing each time a new patch of skin was visible to the eye, paying homage with lips and hands to the warm flesh he uncovered.

With her aid, his clothes melted away. They lay bare beneath the sky.

"You're so beautiful it hurts to look at you," he said.

"Come here," she whispered, locking her lips to his. Slow, sure, soft, hard, frantic, gentle. They caressed each other's mouths and bodies. Passion heightened, threatening to burn them to a cinder.

313

"Tell me what you want, sweetheart," he whispered against her lips.

"You," she breathed. "I want you."

Rolling over onto his back, he brought her with him. He groaned when her warm, moist skin kissed his belly. His hands slipped over her hips, down her thighs, until they rested on the backs of her knees. Gently, he pulled her legs farther apart.

She rose high above him, like a sea-goddess rising from the ocean floor, tossing her head from side to side. Her thighs cupped his waist; silken curls tickled his stomach. Fairly purring, she massaged him with her body, trying to ease the low ache he had caused.

"Keep doing that and I'll be yours forever," he whispered roughly.

She dropped her head forward, staring into his eyes. A poignant look touched her face. Her hair formed a curtain around them, brushing the ground on both sides of his head. She drew a deep, shuddering breath. One lone tear slipped down her cheek. "Will you, my darling? Forever?"

She regretted the words as soon as they slipped past her lips. What had come over her to ask such a leading question? Aware that Brad had become very still, she buried her face in his neck. "Idiot," she exhaled, scolding herself bitterly.

"Kat. Look at me, sweetheart."

She shook her head, no.

"Come on, baby, look at me. It's all right, honey." He rolled to his side, tucking her under his arm. "Do you want me to be yours forever?" he asked, his voice ragged with emotion.

"Please just ignore that. I didn't know what I was saying." Embarrassed now, she turned her back to him. "I just got carried away," was her muffled excuse.

He fitted himself around her like a spoon. Pulling her close, he settled her bare bottom against him. He was still fully aroused. "Does that feel like I'm going anywhere?"

She laughed as he intended. Silently, he stroked her

heated skin; cheek, neck, throat, breasts, hips, thighs—
and back again. Her tension dissolved. She relaxed in
his arms, resting her head on his shoulder, shifting and
angling her head back to receive his kiss.

With the sky as their canopy, the forest as their bedchamber, a plush, green carpet as their bed, they
kissed, caressed, and whispered endearments as lovers
are wont to do. He splayed his hand over her stomach,
massaging her belly, aping her earlier actions.

Her sense of peace dimmed again. The feel of his
hand caressing where their child had slept so long ago
renewed her emotional turmoil. Talk about rotten tim-
ing, she groaned silently. She didn't want to think of
the past, of the pain she had suffered. That was a lifetime ago, she lectured herself. This is reality. Brad.
Her. Together. Playing Adam and Eve in the great outdoors. That's reality. The lecture continued; now is not
the time to dredge up past hurts! It is not the time to
wallow in self pity.

"Sweetheart?"

Naturally, he had noticed the difference in her response to his lovemaking. He was looking down at her
with concern in his eyes. And something more. The
something more proved her undoing. She placed her
fingers over his mouth. "Don't say anything, Brad. Just
kiss me."

He did better than that. Growling, he captured her
lips and slid into her body in one fluid motion. She
breathed his name in wonder; her breath stilled. Reality, memories, and sanity burned up in the fire of their
combined passion.

"Put your legs around my waist," he said, lifting her
hips with his gentle hands.

They were like tongues of fire. Writhing and flaming, blue-hot waves of energy. They moved together in
a dance as old as time itself. Yet the impossible
passion they shared was fresh as a newborn babe.
They were certain with each movement, that each
incredible sensation they experienced had never been
felt before. By anyone, anywhere, anytime, through-

out the history of living and loving on this earth.

"Oh, Brad," she gasped. "Please, sweetheart, please." He could ease the ache threatening her sanity, the delicious yearning he had created. She knew he could. "It's so good. Oh please!"

"You're almost there, baby," he rasped. He could feel the pressure building in her. It threatened his control, but somehow he held on. This was his woman and she would be loved long and well before he allowed his own release.

She plunged over the edge then, shouting his name, scattering the birds in the trees around them. He was one heartbeat behind her. Still feeling the shock waves in her depths, he sailed over the abyss, moaning her name, over and over, clutching her to him with ebbing strength.

Then all was silent. The birds settled in the trees once more. Brad and Kathlyn returned from the place lovers go . . . together . . . never alone.

Chapter Thirty-five

He eased to her side, wrapping an arm around her bare shoulders, resting his other arm across her hips. "Sweetheart, we have to talk."

"Talk?" She was still a bit fuzzy. "About what?"

"Forever."

Her mind cleared. "I told you to forget about that. I don't know why I said such a thing." She laughed self-consciously.

"I think you do. I think you realized before we made love again that we needed to talk about the future, to deal with our past." He smiled sadly, staring into the night. "And we really do need to"—he dropped a kiss on her forehead—"but you kinda distract me."

"My pleasure," she said.

He chuckled. He loved her so! Tenderly, he traced her red, swollen lips with the tip of his tongue. Then he dipped inside her sweet cavern. Finally, he held her gently, his face buried in her hair. "We've wasted so many years," he said.

She raised up on her elbow. "If you could do one thing different, to change the past, what would it be?" She knew it was a loaded question. Obviously, he would say, 'I would never have written that note.' Still . . . she needed to hear it. That way, she could forgive him and they could move on with their life.

"I don't know." His voice had a slight edge. "What about you?"

Kat was disappointed. Why didn't he say it? All he had to do was apologize for writing that damn note, for saying he didn't want to see her again; she would put it all behind her; she loved him that much. *Just say I'm*

317

sorry, please. For a moment, she didn't speak. "If I could change one thing, I would have tried to be more forgiving," she said.

"What an odd thing to say." Brad hadn't meant to speak it aloud.

"Did I say something wrong?"

Brad shrugged. "Just what you said about forgiveness. It struck me as odd."

Kat felt his tension, though she didn't understand its source. She didn't want any unpleasantness between them. It would cheapen what they had shared, to argue now. Quietly, she said, "I would think you might appreciate it."

He ran his fingers through his hair. "Sweetheart, I'm missing something here. We don't seem to be communicating very well. Who do you need to forgive?"

"You."

"Me?" Brad asked incredulously.

Kathlyn grew frustrated. "Brad, don't you regret what happened the morning after we made love that first time?"

"Of course I do," Brad said. Supposing she was referring to the note she sent him, he expected her to explain why she rejected him. She surprised him.

She kissed him quickly. "That's all I wanted to hear." It wasn't an apology, but to Kathlyn it was close enough.

Brad was truly confused now. Well, he would come right out and ask her. "Baby, why did you write me that note?" he groaned. The pain of the past was evident in his tone.

Kathlyn gasped. "What note?" Now she was confused.

"I know it was eleven years ago, but it changed so much."

"What note?" she whispered again.

He turned her face so that it was bathed in liquid silver. "The note saying you didn't want to see me again."

"I didn't," she answered simply.

He could see the truth in her eyes. He didn't know

318

whether to shout for joy or curse a blue streak. A thousand possibilities ran through his mind.

"Did you send me a note?" She hardly breathed, waiting for his response.

"No."

"Oh God!" she exclaimed, squeezing her eyes shut. All those years, all that heartache, and it was over. With one word, it was over. Brad had never rejected her. It was almost more than she could fathom. "Who? Why?" she wondered aloud.

"I don't know." He came to a sitting position. "Unless . . ."

"Who?" she asked.

"Rachel."

"Rachel?"

"Who else?"

"I can't think of anyone else, Brad. But why Rachel?"

"Because she had been throwing herself at me for a year before I met you. I tried not to hurt her feelings, but I let her know I just wasn't interested." He shrugged. "I've been told there's no limit to what a spurned woman will do." His laughter was devoid of humor. "God. She found a very effective way to get revenge, don't you agree?"

"Very," she sighed. "I didn't know Rachel wanted you. I probably would have stayed away from you, if I had," she said as if to herself.

He leaned over her. "Then it's a good thing you didn't know." He smiled gently, dropping a kiss to her lips.

Kathlyn tensed and Brad raised his head.

"Oh no," she breathed.

"What's wrong, sweetheart?"

She sat up beside him, dropping her head into her hands. "What is it?" he asked again, massaging her back, trying to comfort her.

His tender strokes fanned her guilt. "After the ball the other night, when I found the two of you in the greenhouse, you were telling the truth, weren't you? Rachel arranged the whole thing. You were innocent."

319

Brad nodded, remembering how hurt he had been that Kathlyn could think he would molest Rachel.

Her hands drifted up, circling his neck. She pulled him against her. "Can you ever forgive me? For not believing in you."

Gently, he brushed her lips with his own. It was a very sweet answer.

"Now I have to ask for your forgiveness," he said.

"Whatever for?"

"For my lack of control—eleven years ago. Taking you like that was totally out of character for me. I wasn't myself. I just lost control. Hell, as I recall I didn't exercise a great deal of control with you all summer." His ebony eyes softened. He caressed her cheek with the backs of his fingers. "You were so young, Kat. So damn beautiful. And I wanted you so much. Is it any wonder I lost my head?"

Lowering his face, he kissed her. Like a bee sipping nectar from a flower, he drank from her mouth. His sweet breath fanned her face, evaporating the moisture that remained on her lips. "I'm sorry I didn't make it better for you that first time, sweetheart. When you lost your innocence it should have been in a feather bed, with satin sheets . . . with your husband."

She closed her eyes against this last. "I found no reason to complain," she whispered finally. Initiating a kiss of her own, she disappeared into his embrace. He lay her on the green carpet once again. She nuzzled his neck. The smell of summer grass, saddle leather, and a fragrance that was undeniably Brad filled her nostrils.

"Oh baby, think of all the wasted years, of all the happiness we were denied because of that twisted woman's jealousy," he said.

"We were denied more than you know." Her voice was muffled against his chest.

"I tried to see you." He had not heard her last remark.

She pushed him away slightly. "When?"

"About three months after you returned to Union Point. I came to your home, but your parents turned me away. They said you were sick. I assumed you didn't want to see me. After that, I didn't try again."

She wanted to cry for him. How it must have hurt, to reach out to her only to be turned away.

She had not been ill when he had visited, but bedridden from her miscarriage. She wanted desperately to share that with him, to tell him of their loss, to mourn with him, but she couldn't find her voice. Her eyes burned with unshed tears.

Misunderstanding her stricken expression, he soothed, "It's all right, honey. I don't blame you for not wanting to see me. I understand. You thought I had used and rejected you." Lovingly, he smoothed his hands down her sides, molding her to him, dropping light kisses on her brow.

"You don't understand." Her voice was thick even to her own ears. She pushed away again, imploring him with her eyes.

"Understand what, honey?" He was kissing her cheek now.

"I wasn't ill."

"I didn't think so." He stilled. Even after all these years the truth hurt.

"No, you still don't understand. I *was* in bed." She breathed deeply, whispering as she exhaled, "I had had a miscarriage."

"Are you saying . . ."

"Yes. I lost your baby."

He sat up and circled her arms with white, bloodless fingers. His eyes searched her face. When tears slid down her cheeks, his hands loosened their grip.

Finally, he released her. She rose to her knees, and encircled him in her embrace, pulling him against her. Quietly, she sifted her hand through his tousled hair, rocking with him back and forth as he mourned the baby they had lost so many years ago. No one could understand the pain he was experiencing. Not like she could. Their shared grief cemented the bond between them as nothing else could.

Regaining his composure finally, he faced her. His

eyes were unnaturally bright. "How?" His whisper was rough with emotion.

She knew what he was asking. Clasping her hands against her thighs, she fixed her gaze on him. "When I arrived home in Union Point, I was upset." She cleared her throat so that she could continue. "At first I couldn't eat; I didn't want to go anywhere; I guess I just felt sorry for myself."

Her pitiful smile was like a knife in his heart. He wished he had not asked her to explain the circumstances of their loss. But he needed to know. While she spoke, he wrapped her in a blanket and pulled her onto his lap.

"After I had been home a month, I suspected I was pregnant. I had missed my flow." Her cheeks flushed and she fluttered a tiny white hand, obviously discomfited by discussing such things with a man.

Brad made a noise, signifying he understood.

"One day I couldn't stand the seclusion any longer, so I decided to ride my horse. I was distraught, I guess, and weak from not eating. I tried to jump the fence bordering our farm. I didn't make it. Next thing I knew, I was at home in bed, and the doctor told me that I had lost my baby."

Though her tears had ceased, she finished on a sob. He rocked her in his arms, blinking rapidly to clear his eyes. "There will be other children," he whispered thickly.

Kathlyn felt as if her heart would break.

"That is, if you'll have me," he said.

She stopped breathing for a second. He was asking her to marry him. Her sense of honor told her to say no. He deserved a wife who could give him a family, brothers and sisters for Dru. Her heart screamed for her to say yes. *Yes. Marry him. Take what he's offering and forget how little you have to give in return.*

But she loved him too much to cheat him; to tie him to half a woman for the rest of his life. "You don't want to marry me, Brad." Her voice sounded as if she were dead.

322

He raised a questioning brow. "I don't?" He spoke with deceptive calm. What did she want from him? His undying love. God knows she had that. Fear of losing her made him weak.

"I had an infection after I lost the baby. The doctor said I won't have anymore children."

He brushed a thumb over her lower lip. "I'm sorry about our baby, about all you suffered; you have to know how much it hurts." He cleared his throat forcefully. "But whether you can or cannot have children is unimportant to me. All that matters now is that you say you'll be my wife, for the rest of my life."

He sounded so sincere, if only she could allow herself to believe him. His next words convinced her.

"With all my heart, I love you, Elora Kathlyn McKinney. Say you'll be my wife. Say yes."

The radiant smile on her face gave him the answer he desired.

Still, he teased, "If you don't, I'll kidnap you and hold you hostage." He pulled the blanket away. "And I won't give you your clothes until you say, yes."

"How can I refuse?" She threw her arms around his neck, kissing him with all the passion she possessed. When they came up for air, she added, "And Brad, I love you too."

He threw back his head and laughed. Just for the pure pleasure of it. "Say it again."

"Yes, I'll marry you."

"No, the other."

She giggled. "I love you. I love you, Brad Hampton. I love you. I love you."

He lowered her onto her back. With the sky as their canopy, they sealed their vow by making love again.

It never occurred to either of them that she now had two fiancés; the man who held her close to his heart, and the young lieutenant who was planning to kidnap her in earnest.

Chapter Thirty-six

Kathlyn experienced a myriad of emotions when she saw Fort Smith in the distance.

She sighed wistfully, a ghost of a smile tugging at her lips. Due to a problem at the relay station, she and Brad had been forced to travel on horseback rather than catch the stagecoach as planned. And if she lived to be a thousand, she would never forget the past few days. They had ridden hard by day and made love every night, falling asleep in each other's arms. It was as if they were trying to make up for the last eleven years, to recapture the happiness that had been stolen from them. They knew it was impossible, but had a wonderful time trying.

She was strangely sad, yet a feeling of anticipation pulsed through her veins. Now that their trip was at an end, she could hardly wait to see Dru. Not to mention, avail herself of the creature comforts this bastion of civilization offered. She wanted nothing so much as a hug from her future stepdaughter, a hot bubble bath, a change of clothes, and a decent meal. In that order.

"You're awfully quiet all of a sudden," Brad observed.

"Am I?"

Reining in, he swept her off her horse, settling her onto his thighs. "Sorry our pre-honeymoon-honeymoon is almost over?"

"Mmmm."

"Me too," he admitted. "Still love me?" Lowering his head to capture her lips, he slid his fingers inside the bodice of her gown and caressed her breast.

When he finished his passionate ministrations, she

asked, "What was the question?" She kissed him soundly.

"What question?"

"I do love you, you know." Staring into his eyes, she raised her hand to caress his dimple. "And you don't even have to marry me. I'll live with you in sin, if need be. Just to show you the depth of my devotion."

His eyes darkened. "Forget that! We're getting married today. I don't think I can be held responsible otherwise."

"Today?" she interrupted, sounding somewhat alarmed.

"Today! There's no way I can maintain a respectable distance from this delicious little body." His hands paid homage to her *delicious little body*.

"You don't think that's rushing it a bit? Shouldn't I meet Chase and Lacy first, or something?"

"We have your reputation to consider." His tone was light, but there was a hint of vulnerability in his eyes.

Her heart warmed. "How noble of you, to rush into marriage," she teased. "Just to protect my reputation. You're a prince among men, Mr. Hampton. A true prince."

"Well, what can I say?" He winked in a disgustingly attractive manner. "Some of us were born to be gentlemen 'til the end."

"A gentleman?" She looked pointedly at his hand cupping her breast.

"Well a man, anyway."

She wholeheartedly agreed.

"Say you'll be mine . . . today," he prodded.

She laughed at his pleading tone.

"Heartless woman," he teased. "All right. It's on your head if I scandalize polite society by throwing you on the ground and making love to you every five minutes." A sharp hiss escaped his lips when she shifted on his lap, ostensibly to attain a more comfortable position. A painfully pleasant sensation pooled below his waist. "Please be still," he groaned.

She chuckled at the pained look on his face. "Whatever is the matter? You look as if you're in pain."

"Witch." He bit her lower lip lightly. "I won't be able to help myself, you know. In addition to being the quintessential gentleman, I'm also inordinately virile. It's a heavy cross to bear."

"Poor dear, I had no idea you suffered so." She shifted in his lap again and he groaned. A devilish light flickered in her eyes. "In a minute you'll tell me it's a *hard* job but somebody has to do it."

He grinned. "How did you know?"

"How indeed." She arched a brow. "There are some things a man can't hide."

"Tell me about it," he muttered.

"Shouldn't we proceed?" She winked impudently.

"I'm game, but wouldn't it be difficult on horseback?" he asked wryly.

Fluttering her lashes, she kissed him lightly. "Why how else would we proceed into town, if not on horseback?"

"I had hoped you meant something else," he said.

"I can't imagine what," she feigned innocence, enjoying their sexual banter.

He whispered in her ear, outlining what he meant in great detail.

Kathlyn's eyes widened. Brad was very adept at describing lovemaking, she decided. Almost as adept at describing the beautiful act as he was at doing it. "Oh that," she breathed.

He grinned seductively. "Yes that. All . . . night . . . long."

"All night, huh? You *must* be extremely virile."

He bit her neck lightly and nibbled her ear lobe. "No, you're just extremely desirable."

"So are you."

He kissed her passionately then. Over and over. "Whoa, we better stop while I still can." Brad shook his head, trying to regain a measure of control. It wouldn't be seemly to take her on the back of a horse, in full sight of Fort Smith. Eventually his senses stopped whirling. Prompted by single-minded determination, he

326

asked, "So, will you marry me—this afternoon?"

She nodded. "But I have a couple of favors to ask."

He stared into her beautiful face. Her eyes were the color of purple mountains, with the softness of pure white clouds around the edges. "Sweetheart, when you look at me like that . . ." It wasn't necessary for him to finish.

"First, we get Dru's permission."

He hugged her to him. This was just one more reason to love her. Here they sat, horny as hell, discussing their impending marriage, and the thought uppermost in her mind was his daughter's happiness. Not trusting his voice, he nodded his assent.

All teasing aside, she continued, "Second"—she took a deep breath—"on our way to Chase and Lacy's you take me by Fort Gibson—to talk with Glenn."

"Why?" His voice wasn't unpleasant. It just didn't contain the warmth it had a moment before.

It was very important to Kathlyn that Brad understand her motivation. "The least I owe him is an explanation about us, Brad. I doubt he'll care very much that I'm not marrying him. But I owe him an explanation," she repeated.

Brad nodded gravely. "He must be a damn fool."

"Why Mr. Hampton, I believe that's about the nicest thing anybody ever said to me." She cupped his smiling face in her hands. "I love you, my darling, only you. You do know that I've never loved anyone but you? Don't you?"

"It took me eleven years to discover it, but, yes, I know that, sweetheart."

"Eleven years," she said. Eyes turning to lavender ice, her tender expression hardened.

Brad was duly impressed. His sweet Kat had a "hit the deck if you value your neck" look written all over her face. He suspected he knew why. She confirmed his suspicion with her next words.

"Rachel's mine." Over the past several days they had come to the conclusion that the infamous notes could have come from no one, save Rachel. She was the only one who knew the extent of their relationship, the only one with a grudge against Brad.

"Done," Brad said, smiling. The rage flashing in Kat's iris eyes did not bode well for Rachel Jackson. If and when she meted out Rachel's punishment — punishment long overdue — he wanted to be around. It would be a sight to behold.

"You promise? You'll leave Rachel to me?"

"I wouldn't think of getting between the two of you." Grinning, he added, "it wouldn't be a very safe place to be."

She smiled then. "No, it probably wouldn't."

Anxious to be reunited with Dru and begin their new life as husband and wife, they made their way toward town. They galloped past the high-walled military fort which faced the wilds of Indian Territory. The river front was to their left a few hundred yards from the fort.

"The boat's in," Brad said, jerking his head in the direction of the *Robert E. Lee.*

Kathlyn nodded and smiled. "I can't wait to see Dru."

Brad chuckled. "I imagine she'll have a few million questions."

"At least."

Fort Smith was a typical western community, consisting of several hotels, a couple dozen saloons, a few general stores and livery stables, ten or fifteen private homes, and an assortment of other establishments.

The muddy streets were crowded; cowboys milled around the square, farmers and their families moved in and out of stores, roughnecks lined the boardwalks. All paused to look at the trail-worn couple heading toward the hotel.

Likewise, Brad and Kathlyn noticed everyone they passed, looking for a familiar face, hoping to find someone who had been on the boat with them. They came up empty.

Finally, they reined in at the Cherokee Trail Hotel, a

328

respectable looking establishment. Brad hopped from his horse. With a lovestruck smile on his face, he hurried around the animal and helped Kathlyn dismount. He grasped her around the waist and slowly slid her down the length of his body. His desire for her was physically evident.

She widened her eyes; her cheeks grew flushed.

"I told you we better rush this wedding," he whispered, tucking her arm into the curve of his elbow.

"And the honeymoon?" She fluttered her lashes saucily as they mounted the steps to the hotel.

He smiled down into her face. "Oh no. That we'll take slow and easy." His whisper warmed the whorl of her ear.

The first person they saw in the lobby was Jacob Shelby. Frankly, he looked like hell. At least that was Brad's opinion. Millie's daddy needed a shave; his usually impeccable suit was rumpled, and he looked as if he had not slept in a week.

"Jacob," Brad called from across the room. He raised a questioning brow, when Jacob didn't return his smile or his greeting. Instead, he merely walked in their direction, moving as if he had a ton of rocks strapped to his back.

"Brad?" Alarmed, Kathlyn squeezed Brad's arm. She had noticed Jacob's appearance and strained expression as well. "Something's wrong."

Brad placed a reassuring arm around her waist.

When Jacob reached them, he folded them into his embrace. "Thank God you two are all right. Hannah and I have been worried sick."

Brad smiled, though not as brightly as before. His eyes searched Jacob's face. "I ran into a little trouble, but Kathlyn came to my rescue."

Kathlyn stood deadly still at Brad's side, scarcely daring to breath. She wanted desperately to ask about Dru, but fear paralyzed her.

"I appreciate you and Hannah seeing after Dru for me. Where is she?" Brad allowed his gaze to roam the lobby before returning to Jacob's strained expression.

"Hannah and I have taken a room upstairs. Why don't you come on up," Jacob said.

"Is Dru there?" Brad's tone was sharp, betraying his rising panic.

"Come on up," Jacob said softly.

Kathlyn began to shake at Brad's side, but he didn't notice. His attention was riveted to Jacob. "Dammit, Jacob, answer me. Where's Dru?" He was shouting now. The color had drained from his face; his fists were clenched. Other passengers from the *Robert E. Lee* looked on sympathetically.

"She's dead, Brad." Jacob's hoarse whisper cut like a knife through Brad's heart.

"Nooo!" he roared from the depths of his soul. It wasn't true; Brad knew it wasn't true.

Kathlyn fainted at his side, sliding to the floor.

Brad lunged forward, grabbing Jacob by the lapels. "Damn you, where is my daughter?" He shook a white-faced Jacob like a dog shaking a rabbit. Tears were streaming down both men's faces. "Where is she? Where is Dru?" Finally, Brad crumbled to his knees, dropping his head into his hands, sobbing quietly. Instinctively, he gathered Kathlyn's unconscious body into his arms. Somehow, he couldn't believe it; Dru wasn't dead.

Jacob lay his hand on Brad's shoulder. "Brad, please, let's go upstairs." His voice was little more than a raspy whisper. When Brad seemed oblivious to his presence, Jacob shook him gently. "Brad, we have to see to Kathlyn."

Hearing Kathlyn's name penetrated the cocoon of horror and grief engulfing Brad. He swiped tears away with the back of his hand; his eyes settled on her face. Several women knelt beside them, slapping the tops of Kathlyn's hand, trying to awaken her.

"Thank you, ladies. We'll take her upstairs now," Jacob said, reaching down to take Kathlyn from Brad.

Brad pushed him away. Coming up on his knees, he clutched her to his chest. Tears streamed down his cheeks, dropping unheeded onto her face below. Rising, he walked as if in a dream, a horrible nightmare that he prayed God would end. He fully expected Dru to come running up to him, to grab him around the legs and hug him tightly.

A full thirty minutes had passed before he was composed sufficiently to question Jacob. He sat in a chair in the Shelby's suite, still clutching Kathlyn's unconscious body against him. Jacob and Hannah suggested that she be laid on the bed, but Brad refused to release her. They suspected she had fainted due to the shock of Dru's death, but had sent for the town doctor anyway. He had not yet arrived.

"What happened?" Brad whispered past the tears clogging the back of his throat. With a strength of will that had seen him through many a tragedy, he kept his sobs at bay.

"She was with Miss Jackson."

"Rachel?" Brad spat, hatred visible on his face.

"Yes. She sneaked away from our stateroom. We thought she and Millie were asleep. Millie said Dru just went to get Ishta." Hannah answered with a surprisingly strong voice. Her face was heavily lined with grief and not a little guilt. Her pale cheeks were damp, her eyes red and swollen from days of crying.

Brad didn't blame her for this tragedy, but he was too distraught to reassure her. "And?" His lips moved. No sound was heard.

"Miss Jackson . . . Rachel said she was escorting her back to our stateroom when Dru lost her balance and fell over the side of the boat. The captain heard the splash. Naturally, he stopped the boat and sent out a rescue party."

It was too much. Brad buried his face in Kathlyn's hair and cried.

"Brad?" Kathlyn stirred. She looked around, disoriented. Brad raised his head and looked into her eyes. "Dru?" she asked with a quiver in her voice.

He shook his head and placed his cheek against hers. In the stillness, her sobs joined his. Their tears mingled.

Jacob and Hannah were quite sure they had never seen a more heartrending sight. The feeling that it was somehow their fault made it even worse.

Finally, Brad raised his head. "Where's her bod . . . where is she?"

"We didn't find her," Jacob said.

Brad surged to his feet, with Kathlyn following. "She might still be alive," Brad said, the strength abruptly returning to his voice.

Jacob shook his head. "I'm sorry, Brad, but it's just not possible. Think. Could she swim?" Reluctantly, Brad shook his head, no. "The current was vicious in that area. It was late at night, pitch black. The clouds were so thick there wasn't a star in the sky. Even if she could swim, she couldn't see land.

"I know it's hard to accept. But there's no way she could have survived that. I'm so sorry. I swear to God, if I thought there was the slightest chance that child was still alive, I would be there. But we dragged the river and searched the surrounding area for two days. There's just no way," he finished weakly.

Intellectually, Brad knew Jacob was right. Emotionally, he held out hope. "I sure as hell can't let it go at this. God, Jacob, that was Dru. My baby." Though tears were rolling down his cheeks, he didn't break down again. He wrapped his arms around Kathlyn, pulled her to him, tucked her head beneath his chin, and massaged her back as she sobbed again.

Finally, she stiffened. "Where's Rachel?" she ground out, murder in her eyes.

Jacob and Hannah looked at each other uneasily. "She disappeared while we were searching for Dru."

The implication was more loathsome than either Brad or Kathlyn wanted to consider. Still, it was there. Had Rachel pushed Dru into the Arkansas River? And if so, for what reason? Had she been so jealous of Kathlyn, hated her and Brad so much that she would kill a five year old child? Surely even Rachel wasn't that evil.

Then Brad remembered Roth, the leading statements Jared had made about his suspicious death and Rachel's role in it. He knew then with icy certainty that, if Dru was truly dead, it was not an accident. His precious, innocent, baby girl had been murdered, by Rachel. Rage threatened to overcome his sanity.

He grew deadly still, tightening his grip on Kathlyn until she gasped in pain. "I'm sorry," he murmured, looking down into her troubled gaze.

His eyes widened when a thought hit him like the kick of a mule. Kathlyn's life could be in danger too. If Rachel could murder an innocent child, what would she do to the woman she hated above all else?

Before he found Rachel, he had to see that Kathlyn was safe. God knows he *would* die, if he lost her too. He would take her to the Circle C. She would be safe with Chase and Lacy.

Then he would search for Rachel. And when he found her, he would kill her.

That night Brad and Kathlyn slept together. Propriety be damned! They needed comfort that could only be found in the other's embrace.

He pulled her beneath him. Tenderly, gently, sweetly, he made love to her, whispering how much she meant to him, how very much he loved her.

Their physical union reaffirmed that there was life in the world, even if the person they loved most — other than each other — was dead.

After they reached the glorious pinnacle of completion, they tightened their arms around each other . . . and cried again.

When Kathlyn fell asleep, Brad dressed and went downstairs. As if in a daze, he made arrangements for them to take the morning stage to Fort Gibson. Lost in thoughts of the daughter he loved more than life itself, he failed to notice the shadowy figure that slipped out the front door after overhearing their travel plans.

Chapter Thirty-seven

The first rays of morning slanted through the curtains, heating Brad's face. He was not fully asleep, yet not completely awake. In that blissful moment of half-wakefulness he was cognizant of nothing save the warm, soft woman cuddled against him. Tightening his arms around Kathlyn's bare body, he sighed with pleasure. Her silken hair cascaded over his skin and he shivered.

Still groggy, he sipped from her partially opened lips. "Sweetheart," he whispered in his blissfully numb state. Heavy lashes fluttered open, revealing clear iris eyes. The love contained in them caused the breath to lodge in his throat. Then as she came fully awake, pain clouded her gaze.

Brad was snatched back to reality with a force that caused him to groan. He had forgotten that Dru was dead. He closed his eyes against the pain.

Kathlyn buried her face in his chest. "I'm so sorry." Her voice was muffled.

"Me too. Oh God, me too."

"Do you hate me?" she asked.

He placed a trembling hand beneath her chin and tilted her head back. "Hate you? I love you, sweet baby. How could you ask if I hate you?"

"It's all my fault." The tears clogging Kathlyn's throat threatened to choke her.

"It's not your fault, baby."

"If I had stayed on the *Robert E. Lee*, she would be alive. If only I hadn't left her alone. Oh Brad, I'm so sorry. You have to know how sorry I am. I loved her."

"Shh. I know. And you didn't leave her alone. You left her with the Shelbys. Is it their fault she's . . . that Rachel got to her?"

Kathlyn shook her head, no.

"It's not your fault either. Besides, if you hadn't come into Arkansas Post, I would be dead. And more than likely you would have been killed along with Dru." His grief hardened; his arms tightened around her shoulders. "Damn Rachel to hell!"

"Do you really think she killed her?"

"Don't you?" he asked through clenched teeth, trying to tamp down the murderous rage that threatened his sanity.

"I just don't know." She tilted her head back, looking into his eyes. "But when we find her, I intend to find out."

"Sweetheart, I'm not about to let you near that woman!"

Kathlyn pulled away. "You promised, you said Rachel was mine! Brad she ruined our lives, I owe her for that. And now, if she did that to Dru . . ."

"Dru is my daughter, sweetheart. It's my obligation to deal with Rachel, if I discover that she killed my child."

"But I *know* that she killed my child. If it hadn't been for those notes she sent, my baby might be alive today."

"I know, honey. But the baby you lost was mine too," he reminded her.

"But . . ." she began.

He placed a gentle finger over her lips. "It doesn't matter who has the right to punish Rachel. What matters is that she's dangerous. And she hates us. I won't let you put yourself in harm's way."

"Brad . . ."

"No, honey"—he cut her off—"you'll be safe at the Circle C. Chase will see to it."

Kathlyn wanted to argue further, to tell Brad that she was going with him to find Rachel, but a wave of nausea rolled over her. She was barely able to scramble out of bed before she retched in the chamber pot.

"What the"—Brad was horrified—"Kat, you've made yourself sick." He leaned over her, holding her up as she emptied the contents of her stomach. Then he lifted her into his arms. Returning her to bed, he moistened a cloth, and gently bathed her forehead.

He pulled her against him. His whisper was thick with emotion, "Sweetheart, you're all I've got in the world now. Please understand, I can't lose you too."

Kathlyn thought her heart would break. "All right," she said. "But please, please be careful." Raising her hand to caress his dimple, she whispered, "You're all I've got too."

"I promise." They rose from the bed and dressed in near silence. Though they didn't speak a great deal, they touched constantly. Reassuring, comforting, loving. They couldn't bear to be more than a few inches apart. He continued to reach for her, as if to reassure himself that she was truly all right. She went to him readily, trying not to think of when they would part. Finally, they went downstairs for a light breakfast.

On their way out of the dining area, they met Jacob and Hannah. The sight of Millie, standing between her parents, was like a knife in their hearts. The pale, precious child reminded them of Dru. Still, they halted, wanting to reassure the Shelbys that they held them blameless.

Brad placed his hand on Jacob's shoulder. "I appreciate everything you did. And want you to know that I don't blame you . . . either of you . . . for what happened."

Jacob hugged Brad unashamedly. "You have to know how sorry we are," he whispered. Hannah added, hugging Kathlyn, "So sorry."

"I know." Brad nodded.

"What are you going to do?" Jacob asked.

"Make sure Kathlyn's safe, then go find Dru."

Jacob looked as if he would speak, then thought better of it. He slipped a piece of paper from inside his waistcoat pocket and handed it to Brad. "We'll be staying at my sister's spread while we look for a place of our own. She and her husband have a ranch just this side of the Nations. You'll get word to me, if I can do anything to help?"

336

Brad leaned down and touched Millie's hair affectionately. The little girl who had been so active the last time Brad had seen her just smiled sadly. With a catch in his voice, he answered Jacob, "Thanks. I'll let you know."

After they said their goodbyes, he led Kathlyn out onto the veranda to await the stage.

The jehu drove up in a relatively new Abbot-Downing Concord coach. It was pulled by six horses. The body was painted blue with shiny black steps and top railing; the wheels were yellow with fine red pinstriping on the spokes. Ornate scrollwork and gilded leaf decorated the exterior doors. The conveyance was quite impressive, but not to the two grief-stricken passengers who boarded, hand in hand.

Kathlyn was oblivious to everything around her, except her grief for Dru and her fear for Brad. She held onto his hand like a lifeline.

He tightened his grip, noticing everything around them. His protective instincts were razor sharp. Losing Dru burned the edges of his mind, but he was determined to keep a clear head. Kathlyn's life might well depend on it. He would grieve for his baby girl when all this was over. When the guilty were punished, and Kathlyn was out of harm's way.

They settled inside the coach and two benign-looking young men joined them. Brad questioned them, not rudely, but firmly. Unoffended, they informed him that they were new recruits headed for service at Fort Gibson.

A third man boarded the stage. He was a large, middle-aged man. A gunslick. Shifty-eyed would describe him. Slung low on his hip, he wore a .44 caliber, Walker Colt six-shooter.

The monstrous four pound, nine inch gun looked ominous to the uninitiated, but to Brad it was so much dead weight. Decidedly, its appearance was more frightening than its performance. It was the look in the man's eyes that was lethal, however. Brad distrusted him on sight.

"Something bothering you, mister?" Shifty asked Brad.

"Not yet," he answered coldly.

The tense silence in the coach was broken by Shifty's menacing chuckle. He leaned his head back against the coach and pulled his hat low over his eyes.

By noon the summer sun had melted away the cool of the day. Inside the coach the five weary travelers appeared to be dozing in order to escape the sweltering heat. Two occupants, however, were fully awake. Brad and his shifty-eyed nemesis.

Kathlyn — although asleep — moved closer to Brad's side. She awakened when the stage drew to a halt. The stillness awakened the others as well.

"Sweetheart, stay here. I'll go see if the driver needs help." Brad touched Kathlyn's cheek.

From the far corner Shifty sneered, "That's a good idea, mister." Drawing his Colt, he aimed the ponderous weapon point-blank at Brad's chest.

"Oh dear God," Kathlyn breathed.

After relieving all three men of their guns, the brigand gestured toward the door. "You two follow him. Out," he ordered the young recruits.

Kathlyn slid across the seat. "I'm coming too."

Poised with one hand on the door Brad turned to her. "No," he ordered forcefully. He touched her hair gently, softening his directive. "Please honey, stay here. I promise, everything will be all right." He pulled her to him for a short kiss. She circled his neck to hold him back.

"How touching!" Shifty sneered, shoving Brad through the opening.

Kathlyn fell back against the seat as the two recruits followed behind Shifty and Brad. The door slammed and the leather flap snapped in her face. She strained to hear what was occurring outside. It sounded as if in addition to Shifty there were two other outlaws. With a great effort, she ignored her mounting fear.

"Shephard! What the hell?" Brad exclaimed.

"Good afternoon, Mr. Hampton. It's been a long time." Stuart's warm drawl was taunting.

338

"What are you doing here? What do you want?" Brad asked.

"I would think to a man of your intelligence, that would be obvious. You have something I want. And after I kill you, I plan to take it. Is that clear enough?"

"I don't know what you're talking about. But just take whatever it is and let us be on our way. Robbery is one thing, but you'll hang for murder," Brad spoke calmly, concealing his fear. He wasn't afraid for himself. All he could think of was what would become of Kathlyn, if he were killed. It seemed that the men weren't concerned with her at the moment, but who knew what would happen to her after blood was spilled.

"No." Stuart struck a relaxed pose, bending his right leg and hooking it around his saddle horn. "I imagine I'll have to kill you first." He paused for effect. "Before I take Miss McKinney."

Brad wanted nothing more than to dive for Stuart, to squeeze his throat until the life left his body, until he was no longer a threat to Kathlyn, but he knew he had to remain calm; he had to buy time.

The young recruits weren't as wise, however. Thinking Brad had the gunslicks distracted, they foolishly lunged at their captors. Before Brad could assist them, Stuart moved his horse between them, cutting them off from Brad's view. Two shots rang out. The recruits slumped to the ground, dead.

"Now you." Smiling down at Brad, Stuart took aim, and fired. His horse bucked just as he pulled the trigger. The bullet grazed Brad's head, making a deep furrow alongside his temple. Brad hit the ground, raising dust.

While gun smoke still floated in the air, Kathlyn thrust her head through the covered window and found herself staring into Stuart's eyes. They were cold and his lips were cruel. A jagged scar ran from his eyebrow to the corner of his mouth. He was huge, dressed in unrelieved black. He looked familiar.

Tearing her gaze away, she scanned the area. She panicked at the carnage on the ground. Not immediately seeing Brad, she threw the door open and jumped from the coach.

"Come here," Stuart shouted to Kathlyn. "Hurry it up . . . I'm not looking to get my neck stretched." With his last words he backed his horse away and wheeled in her direction, revealing Brad's body to her view.

"Noooo . . . Braddd!" she screamed in horror, throwing herself into the dust beside Brad, clutching his bleeding head to her chest. She rocked back and forth, keening so loudly that the sound of thundering hooves of an approaching band of Comanches was muffled.

Stuart leaned over the side of his horse. Without a word, he grabbed her by the hair.

"Nooo," she shrieked, her eyes wide, wild with grief and fear. She jerked away, burying her face in Brad's blood-matted hair.

A muscle in Stuart's jaw twitched with barely suppressed rage. He said cruelly, "He's dead." But when he tried to pull her to her feet, she fought and screamed as if the thread of sanity had snapped.

Shifty came to Stuart's aid. He approached Kathlyn on foot and tried to pull her off Brad. She turned into a snarling beast. Holding Brad to her breast, she struck out with her feet. "You touch him and I'll kill you!" she shrieked hysterically.

Balling his fist, he hit her alongside her jaw. Her head snapped backward, then she fell unconscious at his feet. Lifting her, he threw her over Stuart's saddle.

"Let's get the hell out of here!" Stuart shouted to his men.

The dust of the retreating outlaws had barely settled when a band of Comanches descended upon the site. Sliding from their pinto ponies, Red Feather and his braves examined the fallen men, looking for survivors.

"Over here," Spotted Wolf called in the Comanche tongue. "This white eyes is still alive."

Red Feather padded over to Brad's side, issuing orders to his men to fashion a travois with which to transport the injured man. Within thirty minutes the Indians

340

headed back toward their village, pulling Brad along behind them.

Red Feather's camp burst with excitement at the war-
rior's return. In and around the tall, conical lodges,
dogs barked, children whooped, and laughing women
greeted their men. For a moment, they overlooked the
unconscious white man lying upon the litter. Then a
dusky-skinned woman, heavy with child, bent over him.

"Brother," Sunrise addressed Red Feather. "This man
is very ill. Take him into your lodge. I will care for
him."

Red Feather smiled warmly at his sweet sister. "Will
my sister's husband, Brave Eagle, object?"

"My husband would not have me let a man die—even
if he is white."

Without looking at Brad, Red Feather's other sister,
Thunder, asked disdainfully, "Will you have me share a
lodge with a filthy, white dog?"

Thunder and Red Feather had lived alone, since their
parents died of typhoid pneumonia. Their lodge was
not always peaceful. "Do you forget that my blood
brother, Stalker, is half white?" Red Feather ground out
between clenched teeth.

"No! How could I forget the way you disgrace The
People by calling that white man 'brother'?" She spat on
the ground at her brother's feet.

"You weren't always opposed to Stalker. Not until he
brought his white wife home."

"Please!" Sunrise stepped between her quarreling sib-
lings, placing a quelling hand on each of their chests.
Like Red Feather, she knew Thunder's hatred of the
half-breed Cherokee whom Red Feather called brother
stemmed from Stalker's rejection of her, rather than his
white ancestry. It was a long standing argument between
brother and sister. "Brother, I will care for this man in
my husband's lodge . . . but Sister, perhaps you should
look at this white eyes before you cast him from you,"
Sunrise said.

341

Reluctantly, Thunder dropped her gaze. She had never seen a man so blatantly virile, red or white. His strong body dwarfed the narrow travois. Red Feather had removed Brad's shirt and tied it firmly about his head in an attempt to stop the flow of blood. Even in his unconscious state, the corded muscles of his naked arms seemed to be bursting with barely contained energy. His full, red lips were slightly parted, and his breathing was shallow. Thunder jerked her chin, calling forth as much dignity as possible. "Very well. I will care for him."

Red Feather coughed a dry laugh, directing two of his men to carry Brad into the lodge.

Standing behind Sunrise, her husband, Brave Eagle, sighed with relief. It was good that his wife would not have to care for the handsome white man.

Once the men had placed Brad on a pallet, Thunder cleaned his head wound, then coated it with a spicy-smelling salve. She removed his remaining clothes and washed his body, becoming more interested by the minute.

All the while, Red Feather hovered nearby. There was something about the injured man that was vaguely familiar to him.

"I have brought food," Sunrise spoke as she bent to enter. Knowing that Thunder would be busy with her patient, Sunrise had prepared Red Feather a quick meal of corn mush and rabbit stew. For the patient, she had cooked a thickened broth. Close on their mother's heels were two black-eyed, naked urchins, four-year-old, Raven, and her five-year-old brother, Wind Dancer.

Brad began to thrash about on the pallet. His skin was dry and hot to the touch. "The fever has begun," Sunrise observed solemnly.

"Will he die?" Wind Dancer asked his mother.

"He is weak and infection has set in. But if he does not die before his skin becomes moist, he will live," Thunder cut in, not sparing her nephew so much as a glance.

"How long do you think the fever will last?" Red Feather asked of no one in particular.

342

Sunrise answered from her position beside the cook-fire in the center of the lodge. "It could last hours or days."

"Kathlyn . . . Dru . . . Kathlyn," Brad moaned.

Raven gingerly reached forth a small finger and touched the dent in the white man's cheek. "I wonder who he's calling?"

"His wife and child?" Sunrise suggested, cradling a golden disc in her palm.

Sunrise moved to her sister's side. A stream of golden light reflected off the object in her hand. She handed Thunder the golden disc.

It was an ornately engraved watch. Inside was a tiny picture of a platinum-haired little girl. Her ethereal beauty seemed to reach out from her image. Thunder hated the little girl on sight. "Hmpf," she snorted, snapping the watch shut and tossing it to Red Feather.

"There is writing on the front," he said. "B.H."

Just then Brad's eyes opened, his raspy voice broke through the stillness, sounding like a sob. "Kathlyn . . ."

"Brad . . ." Kathlyn whimpered, clutching the delicate locket suspended from the filigreed chain encircling her neck. The thunder of pounding hooves sounded in her ears. The earth shook and jarred her stomach with each step the mount took.

The terrible bouncing made her deathly ill. She opened her mouth to retch and a groan emerged. Her jaw felt as if it were on fire, as if the fragile bone had been shattered.

White-hot pain snatched her from the murky depths of unconsciousness. Just as she opened her eyes, the horses halted. The ground rushed up to meet her face.

sva bq on Ta Ta Ta Ta wa nood loo

l'adilanw asilina atuat silt
wa aulla nool ngioni midiyol nal-

Ta gairsqua bna gurta
woy lagisonl

ylbbab ym 158 1 oge wa

oce noed

Chapter Thirty-eight

"You damn fool, don't throw her on the ground like that. How much do you think she'll be worth with cuts and bruises all over her?"

The voice was harsh, but familiar to Kathlyn. It was too horrible to believe. He couldn't be responsible for this. *Please, God, don't let it be him*. She felt him hovering over her, willing her to open her eyes. For as long as she dared, she kept them firmly shut, trying valiantly to postpone the inevitable.

"Come on, Kitty Kat, open your eyes. Is that any way to greet your betrothed?" he purred sarcastically.

Choking back a sob, she moaned, "Glenn?" Reluctantly, she raised her gaze. His head was limned by the sun, his face cast in shadow. He looked dark, evil, his sadistic laugh completing the image.

"Get up Kitty Kat, there are some people I want you to meet."

Glenn Crutchfield hauled Kathlyn roughly to her feet. Jerking her jaw with a rough hand, he turned her head toward a weather-beaten shack.

The lightning sharp pain in her jaw caused the world to fade in and out of focus. Finally, the picture cleared. Twelve beautiful girls formed a solid line, standing outside the front door. They were disheveled, dirty. The fear in their eyes was haunting.

"May I introduce my fiancées?" Glenn and the other brigands laughed at the incredulous look on Kathlyn's face.

The girls all stared at the ground. Then two young women in the center of the line stepped apart, revealing a child behind them.

Kathlyn grasped her throat. The stress had been too much to bear; she had snapped.

"Miss Kathlyn," Dru sobbed, running across the yard, stumbling over a root, sailing into Kathlyn's outstretched arms.

Kathlyn was laughing and crying and squeezing the child so hard Dru gasped for air. "We thought you were dead," Kathlyn cried.

"Daddy, where's my daddy? I want my daddy."

Kathlyn was spared having to respond for the moment. "Well, cousin, you don't look so good," Rachel said.

Kathlyn pushed Dru safely behind her back and lunged at Rachel. Rachel drew back a tight fist, but a member of the band, whom Kathlyn had not seen until now, stepped between them.

With surprising gentleness, he wrapped his arms around Kathlyn's waist. "You don't want to do that." He spoke firmly, but not unkindly into her ear.

Kathlyn struggled in his arms. "You!" she shrieked at Lucky. "Why?"

He shrugged, saying loudly enough for everyone to hear, "A man's gotta make a living." Pretending to nuzzle her neck, he whispered, "I can't explain now. Just see to the child."

She pulled away from him, gathering Dru into her arms. "Stay away from me," she hissed at Lucky.

When they were all assembled in the cabin, Rachel noticed Brad was absent. "What happened, did your incompetents let him get away . . . again?" she asked Stuart.

Kathlyn tensed as she sat on the floor, leaning against the wall. Dru was sleeping in her lap.

"You should eat." Lucky bent to offer her a plate of food.

"He's dead," Stuart said.

Through her tears Kathlyn thought she saw a spark of pity cross Lucky's face. It was gone as soon as it appeared.

His face passive now, he placed the plate on the

345

floor beside her hip. Quietly, he slipped from the room.

"Where the hell have you been?" the handsome young man asked Lucky as he approached him on horseback. "I'm fit to be tied, waiting here on this hill, wondering what's going on down there. I don't like having to stay out of sight with nothing more to do than polish my badge."

Lucky had heard his partner's complaints many times in the past few days. Both men were used to action. Lucky sympathized. "They robbed another stagecoach," Lucky said, dreading to tell his friend the rest of the news.

"Any women aboard?"

"Yeah. One. They brought her in 'bout an hour ago. She's the one I told you about . . . the one on the boat."

"Kathlyn McKinney? The one traveling with Brad?"

"Yeah."

The blond lawman rose quickly. "Is she all right? They didn't hurt her, did they?"

"No, she's all right," Lucky said.

"Thank God. Have you gotten to talk to her? Did she find Brad when she went into Arkansas Post?"

"I assume so."

"What the hell is that supposed to mean?" Lucky's partner was agitated.

Lucky drew a deep breath and placed his hand on his partner's shoulder. "He's dead. Shephard shot him."

"God, no!"

Lucky stayed by his partner's side for as long as he could, saying nothing, trying to absorb his grief. "I've got to be going," he said finally. "They'll wonder where I am."

The young man looked up, his eyes unnaturally bright. "When will they leave for California?"

"The plan's to lay low for a few days. Moving that many women would be too easy to track. We

346

still have a while, before we make our move."

"You know I have to kill him," he spoke evenly.

"Have you forgotten that you're a lawman?"

The young man gave Lucky a look that he understood. "If Chap or Rad had been killed, what would you do?"

Lucky didn't answer; it wasn't necessary. He mounted his horse in silence.

"Heath," the blond marshal called to Lucky. "Be careful. Those bastards are dangerous."

"Don't worry 'bout me. I'll be fine." Lucky offered his partner a crooked smile. "They don't call me Lucky for nothing."

Brad moved through the murky darkness as if he were trudging waist high in quicksand. A dense fog blanketed his mind; the only clear thought he possessed was the realization of severe pain. His head was pounding, nausea flooded over him in waves, his body pulsed with agony. Even his teeth hurt!

Where was he? he wondered. The sounds that met his ears were foreign to him. Dogs barked; horses thudded against hard-packed earth; children shrieked; men and women laughed and talked. Strange. The language they spoke wasn't English. The bed he slept on was made of layers of furs and animal skins. His nakedness was covered by a heavy, scratchy robe. And the scent of wood smoke, leather, grease, and wild onions filled his nostrils.

He opened his eyes. He looked about, shifting slowly in deference to his throbbing head. He was in a tall tent of sorts. It was cluttered with bags made of animal skin and crude vessels that reminded him of turtle shells. In the center of the tent a small fire smoldered. Its smoke spiraled upward, escaping through a hole some fifteen feet above.

He sat up abruptly and was blinded by the brilliance of sunlight pouring through an oval door. Pain and dizziness caused by his abrupt movement sent him back to the mat. He lost consciousness again.

Sometime later, a soft, warm hand, fluttering against his face, brought him awake in degrees. The tinkle of childlike laughter, completed the process. The carefree sound tugged at his heart. When he turned his head, he stared into the liquid black eyes of a little girl.

The room shifted. Brad clamped his eyes shut. Again he felt something soft rub against his hair-roughened cheek. It was the downy smooth skin of a child. Back and forth, she rubbed her palm across his face. He reached out and pulled her to his chest, moaning, "Dru."

She smelled of smoke and the musky odor of damp earth. It wasn't an unpleasant smell, though it was unfamiliar. The child in his arms was not his sweet-smelling baby girl. He knew that. She wasn't his Dru.

Lifting his hand, he touched her head. Strangely, he drew comfort from her coarse, straight hair as it brushed the back of his hand. He held her tight. She was warm and affectionate. Her mere presence was a balm to his grieving heart.

Even in her innocence, Raven sensed that the white man needed comfort, much like the comfort her mother provided for her when the *posa bihia,* mischievous boys, teased her. So for a long moment, chubby brown arms encircled Brad's neck, while strong hands stroked Raven's head and back.

When Raven slipped into her uncle's lodge earlier that day she was elated to find the white man alone. She was fascinated by the prickly black hair growing from his face. Hair did not grow from her father's face like that. She wondered how the black twigs would feel against her skin. They weren't sharp like shards of bone as she'd supposed, but scratchy like frozen blades of grass. It was a worthwhile discovery for one so young.

A harsh female voice broke the spell around the unlikely twosome.

"Brat," Thunder hissed. Before Thunder could reach the buffalo bone lying by the small fire in the center of the lodge, Raven darted through the oval opening and ran headlong into her mother's arms.

"*Peta,* my child," Sunrise soothed, taking her trembling daughter into her arms.

"*Pia,* Mother," Raven returned, secure in her mother's embrace.

Sunrise stepped into Red Feather's lodge, intending to ask what had frightened Raven so. Before she could speak, Thunder ordered, "Go for Red Feather. The white man is awake."

Sunrise and Raven slipped from the lodge quietly.

Thunder slinked over to Brad's side. Suggestively, she trailed her hand through the thick pelt of black hair that covered his chest. "You have given us a fright, white man. We feared that you would travel to the land of the Great Spirit."

Instinctively, he pushed her hand away. "How long have I been out?"

"Two days." Thunder's voice was cold now.

"Two days!" Brad sat up abruptly. The tent spun around him. He grasped the fur covering his lower body, willing the world to right itself. "I have to leave." He tried to stand but his injury coupled with inactivity had made him weak. Once again, he fell back onto the mat. "Where am I?"

A noise from the doorway announced the arrival of Sunrise and Raven. They were followed closely by Red Feather.

Sunrise knelt beside Brad. "You are in the camp of the *Kotsoteka* Comanche. I am Sunrise and my daughter is Raven." When Red Feather dropped down on his haunches, she touched his arm. "This is my *Tah-mah,* brother, Red Feather."

Raven sidled closer to Brad, laying her hand on his bare shoulder. His frown dissolved. He covered the child's hand with his own.

"I found you beside a stagecoach. You had been shot in the head. Three other men had also been shot. They were dead; you are lucky to be among the living," Red Feather said slowly.

349

"Did you find a woman?" Brad's voice was soft, husky, betraying his emotion.

Red Feather shook his head, no.

Despair showed clearly on Brad's face. Sunrise spoke to him in her soothing, musical tone. "When you are able to travel, my brother will take you to a white man who is his friend. He will help you find your woman."

Brad nodded tersely. "Soon," was all he said.

When Kathlyn awakened in the cabin, thoughts of Brad returned. The emptiness in her heart threatened to suffocate her with its intensity. She feared that she was going to be sick to her stomach again.

Then a soft snuffling sound drew her gaze to the side. Dru lay awake at her side, her head cushioned in a profusion of platinum curls, her pale blue eyes wide, frightened, brimming with tears, her breathing that of a child who had cried long and hard.

"Come here, precious." Kathlyn opened her arms to the grieving child. Dru snuggled against Kathlyn's heart.

During the night Rachel had crowed to Dru about Brad's death, breaking the child's already battered heart. If not for Lucky's intervention, Kathlyn would have killed Rachel.

It was just as well that Lucky stopped her, Kathlyn had realized once she was calm. If she hurt Rachel, they might kill her. Then what would become of Dru?

"Daddy," Dru sobbed thickly.

"I know, I know," Kathlyn soothed, her own tears streaming down her pale cheeks.

Through the blur of tears, Kathlyn saw Lucky approaching. He was the only outlaw present in the cabin.

Casting a glance toward the door, he whispered, "Is she all right?" He placed a strong hand on Dru's shoulder.

"What do you care?" Kathlyn pulled Dru away from him.

350

Dru turned her eyes toward the man Miss Kathlyn didn't like. Ever since the bad lady brought her here, he had been nice to her. In childlike innocence, she had decided he was a good man. "My daddy's in heaven," she said simply.

"I'm sorry, baby," Lucky said.

"Why are you being kind to us? Is this some sort of trick?" Instinctively, Kathlyn tightened her hold on Dru.

He shook his head, no. "You've got to trust me."

"I don't have to do anything of the sort. You're one of them."

Lucky implored her with his eyes. "Look, I don't have time to explain. Just do what they say. And for God's sake, stay away from your cousin. She's looking for a chance to hurt you. If she starts anything, yell for me."

"We will," Dru answered for Kathlyn.

Lucky smiled.

Then Glenn strode into the room and Lucky moved away, his stoic facade falling back into place. Confused, yet slightly mollified, Kathlyn glared at Glenn.

He met her stare, then laughed harshly when she turned her face toward the wall.

Brad placed one moccasined foot in front of the other, slowly pacing the confines of Red Feather's lodge. He had been in the Indian camp for a week, and was finally ready to travel.

A flash of light from beneath Thunder's raised bed caught his eye. Bending down, he saw that it was caused by the sun reflecting off a metal object. He grasped it and stood.

Turning the gold pocket watch over in his hand, he ran his thumb over the ornate engraving and flipped the lid. He touched Dru's picture with an unsteady finger.

Slipping the watch into a leather pouch he wore at his side, he raised his eyes. Thunder stood in the doorway of the lodge. "Where's Red Feather?" Brad asked.

She closed the distance between them before answering. "He and the others are at council. They leave tomorrow. We will be alone in my brother's lodge, white man."

"No, we won't," Brad said, ducking through the oval door, stepping out into the clear night. As he approached the large structure that served as the meeting place for the tribe, men began filing out of the low door.

Red Feather's face spread in a smile when he saw Brad. *"Hi, haitsi,* hello friend," he said.

"Hi, haitsi," Brad returned his greeting.

Red Feather sensed Brad's restless energy, boiling just beneath the surface. "Let's walk."

Brad nodded and fell into step beside him.

Together, they made their way through the camp of identical, cone-shaped tents, skirting the meat racks placed haphazardly beside each lodge, winding through the oak and mesquite brush, past the prickly pear, arriving finally at a quiet stream.

They dropped down onto the red sandy beach. Red Feather stretched his long legs in front of him. Dropping his hands at his side, he sifted sand through his fingers. "I think, *Haitsi,* you are ready to leave us," the Comanche leader observed quietly.

"Yes," Brad said.

"Very well. You will find your woman?"

"I will try."

Both Brad and Red Feather knew that would be a monumental task, considering the vast expanse of Indian Territory. "We will need help."

Brad smiled at Red Feather's inclusive term. "You have someone in mind?"

"Yes. Tomorrow we are driving some of our horses" — Red Feather gestured toward the remuda — "to my blood brother's ranch. If anyone can find your woman, Stalker can."

Brad was encouraged. "Will he help us?"

352

"He will." There was no doubt in Red Feather's voice nor in his expression. "We leave at daybreak."

Brad drew a deep breath. "At daybreak," he whispered.

Chapter Thirty-nine

Red Feather, Brad, and a band of Comanche braves approached the ranch, leading a pack of horses, elaborate paints, muscular roans, ethereal palominos; they were all magnificent, some of the finest horseflesh Brad had ever seen.

He reined in on a hill overlooking the picturesque valley and turned in his saddle, taking in the panorama with an appreciative gaze. It looked as if it were painted by the mighty hand of God. Right down to the sprawling mansion cradled in the valley.

When he found Kathlyn, he would bring her here. He smiled wistfully. Together, they would stand on this hill. He would hold her in his arms and show her this beautiful sight. Perhaps they would buy a ranch and build a home like the one below him. And they would never, ever be separated again.

He wouldn't even consider that she might be dead. He held strongly to the belief that God would not make him suffer more than he could bear. And since he could not bear to lose both Kathlyn and Dru, God would not take Kat from him. It was as simple as that.

"Stay with the herd," Red Feather shouted to his men, drawing Brad from his reverie. "Let's go," he threw over his shoulder, galloping down the hill toward the ranch house.

Brad was stunned when they passed through the gate. Suspended overhead, was a perfectly round circle, the letter "C" dangling from the top. *The Circle C.* "I'll be damned," he muttered.

Leaning against the portal railing of the sprawling

354

ranch house, Chase Tarleton smiled up at Red Feather. Brad had not seen his brother-in-law since before the war, but the six foot, four inch, half-breed Cherokee had changed little. His shoulder length hair was still raven black, his eyes the palest blue Brad had ever seen.

When they reined in, Chase paid Brad little mind. *"Hi Haitsi,* Red Feather. At long last," Chase said as he pushed away from the rail. Sauntering across the yard, he moved with the ease of a stalking panther.

Red Feather slid easily from his horse, jerking his head in Brad's direction. *"Hi Haitsi,* Stalker. I have brought a friend."

Chase cast Brad an interested glance. The expressions of shock, relief, then undiluted joy passing across his handsome face were almost comical. "Brad, thank God!" He stepped forward, eye-to-eye with Brad. For a long moment the two men stared mutely at one another. Then in tandem they closed the narrow space between them. Emotion crackled in the dry Oklahoma wind as the brothers-in-law embraced.

"Thank God," Chase said again, emotion deepening the last vestiges of a Southern drawl.

"Where's Lacy?"

"In the house. I'd better prepare her for you. She's been in bed since we heard you were missing."

"You know about the trouble then?"

"Yes . . . and about Dru." Chase cleared his throat, placing a hand on Brad's shoulder. "I'm so sorry," he said softly.

Brad nodded. He was silent a moment. "Kathlyn?" He held his breath, waiting for Chase's answer.

Chase knew what Brad was asking. He had traveled to Fort Gibson when Brad and Dru failed to arrive as planned. He had been told of the stagecoach robbery and had gone on to Fort Smith, hoping against hope that Brad and Dru had not been passengers on that particular stage. It was there that he learned of Dru's death and discovered that Brad and a Miss McKinney had taken the stage.

"She's missing. The Army sent out a search party. But so far, no luck. I was told her fiancé is devastated." Chase elevated a brow.

The violence of Brad's oath surprised Chase. "I'll just bet he is. When do we leave?"

"Perhaps we better tell your sister you're alive first." Chase gave him a wry smile.

Brad agreed, but his mind was still on finding Kathlyn. "Red Feather has offered his help."

Chase nodded. "We'll reach Fort Gibson by nightfall. Red Feather, you and your men camp here while we're gone. I'll send someone back with instructions for you after we check with the Army."

Red Feather agreed.

Then Chase went inside to break the news of Brad's arrival to his heavily pregnant wife. Easing into the bedroom they shared, he crossed the room silently. He found her asleep in the middle of their big bed.

With her pale blonde hair tied back, dressed in a pale pink nightgown, Lacy Hampton Tarleton looked as young as she did the first time he saw her, hiding behind a pine tree, watching him bathe in the lake on Paradise plantation. As always, he chuckled when he thought about that day, his virginal wife trying to hide her six foot wide hoop skirt behind a ten-inch Georgia pine.

"Chase?" Her voice was husky from sleep.

He sat on the bed at her side. Instinctively, he caressed her swollen abdomen, where his babies slept beneath her heart. "Sweetheart, I have a surprise for you."

"Mmm, in the afternoon," she purred, always the seductive imp.

Chase laughed deep in his chest. "That's a tempting thought." As usual, making love to her was what he wanted to do more than anything. But alas, Brad was waiting. He dropped a gentle kiss to her lips. "But that's not the surprise."

She pouted prettily.

"Brad's here, sweetheart."

Lacy's jewel green eyes widened, then filled with tears. "Brad?" she rasped.

"Get dressed. We'll be waiting for you in my study."

"Are you crazy?" Lacy moved rather quickly for a woman seven months pregnant with twins. Barely a moment later, she was sailing down the portal steps, her gown tail flapping behind her, revealing bare feet. She threw herself into her big brother's outstretched arms. They laughed and cried as very carefully Brad spun his baby sister around.

Chase filled the doorway to the ranch house, grinning indulgently. "Brad, has it escaped your notice that my wife is in the family way and probably shouldn't be tossed about like a sack of feed?" His tone was anything but censorious.

Brad set Lacy from him and smiled down into her upturned face. "Is that true, Princess? I thought maybe you'd just gotten fat out here on the ranch." Gently, he laid his hand on her tight abdomen.

Lacy was unable to speak. She buried her face in Brad's chest. He was the first member of the Hampton family she had seen in six years. Distance and the war had separated her from the family she loved more than life itself. She was afraid if she let Brad go, he would disappear.

But she was soon to find out that she had to let him go, albeit temporarily. When she heard Brad speak about Kathlyn, saw the pain in his eyes, and witnessed the love on his face when he said Kathlyn's name, she sent him and Chase on their way.

Brad and Chase passed through the Cherokee encampment surrounding Fort Gibson. They entered the stockade, pulling rein at the Adjutant General's office.

The barely veiled hostility with which he and Chase were regarded was blatantly obvious to Brad. No doubt, the soldiers didn't care for half-breeds like Chase. And since Brad was tanned, dressed in buckskin, and traveling with a Cherokee, they assumed he was Indian as well. Their prejudice was a hell of a note considering that Fort Gibson's main function was to protect the Cherokees from the less-civilized Osage.

Brad was more than a little put out when he approached the officer on duty. "I would like to talk to someone regarding the search for Miss McKinney."

"That would be Lieutenant Crutchfield." A baby-faced private informed Brad. "He ain't here right now."

"Announce us to the officer of the day." Chase's low, steady voice carried an air of authority.

"Just a minute." The young man disappeared through a doorway behind his desk.

A gray-haired gentleman followed the private into the room where Chase and Brad waited. "Can I help you?" His gray eyes looked tired, though they were free of the kind of derision the other soldier's exhibited.

"I hope so . . ." Brad began.

The outer door burst open and three men rushed into the room.

"You!" Brad lunged at the shifty-eyed man who had been on the stagecoach with him.

"That's him. That's the one." Shifty side-stepped Brad.

His mind clear, analytical, Chase noted that Shifty turned Brad's accusation around rather quickly. Almost too quickly to be believable.

A tough-looking man with a star on his vest grabbed for Brad.

"What the hell?" Chase hissed.

It took three men to wrestle Brad to the floor. Shouting and bucking, he was handcuffed and hauled to his feet.

"What's the meaning of this, marshal?" the officer-of-the-day queried, totally baffled.

"This man is under arrest for the murder of a stage-coach driver, two recruits, and the abduction of Miss Kathlyn McKinney. Under orders of Judge Harper he will be jailed at Fort Smith until his trial can be arranged." The lawman's response sounded like a rehearsed speech. Even more suspicious than Shifty's quick response.

Brad pulled away from his grip momentarily. The lawman grabbed him again, pulled his gun, and aimed it at his head. "You made one mistake, mister. You didn't kill all the passengers."

"And you kidnapped my fiancée." The third man spoke with such hate that every eye turned his way. "Where is she? What did you do with her?" he snarled into Brad's face.

"Glenn Crutchfield," Brad ground out.

"I see you've heard of me." His icy smile was insolent, taunting, sadistic. "Then you must know the woman you kidnapped is my future wife. What have you done with her, you bastard?"

The look of violence on Brad's face worried Chase. He lay a restraining hand on Brad's shoulder. "Don't let him get to you, Brad. Can't you see that's what he's trying to do? What they're all trying to do? It's a set-up. But go with them. I'll follow along. I have a friend in Fort Smith—a lawyer. He'll help us."

"No! You have to find Kathlyn," Brad said.

"How pathetic," Glenn spat.

Chase stepped between Brad and Glenn. "I'll find her, Brad. I swear to God I will. But not now. Not until I get you an attorney."

Brad looked as if he would object.

"Brad, if you're found guilty, you'll hang." Chase shook Brad's shoulder for emphasis.

Brad knew Chase was right. He nodded reluctantly. "Then you've got to find her. Promise me, Chase?"

Chase nodded solemnly and Brad allowed himself to be led away.

Chapter Forty

It was apparent that something was wrong. It had all started when Glenn returned to the cabin just after dark.

Kathlyn, Dru, and the other young women could feel the tension in the air. Frightened, they huddled together in the shack. Their captors were meeting outside, around a fire. There was a great deal of shouting and cursing. And they were drinking. Heavily.

The vulnerable women tried to make themselves invisible, fearing that the anger of the outlaw band would be vented on them. Kathlyn was particularly frightened for Dru. She pulled her closer to her side and looked down into her widened eyes. Softly, she slid her fingers across the face that had become so dear to her. Dru smiled weakly. She was a game little thing, obviously trying to hide her fear.

The cabin door was kicked open with such force that it all but flew off its hinges. In reaction, the women jumped. Rachel headed their way. In Kathlyn's estimation, she looked like a female incarnation of the devil.

Stomping across the room, she growled, "Bitch!" She kicked Kathlyn's hip. Panting, she spat, "He's alive!" She slapped Kathlyn then.

Kathlyn rose up on her knees, shielding Dru. The other women whimpered, holding Dru back when the child tried to lunge at Rachel. "Stop it, you bad lady," Dru cried, champing at the bit to get to Rachel.

Dru's words didn't penetrate Rachel's rage. Doubling her fist, she swung and clipped Kathlyn's jaw. "You hear that, bitch, he's alive."

Kathlyn reeled from the blow. Instinctively, she raised her arms over her head, protecting herself the best she could. *Who?* What was Rachel saying? *Oh God, please let it be.* Kathlyn groaned when Rachel kicked her again. Her head jerked up.

"Brad?" she whispered through swollen lips.

"That's right. Your lover's alive."

Tears of joy streamed down Kathlyn's face. She turned to Dru, folding her into her embrace, leaving her back vulnerable to Rachel's attack. "He's alive, baby. Your daddy's alive."

"He's alive." Rachel bowed low over Kathlyn and Dru. The other young women cowered away from her.

Lucky rushed into the room. Having just arrived in camp, he was out of breath. His hand was on his gun. He took a step forward.

Rachel grabbed a handful of Kathlyn's hair and wrapped it around her wrist, pulling her face close. Bare inches away, she hissed, "But not for long."

The look of sheer terror on Kathlyn's face caused Rachel to roar with laughter. Kathlyn covered Dru's ears in anticipation of what Rachel would say next.

"He's going to hang!"

Kathlyn groaned. Dru was forgotten now. Just as she was about to lunge at Rachel, Lucky caught her eye from across the room. Almost imperceptibly, he shook his head in warning. Kathlyn sucked in a vast amount of air. She bit her bottom lip until she tasted the metallic flavor of her own blood. Somehow, she remained still. It took every ounce of restraint she could muster to keep from attacking her cousin.

Rachel was disappointed. She wanted nothing more than to vent her anger on Kathlyn. She taunted her further. "He's been arrested for murdering those recruits and the driver of the stage. His trial with hanging Judge Harper started today. They expect a verdict late tomorrow.

"Sorry, but you won't be able to attend the trial with us. You see, he's also charged with kidnapping Miss Elora Kathlyn McKinney. He'll hang by nightfall."

"God, please no," Kathlyn said softly. The days of constant terror coupled with this emotional upheaval was more than she could bear. All the fight drained from her.

Sensing this, Rachel knew there would be no fun, baiting Kathlyn further. She enjoyed it when Kathlyn tried to retaliate, but the blank look in her eyes told her that that wouldn't happen. Spitting on her in disgust, she left the room.

Kathlyn and Dru moved away from the others, wanting to be alone with their grief. Kathlyn placed Dru on the floor next to the wall. Protectively, she curled her body around the child.

"Will Daddy really die, Miss Kathlyn?" Dru's whisper was so soft that Kathlyn thought she might have imagined it. "Will he?"

"No, sweetheart. You know how smart your daddy is. He'll get out of that jail in no time; then he'll come get us."

"Will they put that bad lady in jail then?"

"Definitely."

"Good."

Through her tears, Kathlyn smiled. "Go to sleep now, sweetlin'."

The tears in Kathlyn's voice reached across the room to where Lucky sat. He was drawn to her. "She'll be all right, you know."

"Will she?" Kathlyn asked tiredly, turning over onto her back, staring at the ceiling.

"Of course she will." He touched Dru's hand as it rested in Kathlyn's. For some unknown reason, Kathlyn didn't pull Dru away from him. Lucky hoped that meant that he had gained her trust. "She gets her strength from you," he said.

"Frankly, I don't have much left to give her. And she needs it so desperately." She turned tortured eyes on him. "Do you realize she's five years old and she's never known life before war and Reconstruction. Can you imagine what that must be like? To be so young and see all that pain?

"She's lost her mother, her grandfather, her baby brother. The uncle she's been told so much about is missing . . . and now Brad." Her voice broke. "Her daddy was dead. Now he's alive. But he might hang. How can she be all right again, Lucky? How can either of us ever be all right again?"

Kathlyn's sense of despair worried Lucky. He needed her to hold on a while longer.

There was the sound of footsteps on the porch.

"Damn," Lucky muttered. "Kathlyn, I don't have any answers for you right now. All I can do is ask you to hold on. I promise everything is going to be all right. Please trust me." He squeezed her hand. "I have to be gone for a few hours. Just hold on," he whispered urgently.

"I'll try," Kathlyn whispered to his retreating figure. "I'll try," she told the moon shining just outside the window of the shack.

Brad lay on a narrow iron bed in the Fort Smith jail looking at that very same moon. He knew he could hang tomorrow. Indeed, from the way the trial progressed today, it seemed a sure bet.

Notwithstanding, all he could think of was Kathlyn. Was she safe? Was she cold? Was she hungry? Had she been hurt? Molested? On this last thought he groaned and threw an arm over his closed eyes, as if to block out the terrible scene that tortured his mind.

"Brad," a soft Southern drawl reached his ears.

Brad jerked his head toward the bars of his cell. "What are you doing here?" He jumped to his feet. "God, Princess, this is no place for you."

Lacy smiled sadly. Her big brother was still looking out for her. Tomorrow if they sent him to the gallows, he would probably scold her along the way for standing out in the sun without her parasol. The thought of a possible hanging brought tears to her eyes. "Brad," she choked, reaching through the bars.

"It's going to be all right, honey." Then he asked the

question uppermost in his mind. "Any word from Chase? Has he found Kathlyn?" He hoped against hope.

Lacy shook her head. "No, but he sent word to Red Feather and his men. They're all out searching." She touched her brother's cheek. "It's just a matter of time. They'll find her."

He kissed the palm of her hand. "Thanks."

"What does Matthew say? How does he think your defense is going?" Matthew, Brad's attorney, was a close friend to Chase and Lacy. They trusted him implicitly. He had a brilliant legal mind. If he could just work a miracle this time . . .

"He doesn't have a lot to work with. It's my word against theirs." Brad shrugged nonchalantly.

The tears filling Lacy's jewel green eyes welled and spilled over, sliding down her pale, porcelain cheeks. Brad noticed then how fragile she looked, how dark the smudges were under her large, expressive eyes.

"But there's no need to worry, Tadpole." Brad's use of their brother, Jay's, pet name for Lacy caused her tears to flow even faster.

Brad thought of Jay then, too. If he hanged tomorrow, he would never know what happened to their brother. He wouldn't be there to welcome Jay if he returned to his family. *When* he returned to his family, Brad corrected himself automatically.

God. He couldn't bear to think of Jay now. He had to stay calm, to reassure Lacy. "Hamptons always land on their feet." He touched her dampened cheek gently. "I plan to be here when my nephews are born." He winked and glanced at her expanding waistline.

"You will be."

They talked softly about inconsequential things then. Laughing and teasing each other as brothers and sisters are wont to do. Despite the devastating circumstances of their meeting, they conversed as if they were on the portico at Paradise, watching the sun set over the crystal blue lake in the distance.

Then all too soon, reality intruded. "Time's up, Mrs.

364

Tarleton," a young deputy told Lacy regretfully.

Brad smiled nostalgically, noticing the lawman give his sister the once over. There was such adoration in his eyes. Brad wondered how many men he and his brothers had run off Paradise for looking at Lacy just like that? Too many to count.

Lacy drew his attention when she placed a delicate hand on his arm. Squeezing, she whispered, "I'll see you in the morning."

"Princess, don't." He sighed heavily. "Please don't come to the trial tomorrow," he implored. He feared what would happen to her if he was convicted. He feared for her and her unborn children.

But when Lacy tilted her head stubbornly, he knew there was no need to argue. Her mind was made up and nothing short of a commandment from God would change it. "Very well. If Chase says it's all right, you can come," Brad relented.

Leaning her face through the bars, she kissed his cheek. "I should say I'll be there! You'll need a ride back to the Circle C after you're found innocent."

Brother and sister stared at one another through a veil of tears. "I love you, Princess," he said thickly. "Please tell Kathlyn . . ."

She placed her fingertips over his lips. "You tell her."

He nodded sadly.

"I love you," she whispered, then ran from the room.

Chapter Forty-one

Brad stared through the window of his jail cell at the picturesque sunrise; the cerulean sky was streaked with a rainbow of colors, from vermillion to scarlet. It was a beautiful day. A day hardly suited for an execution.

Thirty minutes later, they came for him. Shoulders erect, head back, hands bound behind him, Brad was led into the courtroom. His steps faltered when he passed the bench upon which Lacy sat, crying softly into her handkerchief. Chase hovered close by her side, a comforting arm draped around her shoulders.

Brad questioned him with his eyes. A gentle shake of Chase's head told Brad there was no news of Kathlyn. So much time had passed. Brad knew there was little hope that she would ever be found now. His heart ached.

When he reached the front of the courtroom he was shoved unceremoniously into a chair. He heard a low, familiar laugh. It was feminine, mocking. Rage rose in him and he swiveled his head. Seated across the room, surrounded by a crowd of rough-looking men, Rachel threw him a gloating smile.

Brad gathered his feet beneath him and jumped up on the desk. Springing into the air, he pulled his knees into his chest. He straightened his arms, passed his cuffed hands beneath his feet, and landed on the floor, bound hands in front of him. Growling, he lunged forward.

"You bitch, you rotten bitch. What did you do to Dru?" he shouted. Grief from Dru's death and worry over Kathlyn's disappearance had unhinged him. He was totally out of control now. He bucked and shouted, elbowing his captors in the stomach, kicking their shins. Desperately, he swung his doubled fists, fighting his way over to Rachel.

Judge Harper rushed into the courtroom, alerted by the din. "Subdue the prisoner!" he shouted to the marshal. Then to Brad's attorney, "Counselor, control your client!"

A host of armed men tried to overpower Brad; Lacy sat white-faced in the shelter of her husband's arms.

The jury was shocked by Brad's outburst. If they needed evidence that he was capable of violence, he had just provided them with it.

A black-clothed brigand grinned with satisfaction from his hiding place at the rear of the courtroom. Even after all the scheming Stuart Shephard had done to bring Brad low, it was sweet irony that Brad's outburst would be his downfall. With that ferocious display, the high-and-mighty Brad Hampton had hung himself.

Stuart was right. After making a few more threats to Rachel and Shifty, Brad was finally subdued and the trial began. Slowly, methodically, the farce was played out. The contrived testimony was presented, the jury excused from the courtroom, then readmitted; they had deliberated less than five minutes. A guilty verdict was certain.

But Brad no longer cared. With Dru dead and Kathlyn gone, his life had little meaning. Still, he regretted causing his family pain. He turned one last time to Lacy. Apologizing with his eyes, he mouthed, "I love you, Princess."

Instead of dissolving into tears, his baby sister showed the spunk she was well known for. Summoning a watery smile, she blew him a kiss. He smiled in spite of his devastating circumstances.

"Have you reached a verdict?" Judge Harper intoned.

"We have, your honor."

"Will the prisoner please rise?"

Brad and his attorney stood and faced the jury. The courtroom was completely silent. All breathing ceased. As one, the gallery leaned forward in their chairs.

Slowly the foreman of the jury unfolded the scrap of paper upon which the words *guilty* or *not guilty* were scrawled. He seemed to move in slow motion, milking the suspense for everything it was worth. He opened his mouth to speak.

The door to the courtroom burst open, sounding like a gunshot. Instinctively, Lacy and Chase moved to Brad's side.

"What in hell's the meaning of this?" Judge Harper shouted.

Leading the rag-tag group of Southern belles, Lucky made for the front of the courtroom. When the gang all left for the trial that morning, Lucky could hardly believe their stupidity. Being left alone with the women was the opportunity he had been waiting for.

When he reached the judge, the women closed ranks around him. His voice was strong and sure. "I'm Heath Turner, United States Marshal. That gang of outlaws"—he pointed toward Rachel, Glenn, and the men sitting around them—"kidnapped these young women. I have warrants for the perpetrators' arrest." He turned toward Brad. "Mr. Hampton is innocent of all charges. I have proof that he"—Lucky singled Shifty out from among the raging brigands—"is the guilty party."

By then the courtroom was in an uproar. The men surrounding Rachel were on their feet, shouting that Lucky was a liar. Rachel's face was ashen white. For once, she was silent. When brigands cast about for a way to escape, they were surrounded.

"Approach the bench," the judge instructed Marshal Turner.

Lucky did as he was told. Removing his badge from his vest pocket, he tossed it onto the judge's table. Then he showed him a letter from the U.S. Attorney General, commissioning him to infiltrate the gang of kidnappers in addition to the warrants.

368

Judge Harper perused the documents. He recognized their authenticity immediately. "There are two marshals named here."

"My partner will report to you shortly."

"See that he does," Judge Harper said. He pointed to the warrants on his desk. "Are all the perpetrators accounted for?"

Lucky made a quick visual survey of the outlaws. "Stuart Shephard is missing. My partner and I will find him."

"Very well." Judge Harper turned to the local marshal. "Release Mr. Hampton and take these men and Miss Jackson into custody." With a minimum of effort, Rachel and the others were led away. Noting Glenn's uniform, the judge instructed, "Hold Lieutenant Crutchfield for the Fort Gibson authorities."

Lucky turned toward Brad, Lacy, and Chase then.

"Marshal Heath Turner? Lucky?" Brad asked.

"We meet again." Lucky smiled at Brad. "I gave you a hard time on the *Robert E. Lee*, didn't I?"

"Consider us even." Brad smiled.

"Not quite." Lucky's gaze fixed somewhere over Brad's shoulder. He winked and nodded.

In two long strides, Lucky's partner closed the distance between himself and Lacy. "Tadpole," the blond marshal drawled softly. "I believe you've put on a little weight." He reached out a trembling hand to stroke her cheek; tears glittered in his eyes.

Just before she fainted into Chase's arms, Lacy breathed, "Jay!"

Holding his wife against his chest, Chase grinned at his long lost brother-in-law. "Before she wakes up, you better think of a hell of a good excuse for being away all these years."

Jay Hampton nodded and squeezed Chase's shoulder. Then he turned toward Brad, capturing him in a bear hug. The brothers embraced for a long moment. Reluctantly, Jay stepped back. "Well, big brother, it's been a long time since I've gotten your ass out of a sling."

His voice was husky, betraying his emotion. "If I had a nickel for every time I . . ."

Brad feigned a punch at his brother's stomach. "You'd have a dime," he interrupted. "No. Not even that." Brad clamped on to Jay's shoulder as if he couldn't believe he was real. "In fact, I can't remember you ever getting my ass out of a sling," he teased, unashamed of the tears rolling down his cheeks. "As I recall it was the other way around."

"Think so? Well then it's high time I paid you back. I brought you a little present." Jay gestured toward the rear of the courtroom.

"Daddy," Dru called, barreling down the aisle.

"Oh my God," Brad choked out as his daughter sailed into his arms.

Kathlyn watched the reunion from the doorway. Lacy regained consciousness. Her husband placed her on her feet and immediately she disappeared into Jay's embrace. Then Brad presented his daughter to her extended family. Dru finally met her Aunt Lacy and Uncle Chase, getting hugs from both. Jay ruffled Dru's curls while Brad looked on proudly.

It was a tender sight. Kathlyn was glad she had insisted that Jay be reunited with his family before she and Dru approached Brad. And it was good that she had instructed Dru go to her father next, telling her she would be right along. Knowing all three of them at once would have been a shock to anyone, even Brad, she had bided her time. But now it was her turn. Smiling, she took a step in his direction.

"Where do you think you're going, slut," Stuart hissed into her ear, circling her throat with his arm.

Kathlyn screamed, gaining the attention of everyone in the room. The assemblage was thrown into pandemonium. Stuart held a gun on the crowd at large, dragging Kathlyn out the side door.

The color drained from Brad's face. He hugged Dru one last time. "Stay with Uncle Chase and Aunt Lacy, honey." He turned toward Chase. "A gun." Chase nodded, tossing Brad his weapon.

"Get Miss Kathlyn away from that man, Daddy. He's mean," Dru called to her daddy as he dove through the open window in pursuit of Kathlyn and Stuart.

"Let's go," Jay shouted to Lucky, running toward the backdoor of the courtroom.

"Right behind you, partner."

The blazing sun was directly overhead. Squinting against the glare, Kathlyn searched the alley, looking for an avenue of escape. She had to get away from this madman before Brad found them. Her captor was unhinged; she didn't want Brad anywhere near him.

"If you don't pick up your feet and get moving, I'm going to shoot you where you stand," Stuart threatened, tightening his arm around Kathlyn's throat.

"Why don't you just leave town," she rasped. "You don't need me. I'll only slow you down."

"You misunderstand. I'm not going anywhere." His sing-song voice evinced a serious lack of sanity. "And I do need you, Kathlyn, my dear. Otherwise, your knight in shining armor won't follow me. And if I'm going to kill him, Brad must follow me." He spoke softly now, as if she were a child.

"No!" Kathlyn shrieked.

"That's right, scream." He squeezed her throat tighter. "Scream so he can find us." Stuart kicked the doors of a barn open and shoved Kathlyn inside.

She fell on the floor, massaging her throat, gasping for breath.

"Now we wait," Stuart hissed. Taking his place beside the door, his gun cocked and ready, he grinned into the cool darkness of the barn. He had chosen this place carefully. It was perfect for an ambush. The only entrance was through the door. When Brad came in to rescue his damsel in distress, he would blow him to hell.

* * *

371

Brad slipped into the mouth of the alley, following Stuart and Kathlyn's tracks. It was all he could do to maintain control as he inched his way down the street. He had thought Kathlyn was lost to him forever. To catch one glimpse of her, with that low-life's hands on her . . . it was almost more than he could bear.

If Stuart harmed one hair on Kathlyn's head, Brad would kill him. Prison would be too good for a man who would hurt Kathlyn. Clenching his back teeth together, he turned the corner. A wide lane, leading to a barn, stretched out in front of him.

Were they inside? Brad wondered, crouching behind a cottonwood tree some twenty feet from the door. Shifting to the left, he surveyed the lane fronting the barn. There were no visible hoof prints in the soft mud. Only two sets of footprints, one large, one small.

They had to be inside. Kathlyn was holed up with a maniacal killer. Brad leaned his head against the tree, fighting for control.

"He's going to kill you," Kathlyn said softly. "He'll blow your brains all over the wall."

"Shut up," Stuart hissed, turning on her. "He'll never get the chance. There's no way he can get to us without me seeing him. As soon as he sticks his head out, I'll put a bullet between his eyes. He won't get away again," he sneered.

"Yes he will. Because he's better than you."

Suddenly, Stuart backhanded her across the mouth.

"You're scum," she continued, unafraid of the rage in his eyes. Her fear was reserved for what he might do to Brad. All that mattered to her was that she protect Brad. She spat the blood from her mouth, showering his face. "You're trash." She ducked his meaty fist. "You're not fit to wipe his boots," she taunted.

With a blood-curdling yell, Stuart lunged at her. She side-stepped him as Brad burst through the door and tackled him from behind. Both men lost their guns on impact. Stuart rolled aside, grabbing a pitchfork and coming to his feet in one motion.

372

"Brad, watch out," Kathlyn shrieked. She dropped to her knees, searching the straw for a gun.

Brad and Stuart circled each other, Brad careful to avoid the razor-sharp tongs of the pitchfork.

"I've got you now, Hampton. I'm going to run you through, then I'm going to take your slut with me to California."

Brad growled low in his throat and rushed Stuart, barely avoiding the deadly weapon. Stuart dropped the pitchfork. They fell to the floor then, snarling, wrestling in the hay. Stuart shoved Brad to the side, slamming Brad's head against a post. Taking advantage of Brad's momentary disorientation, Stuart retrieved the pitchfork. He raised it high over his head.

As if in slow motion, Kathlyn watched it slice through the air, moving closer and closer to Brad's throat. Brad was dazed, unaware of the grave danger. Terrified, she squeezed her fists. And felt something cold, hard, against her right hand. It was Brad's gun. Without thinking, reacting purely on instinct, she raised the gun to her side, aimed it at Stuart, and slowly squeezed the trigger. He was dead before he hit the floor. The pitchfork fell harmlessly at his side. Throwing the smoking weapon aside, she rushed forward and launched herself into Brad's arms.

"Oh God, I killed him," she wailed. "But I had to. I couldn't let him hurt you."

Brad pushed her head into his shoulder, muffling her sobs. "Shh, baby. It's all right. Of course you had to."

He was worried at the hysteria in Kathlyn's voice. She was so gentle, so delicate. Could she live with killing someone? He angled her head back. Staring into her face with all the love he possessed, he whispered, "You saved my life, sweetheart."

Calming slightly, she buried her face in his neck. "God help me, I'd kill him again to protect you."

"I appreciate that. But I was supposed to be protecting you," he feigned levity.

The barn doors opened then. Jay and Lucky stepped inside and assessed the situation. "Take your lovely

373

lady back to the Circle C, Brad. We'll clean up here," Jay said gently.

"Thanks, brother. I'll do that." Brad helped Kathlyn to her feet. Grateful that they were free of Stuart Shephard forever, he walked away without a backward glance.

"A U.S. Marshal," Brad said to Jay, holding Dru in his lap. "I still find it hard to believe."

They were all safe at the Circle C now. Had been for two hours. Brad, Kathlyn, and Dru had not broken physical contact with each other since returning from town. He dropped another kiss to Kat's lips. Her sigh touched everyone in the room.

Jay cleared his throat. "Me too, sometime."

"What made you become a lawman, professor?" Chase teased.

"After the war, I needed a job. I sure couldn't return to Georgia. Somehow I didn't think I would receive a warm welcome after serving Lincoln for four years. I didn't have the desire to teach anymore. So when I was offered a job as marshal, taming the wild west"—he winked at Lacy sitting beside him on a low sofa—"it seemed a good idea."

"Oh Jay," she breathed, thinking of all the time that had passed, not knowing if Jay was alive or dead.

"I know, Tadpole, I know," Jay said. Lacy didn't need to explain her thoughts to Jay. They had always been close enough to read each other's minds. He knew she was hurting. Regretting. And so was he.

To lighten the mood, he teased, "It's Heath's fault." He smiled, jerking his head in Lucky's direction.

"Me?" Lucky feigned indignation.

"Yeah. You're the one who talked me into this." Jay tapped his badge, turning to Brad. "We were in Libby together. Those were pretty dark days. There wasn't much to do but talk about the future. You know, what we would do when the war was over. Heath had his whole life mapped out. His plan didn't sound half bad. Then when his sister-in-law rescued us, saved our lives really, she talked me into watching out after Lucky."

"Wait," Lacy interrupted. "Back up a minute. Heath's . . . Lucky's sister-in-law broke you out of prison?"

Lucky groaned and Jay threw him a look. "Save it. You were as smitten with her as the rest of us," Jay said wryly. Then to Lacy, "Ever hear of the Vixen in Gray?"

"The rebel spy?" Brad inserted.

Jay nodded. "The female rebel spy. With the emphasis on female. Anyway, she rescued us and then exercised poor judgment and fell in love with one of Lucky's older brothers."

"What? Is he making this up, Lucky?" Kathlyn laughed.

"Afraid not," Lucky said wryly.

"Her name's Kinsey" — Jay looked down at Lacy — "and she reminded me of you, Tadpole. She's something else." He chuckled, remembering the unusual woman he'd met during the war.

"Anyway, the whole family kind of adopted me. So when Lucky said he was going west and invited me along, and Kinsey asked me to watch out for him, well, how could I refuse?"

"Sounds like a pretty lame excuse to me." Chase chuckled, shaking his head.

"Why didn't you contact us?" Brad asked seriously.

Jay winced; his light-hearted explanation had been an attempt to avoid this painful question. "I should have. I don't have an excuse except that I knew you would insist I come home. No matter how inconvenient it would have been to the family, or how much abuse you would have been forced to endure because of me — because of my political leanings. You would have demanded that I come home.

"I just didn't want to put you all through it. I know now that I hurt you by staying away and not contact-

375

ing you, but I didn't mean to. I hope you believe that."

Kathlyn smiled at Jay. She liked Brad's younger brother, quite a lot. Especially since he had served the Union like her father and brothers. "The people of Athens would scarcely have noticed your presence, Jay." She winked at Brad. "Since Brad ran off with the Confederate treasury at the end of the war. Everybody was hot on his trail."

"Particularly you," Brad whispered in Kathlyn's ear, nibbling her lobe.

"Well, that's true," she murmured, kissing him boldly. Laughter lit her eyes when she returned her attention to Jay. "There was some talk about tar and feathers as I recall."

"Tar and feathers?" Jay laughed.

Brad wrapped his arms around Kathlyn's waist and squeezed. "You scamp." Acting like lovestruck kids, they wrestled on the sofa, with Dru right in the middle of the fray.

"The Confederate treasury?" Lucky whistled through his teeth.

"It's a long story," Brad deadpanned, resettling Dru on his lap.

Jay grinned as Dru cuddled closer to her daddy. She caught Jay's eye and smiled over a tiny yawn. "You should have come home, Uncle Jay. I would have protected you. If anybody was mean to you, I'd have blacked their eye."

"I believe you would have, honey. I surely do."

Some months later Jay received a telegram that would send him on an adventure. An adventure that would make his previous work as a United States Marshal seem tame in comparison. An adventure fraught with danger and excitement. An adventure on which he would find the kind of love and passion that all men dream about, but rarely experience.

376

Telegram
Attn: Jonathan Hampton, U.S. Marshal
July 1, 1867
Marshal Hampton:
   On June 25 Rachel Jackson killed two guards and escaped from Arkansas Territorial Prison. STOP I require a man of exceptional courage to pursue this dangerous escapee into the Indian nations. STOP I believe you are that man. STOP I look forward to hearing from you.
Judge Harper, Fort Smith, Arkansas Territory.

Epilogue

River's Edge Plantation
July 4, 1867

"Come with me." Brad grabbed his wife's hand, startling her.

"Brad, the babies . . ."

"Now, Kathlyn!"

His frantic order gained a chuckle from her. He looked a bit crazed in her estimation. He had to be off-balance to ignore her concern for their babies, she mused wryly. Quintessential husband and father, that was her Brad. Ever since the babies came screaming into this world Brad had been as protective, as obsessed, as Kathlyn herself.

And was it any wonder? No one had been more shocked, or more thrilled, than Kathlyn and Brad to discover that she was pregnant. Despite the doctor's declaration that her miscarriage had made her sterile, she had given Brad twins. Two beautiful boys. Winter and Ash.

Another set of Hampton twins! That made three in the family now; Jared and Melinda's, Chase and Lacy's, and now her and Brad's.

Thank God for virile Hampton men, she thought, almost running to keep up with Brad's long strides.

This last set of twins had been a source of amusement for Jay, Kathlyn remembered, smiling. When Ash and Winter were born, Jay had sworn the family to secrecy. Women would be afraid to sit next to him with a family history like that, he had quipped. Much less have a relationship with him.

As Kathlyn recalled, Jay had no problem attracting women. The last time they saw him had been three days ago, just before he left Athens for the wilds of Indian territory. She already missed her handsome brother-in-law. Just as she missed Chase and Lacy. She had come to love her new family. The Hamptons. But now with Winter and Ash, she, Dru, and Brad were a loving family all on their own.

"Mammy Mae's in the nursery with them," Brad broke into her thoughts.

Kathlyn suppressed a giggle. "Good." He had planned this little foray into the great outdoors carefully, it seemed. She wasn't surprised Mammy Mae was watching the boys while their father kidnapped their mother. Mammy doted on them.

She had been thrilled when Brad, Kathlyn, and Dru returned to check on her in Memphis. One word from Brad that another little Hampton would soon enter the world, and would need the love and care she alone could give, was all it took; Mammy packed and was ready to leave for Athens within the hour.

"What about Dru? I promised to help her name the new birds this afternoon." Actually Dru had already suggested names for her parakeets. Porta and Jupe. The child's sense of humor was a constant delight to Kathlyn and Brad.

Smiling, Kathlyn acknowledged that she was teasing Brad shamelessly, coming up with these lame excuses. She wanted to spend time with him just as much as he wanted to spend time with her. Frantic now, he didn't even acknowledge her teasing, rushing across the verdant lawns like a runaway train.

Her lips twitched with the urge to laugh at the look of sheer determination on her husband's face. She knew quite well what was driving him. Six weeks of sexual abstinence.

This morning at breakfast she had whispered to him that they could finally make love again, now that the

380

babies were six weeks old. The look of raw lust on his face had made her doubt he would wait until tonight. At least she had hoped he wouldn't.

But where was he taking her? Why didn't he just carry her up to their bedchamber and lock the world away? As always, her heart accelerated at the thought.

Suddenly, he stopped, as if her words about helping Dru had just registered in his lust-dulled brain. "Mrs. Hampton, I need you to help *me* this afternoon!" he growled. He pulled her body flush with his. Placing his hands on her hips, he rubbed himself against her. "With this." He kissed her with all the pent-up passion of a man deprived. Long moments later he broke the embrace.

Without allowing her to catch her breath, he closed the distance to the glasshouse. Throwing the door open wide, he stood aside to allow her entry. "Surprise," he said softly.

Her eyes filled with tears as she stepped into the room. Delicate, aromatic gardenias spilled over every available surface, floor, table, bench, shelf. The entire glasshouse looked like one, big, beautiful bowl of gardenias. "Oh, honey," she whispered brokenly. "You remembered."

"If I live to be a hundred, I'll never forget making love to you here," he said, his voice unsteady. "The smell of gardenias. The feel of you moving beneath me. The sensation of being inside your body. It was beyond exquisite."

"But this time, it'll be even better. I promise." He looked deeply into her eyes.

For a moment she couldn't speak. His words had affected her more than he knew. Raising her hand, she fingered the fetching indentation in his cheek. "It *was* quite wonderful back then." She cleared her throat. "*You* were quite wonderful."

He traced her face with his fingertips. Kathlyn was stunned that a look of such tenderness could come from a man with such strength. When he spoke, that tenderness was evident in the timber of his deep, husky voice. "This time, it'll be even better," he repeated. "Because this time you're mine, precious. You're my wife. And nobody can take you from me. Ever, ever again."

Taking her hand, he led her to a bed made of white satin pillows and sheets, at the exact spot he had made love to her twelve years before. He pulled her down with him and embraced her from shoulder to ankle. Flowers crushed beneath their shifting bodies. The sweet, pungent smell exploded around them.

It was a familiar smell, a heady smell, the smell of love.

Slowly, reverently, Brad undressed his wife, kissing and caressing every inch he bared, praising her beauty, worshipping her flesh. After she undressed him, he tangled his fingers into her hair and angled her head back. "Kat, I love you with all my heart," he vowed with a hint of reverence.

"And I love you, Brad," she said, tears of joy shining in her eyes.

With a groan, Brad joined his body to her. "Sweetheart," he whispered against her lips, "this time our night of gardenias will last forever."

"At least forever," Kathlyn agreed.

And it did. Each night for the rest of Brad and Kathlyn's lives, they reaffirmed their love. A love first confessed beneath a hot, July moon, in a riverside glasshouse — redolent with the sweet scent of gardenias.